RON CLARK BALL

GROUPE PRIVÉ

Kickback Books

GROUPE PRIVÉ

Published by Privé Publishing

First Published in 2007

SECOND EDITION

May 8, 2009

10 9 8 7 6 5 4 3 2 1

Library of Congress Catalog-in-Publication Data

Ball, Ron Clark

Falcon on the tower / Ron Clark Ball.

p. cm.

ISBN 978-0-6151-4016-2

ISBN 0-615-140162-5

1. Geopolitical thriller   2.   Fiction   I.   Title

PRAISE FOR FALCON ON THE TOWER

"A crackling good read by an author with both a finely tuned sense of history and the ability to twist a plot like a sharpened knife —-read it!"

> - *James G. Stavridis, author of "Destroyer Captain"*

"Incredibly accurate and detailed view of the Global War on Terror. I felt like I was 'back in the seat' as a Task Force Commander again (TASK FORCE FIFTY- ENDURING FREEDOM)."

> - *Tom Zelibor (RADM U.S. Navy, ret.) Dean U.S. Naval War College & former Director of Global Operations, United States Strategic Command*

"(Falcon On The Tower's) characters are intriguing and the prose flows nicely, bringing me deeper into the story."

> - *Laurence Kirshbaum, former CEO & Chairman of Time Warner Book Group, and 2005 Publishing Person of the Year.*

"A gripping novel! Reading it made me feel like I was right there in the middle of the action. A definite must read!"

> - *Rich Mentemeyer (Major General United States Air Force, ret.) former Director Mobility Forces – Enduring Freedom*

"Masterfully done! A frightening scenario is painted with keen insight, timely alacrity, and page-turning dispatch... I couldn't put the book down. Mr. Ball's knowledge of the terrorism financial structure is evident... it's an outcome that's all too plausible, and must be avoided!"

> - *Hon. A. Paul Anderson, Federal Maritime Commission*

FOR   HKB

I wish I was dead 'fore I done what I did,

Or seen what I seed that day.

— RUDYARD KIPLING

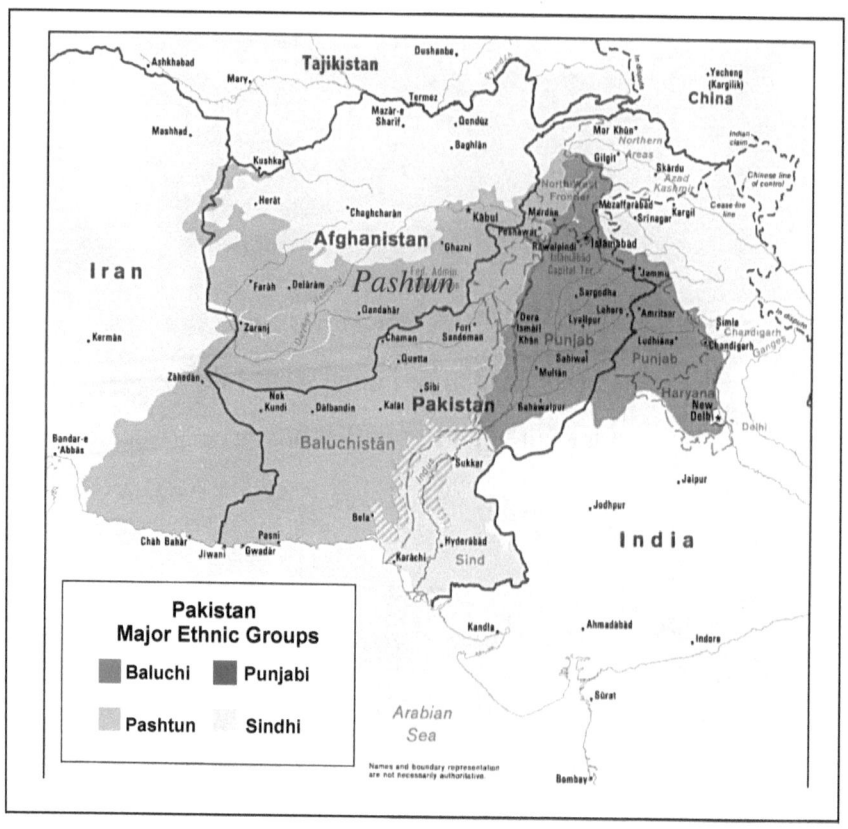

(PD)

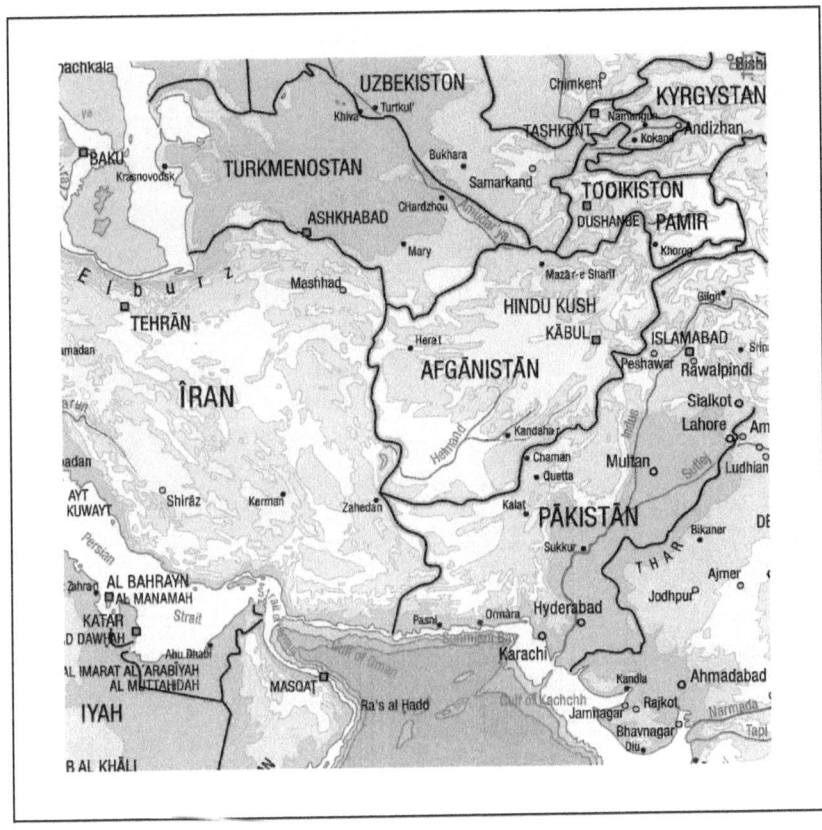

(PD)

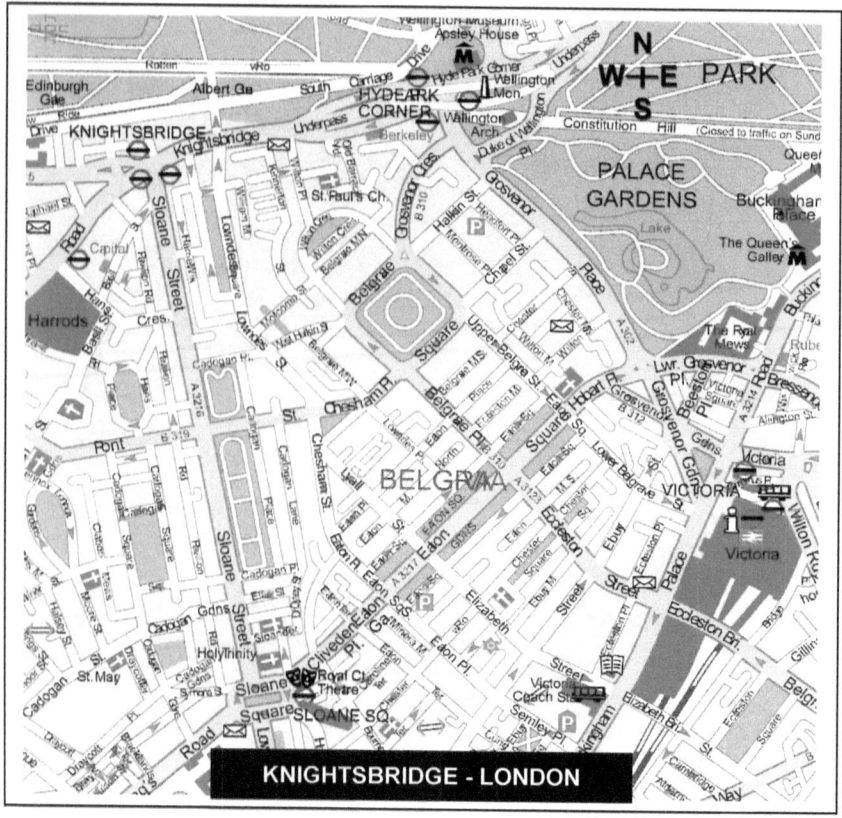

KNIGHTSBRIDGE - LONDON

(PD)

PROLOGUE

DECEMBER 25, 2001

HINDU KUSH MOUNTAINS

H ANIF ZAR WALI WAS TWENTY-TWO when he was found hiding in back of a stone Pashtun outhouse. Filthy, hungry and near hypothermic, he was curled up asleep under a pile of dried goat bladders that were used to carry water. He'd been there for twelve hours, and was awakened by the warm splatter of urine from a man now accustomed to relieve himself outdoors rather than in.

The sudden movement of the pile got the attention of the Special Ops commando, who without interrupting his stream, lowered the business end of his M4 assault rifle and kicked away the bladders, revealing prey. The sleeper's eyes opened to see a bearded hunter looking down at him, expressionless. The Navy SEAL continued on with his job at hand, but now had a tan, well-worn boot placed firmly on the dreaming man's throat. Hanif Zar Wali tried to speak, uttering "_Baaz_," before the SEAL shifted his weight, spun the rifle, and dropped the butt squarely on the sleeper's forehead.

PART I

THE CRUSADE

CHAPTER I

JULY 10, 1892

HINDU KUSH MOUNTAINS, BRITISH INDIA

CONQUEST WAS HIS CALL. The blood that coursed through his veins screamed with it. He let the symbol fly. Rising towards the midday sun, the aerial master displayed innate abilities and instinctive skills like no other. Watching its flight closely from nearby, Kipling believed the bird was closer to perfection than any animal he had ever seen.

"I say, Mister Kipling, look - he's flying higher," Captain Robinson noted.

"It's easier to find prey. With his vision he can see miles, but when he attacks, it's altitude that gives him the lethal advantage," Kipling said confidently.

Kipling adjusted his spectacles and shielded them with his hand from the solar glare. As he looked up in admiration, he was intrigued by the mechanics of its motion, marveling at the effortlessness of the bird's flight. The falcon rapidly flapped short, narrow wings with brief thrusts, causing it to quickly accelerate. Once it had achieved its desired speed the wings would fully extend, giving them the maximum surface area possible. Then it would glide for several moments, its head only moving slightly as it scanned the horizon and ground below with keen eyesight. Occasionally it would adjust its long tail or the tips of its pointed wings to fine-tune the course and altitude. Larger turns were sudden, almost violent, when it would abruptly reverse direction, appearing to literally stop in mid air, then immediately regain velocity and repeat the patrol.

An older man with thick beard, a boy by his side, signaled with a wave of his hand to an attendant in the distance. The attendant, a Hindu, was standing on the shore of a glacier-fed lake with a British soldier in red jacket and white pith helmet. He had a small wooden cage and upon being signaled, opened its gate releasing a white-throated swift that immediately took to the air. The swift was half the size of the circling hunter, but in level flight it was the faster of the two. The attack however, wouldn't start from level flight, where the swift had the advantage, but instead the hunter would stoop to its prey from above, attaining speeds two times the quarry.

"Watch very carefully Shuja," the old man said guiding the boy's shoulder with a gloved hand to follow the flight of the smaller bird as it sprinted across the lake.

"The swift senses the falcon's presence, and it sees the rock walls that would give it refuge. It's a contest, but our hunter is smarter," the falconer explained to Shuja.

Robinson saw the small black bird, now at the lake's center. It turned upward sharply, climbing towards cliffs that rose from the edges of an icy cirque. Losing the swift momentarily as its fleeing body grew smaller, and camouflaged by the colors of the surrounding mountains, he thought the falcon had also lost sight of the prize, now almost home free.

"I do believe he's lost him Mister Kipling," Robinson said, running across the rocky bank, searching the sky for the swift.

"No, Mister Robinson. The falcon knows the swift. He'll predict its flight path, and in good order, position himself for the best angle to attack," Kipling explaining stoically that the game was far from over.

The falcon rapidly flapped its wings, ferocious and powerful strokes, his majestic head slightly cocked to keep the swift in sight. Panicking under the dire circumstances, the swift foolishly changed direction and started returning across the lake to the rocks near the boy and his father. As if by a miracle the spectacle would take place on nature's arena right before them.

The raptor tucked his wings and fell from the sky, initially stooping at an almost vertical angle to attain a speed faster than any creature ever. It was accelerating towards critical velocity, its mass being aerodynamically pulled to the earth by the force of gravity. Timing had to be perfect. Come in too fast, it would be out of control and risk injury, or possibly a fatal, catastrophic midair collision; too slow, miss a meal.

Climbing once again, if the swift could get close to the rock culverts, it would survive the attack; the falcon would disengage from the dive for its own safety. But the falcon's aim was precise; it's trajectory on target. It cupped its wings under the attacking body ever so slightly, increasing drag and decelerating the plummet, the new shape providing the maximum lift possible on pull out.

Like a bolt of lightning, the falcon came in from behind, striking the prey with a glancing, but lethal punch of talons, closed like fists. A direct hit, the contest was over. The victor circled back to claim its prize.

"Smashing, positively smashing," Robinson's voice echoed across the lake and glacial valley. He yelled his enthusiasm at the falcon's brilliant display of predation and slapped Kipling's back to share in his excitement. Kipling smiled.

The falcon stood triumphantly on top the dead swift, calling for the reward of his conquest; it was just seconds away, but still he poked impatiently with a curved beak at the bird under his talons.

Kipling watched as the old man held up his left arm, covered from the fingers to the elbow with a thick leather glove. Recognizing the invitation, the champion took off again, this time for a short flight to the leather perch and a better meal.

"This hunter is the greatest of them all, my friends," the old man bellowed in triumph, as he carefully hand fed a small piece of meat to his beloved warrior.

"Shuja – study the hunter and learn. I will teach how to properly use this weapon, to be its master," the old man said to the son by his side. He handed the bird another morsel. "Hunting with this beauty is a skill my boy - an art. The art of life and death."

Shuja nervously looked up at his father's mercenary as it devoured the reward while perched on the glove, its large eyes surveying the surroundings as it ate. The falcon was cognizant of any movement near or far, especially coming from the boy standing beneath him.

"Don't be afraid, Shuja," the father said, seeing apprehension in the boy's eyes. "He'll respect you soon enough, but understand me when I say that he will never fear you. He is a falcon," the father looked directly in the boy's eyes as he spoke. "Remember that."

He pulled a small ornate hood over the bird's head and secured it with silk ribbon. The hood had been carefully designed to delicately cover its head and large eyes, yet expose both the beak and nostrils. Without the hood, the falcon might become excited at the sight of a rodent or bird. Should instinct kick in, he may try to attack. The hood calmed him. The father had sixteen birds of prey with him always, some larger than others, but this particular predator was his favorite.

"Think of the falcon as an extension of you," he proclaimed to Shuja, laughing and putting his arm around the boy's shoulders. He moved the bird close to the boy, who gingerly stroked its breast feathers. "Together, you become one weapon." Shuja looked closely at the winged gladiator, its hood similar to the crown of a king.

The boy believed his father, understanding his wisdom. He commanded great respect from many people, and was continually asked advice. Something else that Shuja understood as well; his father commanded a great deal of power and fear. He was Mehtar Aman ul Mulk II, King of Chitral.

Kipling and Robinson, who were admiring the falconry from nearby, approached Aman and his son. Friends of the Mehtar, the son liked them both, and thought the officer's uniform magnificent. Officers of the British Army were always impeccably dressed. Predominately red, the clothing was not well suited for camouflage in the mountains, in fact they were easy to spot from great distances, but it gave the man an elegant air. Shuja liked that.

"Simply brilliant. Jolly good show your Majesty," Robinson said excitingly. He had a thick brown moustache, neatly groomed, his hair closely cropped.

"Crivens. Meh thet's soom barry bird ye've goat therr, watch oot fewrr heem oer the loch," agreed the Scot, limping from an old war wound in his calf as he approached with the Hindu man holding the cage. He was a Sergeant Major by the name of Duncan MacLean. His annunciation was not as clear as the Captain. Older than his superior officer, his moustache was the larger, streaked with grey, and it partially covered his upper lip, fluttering when he spoke. His "sideboards" were thick, extending to mid jaw. Shuja wondered why British soldiers sometimes shaved a portion of their beard.

"Whit're think aboot that laddie – ah mean yer 'ighness?" The Sergeant Major asked Shuja.

"I agree. It was indeed splendid," Shuja said in his best English, while petting the bird again.

"Ah suppose yer larnin falconry, are ye? O am ah rrang?" The Sergeant Major asked Shuja, smiling. He was missing his left canine tooth.

"You are correct. My father's teaching me now," Shuja said. Sometimes he found it difficult to understand the Scot.

"Superb my boy," Robinson said. "Your Majesty, that's a fantastic hunter you've got on your hand."

"Couldn't agree more. What sort of falcon is that Mehtar Aman? A Peregrine?" Kipling asked, holding a pipe under his moustache as usual, and walking with a strange club, that lately he was seldom seen without. Looking somewhat like a walking stick, it had a grooved brass plate on a clubface perpendicular to a wooden shaft, and a leather grip at the other end.

"You are correct Mister Kipling, and what is it that have you in your hand? It seems to be a curious tool," the Mehtar said, commenting on the unusual stick.

"This, your Majesty, is a brassie," Kipling said as he puffed his pipe and handed the club to the King.

"A brassie? A weapon of sorts?" Aman asked.

"Of sorts, perhaps," Kipling said, his hand reaching into his wool coat, producing a small gray ball. "A weapon for this," he added holding it up for Aman to see.

"That would be a gutta, wouldn't it Mister Kipling?" Robinson asked, looking closely at the ball.

"Precisely. A gutta-percha ball made from packing material used for shipping," Kipling said.

"And what is the purpose for this ball and brassie Mister Kipling?" Mehtar Aman asked.

"Gouf, yerr Majesty. Grrit, auld Scotsman's gam," MacLean said.

"A frustrating folly of the idle actually. For your own sake, avoid it completely," Kipling said, followed by laughter from the Brit and the Scot. The Mehtar studied the golf club curiously, and then gave it back to the Englishman from Lahore.

The English journalist and the aristocratic officer of the British Army soon learned they enjoyed each other's company immensely. Kipling and Robinson, both Christian English gentlemen, did what gentlemen adventurers enjoyed most when at leisure; engage in intellectually stimulating conversation for hours on end, British imperialism being their favorite debate. Virtually every evening after dinner they'd sit around a campfire near the lake, enjoying tobacco, maybe a rare bottle of booze, discussing at length the virtues of Great Britain's Asian direction, the policies implemented for the Indian subcontinent, or lack of them, particularly as those policies pertained to Afghanistan, which had proven to be in terms of money and lives, very costly. Kipling, usually taking the side of the devil's advocate, would ask, "Was the Empire better off now?"

"We stay on course," Robinson would say. "The heathens will come around."

"You say - but how long will it take, and how many more lives will it cost?" Kipling countered in their pugilism of debate.

"It is ironical, the history of your country - what seems to cause your empire the most trouble is the imposition of imperialism on people who don't want it," Mehtar Aman commented one evening during a spirited debate. "After all," he added, "How many times has British India attempted to depose Afghanistan's ruler with a puppet?"

Kipling pointed out how accurate the Mehtar's assessment of the policy had been. "A chess game of sorts was underway between the reigning world power, Great Britain, and Russia," he said. "Russia, a country with ideas of expansionism, was attempting to assert its own sphere of imperialism, especially in Afghanistan."

"We needed Afghanistan as a buffer state. It was a strategic choice because of the recent problems in India with the rebellion," Captain Robinson emphasized. "It's for Afghanistan's own protection from the expansionist goals of the Russian Czar." And as he put it "But more importantly, the Russians had taken over all the lands of the Caucasus, between Turkey and Iran."

Russian expansionism was "A legitimate concern," Kipling agreed. He was correct; the Caucasus would one day become post-

Soviet states of Georgia, Armenia, and Azerbaijan." The Indian rebellion, on the other hand, "was purely a comedic clash of eastern and western cultures," Kipling countered Robinson euphemistically "triggered by the introduction of a new rifle," the Snider-Enfield, which required the gunpowder to be manually inserted into the muzzle. Troops were drilled to bite open the gunpowder cartridge, greased with lard and beef fat, which was forbidden to be consumed by the Sepoy Indian religion. This cultural ignorance resulted in a violent revolt, followed by the standard massacre of innocents, both British and Indian, and the subsequent execution of the perpetrators; standard fair for nineteenth century British imperialism.

Robinson got back on track with the Russian issue, adding, "They'd begun to influence the Iranian court, and posed the only direct threat to India. Movement into Afghanistan simply was to prevent further military expansion by Russia into British territory." Russia, for its part feared further absorption of Central Asia by the British Empire. It became a chess game and the Russians dispatched an envoy to Kabul to advise Dost Mohammad.

Uncharacteristically sarcastic, Kipling commented, "It seems to be mostly about the tea and beating back the Bear, ay? In this great game of world domination, the lesser countries become the pawns."

One evening after a dinner of Rainbow trout Kipling produced a clipping for Robinson from one of his notebooks, a political cartoon circa 1878. "I believe this is from 'The Times.' Save poor Afghanistan from the imperialistic designs of 'The Bear' and 'The Lion,'" Kipling said.

"'Friendship is but a code for domination," Robinson added.

"It's uncanny how much the Afghan caricature looks like King Aman," Kipling said as he studied the cartoon for the first time in months.

Auckland's new policy first required his own envoy be sent to Kabul to counter the Russians. His choice Alexander Burns, a career diplomat, cut from the "foreign service mold." The Russians of course countered with an envoy of their own. Lord Auckland believed he ultimately had no choice but to send troops, and he did. An army was dispatched from Punjab to Afghanistan in December 1838 under the command of an icon of sorts, General William Elphinstone, but who also was a commander who hadn't seen a battle in decades. Robinson, forever the young idealistic military man, noted what a complete mistake it was to send, as he put it, "Such an indecisive, incompetent leader. Mister Kipling, I tell you that he was a General only because he was the son of a director of the British East India Company. Nothing more."

Kipling remarked that, "It was true he was old, and he'd been out of practice for real command, nevertheless, he'd seen war firsthand. Didn't he have battlefield experience at the battle of Waterloo? I believe it's there he led the 33rd Regiment of Foot."

Robinson argued, "That Auckland's choice was horrible," given the ultimate results, and the fact that Waterloo was the last battlefield experience that he had. "Victory against Napoleon at Waterloo, certainly wonderful for God and King in 1815, proved meaningless in Afghanistan in 1840. Two vastly different circumstances and very different foes," he adamantly countered.

Elphinstone crossed into Kandahar in April 1839, attacking the Muslim forces of Dost Mohammad Kahn, the ruler of Afghanistan. The Dost's son, Mohammad Akbar Kahn, commanded troops at the plateau fortress of Ghuznee. "A remarkably enchanting place," Kipling said of Ghuznee. "The tombs and the grand twin minarets from the 10th century, simply historical. It would be a shame if they were ever lost in a war."

Akbar Kahn faced the British but was completely routed by the superior forces. After having been exiled for thirty years, the British puppet leader, Shah Shuja was then enthroned in his old Kabul palace, as the Dost fled with his followers to Bukhara, and ultimately surrendered to the puppet. The Dost Mohammad was imprisoned immediately, however his son managed to evade capture, allowing him to irritate both the British and the Shah through typical insurgent tactics; protests, demonstrations, riots, and murder.

Chasing uncertainty, Auckland measured his options. "Put a second knight on site," he decided, a diplomatic professional for Burnes the explorer to report to. Lord Auckland appointed a British administrator in Kabul, Sir William Macnaghten to support the newly installed government. Macnaghten, recently nominated to be the governor of Bombay, had the support of Elphinstine's troops, which by then became a resented occupational force, although necessary to prevent the ousting of the Shah by the Afghan people, who deeply resented him as well. Kipling noted that it was "Sir Macnaghten's sense of duty to the Crown that doomed him. If he'd only taken the post at Bombay sooner."

Robinson, again thinking of what's required for an occupational force to be successful, stood his ground on the question of Elphinstone "The incompetence of the old swaddy, and an army too few in numbers, led to a complete degeneration of the occupation. Without leadership and reinforcements from India, the men became demoralized, mob-like, easy game for insurrectionists."

In November of 1841, Macnaghten's number-two in Kabul, Sir Alexander Burnes, was murdered by a Muslim mob.

"A grit Scotsman thae he was," MacLean noted.

"Trekked the majority of known lands here. Responsible for what knowledge we have for the language and cultures on the subcontinent," Kipling added. "A tragedy to eliminate the very one that supports your cause."

Shocked by the brutal murder and fearing complete chaos, Macnaghten frantically sought to buy protection from Tribal War Lords, but only bought time.

Sergeant Major MacLean commented "Thae non moosleem wawrr Lords ay canbeabaht fewrr a fuuw quid." Unfortunately the financial drain on British India became more than was bearable, the subsidies to the War Lords stopped. In a last ditch effort to save a dire situation degenerating at an alarming rate Macnaghten vainly attempted a negotiated peace with the Dost's son, Akbar Kahn. Instead of following up with diplomatic negotiations, Akbar assassinated the newly nominated governor of Bombay just two days before Christmas of 1841. In a grizzly display, his corpse was dismembered and paraded throughout the streets of Kabul.

Elphinstone, now panicked, hastily evacuated the 44th Foot from the capital. A British column of four thousand five hundred troops and twelve thousand camp followers retreated from Kabul, but were met by Ghilazi Pashtun warriors at the Kurd Kabul Pass of the Hindu Kush Mountains. There, between Jalalabad and Kabul, the 44th were massacred in the snow at Gandamak, the largest of any British Regiment during the 18th or 19th centuries. What few that survived were either executed or forced into slavery, with the exception of one sole survivor. British troops waiting for the column to arrive were shocked to see only Doctor Brydon carried by a tired horse to the gates of the garrison at Jalalabad. Several months later the British puppet leader was also assassinated, and Dost Mohammad returned to gain control.

An uneasy equilibrium existed between Afghanistan and the British Indian government over the course of the next thirty-five years. Hardly a diplomatic truce, the British failed in every attempt to place an envoy in Kabul. Patience exhausted, Lord Lytton, the new viceroy of British India, ordered a final diplomatic mission to Kabul in 1878. Again denied entrance to Kabul by Sher Ali Kahn, the third son of Dost Mohammad, Lord Lytton initiated the 2nd Afghan-Anglo War. With an army of forty thousand, the British again succeeded in becoming an occupying force, yet repeated their previous poor performance in winning the hearts and minds of the Afghan people, who refused to have the will of a foreign government forced upon them. Self-determination was their desire. During the next three years, British and Afghan forces engaged each other in nineteen separate battles as Great Britain fought to bring the Afghans to their knees.

Kipling discussed the historical details of the 2nd War vividly one evening with the two soldiers while sharing a bottle of Russian vodka. "I recall at boarding school in England, a number of boys just a few years older than I also joined the fight. I've always fancied the tales of the 66th at Maiwand," he lamented.

British and Indian troops from Bombay led by Brigadier General Burrows engaged Ayub Kan on July 27th, 1880. Greatly outnumbered, twenty five hundred British and Indian troops met an Afghan force of three thousand cavalry and nine thousand infantry, including thirty-six cannon. The place was just west of Kandahar.

Robinson studied the battle in hopes of learning critical errors employed by the British commander. "The bloody Afghans used the ravines to flank the chaps of the 66th putting the regiment perpendicular to the Jacob's Rifles and the Bombay Genadiers. The mistake created a horseshoe and the Afghans could capitalize on the weakness in the center. By Jove, the old boys almost ran out of ammo and the Afghans cut them to pieces."

Kipling remarked that although the battle was a terrible defeat, and resulted in yet another "last stand," the remainder of the 66th, eleven men and a dog, named Bobbie, managed to hold off the Afghan hoards. Badly shot up, including the canine mascot, the rag tag elements escaped to Kandahar. Months later, upon returning to

England, the eleven survivors, including Bobbie, were awarded the Afghan War campaign medal by Queen Victoria. Kipling embraced the story of the battle with great affection.

The battle at Maiwand set up the circumstances of the Afghans biggest defeat during the 2nd Anglo-Afghan Wars, and Great Britain's greatest victory coming at the Battle of Kandahar in September of 1880.

"Sergeant Major MacLean was there. In fact, fought gallantly," Robinson said, pointing out the non-commissioned officer's experience.

British forces numbering ten thousand met head on with twelve thousand eight hundred Afghans under the leadership of a twenty three year old Emir, Ayub Kahn. Engaging the British Commander General Roberts, a future Field Marshall of the British army, the Emir bombarded British reconnaissance troops with artillery positioned from above. The opponents went at it that day on September 1st, but in the end, the Afghan army was routed handily, suffering two thousand five hundred causalities; the British only thirty-six killed and two hundred eighteen wounded, including MacLean.

Although the British displayed military superiority over the Afghans in the battles of the 2nd Anglo-Afghan War, ousting Ayub Kahn in the process, they no longer had the stomach for costly post-war occupations. Fortunately a new Afghan ruler, Abdur Rahman Kahn, the "Iron Shuja" came into power and became a tentative friend of British India. Thus began a twenty-year courtship to finally forge a nation out of the numerous splintered tribes of Afghanistan. The unification effort became increasingly difficult though, when Abdur Kahn was encouraged to agree with newly created borders between Afghanistan and British India. The borders were as controversial then as they would be more than a century later.

Along the mountainous northern reaches of the North West Territories of British India and Afghanistan was a new border, a two thousand six hundred kilometer line proposed by the British Empire. Known as the Durand line, it had been drawn by Sir Mortimer Durand, the foreign secretary of British India. It was a boundary that would literally split the Pashtun territories in half. Although following clearly defined topographical features, the line disregarded demographic realities and cut a swath straight through villages and tribes, setting the stage for future tensions between Afghanistan and Pakistan. Great efforts were underway to gain the support from numerous indigenous tribes of the area, especially those of Chitral at the base of Tirich Mir, the highest mountain of the Hindu Kush at over twenty-five thousand feet. Many tribes would be cut in two within site of the peak. Mehtar Aman, the King of these tribes in the hard to reach mountain region, had begun to express a willingness to aid the British. However, in the western Hindu Kush of Chitral were factions much less agreeable with the foreign definition of the border. One such faction was the Hindu Kush Kafirs.

Distinctively warlike and independent, a unique language, culture and religion, the Kafirs were adamant in their opposition to British guidance they likened to subjugation. In 1892 the Kafirs had yet to be completely converted to Islam. Yet regardless of their religion, one constant was their determination to fight, and fight to the death if need be, defy foreign rule, stand on their own. They could be brutal in that determination.

The Mehtar, already an Islamic convert himself, did his best to appease various factions, and there were many: Kata Kafirs of Kati Valley, of Bashgul Valley, of Kulam Valley. There were Black-Robed Kata Kafirs, and Black-Robed Kom Kafirs, considered the most intractable and capable of keen military strategies. There were Black-Robed Mumo Kafirs, Istrat Kafirs, Vasi Kafirs, and so forth. The Kalasha Kafirs were the most hospitable, handsome, and said to be descendents of Alexander. Many Kalasha had light hair and light eyes. The Kalasha Kafirs were Mehtar Aman's ancestral tribe, and although considerate of those people, his responsibility as a Mehtar was to unite all Kafirs. Unfortunately feuds between the clans were commonplace, and the Durand line not only added fuel to an already brewing fire, it ignited a full-blown ideological and intertribal war.

Their encampment was on the bank of a mountain lake, surrounded by massive glaciers, cirques, ice flows and crevasses, the month was July. Captain Robinson, attached to the Corps of Royal Engineers, also known as the Sappers and Sergeant Major MacLean of the 92nd Highlanders were there with a partial platoon of twenty Sikhs. They'd ventured to Chitral in an effort to cajole Aman to agreement, and offer the services of the Royal Engineers as well. They proposed a road be constructed from his capital to Peshawar, which the Royal Engineers would undertake. He was given an annual subsidy, five hundred Snider-Enfield rifles and 100,000 rounds of ammunition.

Mehtar Aman was a magnanimous leader, yet could be ruthless, not hesitating to personally kill his own soldier for a severe infraction such as rape. And Aman was suspicious of the British, but willing to learn more, so he accepted the group for the time being, and certainly accepted the arms. He would be their generous host and offer protection, safe haven from any enemy; that was after all, the tradition.

"How's the trout today?" Kipling asked Captain Robinson sarcastically, as the soldier ate his catch one warm afternoon.

"Mister Kipling - exactly as it was yesterday, and the day before that," Robinson said, looking up from the plate on his lap.

Fables of Rainbow trout literally jumping into men's hands as they fished came to Kipling's mind, and weren't far from the truth. Unfortunately after days of the same main course, all wanted a change. Robinson wished for steak and chips as he took one last bite. Tossing the metal plate and utensils on the rocks next to his pith helmet, he looked at Kipling, now gazing stoically at the lake while puffing his pipe. Robinson, wondering what the intellectual was thinking, asked, "Mister Kipling is there a story that comes to mind, or perhaps a poem?"

"Perhaps," Kipling murmured as he watched the Sergeant Major struggle with a hooked trout on the bank of the lake. Shuja was in the distance, preparing to send his falcon on an afternoon hunt.

"Tell me old chap, what do you know about the Black-Robed Kom Kafirs?" Kipling asked, getting to the point of his original thoughts.

"Fierce lot, they are. Barbaric. Pagan actually."

"Not Muslims?" Kipling asked motioning to a Sikh to bring him a wooden stool.

"Not at all old boy. Brilliant bastards at outright murder though, in fact, their favorite sport is killing Muslims."

"Please, you're joking," Kipling exclaimed while sitting down.

"My man, as good at it as a falcon killing a swift," Robinson asserted, pointing at the predator now airborne.

"Rrayht Mesta Kepplin, an for kallin wan they danz a jig taer warr gawds. They git shawls for kallin twoo," Sergeant Major MacLean added, joining them with catch in hand and tossing the fish at the Sikh to clean.

"Good God man, a dance to war gods for murder and robes for multiple murders? Absolute bloody heathens," Kipling proclaimed, opening up his journal to take notes. "You've witnessed this first hand?"

"I dare say - the Sergeant Major definitely has experience in this matter. Don't you MacLean," Robinson confirmed as he packed his own pipe with tobacco, lighting it and taking a puff.

"Ay Sahrr, ah doo. Kafewrr fight tae the daith an' live for revenge. More tan moosleems - ne'er forget a thing. If wan Kafewrr es shot deid en the clan – the rest'll kep after the mon that doon it, til they catch the bastart. Na matta ow lang it taks," MacLean said, emphasizing their elephant-like memory when it came to retribution. He went on to describe the particular combat strategy of the Kafir. Employing guerilla tactics initially, followed by an attack of the enemy from all sides simultaneously, similar to a swarm of bees, they had an utter disregard for their own losses.

"They prefer to attack en masse rather than first exploit the enemy's weaknesses," Robinson said.

"Trroo, also they is thieves an' canbeabribed. Wisnae an 'onest wan," MacLean added.

"The Sergeant Major's right - they can be bribed, but never bought. Especially when it comes to honor, not for any amount of gold. Jack the Ripper could hide here and they would never give him up," Robinson pointed out. "Other than that - good natured lot," he added with a laugh.

"Noo, except fewrr auld wifies, Mesta Kepplin," MacLean corrected, pulling out his pipe and joining the smoking party.

"And the problem with the women would be?" Kipling asked with a grin. He was expecting a good one from the colorful Sergeant Major.

"Yer have nae problem sahrr – if ye fancy a face lak a backdewrr. They is hideous ewgly dewgs - rrahtwhylers – wean eatin monstahrrs they is. Heids brroon an' black es bewll tahrriers," MacLean said wincing. He pondered a moment as he lit his pipe, and added, "They newt pure hacket at furrst - ah mean, the lassies urr brraw an' bonnie…"

Robinson interrupted the Scot's nonsensical rambling "Sergeant Major MacLean's quite opinionated on the subject Mister Kipling. Afghan girls are very beautiful, yet their life is miserable. Now, though they're all slaves, they're treated much worse. We're kinder to our dogs. Bought, sold, and worked to the bone – then the mountains and wind get hold of them - takes its toll. Before they turn twenty-five, they're washed up, faces dark and haggard, coarse with wrinkles and filthy from head to toe."

"Twelve pints isnae enough whiskey tae git yirrsel pished enough tae poke er Afghan airy pie. Guid reason tae bea moosleem daer think? Ah mean thaer dewgs uv tae wear burqas an ye coont see thaer faces," MacLean said with a chuckle.

"This has all been quite interesting, to say the least. By chance do you have anything else to add?" Kipling said, chuckling while looking at Robinson. He wrote down every word.

"Mister Kipling, old boy, don't make them angry and you'll be quite fine," Robinson answered, half joking.

"Rrayht sahrr – ne'er convert tae moosleem an ne'er tetch em gauf Mesta Kepplin," the Sergeant Major added seriously, causing the two Englishmen to erupt in laughter, echoing across the lake.

"One point of the conversion to Islam however," Robinson said, becoming very serious as he spoke. "Amir Abdur Rahman is determined to convert this hoard. It's believed that he's been kidnapping large numbers of young boys, taking them to Kabul and converting them. Rumors abound that he already has fanatical converts amongst the Kafir today – and they're ready for the word to sack the Pagans."

"Do you think they've operatives in hiding amongst the Kafirs?" Kipling asked.

"Old chap, I believe that's very possible."

CHAPTER 2

JULY 17, 1892

HINDU KUSH RANGE, BRITISH INDIA

THE WEEKLONG SOJOURN OVER, they broke camp at the lake. It was time to move south and rendezvous with another clan of Kafirs at a valley south of Tirich Mir. Before they departed, however, Kipling had a surprise for the Mehtar and his immediate entourage of sons. A corporal from the 51st Sikhs Frontier Force brought something few of Mehtar Aman's men had ever laid their eyes on before, a wet plate studio camera that had been hauled up to the lake.

"Please, your Majesty, please group close together in front of the rocks. I vill make the portrait of your court. Tank you please sahr," the Sikh corporal requested of the Chitrali King. Aman complied without questioning. The corporal, overly polite, methodically directed Mehtar's entourage in position, asking each to be very still, as he prepared to expose the photographic plate. The corporal noted to himself that the sun was close to disappearing behind a cloud. If he waited a moment, the tintype would be absent of any shadows, yet brilliantly lit by the bright snow of the glacier and cirques. He made two exposures, both perfect.

The band of travelers made their way down from higher ground of the Hindu Kush, moving southwest toward the border of Kafiristan, modern day Nuristan. They crossed numerous small tributaries and creeks that ultimately merged, finally flowing into the Kabul River well beyond them, arriving at a small Kalasha Kafir village set in a high mountain valley. The steep hills surrounding the village of twenty or so houses were sparsely covered with trees and shrubs. The British officer and English gentleman followed the Mehtar into a small ornately carved structure built onto the side of one of those hills. There, they were joined by five of the Mehtar's sons and his younger brother; all entered the multi level wooden enclosure.

The Kafirs were stern, imposing, and ready for serious discussions. As somber as they were, Kipling thought they were also a colorful society, both in their approach to life and appearance. The Mehtar was at the center of the troupe. A big, tall man, with a large dark beard and moustache, highlighted with gray, his head was covered with a red turban, similar to Sikhs, and indicative of the cultural influences on the Kafir. He wore a large light blue and green wool coat that fell to the ankles; his knee-high boots were standard Russian issue. The Mehtar's sons, and he had many, varied in age from thirteen to late twenties. Aman's younger brother, Shir, was thirty-something, yet looked much older a scowl permanently etched on his face. All family members were dressed equally as colorful as their leader, multi-colored turbans, scarves, and accents of ammo belts for the Snider-Enfield rifles carefully leaning against the rock walls of the enclosure.

The Mehtar, who'd been the Chitrali monarch for thirty-two years, studied Robinson with piercing blue eyes that denoted those years of wise rule. Aman was concerned with the proposed border and the resulting division for Chitrali tribes, his tribes. British India had graciously offered services, food, engineering, even weapons as carrots. The Mehtar said, "the British on one hand have offered to build a road from Chitral to Peshawar. Your Queen shows great magnanimity, but how are the British designs any better for the people of Afghanistan and Chitral than Russian ideas?"

"Your Majesty, the Russians attacked Afghan troops and have settled permanently in Penjdeh," Robinson pointed out. Penjdeh was a village in the northwest desert of Afghanistan.

"And the British have attacked Afghanistan in the east. You have had seventy thousand troops occupying this country. What do you propose to be the difference?" Aman asked, noting the hypocrisy.

"Autonomy. Great Britain, the Queen, all believe in self-destiny for the people of Chitral and Afghanistan," Robinson said.

"But you've given us a border that divides," the Mehtar stated, unimpressed. "And we are already autonomous. No one rules us," he added.

"The Amir in Kabul, your Majesty, he's in agreement with Britain and encourages you to join with him. I implore you to consider."

"My place is here, after all, what will happen to Kafiristan and Chitral otherwise? All Kafiristanis are not in agreement with a border that would make them subjects of the Amir," Aman pointed out.

"They unfortunately, would be required to comply with the Amir your Majesty."

"And taxes, to the Amir as well?"

"The Kafir would pay taxes - as required by the government in Kabul and they'd be required to become Muslims, well, as is mandated by Amir Rahman, to convert that is," Robinson said.

Kipling observed the reaction of the entourage, seeing Aman's younger stepbrother immediately lean over to the Mehtar and whisper in his ear. Listening to Shir Kahn, the Mehtar looked back at Robinson and continued, "What would happen to the people on the British side of your Durand line?"

"The Kafir would not be taxed by British India, and would not be forced to convert to any particular religion. It's up to the people to decide, "Robinson said.

Robinson went on to explain the Kafir would be masters of their own destiny based upon the British parliamentary system of government, but enforced by the Mehtar in the North West Frontier. The current local form of law would still apply, which consisted of an elected magistrate and twelve assistants, similar to a mayor and city council. The magistrate would have the onus to enforce religious tolerance, allowing people to worship how they pleased, so long as they didn't violate the law.

Publicly, Robinson put on the best game face he possessed, while making his argument to the King. Privately, both he and Kipling thought that armed conflict would be forthcoming between Mehtar Aman, and the non-Muslims, that ended up on the wrong side of the border. And there was the ever, present Russian, looking for the opportunity to profiteer by stirring the pot. Safe to say, both Kipling and Robinson thought the situation would grow worse before it got better. As they stepped out to the rock and dirt road, Kipling asked Robinson his impression of Aman's attitude.

"Excellent question Mister Kipling. My impression? My impression is that he appears to favor the British point of view, and yours?" Robinson asked.

"I must side with you, Mister Robinson, however - my thoughts on his brother, and two sons, are quite the opposite," Kipling said, pipe in mouth, addressing an imaginary ball with his brassie.

"You must be referring to Shir, Nizam and Afzal."

"Precisely," Kipling said, swinging with his finest follow–thru.

"Ay am inclined to agree with your astute observation, Mister Kipling, however; ayy fear... there're influences...outside of our own - at work here."

"Perhaps...Russian?"

"Perhaps, - perhaps indeed, old chap. But, likely not only them," Robinson said.

"Likely, being whom?"

"Fanatical Muslims, who else could they possibly be?" Robinson spewed, miffed at the obvious.

"Muslims? For what purpose?"

"My God old man, perhaps you've spent too many years displaced – our Afghan friend has it in mind - to turn the entire world into converts of Mohammed," Robinson said.

"Muslim, against Muslim, I take it?" Kipling asked, rhetorically.

"Kipling? Please, spill me some of your vodka – an' I'll tell you Shakespeare's version," Robinson said, as he held out his tin cup for a pour. "Absolute domination, chap. Absolute domination."

"The new caliph," Kipling confirmed, handing over the flask of Russian booze usually in his coat on colder days.

"Unfortunately, I'm afraid so - and time is on the side of their plans," Robinson said, disturbing a small ant mound with his boot as he sipped his hooch.

"I can understand your sentiments – I do. In fact, I recall the history of these lands – but we...we, my friend, are not doomed – unless...unless, of course – we plan it that way – unintentionally, mind you," Kipling said, then repeating his swing with a new grip. "A young man named Vardon taught me to hold the brassie in this manner," Kipling added as he dual tasked.

"Oh really Mister Kipling, that's all very interesting," Robinson commenting on his companion's distraction. "But you said unintentionally?"

"Absolutely," Kipling said, motioning the brassie's face in the direction of his practice shot. He swung at an imaginary ball; and after the follow-thru, placed the brassie head on the ground, leaning on the shaft. "Ye've gotta kep yer ay 'en tha bardie – Mesta Robinson," Kipling said in his best impression of MacLean.

"Ignorance is what your implying Mister Kipling," Robinson said, giving the flask back.

"Thank you, man," Kipling said holding up the flask as in a toast. He knocked back a swig himself.

It became increasingly clear to them that the intertribal bickering that had persisted for years was ultimately going to cause the downfall of all Kafir. The Amir from Kabul would find it easy to divide and conquer people that had essentially divided themselves, regardless of an imaginary line invented by an English surveyor. The people in the village were warlike, and all were slave owners. The slaves themselves came in two varieties, the domestic, or house slaves, and artisans. All women were domestic slaves, the wives and mistresses; and the men could own more than one of each. Adultery was permitted in the pagan clans as well. The women also worked in the fields and gardens, and if a pack animal was not available, women were responsible for hauling loads, regardless of the weight. Artisans were the second classification of slaves, and included woodcrafters and musicians.

The matter of the Kafir reputation as a fierce warrior came up on more than one occasion while the three British subjects stayed in the mountains. Since having an opportunity to live amongst the Afghan and Chitral Kafir for several weeks, the power of observation gave great insight as to the true character and nature of these unusual people. The manner in which they lived, Kipling believed, was of some importance. Slavery, high altitude, paganism aside, Kipling noted their permanent habitat. For a Christian and gentleman, educated at the finest schools, used to a strict observance of personal hygiene that extended to one's shelter, he found the Kafir habits very unappealing and unsanitary.

Houses of the villages in the mountains tended to be clustered together on the side of a hill and designed with a foundation that allowed for a small basement, or additional room. With multiple levels, they tended to be grimy and dirty, littered with slaughtered animal bones and horns. The bottom level was usually used as an open pit latrine, and the smell of urine and stored manure would emanate throughout the additional levels. Weapons and other family valuables were kept on the middle level, and the actual living spaces on the third and final level.

"I believe it's quite possible that part of their fierce reputation may stem in part from their appearance, and the manner in which they live," Kipling remarked to Robinson.

"I see your point Mister Kipling. They do posses a sinister look, don't they?" Robinson replied as they observed a band of warriors enter the village one afternoon.

Unlike the Kalasha Kafir, the Black-Robed Kom Kafir from the west were not fair-haired with light eyes, but dark skinned, with heavy eyebrows and low foreheads. Known as plunderers, assassins, and opportunists, they lived by the sword and died by it. Fighting was a way of life; seeking revenge and killing was sport.

As the band of six men passed them, Kipling couldn't help but notice how curious and crafty their furtive gaze was. It reminded him of the falcon, quick and shifty; however, rather than being majestic as the falcon, these men appeared criminal, peering at them from below their furry eyebrows. Kipling commented that the marauders were armed to the teeth and carrying Russian Berdan rifles.

"Well Mister Robinson, I don't believe they purchased those from traders on the Caspian. Perhaps the Russians are giving their weapons away these days? The Czar isn't courting the Kom Kafir is he?" He asked sarcastically.

Robinson agreed wholeheartedly with Kipling that there were probably a few dead Russians lying in the Hindu Kush. Kipling confirmed Robinson's story of Kom Kafir battle tactics in conversations with Aman's sons. Conflict hardened and fearless, they would fight to the last man. Loyalty to their fellow comrade was paramount, known to never leave their dying or dead on the battlefield. Their skills in business were minimal at best, preferring to carry axes, swords, daggers and guns, rather than an abacus and pen. Black-Robed Kom Kafir were professional killers, their sole motivation and meaning in life was to fight to the death.

As the six moved into the center of town, it soon became clear that an altercation was brewing. The six Afghan Kafir looked fierce in their goatskin tunics, wide leather belt, and black turbans. Their boots were made of hefty leather and goat fur. Each had crisscrossed bandoleer belts around their torsos and pouches of ammo, more than likely from Russians they had robbed and killed. The ever-present I-handled dagger was stuffed between the belt and tunic. Each also had a large, intricately carved walking stick, which could easily be used as a lethal club.

Afzal and Shir, both Muslims and aligned with Amir Kahn, were approaching the six men along with four backup from the Mehtar's small army. The gate of their step meant business. A fifth uniformed man, distinctively foreign, was with them as well. He was a Russian officer, gripping a single action forty-four revolver and apparently very angry.

"Mesta Robinson - whit're ye think thaes daeing ere sahrr?" The Sergeant Major asked. "Ye rooski - awa' an' dicht yer neb ye snottery bastart ye," MacLean added as he stood up, moving his hand toward his Webley service revolver.

"Take your leave Sergeant Major - let's see what happens first with these unsavory chaps. Mister Kipling prepare for anything. There may be shooting," Robinson warned.

Yelling began before the two groups had reached each other, still twenty or thirty feet apart and near the center of the village. Three other men stepped out of a hillside house, each brandishing a new Snider, they were Mehtar's men. The Kom-Kafirs then did something very surprising; they stopped in the middle of the town and began laughing, as if they found something funny about the precarious situation. Laughter from the Koms only served to infuriate the Russian that much more. He was screaming at them in his native tongue, while motioning at the rifles. The Mehtar's sons were translating.

"Mister Robinson it appears that you're assessment was correct," Kipling said.

"They believe the rifles were stolen?"

"Well, I can understand a bit of what Afzal and Shir are saying. Not happy at all. The question of the origin of the rifles has come up," Kipling said.

"Weel ah dinna whit ye think sahrr, bea ah see shootin soon. Mista Kepplin sud it start, muv behind meh," the Scotsman said stepping in front of Kipling and examining his rifle to make sure it was loaded.

When the Russian got within ten feet of the Kom Kafir, he raised his pistol without warning and fired, striking one in the center of his face. The five remaining Kom lifted their rifles; but before any could pull the trigger, shots rang out from the three men flanking the Kom, followed by two more shots from the Russian. The deadly fracas was over in a flash, and all six Kom Kafir lay on the ground in pools of blood collecting in the dirt, dead or dying, as blue smoke rose in the air.

"Good God man, how brutal," Kipling exclaimed. He could smell the spent gunpowder.

The Russian was examining the rifles as one of the Muslims checked each of the gunned down enemy. Two had survived, but of no threat anymore, they would be taken care of momentarily. Several village women that had been hiding now poked their heads out from doorways. Satisfied the fighting was over, the women moved in to strip the dead Koms of any valuables they might have, and for their own safety, repeatedly struck the bodies with the large clubs dropped during the fight. Loud thumps, followed by an occasional grunt from the living could be heard each time a woman made contact.

In the early evening, a seventh Kom was found, one that had been straggling in the mountains. Kipling and Robinson were relaxing with the Sergeant Major when they heard a loud disturbance outside their shelter. The three bolted from the tent to see the Russian, drunk with vodka, staggering towards a group of men near a campfire, sidearm in hand. His boots hastily placed on the opposite feet were buckling at the ankles with every other step as he stormed over the rocky ground toward them. Two Muslims had the Black Robed Kom Kafir pinned on the ground as another held a knife to the man's throat.

"He's a murderer," a Kafir Muslim said to Afzal, the eldest son of the Mehtar, as he too made his way toward the scene.

"Yes Afzal, we caught him with the Russian rifle too," said another.

"Hold 'im darr," the Russian slurred in English, stumbled, and then fell, landing hard on the rocks with his hands and knees. His clumsiness only fueled his anger as he precariously stood back up. Swaying, he resumed the approach.

"What were you thinking - you thieving goat?" He roared in Russian at reaching the campfire. "Stinkink foul. You are dead now, *prishju*," the Russian continued as he raised his pistol in preparation to fire at the Kafir's temple. The man closed his eyes, expecting imminent death.

"No. No," Afzal yelled, trying to stop the Russian from killing the man. He reasoned the prisoner could be useful later and after his usefulness had expired, then the infidel would be killed.

Distracted by the Prince's voice, the Russian turned his head, falling once again, the gun discharging, missing its mark, the bullet ricocheting into rocks. Scrambling to catch his fall, the Muslims let loose of the captured man's arms. Now free, he leapt up and darted away into the shadows of the rock cliffs.

"Ahhh, *govno*. Git 'im," the Russian screamed. A Muslim militiaman managed to run him down, and after tackling the Kom Kafir, held the Kom down while the Russian struggled to reach them.

"No, I said don't kill him. I have other uses for him," Afzal said, imploring the Russian to spare the Kom Kafir.

Tempered by Afzal's persistence, and dizzy from a night of vodka, the Russian finally relented. He stood above the Kom, now cowering, and spoke directly at the man.

"Pig, you're lucky. I spare you for moment. Tonight you make peace, tomorrow you dead," the Russian said, and then staggered back to his tent, collapsing in a drunken stupor.

"Tie the goat over there by the shit," Afzal ordered, pointing to a rocky hole that was used as a latrine.

A touch to the shoulder woke Kipling from an otherwise sound sleep. Shuja was sitting next to him with the falcon on his gloved hand.

"I'm very sorry for disturbing you Mister Kipling. Might I ask a question of you concerning the captured man?" The boy politely inquired.

"My boy - your highness, please do go on. What's your question?" Kipling asked seeing concern in the boy's eyes. Shuja looked completely perplexed.

"You see Mister Kipling, the man – the Kom that was captured -

he will be killed tomorrow by my brother."

"Why, yes of course, I suppose you're right."

"I believe that he should be set free."

Kipling sat up as he put on his glasses. "I say your highness, why pray tell do you believe that should be what's done?" Kipling asked.

"I believe this is what you English call a conundrum Mister Kipling. You see - if I let the man go, it will show that I'm weak but it will also show that I am strong." He stroked the bird's chest with the back of his free hand. "I'm weak for showing compassion for an infidel, but I'm strong for giving life rather than taking it."

"That's very astute your highness. And you can preside over the unfortunate man's sentence without objection?" Kipling asked, impressed by the boy's wisdom beyond his years.

"Well, not exactly Mister Kipling. I am after all the youngest son of the Mehtar. But I am the son that is the falconer and my father will respect my decision above that of my brother's objections."

"I see."

"I would need to secretly let the man go. But it's my belief that in giving him life, I will gain the greatest respect from the people that we are trying to unite. What are you thoughts Mister Kipling?" The boy asked, confident he was on the right track.

"Yes, I see your highness - the 'more flies with honey' approach - a very clever idea indeed. Perhaps it just might work." Kipling was very proud of this precocious Prince. He was already showing signs of being a true leader. Maybe the future would portend success for these people of the Hindu Kush, if Shuja were the Mehtar one day, Kipling decided.

Just before sunrise, young Shuja slipped away from the spoon of his female slave and out of his house, creeping silently to the doomed man. Shuja knew the man had to be set free by morning; it was a certainty that he would be interrogated, tortured, and executed by the Russian before noon.

"What are you doing?" The Kom asked in his native Drardic dialect of Kamviri as Shuja cut the ropes that bound him.

"I'm freeing you, but you must run like the wind and never come back. Do you understand me? Now go. Hurry," Shuja said as he cut the last rope. The man looked hard at Shuja as he clutched the boy's forearm. He thanked him, and escaped.

The high pitched cackles of women slaves woke the rest of the village, including the Russian who after opening his tent could see the Kom Kafir fleeing like a swift towards the safety of the rocky cliffs. Quickly, Muslims were in hot pursuit, but the Kom was much faster. The pursuers rapidly started to lag behind the speedy man.

"Let him go," Shuja yelled at the Muslim militia.

Puzzled, one queried, "But Prince Shuja, he's getting away. We should go after him, shouldn't we?"

"No. Let him go. Look at him – he's running like a swift; let him be one. Anyway, there's nowhere for him to go." A slight smile formed on Shuja's mouth as he watched the Kom disappear. The Russian looked at Shuja and began berating him sternly. Shuja waved him off in disgust.

Robinson, now standing by Kipling's side offered his editorial, noting the blatant act of Shuja, "It appears Mister Kipling that there may be some dissention among the Mehtar's ranks as to the Kafir situation."

"Oh quite more than that old chap. I had quite a conversation with the young Prince while you were counting sheep."

"Don't leave me hanging Mister Kipling, what did his highness have to say?"

"It appears that much more is going on than one would believe. Our Russian here is in cahoots with the Mehtar's brother and oldest son."

"Get to the point dear man, for what?"

"Second oldest racket in the world Mister Robinson – slavery. Only this slave trade is a bit more sinister."

"My God - slavery, ay?"

"And you were right about the Islamic sleepers amongst the Kafir, Mister Robinson. Amir Kahn has agreed to give the bloody Russians kidnapping rights. They're the ones making off with young boys from Chitral and northern Afghanistan. Then they're brainwashed in Kabul and turned into fanatical Muslim ghazis - capable of anything, murder, insurrection, even self-imposed martyrdom. He's planning a Jihad and ghazis will be weapons. Shir and his nephew Afzal are just part of the conspiracy in Chitral."

"Good Lord Mister Kipling, this is how the Amir proposes to convert these heathens to Islam? The consequences for the Durand agreement – what do you imagine they would be?"

"I don't know old boy, but I dare say that I fear a dark curtain may soon fall on Afghanistan and Chitral – for some time to come."

The Black Robed Kom Kafir was no fool. He ran away as fast as could, never daring to stop for a moment. The fear of being captured and killed kept him going. He climbed up the mountains of the Hindu Kush like an Ibex, and then down, until finally exhausted, he couldn't run anymore. He collapsed in a heap by a pile of rocks. There was nothing left. If he was found, then so be it. It was God's will. He simply had to sleep. And he did.

Concluding his Hindu Kush summer sojourn, Kipling prepared a present for the Mehtar, a Hotel Guest Registry that would have been used as a journal or simply a notebook.

"And what's the purpose of this book Mister Kipling?" The Mehtar asked, Shuja by his side with the falcon in hand.

"When honored people travel to your land in peace, they should sign the Registry your Majesty, as an indication of good faith and good will, on the level and square," Kipling said as he presented the gift, along with the portrait of the Mehtar's family. The Mehtar thanked him graciously and asked Captain Robinson to keep it for him while he stayed on.

As for the Captain, Kipling gave him the remaining tintype.

"What shall I do with this, Mister Kipling?" Robinson asked.

Kipling pondered as he smoked his pipe before answering. "I don't know old boy, but hold on to it – it may possibly mean something one day."

CHAPTER 3

THE U.S. NAVY COMMANDER pointed the red "grimes light" on a book-size, portable GPS fastened with a Velcro strap to his thigh. The red lens was used at night to mitigate any negative affect on the flight crew's night vision. Occasionally, he'd look out the cockpit at the stars; or when the pilot called "traffic," he'd try to find the bright strobe light of a nearby plane, always coming back to his task at hand, reading. On the GPS was a sheet of stationary that had been with him since deploying to Afghanistan one month earlier. A poem was printed on the sheet, and he tended to read it often lately, focusing on the final verse. It had long since been committed to memory. He repeated the words to himself over and over as he gazed out the cockpit into the darkness, a verse summarizing a survivor's thoughts of a massacre near Kandahar a long, long time ago, his advice to a young British soldier. The author was Rudyard Kipling.

> *When you're wounded and left on Afghanistan's plains,*
> *And the women come out to cut up what remains,*
> *Jest roll to your rifle and blow out your brains*
> *An' go to your Gawd like a soldier.*

Go, go, go like a soldier,
So-oldier of the Queen.

They were flying at flight level two four-zero, twenty-four thousand feet, and one hundred miles north of Task Force Fifty. The flight had just crossed the coastline, now over the Arabian Sea.

"Commander, we're feet wet. Our ETA is twenty-five minutes. We're on track for the twenty-two thirty recovery," the pilot said over the ICS. "We'll trap right after these guys on the starboard side."

Commander Bryan Craig could see the bright running and position lights of a flight of two F/A-18 Hornets on the right side of their aircraft. Both appeared to be at the same altitude, also on their way to the USS Carl Vinson and Flag Ship of the three-carrier task force. The S-3 Viking Bryan was in was dispatched by the Task Force Commander to fly him to a strike brief. It was also a chance to warm up and get a belly of food. He'd been in the elements on the frigid Hindu Kush for the last three days.

"Viking Two Zero Two take angels one eight, contact approach button eighteen." An E-2C Hawkeye descended their flight to eighteen thousand, handing them over to carrier approach.

"Roger."

Bryan loved the curt response of a sharp aircrew; it was professional, the true sign of a tail-hooker, radio discipline and airway brevity. Communications were short and sweet.

"Approach, Viking Two Zero Two with you on the Zero Five Zero at seventy five."

"Roger Viking Two Zero Two, say angels."

"Angels One Eight."

Several minutes later Bryan felt the plane's speed-brakes deploy, followed by landing gear and tailhook, the induced aerodynamic drag causing the Viking to shudder as the plane decelerated to approach speed. Bryan looked up from the GPS when he heard the call for the aircraft to turn to final. They were getting close. Stowing the GPS in the map case, he cinched the shoulder restraints tight, making sure that the harness of his Douglas zero-zero seat, one that would eject if the plane was on deck or airborne, was locked. He fastened the oxygen mask over a bearded face. Hearing the familiar call over the radio from the Landing Signals Officer, he inserted his iPod earphones – *"Pink Floyd – Dark Side Of The Moon,"* his favorite, his mind clear of what he couldn't control.

"Three quarters of a mile Viking, call the ball," the LSO said listening for verification that the pilot had the "meatball."

Landing a jet aircraft on board a carrier is probably as difficult a task as anything, Bryan thought, especially on a dark night. Zero margins for error. The pilot used the "meatball," a visual landing system, to fly the plane to the deck. Consisting of an array of four orange and one red vertical lens, plus green horizontal "datum" lights, the visual landing system provided a 3° glideslope for the pilot to fly. When flown to precision, the aircraft perfectly "on speed" and the middle orange light lined up with the datums, the pilot would be said to have a centered "meatball," resulting in an "OK three wire;" catching the number three of the four wires. At three quarters of a mile, the pilot referenced the meatball, as opposed to the glideslope information displayed on cockpit instruments. The pilot's scan consists of three reference points: Meatball – lineup – angle of attack.

"Two Zero Two, Viking ball - Seven Point One," the pilot said verifying that he had "the ball" and giving his fuel weight for arresting gear settings.

"Roger ball Viking. Lined up a little right," the landing signal officer said encouraging a flight path correction. Lineup was one of the three.

Operations at sea are conducted continuously. Aircraft are launched and recovered simultaneously, but to do so efficiently, the landing area was designed with an angle. The Carl Vinson's angle was twelve degrees left of the carrier's bearing, the centerline of the landing area constantly moving to the pilot's right. When winds are calm, the landing area will move to the right at an even faster rate as the ship speeds up to twenty-five or thirty knots while making its own wind. The pilot therefore, continually made adjustments to lineup during the approach, all the while maintaining glideslope and proper airspeed, or "Angle of Attack," for tailhook position.

For angle of attack, the plane needed to be "on speed." Come in too fast, or nose down and flat, the plane would "bolter," and miss all four wires. *Miss a meal!* Come in too slow, the tail end dragging, there's a risk of an in-flight engagement, the hook snagging a wire while still airborne. The plane would be yanked down onto the deck with great force, causing severe structural damage to the airframe.

As the aircraft got closer to the stern, the glideslope, or meatball, which is conical in shape, became narrower and adjustments in power and lineup needed to be very delicate, yet more frequent. It was akin to surgery, a life or death event, and the meatball the most important of the three. If he came in too low, below the "red ball," shipmates would be picking up pieces of plane and pilots from the fantail, but the LSOs would never allow the pilot to get that low without calling for a correction.

"POWER, POWER, POWER," would be the frantic call.

The key was to "walk" the throttles. Hold the stick like an open tube of toothpaste. Anticipate the flight path. Correct before the correction was needed, ahead of the plane, ahead of the power curve.

With a tiny wing dip, and a schosh of power, the pilot made the lineup adjustment requested. Ten seconds later the Viking hit the deck and jerked to a violent halt, as the pilot went to full power, anticipating the bolter that didn't come. Three wire. A perfect landing, they'd eat in the carrier's wardroom that night.

Pulling back power, the pilot raised the hook, and followed the plane captain's illuminated wands for taxi directions. Multiple aircraft were still being recovered at sixty-second intervals. The Task Force was in war mode, and sorties were launching and recovering 24/7. They chalked and chained near the island, just below vulture's row.

Though seemingly small from the air, sometimes called a "postage stamp," once onboard aircraft carrier, the actual size never ceased to amaze. The Carl Vinson was five billion dollars of warship, without the aircraft on board. As she steamed that day, CVN-70 was ready for war all by herself, with four surface-to-air missile launchers, four twenty-millimeter cannons, countermeasures, and torpedo decoys. And that was just for defense. For offense, she had an array of ten various radars, three guidance systems and ninety warplanes.

Vis Per Mare - Strength from the Sea. Her keel laid in 1975; the Carl Vinson was commissioned in 1982. She's massive - ninety-seven thousand tons of displacement, three hundred and thirty-two meters in length. Seventeen stories from the top of the island to the nuclear reactors, a floating city of five thousand four hundred and eighty shipmates, able to stay at sea for months, only needing replenishment for aircraft fuel, plus food and water for the crew.

Bryan followed the pilots inside the island to pri-fly, the carrier's version of an "airport gate." Lieutenant Rick Johns, the Admiral's aide and his guide to the War Room, greeted him. He trailed the aide through a number of hatches, up and down various ladder wells, finally arriving in the "Flag Spaces," a series of rooms along a passageway of the 0-3 Level just below the flight deck.

The exterior of an aircraft carrier was steel and non-skid. Painted grey from bow to stern. Inside however, the labyrinth of passageways was kept clean and shiny, sailors busily waxing, buffing, and polishing. The Admiral's spaces were kept extra shiny. Enlisted personnel would literally be scattered along the floor, sitting cross-legged, polishing brass on doorways, or buffing the floor until the surface bore a reflection. Twenty-four hours a day, seven days a week for six months.

"Watch your step there, sir. It's just been waxed," a seaman requested as Bryan crossed over a knee-knocker into the pristine area. Always an obstacle course, Bryan tapped danced on by.

Opening the doorway to TFCC, The Flag Command Center, Bryan's eyes adjusted to the darkness of the cold room. Filled with staff that worked for Rear Admiral Jack "Rabbit" Barnes, TFCC was the mission hub. Distracted by the light, all eyes momentarily looked in the direction of the door. *Who's that guy with the beard?* They went back to work. The Task Force Commander simply smiled.

"Bryan Craig - look what the cat drug in. Great to have you on board," the Admiral said gregariously, shaking Bryan's hand with the strong grip of a weightlifter. The Task Force Commander's mission was a serious one, but the Admiral loved his job, had fun doing it. And it showed in his attitude.

Bryan had known Rabbit since the Gulf War. A very respected leader throughout his career, he'd shot up through the ranks, achieving Flag by forty-two. The callsign "Rabbit" was fitting, but he was also known as the "baby Admiral." He had an easy going personality, often using a person's first name rather than rank, enlisted and officers alike; a disarming, effective leadership style. When the rank led the last name, look out.

Rabbit quickly went around the room introducing the key players on his staff; the Carrier Air Group Commander, his deputy CAG, the Surface Warfare Commander, Air Warfare Commander, the Vinson's skipper, and the strike lead who was also the only woman in the group. Lieutenant Crystal Walker had the callsign "Street." A round of handshakes ensued.

"Good evening sir," came the greeting from the flight lead, a slight southern twang in her voice. She gave Bryan a firm handshake.

Not quite sold on the aspect of women in combat, Bryan believed the opposite sex was more of a distraction, a social experiment that under no circumstance should be conducted in forward deployed combat units. Lieutenant Walker was attractive, even without makeup and when wearing a flight suit rather than women's fashions. Her looks were the basis for more than one possible problem, Bryan honestly believed, the most obvious being that there was one female pilot in a squadron of many men. Sexual harassment charges could be made, or sexual discrimination charges for that matter. A constant in the corporate world, no doubt, but this was war and PC needed to take a back seat to victory, he believed. Her callsign could also be thrown right back in the face of the Commanding Officer that allowed it, even though it was probably innocently adopted by her in an effort to fit into a man's world. Lastly, and what disturbed Bryan the most, the horrible things that she could be made to suffer at the hands of terrorists, or Taliban should she be shot down and captured. That thought could also be in the back of the mind of a fellow pilot, who may take unnecessary risks to prevent such a possibility from becoming reality.

No doubt, she was good looking though, he thought, which made him think of sex and the expense of the training, seemingly wasted should she become pregnant? And that was a definite possibility, unless of course, she was a lesbian. He didn't think so for some reason. *Women in combat, just what the hell was the Navy thinking?* Maybe one day, he'd be proven wrong - a caveman in a modern world.

"You've got to be Admiral Craig's son," a Captain said to Bryan. He read the nametag on the officer's flight suit. He was the CAG - Captain "Wells" Fargo. All tailhookers had callsigns.

"Right, I suppose that'd be correct sir," Bryan answered, thinking he recognized the senior officer from somewhere.

"I was a nugget Corsair pilot when I first met your dad years ago," the Captain said. "He was Commander Sixth Fleet when I was just a Lieutenant JG - and one hell of a warrior, Bryan."

"Yes sir, he sure could be," Bryan said hesitating. Another Sixth Fleet pilot again, he thought.

"How's he doing anyway?"

"Just fine, sir. Probably playing golf," Bryan said, dodging any more discussion on the subject. His father wasn't doing well and he hadn't seen him in three years.

Undeterred, the Navy Captain pressed on "It's interesting, your dad always reminded me of some sort of actor. I'd swear he could have been a western star - and you know something, you're the spittin' image of him, maybe just a little shorter." The Captain laughed. "Anyone ever tell you that?"

Bryan shook his head in denial. "I can't say that they have. If you'll excuse me sir, but…"

Interrupting Bryan, the Captain continued "You're dad ever tell you about the fun we had with Libya?"

Bryan faked a laugh. "Oh yeah – you guys sure kicked their butt," he said. Still laughing, "But if you'll excuse me sir, I've gotta brief."

Years ago, when Bryan's father was still on active duty, the comparisons were rare. Now that the two had swapped places, it was a regular occurrence and irritating. Vice Admiral Craig, a tall man with a catcher's mitt handshake, was both loved and reviled. Bryan disliked being measured against him, good or bad. "Especially by height, now that his spine's fused in old age – we're both six-two," he'd say to laugh it off.

"Alright, let's get down to business people," the Admiral said, motioning the group into the War Room where they could focus on the business at hand, and the reason for Bryan's trip to the Flag Ship. The subject of the briefing was a large Taliban and Al-Qaeda concentration along the Pakistani and Afghan border, the target of the following morning's sorties. They entered the room adjacent to TFCC.

Sitting down at the briefing table, Bryan studied the large projection screen on the wall. A tactical satellite and geo-plot overlay of the North Arabian Sea and Indian Ocean was displayed, duplicating one of the large screens in the room they just left. As the Combatant Commander, the Admiral's immediate tactical staff included a Captain responsible for coordinating C4, the Command, Control, Communications, and Computer Systems.

The Flag Command and Control gave the Admiral a real-time, "big picture" of his airborne assets, surface assets, and submarines, as well as unidentified plots on the surface and in the air. Having the big picture was vital to effectively bringing to bear tactical systems such as attack aircraft or Tomahawk cruise missiles, even nukes. Feeding the massive computers on board was data beamed in by the various intelligence gathering apparatus, satellites, AWACs, and numerous ships in the Task Force. In addition, intelligence was collected and transmitted from Special Operations teams on the ground. All the teams worked for Bryan.

"Rick - kill the lights and bring up the overlay," Rabbit instructed the aide.

"Bryan's spent the last few days virtually on top of a terrorist camp that's number one on our target hit parade," the Admiral said in a southern drawl that gave away Tennessee roots. He trained a red laser on a screen with a satellite image of the Nangarhar province of northeastern Afghanistan.

"His team has pinpointed a concentration northeast of Jalalabad and north, northwest of the Khyber Pass. This is a high value target people. I can't emphasize that point enough. I'll let our SEAL commander take the floor from here - Bryan?" Rabbit passed the baton of the laser pointer.

Bryan vigorously rubbed the short thatch of dark bristle on his head. He looked down at his portable GPS, verifying the lat and long of the target, stood up and moved to podium at the corner of the briefing room.

"Thank you sir." Bryan scanned the audience for a moment and then got right into it. "The training camp of interest is right here." He pointed to terrain displayed on the screen with the laser.

"Latitude 35°01'50.89"north and longitude 71°20'44.93" east - well camouflaged and tucked away in this tiny valley at thirty-nine hundred feet between a small mountain at five K and another at a little over six K. There's a clump of trees in this area here," he said, circling a patch of green with the little red dot.

Bryan went on to explain all aspects of the planned target area. He and his team had spent several days near the camp, surveying or casing, depending on the point of view, yet collecting critical tactical information required for the successful completion of the mission.

"It's been operational on and off since the days of the Soviets. More than twenty years now." He paused for a moment and poured a glass of cold water from a pitcher on the table, took a quick sip and resumed.

"Amassed here are two to three hundred Al-Qaeda and Taliban using the camp to regroup, and developing a supply line over small roads, and a system of caves, and tunnels to and from Pakistan," he said scanning the room.

"Any questions to this point?" Bryan queried his audience. The Admiral shook his head. No one asked a thing. He resumed.

"Asmar is a small village down the river valley to the south. They're supplying the camp. The indigenous there are Pashtun - sympathetic to the Taliban and Al-Qaeda. And I'd say, making matters a helluva lot worse, the Pashtun militiamen are pouring in from the Pakistani North West Frontier, increasing strength at the camp daily." The Pashtuns are considered to be the world's largest tribal group, with a population of forty-five million stretching across Pakistan and Afghanistan, and with a history dating back to Alexander the Great. They were the major ethnic group in Afghanistan and central Pakistan, including the North West Frontier. The Pashtuns have always been considered a very proud and fierce people that adhere to precepts derived from Mosaic code of the Torah known as *Pashtunwali,* which predated Islam. The tenets were unwritten, but one particular code that had proved to be very frustrating to the coalition forces was called *Pannah Warkawel,* the offering of asylum. The code was cloaked in honor, and under no circumstances would tribal elders or Pashtun War Lords violate it, with the one exception being revenge or justice. Money, guns, food, all had zero influence in uncovering the terrorists that were being harbored. Bryan and his men were forced to root out Al-Qaeda and Taliban in an area where the indigenous people were Pashtun, like the Taliban, and they would generally die before giving up the terrorists. It was always an uphill battle.

Bryan quickly scanned the eyeballs in the room. They were fixed on each word he uttered, as they should be. He spoke with authority. He continued with his brief, "A well-fortified base camp. It needs to be softened considerably before boots can be put on the ground. The terrain is mountainous and it's getting awfully cold up there," Bryan said, deciding miserably cold was more appropriate. His men were still up there in the Hindu Kush and he wanted to get back.

Bryan rotated his head about his muscular neck, cracking vertebra. "Taliban and Al-Qaeda have extensive knowledge of the cave systems, which I might add have probably been there since Queen Victoria, maybe before that - Bunker Busters are what's called for, so they'll do the damage first. We have SAS there now. They're painting the camp and will continue to provide Intel through egress and damage assessment. The commandos are positioned here to the northwest - above the camp. They'll handle mop up as needed until relieved by my SEAL team. Everyone's on SATCOM with base - once the camp's pacified, the Rangers can go in, Spec Ops out."

The Admiral took back control, again emphasizing the high value nature of the planned target, and the need to wipe the enemy off the planet. The Task Force Commander was a true warrior cut out of the same mold as Bryan's father, he thought. A favorite expression of his to use at the end of a mission brief being, "Let's go put warheads on foreheads folks."

The other key players put in their two cents to the plan, including the CAG, Lieutenant Street, and the AAWC on the Tomahawk launch that was planned. "Admiral, we'll launch at 05:30, to be on target at 07:00," Captain Wise said, specifying the launch of the cruise missile.

"Okay. Good luck everyone. Remember, warheads on foreheads, so go get 'em." Bryan smiled as he heard the expression once again.

The Admiral stopped Bryan before he left the room. "Got a minute to talk privately about some of this?" he asked.

"Yes sir, I do," Bryan said.

"Good, have a seat – Rick, bring that coffee over and join. You might learn something," Rabbit said.

"Yes sir. Thank you," the aide said, looking forward to the opportunity to listen to the Navy SEAL and his Admiral.

The minute turned into two hours as Bryan and the Admiral discussed various theories on coping with terrorism. The Admiral's aide listened with keen interest as Bryan spelled out an idea he had. "A team focusing on getting the people that are financing the operations, able to deploy Special Ops though," Bryan said. He even had a name based on Greek mythology.

"Commandos and financial forensics," Rabbit said, reducing the concept down to the basics.

"Right on the mark sir, but also a psychologist, someone to help get into the minds of the radicals – like a profiler, and they'd need a lab," Bryan added. He thought for a moment, and added, "It'd be nice if we could counter the propaganda coming from radical Muslim news stations."

"How about your own news reporter?" Lieutenant Johns said offhanded. Bryan and the Admiral just stared at him, silent.

Bryan was led to his guest room, which fortunately was on the same level as TFCC, just around the corner from the War Room. It would be hard to get lost. Unfortunately though, it was also right below the flight deck and noisy as hell from operations going on around the clock. Quiet was nonexistent on a carrier. Between catapult shots, jet engines at full power, and planes landing just above, he would get very little shuteye. He checked his watch. In four hours he'd join the Admiral on "Vultures Row" for the launch of the strike.

CHAPTER 4

NOVEMBER 11, 2001

NORTH ARABIAN SEA

"BRYAN, GIDDAY MATE." He turned his head to see the face speaking the familiar Australian accent. Dylan Sizemore was approaching from the opposite end of the passageway, both nearing the hatch to Vultures Row simultaneously.

"How about that, Dylan Sizemore. What brings a journo newsman like you out to places like this, huh?" Bryan asked rhetorically, thrilled to see Dylan, his favorite correspondent and friend. Dylan was on his way to news stardom, Bryan was convinced, but still hadn't shaken the surfer look quite yet. His curly blond hair still hung over his ears and gave him an even younger appearance than his thirty-six years.

"Journo? Ah'm no journalist, thet's for sure. At'l be War Correspondent, if you will," he said shaking Bryan's hand firmly and smiling wide. Dylan added, "Anyway, good lookin sheila goin in 'arm's way, mate - big news nowadays, you know, the face of the new yank navy. The natework jest loves a juicy story like this one," Dylan said, his heavy accent bursting out.

"And which network might that be? Fox?" He knew war correspondents bounced around. True free agents, "war whores" he called them.

"You guessed it. Fox it is - at least until CNN coughs up more moolah. - And you mate – must be here ta win the war single-handedly, ay?" Dylan said.

"Sorry, can't go there *daaarrrlin*. That'll cost you a round of drinks first - but I'll say this - I've got an interest in the same pilot, but not for news reports," he said with a smile and a pause, before adding, "She's the flight lead for this morning's sortie."

"Well she's supposed to be one of the best pilots - graduated top in her class, and now here bombin Taliban - thet's big news mate. Viewers jest eat it up, no question. Ah can't wait ta interview her when she lands," Dylan said. "Of course, I shall use my refined television voice, clearly annunciating every word," he added, getting a laugh from both of them.

Still laughing, Dylan asked "Jest what's your take on everything, mate?"

"Come over here, let's step out of the way," Bryan said, taking Dylan by the arm through a passage way and into small glass windowed observation room that overlooked the flight deck.

"Off the record?" Bryan asked.

"As always."

"Well, I'll put it this way – militarily, it won't even be a contest. Why, this Task Force alone could do the job - but it's afterwards that counts," Bryan said.

"Win the hearts and minds?"

"Dylan, have you any sense of what's happened here before?"

"Historically? In Afghanistan?" Dylan asked - Bryan nodded his head. "The Soviets and thet disaster, yeah, but before – no, not really," Dylan added.

"Britain had an entire regiment massacred very close to where bombs are being dropped this morning. It was about a hundred and sixty years ago. They were in the middle of a retreat from Kabul after an occupation that turned out to be a disaster," Bryan said.

"Ya don't say. What happened?"

Recalling the history for Dylan, "The British Empire wanted Afghanistan as a buffer to Russian expansionism – so they marched an army from India into Kabul, deposed the current ruler, put in a puppet, and set up shop with an occupying force – one that was insufficient in numbers, I might add. The result was that the British couldn't maintain control and the situation on the streets of the capital got out of hand. The Afghans ended up hating the British troops. Well, the number two diplomat from Great Britain was murdered by a Muslim mob. Needless to say, that got the senior British envoy very worried. He tried to buy protection from tribal warlords, but only bought time. British India felt the pinch and cut off funds," Bryan said looking down at the flight deck. Planes were starting their engines.

"Typical cheapskates. So the Brit's cut their man's funds off, huh - what happened after that?" Dylan asked.

"The Muslims did some cutting of their own – they cut off his head, arms, legs, and paraded his dismembered body around the streets of Kabul," Bryan said with an affected frown.

Dylan grimaced. "Cripes! Bad day – did they cut off his knackers too?" He put his hands over his groin.

"That's not the worst part."

"Come on," Dylan said in disbelief. "How could it go down hill any more?"

Bryan continued, "It turned into the ultimate cut and run - the British General in Kabul decided he'd get the army the hell outa there. He was trying to get forty five hundred troops and twelve thousand camp followers to the British garrison at Jalalabad – never made it. Akbar Kahn and his Ghilazi Pashtun warriors met them at the Kurd Kabul Pass. The General and his second in command, some Brigadier, surrendered, but only themselves. They ended up living. But the 44th Foot army were surrounded and massacred in the snow at Gandamak. The entire regiment and the followers, wiped out. What few survived were either executed or forced into slavery, with the exception of one sole survivor."

"That's what's out there?" Dylan exclaimed.

Bryan nodded. "British troops waiting at Jalalabad for the column to arrive couldn't believe their eyes when only one survivor showed up on a shot up old mare. A doctor."

"What happened to the Generals?"

Bryan furrowed his brow. "Oh, they were released and probably lived to some ripe old age back in England," he said sarcastically.

"Couple of pikers, those pommy Generals," Dylan said chagrined at the tale. "But somethin to think about, ay?"

Bryan had a stern look firmly planted on his face. "First of all – if you're going with military against Muslims, you'd better know your history." Bryan thought for a moment and finally continued, "You know that massacre sent shockwaves throughout Great Britain. I think that the Viceroy to India even had a heart attack when he heard the news - the worst massacre in several hundred years. But the British army did something – they arrived at two very important axioms that I memorized."

"Which are?"

Bryan looked up to remember the words and their author. "And these are quotes from Lieutenant General Sir George McMunn, a Churchillian military man, 'It is wholly impracticable to occupy a country or attempt to impose a government not welcomed by the inhabitants. The only result will be failure and great expense in treasure and lives,'" Bryan said. "The second axiom I subscribe to the most - 'political officers must not be permitted to predominate over military judgments.'"

"So what are the implications here mate?"

"On the QT, right?"

"As always."

He glanced around. "The politicians who push the buttons need to listen to the commanders at the tip of the spear, and they better have the stomach to hold the country's hand for a long time after payback and heads on platters," Bryan warned. "None of this cut and run stuff. If ya put boots on the ground, it's because you're taking something that you're gonna hold onto."

"How long?"

"Not to be cliché, but suffice to say – as long as it takes," Bryan said shaking his head.

"And the Taliban? What about them?"

"Again, same thing – as long as it takes. They're motivated and determined. Once forced out, they'll be even more determined. They'll never rest as long as there's one adversary left alive, including other Muslims," Bryan said, folding his arms. "You can take that to the bank, my oz friend."

"Sounds daggy - and the Al-Qaeda?"

"Pretty much they're all Arab in Afghanistan, just trying to get the worldwide Jihad going, but that'll change over time. We'll do our best to wipe 'em out, starting here, but I'm confident a new group will pop up. They've got splinter cells of Al-Qaeda all over Pakistan."

"No end in sight – sounds like a great story for a journo kid from Queensland, thet's for sure," Dylan said.

"Well, I'll be doing this for awhile, and you'll be reporting on it for a long while. How's 'bout that?"

"Thet's a future alright. Where ya goin' from here?" Dylan asked.

"Back to the snow and rock," Bryan said smiling.

"Good luck ta ya, an' nice beard by the way, mate," Dylan commented.

"Oh, yeah - this," Bryan said, scratching his whiskers. "Blendin' in by goin' native. Now come on, let's go outside and watch 'em launch." He slapped Dylan on the back, put foam earplugs in his ears, and pulled the handle down to open the hatch to Vultures Row.

"After you."

Stepping onto vulture's row was like entering a world all unto its own. The exhaust of turning jet engines stung the eyes slightly; the blended smell of jet fuel and sea salt permeated the air. Located on the port side of the Island, Vulture's Row is a steel balcony sixty feet above the flight deck, one level above the Captain's bridge. From that vantage point, observers could see, hear, feel, and smell flight deck operations.

Rabbit caught the hatch opening from his periphery. "Mornin' gentleman."

They could see the Admiral's mouth moving as he spoke, but it was impossible hear his voice over the noise of turning jet engines. They squeezed in next to Dylan's cameraman, already capturing digital video for the day's hot war story.

"Not normally out on vulture's row for launches," Rabbit yelled, smiling. "Dylan's news team is on board. Gotta keep an eye on em – make sure they don't get hurt." Public relations was important for the Navy, and correspondents such as Dylan were welcomed at times, but the brass liked to keep the crews on a very short leash. Media access was going to be tightly controlled.

The sun was still well below the horizon, but a line of clouds were beginning to lighten as the earth spun to greet the morning. Looking further up in the sky, the faint glow of dawn faded to dark gray, then black. The stars were out and as Bryan scanned the millions of celestial bodies, his eyes stopped on the moon, about 30° above the eastern horizon, a bright waning crescent, a star distinctly in its field. The sign of the Ottoman Empire was the crescent moon and a star, he recalled. Was this an omen, he wondered?

"Helmsman, come about starboard ninety degrees, heading zero nine zero - XO, you got the con," the skipper said as he waved to the group above on vultures row.

After turning as tightly as the she could, the carrier faced the wind, her bearing on an easterly course. With thirty knots of wind over the deck, the Air Boss was ready to launch aircraft. A helicopter lifted off; search and rescue in the event of a mishap. An E-2C Hawkeye was next, one always airborne for the Task Force's "God's eye view." The first Tomcat taxied to the port catapult. The pilot, Crystal "Street" Walker, carefully followed the directions of the plane captain in his yellow jersey. Street was Dylan's feature story, and the real reason the media was out on the carrier. She was the first female Navy pilot to go into harm's way on an attack mission, although resistance would be non-existent. Of course the fact that she was pretty made the story even more sensational.

The F-14D Street piloted was one of twelve aircraft of the Black Lions, the only Tomcat squadron on the Vinson, and Street its only female pilot. The F-14 had a crew of two, a pilot in the front and navigator in the back. It was Bryan's favorite fighter, although now in the twilight of its career. The "D" version was much improved from the original in the fleet, but deep down it was still the same plane. With engines providing combined thrust of fifty-six thousand pounds in afterburner, the plane was capable of Mach 2.3. Carrying a quiver filled with the best air-to-air missiles and bombs that taxpayers could buy; the F-14D was the world's premier air superiority weapon. And watching it launch off the deck of an aircraft carrier was like attending a well choreographed and rehearsed ballet. All was in motion. Lieutenant "Street" Walker was as skilled at her job as any that came before.

The plane captain, as if conducting the orchestra pit with glowing wands, helped position Street's Tomcat on the catapult. She eased the plane forward, using nose-wheel steering to tweak her spot, all the while hawking the subtle directions of the yellow shirt's body language as he gracefully moved, at times with his head alone, left or right, indicating the need for an ever-so-slight change in position. She felt the familiar bump as the nose-wheel came up and over the catapult shuttle. The plane captain crossed his wands, signaling her to hold the brakes.

A man in a green jersey ran under the nose to check the hold back fitting which kept the jet in place when the engines were run up. He was just several feet in front of the powerful engines' intakes. If the throttles were accidentally jarred forward at that point, he would be sucked into the stator blades and diced like a tomato. Another deck crew moved in view of the pilot, holding a placard above his head. It read "68,000," the aircraft's takeoff weight. She signaled a "thumb's up." The weight was good.

Bryan was simply in awe at the ever-present danger of the sequence unfolding before his eyes. So too were Dylan and his cameraman. No one on Vultures Row was missing a thing.

A red-shirt, or ordinance man, quickly checked the two thousand pound bunker buster, and two air-to-air sidewinder missiles. The pins were pulled, weapons armed and ready. There was something written on the bombs, a message. Bryan couldn't read it from where he was. He didn't need to; he knew what it read.

The jet-blast deflector rose in back of the plane's engines, protecting the deck crew from the intense heat of the afterburners at full power. Satisfied the Tomcat was "good to go, the plane captain uncrossed his wands, signaling for "Street" to release the brakes. With his right wand extended high above his shoulders he rapidly moved a wand back and forth at the wrist.

"Street," now on an open, "hot mike" with her RIO, "Beef" Stuart Wellington, scanned the instrument panel from left to right.

"You ready back there Beef?" She asked.

"Good to go Street."

"Roger that."

She smoothly moved the power levers forward, meticulously checking the fuel flow and RPM of the engines. The plane was at full power, perhaps helping the carrier to move infinitesimally faster through the water. She sucked on the oxygen through her mask harder. Her metabolic rate increased, blood vessels constricted, bronchiole dilated, adrenal medulla kicking into gear, the heart rate twice as fast as only moments before.

Dylan looked at Bryan and smiled. "Pretty damn brilliant mate," he said giving the Hawaiian "shaka" sign, his hand rotating back and forth.

Bryan read Dylan's lips, nodded his head, and returned the smile and gesture. They both looked forward toward the bow. The deck was cycling up and down ten feet against the backdrop of the faint, distant stars. The sun's rays were beginning to pierce the scattered cumulous clouds from far below the horizon, an outline of a light grey hue. All looked back at the Tomcat as every surface area of the plane was now in motion; the pilot checking her controls for free, unimpeded movement. On Vultures Row they could feel the thunder of the jet in their stomachs, deep in the gut as the fighter screamed for release.

"Street" concurring the plane "good to go," turned her head to the right and spotted the plane captain. He was looking aft and under the belly of the jet at green shirts final checking the maneuvering surfaces; both gave a thumb's up which he passed on to the pilot. She moved forward on her harness slightly to test that it was locked, and then smartly gave the plane captain a salute. She was ready to launch. The plane's exterior lights all on.

The plane captain looked over his shoulder and skipped backwards a few steps to clear the take-off lane, the wand still rapidly moving. He crouched down as he looked up the flight deck and back down. Squatting as if stretching, his left leg straight and pointing to the stern, right leg bent at the knee, he moved the wand in front of his "Mickey Mouse ears" and goggles, returning the salute. He touched the deck and pointed the glowing wand at the bow. Everything on the flight deck seemed to be roaring and on fire, afterburners, wand, and lights. Crystal moved her head slightly aft, the back of her helmet resting on the seat cushion.

She counted to herself "one-potato, two-potato, three-po..." The nose of the Tomcat dropped six inches on the olio of the strut, as the steam catapult began the ferocious tug on the sixty-eight thousand pounds of plane, fuel, weapons, and crew. G-forces rapidly increased, the fighter accelerating from zero to one hundred and forty knots in two and a half seconds. At the end of the cat-shot, the fighter flying and the G-forces dissipated, Crystal raised the gear handle and checked her instruments. "No caution or warning lights, plane's flying, gears up. The mission's underway," she thought to herself.

Moments later the wingman was airborne right behind her. On vultures row all watched as the two fighters rapidly accelerated, the afterburners a bright blue-white. Soon they were only silhouettes against the twilight, "dots on the horizon." The flight climbed and turned towards the coast.

* * * * *

NOVEMBER 11, 2001
KONAR, AFGHANISTAN

Morning sunshine warmed them. Two SAS commandos and a guide flattened their bodies in the snow. They were lying between boulders on a ridge fifteen hundred feet above the terrorist compound. It was frigid, below freezing, and for the moment it was nice just to have the warm rays on their faces. But they were careful to keep metal or other reflective objects out the sun. Soldiers assigned to Bryan; they were elite, smart, dangerous, and cold. They'd been there for three days and nights, watching and waiting. That's what they did for a living, and they volunteered for the duty. The ultimate mercenaries, many said.

Fight like you train and train like you fight! Readiness was of the highest import for cold weather combat operations. Being ready to fight in the cold meant training in the cold to fight. SAS commandos and their U.S. Special Ops counterparts knew the essentials to be masters of cold weather combat. Keeping the body fueled with food and water was essential. And staying warm, another big essential.

The team wore insulated undergarments made with silver fibers covered by white cold weather exposure suits. The clothing not only made them invisible on the snow-covered ridge, but also provided microclimates around their bodies, keeping them warm and dry. A byproduct of the silver fibers; silver kills microbial germs so they smelled nice too. And of course: the snow – always the snow, which offered great protection from the wind. At night, when the temperatures really dropped, they dug an ice cave, got in, and huddled up. Naked.

Above all, attack the enemy! Sergeant Major MacLean checked his watch; it was 0645. The compound and their occupants weren't yet awake, but would be soon. They'd be getting an unexpected, early morning wake up call in fifteen minutes, followed by two more uninvited guests. It would be an explosive reveille.

An hour and twenty-fives minutes before, at precisely 0530, a single Tomahawk Missile's engine ignited within its cell on the USS Kane. The exhaust of flames and gas piped into the predawn air as it fired its solid-fuel booster and cleared the vertical launcher. Written in magic-marker near the warhead were two phrases; "For 9/11." and "Remember the Cole - Asshole." It was on a one way, nonrefundable cruise to the foothills of the Hindu Kush Mountains.

The flight would be scenic, passing over the Minarets at Ghazi, and just to the west of the Khyber Pass, but at five hundred and fifty miles per hour it would be short, lasting only an hour and a half. Using Terrain Contour Matching and an onboard contour map, the Tomahawk would stay below the flight of most birds, yet maneuver as necessary to avoid terminating too soon.

Lying atop a snowy boulder, "Wolf" MacLean looked through the telescopic sight of his M4 assault rifle at the terrorist camp. Half the size of a football field, snow blanketed the entire camp, making it almost impossible to see from the air. In the center were five single-story buildings, the snowy roofs rimmed with icicles, surrounded by a rock wall. Each building housed at least forty militants, smokeless gas generators provided power for space heaters to keep them warm. The buildings were inter-connected with underground tunnels and bunkers, stockpiled with weapons caches, mortars and explosives. They had two SUVs and three all terrain vehicles, also covered in white camouflage. Wolf figured a compliment of two hundred and fifty men, but enough arms and other weapons for five times that. As the commando observed the camp, the team's Pashtun guide was sitting just below him eating a chocolate protein bar, his M-16 resting on a boulder. MacLean felt the barrel touch his ribs.

"Meh grit, grit granddad fought close beh here - at Kandahar," Wolf quietly whispered to Raza and Sergeant Ryan. "He was with the ninety two Highlanders."

"Is thet rayght Wolf. Wha appened?" Ryan asked with a smile as he also looked through his scope.

"The battle et Maiwand en eighteen eighty. The biggest defeat for the Afghans en the second Anglo-Afghan wars. His name was Duncan MacLean – he was a Sergeant Major like meh," MacLean said with a cornered grin.

"Runs in the family, does it ay," Ryan said, with a low voice.

"He got wounded there," MacLean said.

"How did that happen sahr?" Raza asked.

"Well, the British forces numberin ten thousand met heid on with twelve thousand eight hundred bloody Afghans. General Gough sent donkey wallopers ta look for the whereabouts of Ayub Kahn's geyzi fighters. Careless fawk - geyzis, they'd began shootin at the regiment. Now the British knew where they'd their big guns," MacLean said, explaining the Afghan commander's major blunder of firing cannon early. "The galloper reported ta the commander, General Roberts, an the shootin was on."

The Sergeant Major rolled over onto his back, now looking at Raza. "Fools haste is no speed Raza. Come daylight the Brits began shootin artillery at Babawali Pass, and the ninety two Highlanders marched rayght into Mulla Sahibdad," MacLean said, as he started rolling up his right pant leg. "Ah'm gonna show ye somethin."

"Ah've 'eard this one before Raza, pay attention," Ryan said. "He's gonna tell ya the circumstances of how his ancestor was shot."

"Sahr-koom-stances – vhat vere they sahr?" Raza asked.

"Bloody dhobi wallah," MacLean said shaking his head.

"He vas shot by Pashtun from Class Regiment?" Raza repeated, embarrassed for his people.

"Thas rayght Raza, rookie dhobi wallah on his own side," MacLean winked at Ryan, unseen by the guide. "Ya see he had his Martin Henry rifle, but oot of ammo. An he saw the little chota wallah lolly-gaggin by his Snida Enfield. Well, he'd loaded an primed the bloody thing, ah mean it was hot," MacLean explained to Raza.

Ryan touched the Sergeant Major to pause. "The Martin Henry was a forty five caliber, Raza. The Snider's a fifty seven."

"Rayght. Anyway, so the bloody rookie picked up the fifteh-seven caliber Snida pointin rayght at meh grit, grit granddad's heid. Now he yelled at him an seid 'Whit're ye doing, man? Would ye watch where your pointin that - ye dunderheid. Ye maht shoot meh,'" the Sergeant Major chuckled. "Well, it made the laddie jumpy an the eejit pulled the trigga. Shot him anyway - rayght en his lahg. Same place as meh." MacLean pointed at a scar on his own leg.

"Who did that sahr?" Raza asked.

"Bloody dhobi wallah," MacLean said grinning, moving Raza's rifle away from his body.

"Sorry sahr," Raza said, further embarrassed. The two commandos enjoyed teasing the Pashtun man.

Wolf saw a man exit a barracks in the camp. "Okay lads, pipe down. The fawkers are oop." He looked at his watch. It was 0657.

"Raza, come over e'yer and huv'a look," Ryan said to their always-present guide, who had become one of them. The Pashtun guide crawled silently over to the two commandos and looked down the ravine at the enemy. It was show time.

As they scanned the camp, Raza couldn't help but finally ask, "Sahr, please why do all persons call you volf?"

"It's meh bloody 'andle, tha's why. Meh favorite footballer's Blevins, 'an tha's Welsh for lit'al wolf. Call meh Sergeant Major 'an ah'l break yer neck," he said giving the guide a wink, grin, and elbow.

Raza smiled back and pointed at the camp. *"Khaow ray da pasar ka,"* Raza said in Pashto.

"Wha' the bloody 'ell does that mean?" Wolf asked, looking up from the scope at Raza, his face only a foot away.

"May the earth cover you up."

"'Ow poetic." Wolf was actually being sincere for a change. He looked back through the scope again.

"Jaysus chrayst, luk the'er et is," Sergeant Ryan whispered, tapping Wolf on the shoulder. This was a first. It was a blur, but they actually saw the twenty-foot long missile in its last moments of flight, and right on schedule. Vertically penetrating tall snowdrifts between two buildings, the thousand pound warhead detonated once its mass was well inside the subterranean bunkers. Wolf and company felt the shockwave emanate deep inside their bodies.

"Da spi zo," the guide exclaimed as the deafening sound rattled their eardrums.

Wolf recognized that Pashtun expression and couldn't have agreed more. "Son of a bitch is right," the Sergeant Major concurred.

A secondary explosion from the camp's munitions followed almost immediately. A dark, bluish-brown mushroom cloud rose up from the small white valley. As the debris started settling, Wolf looked for movement and assessed the damage from the Tomahawk. Three of the small buildings were completely destroyed. Of the two remaining, one was more-or-less intact; the other had significant damage. Bodies and pieces of bodies were scattered across the grounds. Some were still moving. The Tomcats would be on target within seconds to finish it off, Wolf thought as he saw several of the enemy now standing, obviously impaired.

"Bow-EE-KAA, ya' fundie jundies," Wolf said, anticipating the second wave for the walking wounded.

"Please sahr, what's the meaning of that expression?" Raza asked.

"It's spelt B-O-H-I-C-A – 'an no offense tae ya' Raza, but' it means 'ben o'er, ere it comes again ya' fundamentalist Mossulman," the Sergeant Major responded.

"Thank you, Wolf - we say *'kuss di ughame'*."

Strike leader Lieutenant Crystal "Street" Walker banked the flight of two F-14D Tomcats toward the IP of the target. Maintaining tactical combat spread, they descended from an altitude of eighteen thousand feet. Each was carrying a two thousand pound Paveway Laser-Guided Bomb; both had already acquired the targeting laser that illuminated the center of the two remaining buildings and the entrance to an enclave of stored munitions.

Releasing their ordinance at fifteen thousand feet, the pair of Tomcats turned away. The "beam riders" were guided on a laser-designator that used a series of encrypted pulses, each Paveway impacting their target, one right after the other. A split second later, the bunker busters exploded with ferocity. Shockwaves lifted the dust from the previous explosion as they spread outward in perfect circles.

To Wolf's surprise, two of the all-terrain vehicles suddenly appeared from the smoke at the far end of the destroyed compound. He sighted the lead operator with his M-4 assault rifle and squeezed the trigger. The man fell off in the snow, dead before leaving the seat. Wolf aimed at the second surviving militant, firing two quick rounds. Both rounds hit the vehicle. Careening out of control, it jumped over debris, turned sideways, and tumbled multiple times in the air before crashing into remnants of a shattered, rocky wall. The dust and snow silently sprinkled to the ground, settling in a dirty tan haze. Wolf waited patiently for the cloud to clear, dumbfounded by the chance of luck. The second man, still alive, scampered over the snow and then vanished into rocky cover.

"Shite. Lost 'im," Wolf cursed as he pounded the frozen ground with his fist. Before he could react, another man also made it to the safety of the hillside.

"Fawk, thet's bloody two of 'em," he cursed again, now slamming his rifle butt into the ice.

The SAS team surveyed the remainder of the decimated camp. Nothing else was moving, and as far as they could tell, the final damage assessment would be total. Their mission was a complete success and the American Rangers could be dropped in anytime.

PART 2

THE ADVENT

CHAPTER 5

SEPTEMBER 4, 2002

KARACHI, PAKISTAN

A WORN LEATHER SATCHEL bulging with opportunity clutched under his arm, the founder of Dubai-Pak stood in the aisle near the front of a crowded bus hanging onto the frame of a seatback with his free hand for balance. Precariously dancing along pothole-laden streets, shimmering and jingling, the bus was elaborately decorated on the exterior with colorfully painted designs, accented by tiny bells swaying over the tires. Inside though, it was old, worn and tired. Most seats bore scars of torn plastic upholstery, the foam rubber cushioning protruding, splayed like growing fungi. As usual the bus was standing room only, and as usual, minus metal handrails long since surrendered to corrosion and neglect.

Unconcerned about his vehicle's dilapidated condition and oblivious to safety, the driver tightly cornered the turns of the heavily trafficked streets, crashing through large potholes rather than slowing down or going around. Standing passengers often fell onto sitting ones. Stagnant diesel exhaust fumes emanated throughout the interior, collecting thickest in certain areas, watering eyes and causing coughs. The combination of slight G-forces and carbon monoxide made people nauseous, some seeking relief from less polluted air by hanging their heads out partially opened windows. The street was noisy. Cars, buses, taxis, motorcycles, all vying for the same piece of hot asphalt it seemed. Beeping horns and people shouting - just a typical morning in Karachi, Pakistan.

The man with the satchel was standing in back of another holding a morning paper. Noticing a sensational headline of a story on the front page, he leaned forward, pursing his lips as he read the first few lines:

"Suicide Bomber Kills U.S. Diplomat - Islamabad,

September 4, 2002 – An American diplomat was killed yesterday in

a suicide car-bomb attack near the American Embassy..."

The bus came to a screeching, bell-jingling halt, moving the newspaper forward out of his view. It was his stop anyway so he made a mental note to follow up on the story later.

He stepped off the bus and onto a downtown sidewalk of Saddar Town, the business district of Karachi. Pakistan's largest city had a population of twelve million and was one of the most densely populated in the world. Although early, commerce was already in full swing on Karachi's busy sidewalks and in small shops. A few areas of the city were new and clean, this was not one of those; a dirty, heavy foul smell of refuse saturated the air, stinging the olfactory senses. Saddar Town's garbage men had been on strike for two weeks, demanding higher pay.

Shahid Mahmood was a man whose otherwise mundane life had recently been rejuvenated. The company he founded with his uncle two years before had just received a very large labor contract. "It is God's will," he said.

A new construction development was underway in Dubai. In his hands were the first hundred of what would be five hundred work visas for the UAE, all pre-approved, without a single name yet filled in. In fact, not one laborer had even been hired yet, but all would be by week's end. The business was on the verge of taking off, he thought.

Pre-approved applications didn't come without an added price, costing his company a hundred dollars each, but not one name would ever be listed with an official Dubai or Pakistani government labor agency. It was a price worth paying. Once hired and on site in Dubai, the Paki workers would simply become nameless faces in blue uniforms, toiling under the blazing desert sun. As if they never existed.

"I have the forms here with me. It is thoroughly completed. This is a marvelous day for us," he assured his uncle over the cell phone. "God willing, we will have many more days to come like this," he added as he scurried to an intersection. Without a pedestrian signal, he hesitated and looked in both directions before jaywalking between the rivers of traffic. He was careful crossing today. There was too much to lose.

Shahid's office was across the street from the corner bus stop, in the middle of the block. Long queues had already formed in opposite directions from the first floor entrance of the office, and now wrapped around the street corners, extending two more blocks. He estimated that at least fifteen hundred men had lined up to be interviewed. The unskilled jobs would be filled on a first come, first serve basis, as long as applicants met strict, mandatory qualifications. The contractor from Dubai had been very specific.

"This is good, very good, uncle. I will call you later after we have finished," he said before disconnecting the call.

"Please excuse, thank you. Please excuse, thank you," he said in a gruff, high-pitched tone, pushing his way through the crowd of sticky sweat to reach the doorknob. He looked at the clock on the wall in the waiting room. It was 7:10 AM.

"Good morning my friend. Is the doctor here?" Shahid greeted his assistant.

"Not yet. He said he would be here by 7:15, Shahid. I can call him on his cellular if you wish? Do you want to complete the medical screen before the interview," the young assistant asked nervously.

Noting the anxious expressions on the faces of the applicants stacked up outside, Shahid thought for a moment. He had to get started right away, "No, that's not necessary. Open the door for them. Have five at a time in the waiting room filling out the paperwork. When the doctor arrives, send him to my office. Please bring a cup of tea for me, and remember – five at a time, no more, no less. Thank you." He rotated a cupped hand to emphasize the expedient nature of the tea request.

"Right away sir."

"Oh, and one other thing – please find out who is representing the garbage men." Shahid wanted more contacts for his Rolodex. Garbage men were possible clients for Shahid.

"Absolutely sir. Right away."

Dubai-Pak Ltd. leased a small office in the heart of Saddar Town, conveniently just minutes from both the Central Bus Station and the Railway Station. The office was barebones, equipped with only the basics. The waiting area had seating for just five people - secondhand wooden stools. A Formica countertop separated the assistant's desk from applicants waiting their turn. There were two interior offices, one for Shahid, having the only window and the only air-conditioner, the other a vacant room with a ceiling fan, unoccupied. There was an examination room used by a contracted doctor for the speedy physicals. Shahid suspected the man had never been to Medical school, but it didn't matter. There were two phones, two computers, and filing cabinets. The monthly tab, including payroll, cost less than four hundred dollars. Creature comforts weren't much of a concern for Shahid; the office would be there for only two months. But in the process they'd net eighteen hundred dollars per worker, even after greasing the palms of dishonest officials. "It was God's will," he believed.

Shahid positioned himself in back of his desk. Drumming his fingers, he checked the Dubai construction schedule. The new project was an eighty story high rise of offices and condominiums calendared to break ground in two weeks. The construction manager contracted for one hundred fresh laborers to be on site the following week. The remaining would gradually be delivered during the following three to five weeks, depending on weather, construction timetable and equipment procurement. Labor camp housing would soon be finished and awaiting its future occupants.

Paperwork in hand, the first applicant entered Shahid's office.

"Please be seated, thank you," Shahid said, motioning for the applicant to sit down on a collapsible, metal chair. He quickly reviewed the man's paperwork. Drawing a box at the bottom of the first page margin, he prepared an area for his notes. Dubai-Pak was paid bonuses by the contractor for hires that met certain "extra qualifications." The box is where he kept score.

His first question would always be the same, "You will have a medical exam if you qualify, but do you have any significant medical history?"

Usually from areas of Pakistan that had few medical facilities and that were rampant with disease, it was doubtful many applicants were up-to-date for inoculations and immunizations, all necessary for work visas in the UAE. A very crucial service Shahid's company provided was the compliances with "Guest Worker" medical requirements for entry in Dubai, and compliances meant that, as Shahid would put it "all shots, examinations must be current or they will not be allowed to leave Pakistan. Is that understood?" Though the doctor's credentials may have been suspect, the exam was just cursory. No diagnosis, prescriptions, or surgery, the quick exam would verify overall health, shot card, and determine if they were qualified or not qualified.

"No medical history," the applicant answered.

"Very good then – we will get started. You're twenty-four - are you married?" The man shook his head.

"No - alright, I see you're single," Shahid verified from the application. "Are you a devout Muslim?" Devout Muslim was the correct response.

"Yes sir."

"And you're Sunni or Shi'ah?"

"Sunni, sir."

"Pashtun?"

"Yes."

"Yes of course. Do you speak Arabic or any other languages besides Urdu and Pashto?" Hopefully the candidate would say "yes,' which was worth a bonus. English was also another bonus – the largest.

"No sir."

"Any physical problems not significant? Allergies? Sexually transmitted disease?"

"None, sir."

"Okay, very good. Do you have previous experience in construction?" Marginal experience was satisfactory. They weren't looking for labor foremen. The plan was to hire unskilled labor only. Raw recruits.

"I have helped build houses in my village sir."

"That's good. That's good." Shahid had an image of a stone hut with a tin roof. "Have you ever been employed through a union?" A "yes" response to the question was unacceptable.

"No sir."

Shahid spoke for a few minutes more, keeping the conversation light and upbeat. His message however, was deceitful about virtually everything, the job, the pay, and the benefits, everything, with the exception of the wonders of Dubai.

"My friend, you will enjoy Dubai very much. There you'll find everything you have ever dreamed of. And very soon, you'll be able to bring your family there. You can make very much money. Trust me what I am telling you." The trust would do the applicant little good, and everything he dreamed of was in Dubai, but not for him.

He asked the young man if he had any questions. Very seldom did they. Lastly, after running through the long list of benefits, Shahid would spring the bad news. He explained to the applicant that they would be required to pay two thousand three hundred dollars each for a "Workingman's visa. You see the visa for Dubai is very precious and extremely hard to come by. A small pittance in the long run for the opportunity of a lifetime," he would add.

"It's a very, very small price to pay, don't you agree? But if you don't have the money now, or you can't borrow from your family, I can advance you the money for your workingman's visa. You can pay back with installments over two years." Shahid waited a moment and then added, "Truly, I don't mind, and as a good Muslim, I won't charge interest, I will do that for you," explaining to the applicant he was doing him a huge favor. Construction companies in Dubai paid the contracts up front to Shahid, and he in turn secured a two-year note from the worker. It was a sugarcoated scam and very lucrative. He looked over the two-page application one final time and with a thud, stamped the paperwork "approved."

"Congratulations – you have been accepted, barring any problem with your medical exam. Please sign here."

After signing the promissory note, the applicants were sent into the examination room. There, the doctor gave each a quickie "look over" rather than an actual exam, checking only for obvious physiological problems, maladies, or contagious disease, flu, aids, tooth decay, or drug use; if they appeared healthy, the new hires would be on their way to the UAE in five days.

Shahid and his staff of two repeated the procedure until late at night. The following day all completed documentation was sent to the construction company's "Laborer Sponsor," another subcontractor. The sponsor had the responsibility for processing laborers into Dubai, distributing paychecks, and functioning as a go between for grievances at the work site or labor camp. The sponsor also received a ten percent "vig" on the work visa fee. Always cash.

Once the new contingent of hires had either boarded a plane or ship for the UAE, the Dubai-Pak sign would come down, phones disconnected, and the office closed. Minimal sales efforts were required. Shahid liked that fact. They simply screened and processed applicants from "point A to point B. " When a new contract was received, a new Dubai-Pak office would open.

The job and an opportunity for a new life and riches in Dubai, sold itself. Very few ever grumbled over the extortion of future wages for "guest worker passes." Should "undesirables" be uncovered after arriving in Dubai, they were deported - or worse. What happened after the hires arrived in Dubai was something that Shahid didn't really think of or care about anyway. It wasn't his problem; it was Dubai's. The entrepreneur was concerned instead with finding the next construction labor contract, and repeating the same procedure over and over. The money was that good. Especially from the contractor he was working for now; the business would thrive.

"This is all God's will," Shahid would constantly say, especially when he received a new bag of cash from a courier. One day he might need to become legitimate and open a bank account, he imagined. "If God be willing."

CHAPTER 6

SEPTEMBER 24, 2004

DUBAI

MOVING THROUGH THE GATE, the labor camp bus jumped slightly as the driver accelerated over the speed bump, the heads of men sitting in the back seats bounced off the ceiling. Another long day of hard labor was finished. Two hours of commuting, twelve hours of work. But the men would need to be ready to go back to work only ten hours later, when it would start all over again, as it had for the last two years. It was all they had to look forward to now, seven days a week. Their lives were meaningless, simply existing. It was their "groundhog day."

Promises made to them by the employer, sponsor, and the developer were never kept. In fact, not only were they making less money than what had been contracted; they hadn't even been paid in over three months. These were desperate men. Alienated, and without hope. Some were suicidal; several hanged themselves. And just when all hope had vanished, a stranger arrived, a Muslim that said he would help.

The man was Pashtun, as they were, and pious, much more resolute in Islamic fundamentalism and his practice of faith than they. He was a Pashtun Sunni and was there to help other Pashtuns. He said, "They were being persecuted." Adding, "It was unjust - but you can trust me. I am here to help you, God is watching and God is willing," to help the helpless and to feed the hungry. The stranger came through with his promises. He did all that and more, he backed up his words with something the workers hadn't seen before; their families were sent money. Trust him? They loved him. They needed him.

Warning the unfortunate of the necessity to have a stronger faith, he preached a fundamental devotion to Islamic life, a rediscovery, re-birth. They would need to become as resolute in their beliefs as he. They needed to be strong in their faith, preparing for the day of reckoning, or they too would be doomed to damnation like the infidels. Jihad was the plan that Allah had for them, and they were the soldiers. If they committed to Islam and to the Jihad, Allah would be kind, watch over them, accept them and their families into heaven; for the ultimate act of faith, they would receive the greatest glory.

Laborers, with the kind man's direction, built a small, makeshift mosque at the camp. There they would pray, pursue Quranic study, and hold weekly meetings. A meeting was being held that night. They would pray, speak of the great prophets, and plan for the coming Jihad. Workers looked up to him and after a time, believed every word as if coming from the lips of Mohammed himself. The man was very shrewd indeed, and they called him Wazir.

Wazir was very meticulous in his plan for the laborers. He believed that to successfully accomplish a mission, every detail, no matter how insignificant, must be considered. Special events and the training process could not be rushed. Painstaking and time consuming, it was a process of indoctrination to an entirely new philosophy. A Jihad, and a curriculum cleverly designed to push students to the next phase, terrorism. Deprivation was the key as it always was with any form of brainwashing. Laborers were being deprived of money, sleep, food, family, and religion, and their only salvation was through Wazir and a strict devotion to Islam, a perfect formula for creating an army of Jihadists. He was their ticket, and they were his.

The meeting ended routinely just after midnight. Wazir exited the labor camp on foot, walking passed the gate and into the darkness without the slightest glance at the security guard manning his post. He continued on the shoulder of the asphalt road when an SUV suddenly turned on its headlights, spotlighting his frame. Wazir paused a moment, saw the familiar Range Rover headlights, and approached the vehicle which now had a running engine. Opening the passenger's door, he slid in.

The driver lit a cigarette with the car lighter, the glow revealing his face in the shadows. A large face, on the front of a large head, and everything about it was large and ugly; the hairy ears, his bulbous nose, fat cheeks whose roadmap appearance was evidence to years of heavy drinking, and large lips that puckered when he spoke. The only thing that wasn't large was his forehead which ended abruptly on a decline from a protruding, hairy brow ridge. A face not even a mother could love. "Tell me dat everysink's on trrek," he said in his familiar "Runglish" accent.

"It is going as it should be," Wazir responded, with a slight amount of disgust for his companion in the car. He didn't care very much for this individual, but at the moment working with him was a necessary evil.

Wazir added, "Please, these things take time Mister Petrov. Laborers don't simply become martyrs overnight. If that were the case, we could build the army without leaving Karachi. I have a Madrasah here. I will contact you when they are ready. God willing, that will be soon. "

"Gaht willin jes, Wazir, bet I ave new rrequests from client in Iraq. They turn to me - I turn to ju. Deju expect different? Isn't dat da vay it work? I elp ju - ju elp me." Petrov pointed out with a touch of sarcasm.

"Mister Petrov, my friend - please do not patronize me - we are motivated by two completely different forces. You my friend are a slave of money and want wealth alone. It is immediate financial gratification that drives you. I have Allah."

"Prrofits what drrife Leonid Paytrroff - prrofits frem seempul beeznuss - seempul beesnuss of warr, ay Wazir? Warr." He said with a deep guttural laugh followed by a prolonged cough.

"Of course that is the case - as long as there's profit - then you'll provide the services, the people, the weapons - whatever we may need. Am I not correct? Islamists my friend, have something much greater - our Islamic ideology through Mohammed and Allah -

something that atheists and communists have rejected. That is your mistake."

"I far frrom communist - my comrrads and Soviet Union I give up long time ago." He took a long drag on his cigarette and flicked an ash out the window. "I capitaleest, and I rrooshan. I eendependent beeznuss man," Petrov said. He took another drag and continued, "One thing you rright - I go where fuckin money iz. You need me - I do dirty work - I get job done. You want one thousand Pakis. Who do you come? Leonid Paytrroff. You know man can do better jeb – den pay heem."

"You are a lost soul and without Allah."

"Don't make fool of Leonid Paytrroff – you're vant more den Gaht. You vant revenge. Don't fuckin do bulsheet on me. Leonid Paytrroff know Arab never forgit. You need revenge, ya?"

"Please don't insult me."

"Okay, okay, I sorry. I mean Paki, Afghan - but what's difference, eh? All vear rags 'roun' head," Petrov said laughing and displaying the total depth of his disdain for Muslims of any ethnicity. He catapulted his cigarette butt into the night, the hot desert evening breeze returning some of the burning ash back into the SUV cabin.

"Your ignorance is baffling Mister Petrov. And you are right about your role. We do need you, and you are being compensated well for what you provide. Just continue to do that and everything will be just fine." Wazir paused, and then broached a new subject, "And how is our new project coming?"

"New proujit? Take time, *da*? Dhats what you say - don't vorji Wazir, I geaf you what you vant for to make many people suffer – I geaf you blutt – I geaf you 'xaos bomp.'"

"That is your final mission my friend, and when you complete it, you will be a rich man. Are we in agreement?" Wazir asked, again reliant on amazing patience.

"Leaf money in begh – den Leonid Paytrroff agree," Petrov said pulling out a flask of vodka from the inside pocket of his grey silk jacket. He took a swig, put the Range Rover in drive and turned the vehicle around on the dark road. Speeding back toward Dubai, the city's lights stretched before them, across the totality of the evening skyline.

CHAPTER 7

MAY 26, 2008

LONDON, ENGLAND

"LOVE, HOLD MUMMY'S HAND," Julie Perkins said as she tried to simultaneously keep her four-year old son in tow, balance a tray of food, and tote three full shopping bags. She adjusted the rope handholds of the bags to make room for the pint size hand.

"Mummy needs to find a table dear," she said under her breath as she alertly scanned the Food Hall inside Harrods. She knew when her target was spotted the window of opportunity would be very small; she wouldn't have a moment to lose.

"Brilliant, I see one love. O'er there, near the big funny bear." With shopping bags and her son's tiny fingers firmly in the grasp of one hand and tray in the other, she began briskly moving toward her target. "Right away, let's go Danny. Hold tight to Mummy."

Her intended destination was fifty feet and a mob of afternoon shoppers away. The only vacant table in the entire Food Hall was directly below a seven-foot wooden bear located at the far opposite end from where they were. The bear was her mark.

Julie negotiated the crowd with the agility of an Olympic slalom skier. She'd honed her skills on the sidewalks of the city where she grew up, London. Toting shopping bags and darting through crowds in high heels and tight jeans was not a virtue but a necessity, otherwise "one could forget about ever getting a table or taxi," she'd say.

She'd almost reached her goal when the mother of three toddlers spied the same free table and began her own rush, tray, bags, and all, to get there first. The race was on. Julie danced right and left, literally lifting Danny off the ground in the process. At the last second, she pivoted and blocked, putting her body and the shopping bags between the table and the competition.

"Brilliant. Here's our table Danny, just perfect for the two of us," Julie said loudly while setting her tray down on the prize. She affected a victorious smile at her opponent, who Julie tagged right away as a typical American tourist that could afford to go on holiday and shop at Harrods. Unable to frown or express any emotion by a face frozen from Botox, the loser simply waved her jeweled hand at Julie in disgust.

"Sit here Danny," she said lifting her oversized white sunshades to rest on the top of her blond hair. She looked at her watch to check the time. It was just before six. There was barely enough time for a quick bite before they would have to get a move on, she reasoned. She began cutting the slice of pizza into smaller pieces with the flimsy plastic utensils. Smaller pieces would be easier for Danny, meaning a speedier exit. When they finished, she'd get her new, freshly washed and waxed Range Rover from valet and make the short drive to the salon in Chelsea for her appointment.

Fanatical when it came to her appearance, she loathed even the slightest hint of dark roots to show. So it seemed the salon, rather than the gym, had become her second home, and Donna, the salon's owner, was doing her a big favor by coming in late at the last minute. Thank God she'd good friends that she could depend on.

"Perfect timing," she thought confidently.

It had been a wonderful day for Julie and Danny. She relished times just like these, when she could enjoy the benefits of a very fortunate life. She shopped with out a care in the world, spoiling herself and the love of her life, her son.

"Simply marvelous," she thought, tickled over their station. Frankly, Julie had been overjoyed when they'd chosen Knightsbridge as their home. It suited her. A perfect place to raise a family, and

London was an ideal spot for a talented surgeon as her husband. Famous people and those of means, though not so famous, lived in Knightsbridge, home to some of the most expensive real estate in the world. And those who lived there made it a point to ensure its safety and security beyond that of the remainder of London. He hung his shingle. They started a family.

"Dear lord, it's the rest of the world that's violent," she'd say at cocktail parties.

London and suburbs such as Knightsbridge certainly weren't immune to violence. She knew that all too well; the news kept her informed more than enough. In fact who could forget the London subway and bus bombings; and of course there was the crime associated with any large metropolitan area. Even in Knightsbridge, there were at times some random acts of crime such as a pickpocket here and there or a rare burglary, but generally she felt very safe. Knightsbridge residents were an eclectic mix of the wealthy that could well afford the security necessary for their enclave. The violence of Israel and Iraq was inconceivable in a community such as Knightsbridge. And security was everywhere it seemed, not just in Knightsbridge.

Alert levels and color codes that Americans seemed to live by were meaningless to her, as were the problems of the rest of the world. She didn't believe that it was a matter of ignorant bliss, she was after all aware of terms such as "sectarian violence," and "insurgency." And she truly felt sorry for soldiers that had lost their lives to "IEDs" the acronym that anyone who turned on a television now knew. But that was a world away, and really not very relevant to her life here. It was real but distant reality.

"We've the ring of steel," she concluded.

The "Ring of Steel," a surveillance belt cinched around London, strategically placed to thwart terrorists or perhaps at the very least discourage them somewhat. Highways and roads providing entrée into the city had been narrowed, chicanes carved into them, forcing traffic to slow to a crawl, each vehicle and driver captured on one of the four million closed circuit television cameras throughout the UK. London had also set up roadblocks of concrete as well as closed off some streets entirely. A true steel curtain designed to protect. *Provide security.* There was very little to worry about, she thought.

Content in those thoughts she cut another small piece of cheese pizza from the slice on her paper plate and put it on Danny's napkin. He grabbed the piece with his left hand and stuffed it in his mouth, all the while maneuvering a thirty-second scale model F-16 fighter jet on the tabletop with his right.

"Oh Danny, behave and please be careful dear. You'll drop that on your trousers," Julie said as she reached for the messy hand holding his toy. He raced his jet across the edge of the tray and onto the remnants of pizza. She checked her watch again. It was 6:00 PM on the nose.

"Danny dear, do you think we should give Donna a quick ring an' let her know that we're running late?" She asked rhetorically.

"Dunno mummy," he said with a shrug of his shoulders.

Julie looked under Danny's chair for her handbag. The cellular was in there somewhere, she thought. Picking up the designer bag and putting it in her lap, she fumbled blindly with her left hand, careful not to break a nail in the process. She soon felt the thin, now familiar shape of her new phone. Handling the gadget with the dexterity of a card shark, in spite of her long fingernails, she opened the face with her left thumb and punched "contacts" to search for Donna's number. She looked at her son. "You're a handsome devil, my dear sweet thing," she told him.

"Huh?" Danny answered without really hearing her. He'd been transfixed by a young man in Hip-Hop clothing, passing by their table. The man was holding his head down, hiding under his ball cap.

"Danny, hurry now an' finish. We shouldn't keep Donna waiting love," Julie cajoled her son, while she punched in the letter "D," jumping to Donna's number. It seemed she was finally getting the hang of her new phone but her nails still caused a bit of a problem now and then. "It's the keypad – it's so bloody tiny," She thought. She pushed the center button to start the call.

"Bloody hell, did it again," Julie said to herself, realizing after several seconds, the call had failed. She had a good signal though, so she tried once again.

Still holding the phone near her face, she noticed the tall young man directly in her line of sight. She peered at him over the top of her phone. She considered the man. "Something unusual about him," she thought.

Standing just a few feet in back of Danny's chair, he was wearing a large coat that draped to his knees. She reasoned the young man's clothes as nothing out of the ordinary; she was savvy to fashion statements and Hip-Hop was a trend that seemed to live on. Kids loved the oversized, layered look. A walking advertisement, he had "the look from head to toe; ball-cap, and "high water" pant legs hemmed at the calves," she thought.

But what really got her attention were his gestures. His hands moving inside the coat, he was violently pulling or perhaps tugging on something. Another thing struck her as being odd about the man; Julie thought she could hear him saying something, repeating some phrase. She strained her ears to isolate his words over the loud racket of the Food Hall.

"What's he bloody saying?" She wondered. "That can't be right," she thought. "Something like 'Allah - something or other.'"

His eyes suddenly caught hers and for a split second the two were locked in each other's gaze. Despair and contentment met and were linked for but a brief moment in time. She freed her stare from the young man's to mind Danny. He was pulling cheese and pizza sauce off the wheels of the toy jet, stuffing the tasty mess in his mouth with small fingers. The sight made her laugh. And then she smiled one last loving time at her son. Without warning, a blinding flash instantly propelled them into eternity.

* * * *

The bomb was actually two bombs in one. The first part being the *"Shaheed* Belt," or Martyr Belt, which looked more like a small flak jacket and was filled with acetone peroxide, a favorite of Hamas and Hezbollah suicide bombers. The ingredients could easily be purchased from drug stores without raising the slightest suspicion.

The concoction consisted of hydrogen peroxide, a common ingredient used for bleaching hair, plus acetone as the necessary electrolyte, found in most nail polish. Once cooked and cooled, the result was a volatile gel-like explosive. Unlike C4 and other plastic explosives, acetone peroxide couldn't be detected by bomb sniffing dogs. Making the explosive was an extremely dangerous process, one that had resulted in the accidental death of many inexperienced bomb makers.

The expert bomb maker in this case though, had not stopped at the belt. The second part to the lethal device was the "Shaheed Coat." The bomber's overcoat was literally plated with fifteen pounds of much more powerful ammonal, or common ammonia nitrate mixed with coal and aluminum powder, which could easily be detonated by the acetone peroxide in the belt.

With at least twenty pounds of highly explosive material surrounding the body of the suicide bomber, maximum lethal damage was guaranteed up to twenty-five feet from detonation. Yet most of the carnage would result from the shrapnel that sprayed throughout the fragmentation zone, impacting shoppers two hundred feet away.

Inside the oversized coat, the bomb maker had placed an additional ten pounds of ball bearings, screws, nuts, washers, and small pieces of wire that would be fired throughout the entire Food Hall in all directions. Literally hundreds and hundreds of deadly projectiles, as if blasted from a dozen shotguns, at unsuspecting, innocent women and children. He'd completed his guise by dressing in Hip-Hop attire. He applied makeup to cover a severe rash that'd spread across his face, pulling a ball cap to further hide the malady. He went to Harrods.

When in place, the bomber reached into the left hand pocket of his coat and depressed the red trigger. The detonator button, powered by a single AA battery, lit a small light bulb hidden in the "fragmentation jacket," instantly heating a tiny wire coated with the acetone peroxide, detonating the belt. That took hundredths of a second. One hundredth of a second later the coat exploded. The shrapnel, plus the martyr's flesh and bone hurdled in all directions, his blood a microscopic aerosol mist.

Within fifteen feet of detonation epicenter, the air was immediately heated to three thousand degrees Fahrenheit, obliterating all within that radius. Everything else within fifty feet of the blast that was not nailed or bolted down; tables, chairs, food trays, people, was picked up and either ripped to shreds or sent flying down the main hall, where hundreds of shoppers, mostly mothers and children were dining. The crowd was delivered a thousand pieces of molten shrapnel at better than the speed of sound. What had been a gleeful shopping atmosphere became a fiery hell.

Then, what could only be described as macabre irony, heat from the intensity of the blast set off all sprinkler heads high above in on the ceiling. Even though the after-blast had left little remnants of fire, gallons upon gallons of water now showered down upon the carnage below, where pieces of furniture, body parts, blood, shopping bags, clothing, and personal electronic devices were strewn everywhere. The scene was a grotesque red soup of death and destruction.

* * * * *

The concussion shook every square inch of Harrods. The blast could easily be heard at Buckingham Palace and as far as three miles away. A beautiful start to a London summer was violently derailed. Reverberations were global. Unfortunately, the London bombing was just the first in a series of similar horrific attacks that would resonate from UK and throughout the United States in less than an hour. By the end of the day, there would be a total of eight very lethal suicide bombings, killing four hundred and ninety five innocent people, as well as one failed attack resulting in no fatalities other than that of the suicide bomber. The attacks would occur in two countries and across two continents. During the failed bombing, the bomber, believing that he had been discovered by a mall security guard, fled down a deserted hallway and into an empty bathroom. There, he had inadvertently detonated himself. Being contained, the blast obliterated the bomber, killing no one else in the process and causing only minor structural damage and bruises to mall patrons knocked off their feet by the blast.

Beginning with London and continuing on at New Orleans, Louisiana; Newark and Camden, New Jersey; Philadelphia, Pennsylvania; Baltimore, Maryland; Portland, Maine; and Wilmington, Delaware; Newport News, Virginia, the horrors and heroics during the course of the day were sadly familiar, often repeated. The one failed bombing attempt required mop up, but Baltimore had fortunately been spared the human toll seen elsewhere in London and some of America's greatest cities. Within ten minutes of the Harrods attack a chain reaction of emergency response and alerts reverberated across local law, fire, and medical teams at the impacted areas, as well as state and federal law enforcement agencies.

In the United States, at the Federal level the FMCS, or Federal Multi-agency Coordination System of Homeland Security, jumped into action. A division of Homeland Security, the system was created in the aftermath of 9/11 to "combine facilities, equipment, personnel, procedures, and communications, integrated into a common system" and most importantly, to support the management of joint response following a terrorist attack. Basically FMCS had been organized to prevent miscommunications between local, state, and federal field operations responders following a disaster of any origin. Unfortunately the system had failed miserably in the aftermath of Hurricane Katrina.

England's counter-terrorism responsibilities fell squarely on the shoulders of the Home Secretary and in light of the deadly London bombings of 2005, the country passed extraordinary measures designed to specifically tackle Islamic extremists. The bill created an act that was divided into three parts: Part one made it a criminal offense for encouraging terrorism, distributing terrorist publications, planning terrorist acts, training for said acts, making devices for those acts, on down to trespassing on a nuclear site. The length of prison terms was also extended for crimes covered under previous bills now covered by the new one.

Part two was a bit more vague, but suffice to say it allowed for the continued prosecution of a known terrorist group if they changed their name, which made a great deal of sense evidently to all except for the groups being prosecuted, they believing their rights were violated. Of particular interest was the time a suspect could be detained for questioning without bringing about formal charges. Primarily, the bill was meant to deal with homegrown terrorists, or individuals legally residing within British borders. Although it did not address those outside of the borders, there was a provision in section two increasing the powers of the intelligence services for warrants, communications intercepts, searches and seizures.

The additional powers of Part two led to increased funding for collaboration with the United States. Together, they developed a new top-secret counter-terrorism group to forensically examine and decrypt the vast amounts of data compiled through confiscation, or other means of collection, including computers, cellular phones, wiretaps, and electronic monitoring equipment. In addition, the new office would develop additional "High-Tech" tools to exploit the terrorist threat. Other forensic analysis included financial, biological, chemical, radiological, and nuclear. Running the show was an American, Bryan Craig.

Navy Captain Bryan Craig was well aware of the multitude of shortcomings many agencies had in past crises. He was a veteran of the Gulf War and a past commander of elite SEAL teams. He now belonged to a Black Ops, Counter-Terrorism netherworld placed under the umbrella of the DNI, which had consolidated power over the CIA and other Federal Law Enforcement Agencies. He was an operations type that employed specialized skills using very lethal, clandestine means. He was a planner with an aptitude suited for designing and executing a variety of tactical assignments. Particularly involving the war on terror. As part of the top-secret program, Bryan and his team were called in wherever and whenever their particular skill sets were most needed.

Code-named Pegasus, the plan was credited as the brainchild of the Director of National Intelligence, Admiral Jack Rabbit Barnes. Rabbit had vaulted from one star to four in just two years, skipping two along the way. Tapped to be the top military advisor for the Secretary of Defense from his Task Force command, he put on three stars, was in the inner circle of the President but out of the limelight, a job that lasted only two years when he was promoted again and given a "baby four star" joint command as SOUTHCOM.

At dinner with the Admiral and his wife one evening when Rabbit was still at the Pentagon with SECDEF, Bryan asked, "How heady is that?"

"I've finally gotten used to being with the Secretary of Defense. You know I'm with him every day," Rabbit answered between tastes of after dinner sherry. "Now I'm around the President at least two or three times a week – calls me Rabbit – but you just never get used to being around him – never feel totally comfortable."

The Admiral loved to tell one story in particular. The President and the inner circle were meeting at the ranch during a holiday. "The usual suspects were there," Rabbit explained. "Inside the porch, sitting at the conference table you had the President, Vice President, SECDEF, Secretary of State, the National Security Advisor, and the Chairman of the Joint Chiefs."

"Everyone who's anyone," Bryan said.

"Yeah, exactly." Rabbit looked at his sherry as he swirled it in the glass, a smile forming. "Sitting around the outside, where we always sit, were all the Chiefs of Staff, including me. Oh, and Buckshot, his Basset Hound, was in the room. Anyway a four star marine was briefing the President on the capabilities of the Aegis missile cruiser – and the brief was going really bad, he didn't know what the hell he was talking about. So I see the President's eyes start to wander around the porch, and I'm thinking 'Man this is going bad, he's losing the President.' The next thing I know the President says 'Hey Rabbit.'"

"He called on you to finish the brief?"

"That's what I thought too. You know, 'Hey let's get a Navy man to brief the Navy stuff.' I'm thinking 'This is my big chance.' Do you know what he was calling on me for?"

"What?"

"The President said, 'Hey Rabbit, can you open the porch door? Buckshot looks like he wants to get outside.'" The three laughed hard, getting the attention of other's in the cozy Ristorante Piccolo. The job worked out just fine. Rabbit soon moved on.

SOUTHCOM, U.S. Southern Command was supposed to be a steppingstone to Chief of Naval Operations, or Supreme Allied Commander Europe, a command designed, "Just to get your feet wet as a four star," the Secretary of Defense told him.

Not so the case with Rabbit. Already a favorite four star of the President, Rabbit really got the Commander in Chief's attention for deftly utilizing multiple forces and agencies to put an end to a major crisis. The Caribbean nation of Haiti had been overthrown in a coup d'état, and a new military dictator set up shop. The dictator collaborated with Venezuela, whose leadership was unfriendly to the United States, allowing the island to function as safe haven for international terrorists, a conduit for drug smuggling, money laundering, and a distribution point of counterfeit U.S. currency printed in Venezuela. Rabbit successfully deployed assets of the CIA, DEA, and Special Operations, to depose the dictator, reinstate Haiti's previous leadership, and expose Venezuela as being complicit in violating international law. Not one American was ever "officially" on Haitian soil during the operations.

Impressed by Rabbit's skill, the President asked him to become the DNI, a senior Cabinet Level position, and a job he didn't seek nor felt qualified for. "That's bullshit Rabbit, you're the man – there's nobody better suited," the President said. He was honored and obligated to accept. As the new DNI, he put together Pegasus, telling Bryan Craig, "You're the man. Let's implement what we talked about."

Pegasus was designed around three basic principles of fighting terrorism: the psychology of the terrorist, the financial forensics, and the actual counter-terrorism action. Bryan had been tasked with building the operative team to handle that mission, he was very aware of the daunting responsibilities before him, and sometimes, fortunately or unfortunately, forced to get his hands dirty. As a result, Pegasus put Special Operations assets of the United States at Bryan's disposal, and being a collaborative effort with Great Britain, certain assets of MI5, MI6 and the SAS when conducting joint collaborative counter-terrorism operations.

The first task was to assume the role as the senior official on location in the wake of the horrific terrorist attack in London. From that moment forward he'd better do things right from the get-go. There would be little tolerance for errors or lapse in judgment. His mind raced as he hung up the phone with Washington, and he quickly began to formulate the program's action plan. He eyeballed his Cisco IP desk phone, and then punched the top intercom speed dial button that read "Parker."

"Hello?" Responded a soft voice that gave away a slight mid western accent.

Bryan began in a slow and calm tone. "Shannon, we've just had a report of a large explosion right here in London - at Harrods."

"Oh my God. It's happened again, hasn't it?" Exclaimed Doctor Shannon Parker, the FBI's terrorist profiler and behavior analyst assigned to Pegasus.

"Yes, I'm afraid so - lots of fatalities and looks to be a coordinated attack with considerable planning in back of it," Bryan said matter-of-factly and paused to allow time for the gravity of the event to hit home.

He continued, "It's confirmed with home plate. Just happened less than ten minutes ago. And I've just been on the phone with Washington," he paused before speaking the next sentence. "They were hit in the States too – multiple bombings across the country. Homeland Security has issued a nationwide red alert and most airports have been shut down. I'm checking on Heathrow now," he said searching the database of his computer.

"Al-Qaeda, isn't it?" She said, pushing away the remainder of a sandwich sitting on her desk. Her appetite had vanished thinking of the many people that must have just been murdered.

"Don't know just yet, but it looks that way. Professional, detailed, intricate – text book case. Let's get on down to the situation room right away. Okay? And uh, have a helicopter standing by for a trip downtown."

Bryan disconnected the call and slowly rotated his head about his shoulders, cracking his neck multiple times. He carefully contemplated his next call. This time he grabbed his cellular and pushed the radio alert twice. Seconds later a single radio-click responded.

"Bus?" Bryan asked. "Bus" was Gil Bussmann, head of financial tracking.

"Go ahead."

"Very ugly, I'm afraid."

"Color coded?"

"Code red," Bryan spoke softly. Pegasus was activated.

"Roger that. Have you turned the TV on yet?"

"No," Bryan said searching for his remote control.

"It's all over the news. Turn it on. Anyway, I'm ready - so let's roll."

Bryan responded with two clicks and turned on his office TV. CNN News was broadcasting the story with a banner below the reporter's talking head, "Breaking News – Memorial Massacre."

Bryan had one more very important, final call to make. He turned his chair to face the window and its view of the Thames. Reaching into his left-front pants pocket, he pulled out an iPhone nano. This was one of those ultra-cool devices that a key member of his team developed. It appeared to do one thing, but really did something entirely different.

After connecting the USB power adapter to the nano he waited a few seconds for the device to power up. Spinning the dial on his iPhone to "games," he held the center button down until he heard the familiar ping sound that came from the Mac PowerBook laptop stationed on the credenza below the window. A graphical user interface that looked similar to his cellular phone popped up on the screen. Putting the earphones into both ears, he listened for dial tone, selected "Secure" on the skin of the GUI, and pushed "eight, nine, zero." It started ringing.

"Evening," came the easygoing voice from his earphones. The clarity was remarkable for a secure call that used the highest level of encryption possible. In the past, those calls were garbled with background noise and static.

"Hello to you too." For a split second, Bryan thought the connection dropped, but then he heard the familiar voice again. Without the hissing of the old system, a pause sounded like the absolute quiet of a hang up or dead line.

"It seems you're about to get very busy. Better start loading up on those Red Bulls, huh?"

"Maybe so. Like how about right now," he replied as he opened the mini refrigerator below the credenza, removing a small can of the energy drink. "You'll be getting busy as well."

"Yep. Are we a go?"

"Team's in motion, and I'm in contact with state side."

"Sounds good. I'm ready here."

"Stiff upper lip and all that, right?" Bryan said using the old English expression, mockingly.

"You got that right. We can't afford screw-ups like our predecessors. That's why you're in this game now, I'm sure."

"I'd like to believe we've learned lessons from past mistakes. That's for sure," Bryan said.

"Glad to hear that. These bastards have pushed us over the edge, and there's going to be severe pay back." The voice had lost its charm, now angry.

Bryan felt a tingle emanate from his lower back right up the spine to his ears. He listened intently as he popped the Red Bull open and took a small swig.

"Okay, good luck."

"Thanks, I'll know where to find you." This time Bryan knew that the silence from the other end meant the call was over. He finished the Red Bull in two large swallows, tossing the empty into the trash. Grabbing the Counter-Terrorism Emergency Procedures Briefing Guide from his desk he stood up and dashed out of the office toward the situation room.

* * * * *

MAY 26, 2008

NEW YORY CITY, NEW YORK

The eight, forty-two inch flat panel screens were televising the same theme, from nine different locations, and not make believe. Scripted, but definitely not make believe. He reasoned that Hollywood would have to wait years before it could conscientiously tell these unfolding stories.

Expertly, he split the pictures on all screens to view local and national coverage for every bombing. On two screens he had CNN and Fox news on one, Al Jazerra news and CNBC on the other. The destruction appeared worse than it really was. The psychological impact was already taking hold of both nations, and the bombings were not yet an hour old. Financial futures were indicating the next day's opening would be tumultuous, very unpleasant. New York stock exchange curbs would most likely need to be in place, preventing massive programmed and panicked sell offs. The likelihood of an actual trading halt, better than fifty-fifty he calculated. The next twenty-four hours would prove to be challenging for the financial experts on Wall Street and at the London Exchange. A slight, forlorn smile formed on his mouth. His accounts were covered, hedged against losses. Tomorrow would be an ugly day for investors in American stocks.

The Sultan Amir Sika Kahn adjusted the volume between televisions to hear the news anchors' commentaries on the various bombings. Occasionally he switched a channel to a German or French news program, listening to the impressions of Europeans critical of

British and U.S. policies. The universal reaction was that of shock; however opinions varied across the spectrum, for reasons or blame for the foray.

As Amir studied his screens, he became distracted by a beautiful young Euro-Asian looking woman approaching barefooted from across the expanse of the massive room. She was carrying an ornate tray with a plate of fruit consisting of grapes, dates, and orange slices. She also had a pot of coffee and a single eighteen-karat gold cup.

Appearing to glide with very short, abbreviated steps, her movement impeded slightly by a form fitting black and turquoise dress which tapered just below her ankles. The silk shimmered in multiple shades of light and dark as she walked. Gracefully, she knelt before his chair, her knees resting on a priceless fifth century Persian rug. Her delicate face framed by a white silk scarf, she bowed her head slightly as her small bottom came to rest on the soles her tiny feet.

"Would you care for fruit and your coffee now Master?" She demurely asked while offering her tray.

"Thank you my dear. Yes I'd like that very much," he replied in English, with an accent that could have been honed from years of a privileged education at Great Britain's finest schools.

"It's three o'clock after all, isn't it?" His large hand cupped her chin and moved it upward until her eyes met his. She smiled as he leaned forward to kiss her on the forehead.

"Just the coffee Despoina," he said pointing to the spot on the gold leaf coffee table where he wanted her to place the cup.

He enjoyed saying her name. Despoina literally meant "Mistress" in Greek. How "après pro" he thought, as he leaned back in the overstuffed chair.

She set the gold coffee cup next to his computer, poured the hot coffee to exactly one quarter of an inch below the brim, then stood up and waited for his instructions.

"Thank you Despoina. That'll be all," he said smiling at her. She returned the smile, stood, turned and walked away. His cell phone chirped to life. He flipped the phone open and activated the speaker.

"Yes?"

"Your plane is ready as you wished Sultan - flights are permitted from the airport," an aide spoke over the phone in Pashto, a language similar to Farsi. His message meaning the Gulfstream V had been topped with fuel. The flight plan called for London as the destination, but instead they would fly nonstop to Dubai. The pilot would make the flight change en route.

"Get the car ready for the heliport. We'll leave when I've finished my afternoon coffee," he said speaking perfect Pashto. He was a linguist, able to converse fluently in fifteen languages. Pashto he preferred the most.

Putting the phone down, he sat back in his chair and took a sip of coffee. The cup was held gingerly in his right hand with his little finger slightly extended. On it he wore a large ornate ring that would have fit on an average man's forefinger. It was silver with symmetrical designs along the sides; the face was flat and highlighted by a circle of interspersed diamonds and rubies. In the center was a large white image resembling a mountain made from Mother of Pearl.

Finishing his coffee, he set the cup down, leaned forward, reinvesting his study of the scenes unfolding on the television screens before him as he rubbed his chin with his left hand. He was unconsciously caressing the magnificent ring as he took in the images of death and destruction. He looked down at the ring, drawing it to his lips for a soft kiss. It was time to leave the United States once again.

CHAPTER 8

JUNE 1 2008

LONDON, ENGLAND

I T HAD BEEN ONLY one week since the coordinated terror bombings. Referred to as the Memorial Massacre, it was an ignominious but accurate title coined by the media. A handy moniker for hype and prone to be used by cable news channels always hungry for sensationalism, yet sensationalism was inherent in the act itself, with a title or without one.

The national temperament both in England and the United States was clearly in the early stages of the Kübler-Ross grief cycle, vacillating between shock, denial, and anger. The world's resident evil had struck again, this time it happened in the heart of western symbols of capitalism, shopping malls.

Activists, religious leaders, politicians, celebrities; all called for the American and British people to come together in a display of national unity. Demonstrations and remembrances were coordinated in cities and towns around the country, the primary sites being in the cities where the attacks had occurred. Over three hundred thousand people filled Philadelphia's Fairmount Park. Another three hundred thousand gathered on the Mall in Washington D.C., and an estimated five hundred thousand in New York City's Central Park.

Immediate sympathy poured in from governments around the world. Great Britain's Parliament observed ten minutes of silence. The Vatican issued a statement calling for an end to senseless terrorist violence, condemning self-incurred Martyrdom. In the United States, a bipartisan investigative commission was called for from elected congressional members of both political parties. These were the normal reactions that invariably always occurred, but had little or no impact on future events, simply symbolic.

Conspiracy theorist came out of the woodwork, their diatribe parallel to derision of the government and military by radicals claiming sinister plots after 9/11. Statements by officials were taken out of context as proof of the diabolical planning. A small group of theorists deduced that the property owners blew up their own malls to collect insurance. There were at least another dozen or so equally ludicrous theories. One of the most bizarre was the theory that the bombings were planned by retired members of the military as a protest for American's ambivalence to sacrifices made by the armed forces; the very reason why the attacks occurred on Memorial Day.

The bombings occurred on a day of remembrance for all Americans. Remembrance for sacrifices made by those who gave their lives to preserve the freedoms of the living; freedoms that included democracy and the market-based economy that bore those very malls. Although shocking in their scope and the subsequent fear that they spawned, repeat suicide attacks on America's shores had always been expected after 9/11. Those fighting the battle against terror on the front lines uttered that warning over and over.

"They only have to get it right once. We need to get it right all the time" was their mantra. "They were right, unfortunately," Bryan Craig thought.

What was startling about the Memorial Day attacks however, was the precise coordination of the bombings across multiple cities and two continents. The similarities with the earlier successful London and Madrid bombings were easy to see, as well as the similarity with another failed attempt by homegrown terrorist planners in London. Homegrown Islamic schemers were of Pakistani heritage, and planned to blow up twelve airliners over the American cities using acetone peroxide liquid explosives ignited by cell phones or other improvised electronic devices. Each of the schemes had the fingerprints of Al-Qaeda.

Hezbollah or Hamas could be ruled out. Both organizations would have too much to lose by attacking the U.S. inside its own borders and would face harsh worldwide criticism for attacking innocents in Great Britain. They both wanted to gain international legitimacy via political elections, much in the same manner as Sinn Fein had in Ireland years before. They both received tremendous funding from sympathetic Islamic groups in the United States and the UK. A direct attack by either organization would draw unwanted attention to their contributors and jeopardize that funding. In addition, Hezbollah and Hamas had their sights set on the State of Israel, constantly threatening the livelihood of Jews in the Middle East, not on necessarily the punishment of the United States or Great Britain. The Memorial Day attacks were too horrible and senseless. Hezbollah and Hamas were quickly ruled out.

So it was more than likely an Al-Qaeda inspired splinter group. But the fact that the attacks were carried out absent the usual "chatter" or warning of some sort, which was regarded as a precursor to a significant terrorist event, was unusual, startling. Nine times and nine targets, the London Metropolitan Police, Scotland Yard, Homeland Security, the NSA, the FBI, the CIA, the military, local law enforcement, all had the proverbial wool pulled right over their eyes. Or had they, Bryan pondered?

Pondering the prospect that law enforcement dropped the ball again, Bryan prayed that clues hadn't been in front of their faces yet again, but suffering from myopia, they'd failed to connect the dots. The possibility existed though. Maybe a counter-terrorism agent or even a local cop had one or more of the homicidal bombers in his or her sights, yet the warnings were ignored? Had logistical gridlocks of an overly complicated communications system failed as they had on 9/11? Or had terrorists spawned new tactics? Did they have "the playbook," a prospect that concerned him most? Bryan had been on the scene of the mall bombing in London just forty-five minutes after the suicide murderer obliterated himself in the Harrods Food Hall. The bomber killed fifty-two and injured one hundred and thirty. It was a depressing scene, and up to now, one week later, there were no clear-cut answers, only dead-end clues.

The facts were simple enough, nine bombings, nine shopping malls. Scores killed. One botched job. The types of explosives used were identified and well known, very common. But there were question marks. The assailants were as yet still unidentified. What little was left of the perpetrators, physically, was being analyzed by crime scene investigators and forensic labs for DNA. Results had been inconclusive so far.

The Islamic martyrs had popped up out of nowhere at eight locations across the United States, and one in London, and simultaneously blew themselves to smithereens. Most of the malls had security systems that used facial recognition, including Harrods, but the videos were unusable. The few digitally recorded images of a bomber were obscured, their faces never in full view. To make identifying the attackers all the more difficult, each wore oversized, hip-hop clothing that blended with dozens of young people in similar fashions. Security guards were trained to detect suspicious behavior; only one had succeeded in thwarting an attack. Eyewitness accounts from survivors at Harrods who Bryan interviewed, had provided little useful information. Bryan Craig needed a miracle and soon.

* * * * *

He carried out his missions with resolute, noble-mindedness. Some might say like a medieval knight on a crusade. An eternal pragmatist, Bryan was the product of a military careerist and a meek, doting mother undaunted herself, but devoted to her husband's career. An only child, he grew up in the world of Navy bases and Washington as his father climbed the promotional ladder. Eventually rising to Vice Admiral, senior Craig's climb ended abruptly when a torrid affair was unexpectedly uncovered.

Vice Admiral Craig's career had been stellar. Always screening amongst his peers at the top. Over the years the Navy had selected him as commander of a fighter squadron, Carrier Air Wing Commander, a Flag Officer, and eventually promoted to Vice

Admiral as Commander of the Sixth Fleet, a choice assignment based in Naples, Italy; a command of great power during a time of uneasy peace and uncertainty of the Cold War.

Maybe due to the loneliness of separation as his father claimed, he strayed from his wife. She wanted to believe that but knew better. It wasn't the first time. Bryan was convinced it was just his father's nature and the intoxicating effects of power, the misguided belief that some of the rules didn't apply to certain people. In a different place and different time, that might be true, but not in an era when morality was under the microscope. Any hint of infidelity was political suicide, and in government or the military, the infraction was dealt with harshly, usually signaling the end of a career, castigation, and denunciation. Vice Admiral Craig was no exception to that new rule.

His father became involved with a famous Italian movie star. She'd been a sex goddess of the sixties, renowned for her physical attributes, particularly large breasts. Inside joke being, her two, and his three stars made the only five-star in the Navy.

She was attracted to the Admiral's charisma and power, and he to her beauty and impetuous Latin temperament. Their liaison was scorching. Maybe they were even in love, Bryan thought.

The Vice Admiral jetted around Europe on military planes with the sexpot, having the time of his life. As if he were begging to be caught, he was even so bold as to have her ensconced in a hillside Italian villa used as the Sixth Fleet's residence. With panoramic views of Naples, Capri, the Italian coastline, and a household staff to cook, clean and garden, the two carried on like Anthony and Cleopatra. He was oblivious to the transparency of his glass house and romped with impetuosity.

Discretion was a virtue the Admiral had long since disregarded, having "left a trail of breadcrumbs a blind man could follow," the Admiral's aide said. It didn't take long for scandal salivating paparazzi to uncover the juicy tale. What had been a swift rise to Vice Admiral, and the certainty of four stars, was derailed by an explosion of gossip, innuendo, and unfortunately, by photographs, hard evidence right in his face. Plausible deniability vanished with the click of a camera's shutter. Photos and eyewitness accounts of the illicit affair splashed across the pages of paparazzi fed Italian newspapers. Soon he was fodder for the Washington Post and finally called home to face the music, and his wife of twenty-five years.

Disgraced, divorced, his father retired with one less star, the flamboyant lifestyle was over, the power gone.

Bryan was in school at Yale paying his dues and engrossed in study when the news hit. "What the hell was he thinking?" Bryan had first angrily asked himself, then asked his father. They played golf together, talked about Bryan's future, yet no mention of the home life with his mother, who had been devastated. Bryan assumed their communication would be superfluous from that point on. A broken man, he found refuge in golf, followed by long afternoons at the nineteenth hole, in the end never even making it out on the course. Senior Craig died at sixty-two, his once vibrant body debilitated by lungs racked with emphysema from years of smoking. Bryan never married. He didn't want to do the same thing to a woman that his father had done.

An above average student, and all round athlete, he'd participated in sports his entire life, liked football and baseball, and was an excellent rower for Yale, yet rugby was the sport he loved the most though, and at six foot two and 195 pounds played the position of wing with ferocity. After finishing his degrees, Bachelor of Arts in History and Bachelor of Science in Economics, he took the double major and applied for SEAL training via Officer Candidate School, and was accepted. Sailing through training, the experience was more of a chance to shed the mental baggage of his father's shadow, gain inner peace and a new perspective. Soon he was half a world away as Desert Storm began to unfold. Reputation preceding him, he became a favorite of theater commanders, admired for his strong will, determination, and drive. There was something of Bryan's father in him after all, maybe only the warrior, hunter.

The world of intelligence and counter-terrorism was now Bryan Craig's niche. Not a political animal, he was just good at what he did. The world of post 9/11 changed his career path. The military and the intelligence agencies shifted their emphasis to Islamist counter-terrorism and terrorism finance, an expertise where Bryan had no equal. He was specifically handpicked and now in charge of Pegasus.

Bryan's neoteric focus was on the Pegasus' stated mission, "To protect and defend the United States and their allies against terrorists and terrorist threats." He used every means at his disposal to carry out that mission, and his team got results. Successful operations were rewarded. Pegasus was funded further. Bryan also had access and clout previously unheard of in counter-terrorism units. To solve the Memorial Day bombings it appeared however, that he might need something more. He needed technology and a wizard to work their magic.

In the fast paced first week following the bombings, Bryan used mini, two-hour catnaps to catch up on badly needed sleep. His bed was his office couch. He awoke from one of those naps to Shannon's voice over the intercom.

"Hello, Bryan?" Shannon asked.

"Hola," he said eyes still shut.

"I'm at the lab. We have something here you need to see right away."

Bryan opened his eyes, blinking at his wristwatch. It was 5:20 in the morning.

"On my way" he said sitting up. He needed a cup of coffee, or "perhaps one of those Red Bulls, " he thought. Back to work.

He opened his office door and flipped on the light switch to the cube farm, a spattering of fourteen modular cubicles, absent the inhabitants that generally arrived at 6:00 AM. When manned, the hard working Pegasus staff monitored the activities of hundreds of terrorist cells worldwide, surveillance of calls, Emails, websites, and television. He turned right and walked briskly toward the stairwell.

The lab was in the basement, secured and fortified, designed to withstand a twenty-kiloton nuclear detonation. Bryan arrived moments later at the entrance which had its own secure access. He positioned his left hand on a wall-mounted biometric scanner while inserting a key card into an adjacent slot. The device combined a self-contained fingerprint and palm print module with a smart card reader for dual authentication. Maybe a little overkill he thought but definitely secure. The yellow light on the scanner changed to green, indicating that access had been granted. The door clicked open as the lock was released. He pushed it open and walked inside the large frigid area.

It was a top-secret lab and looked the part. Part control room, part communications, part hi-tech analysis, with lots of glass, and monitor screens, but plain concrete walls. All electronic and communications equipment were next generation, having an appearance that belied a design team from Hollywood, Cisco VoIP phones, giant flat panel displays, glass doors, and glass interior office walls. One flat panel was used for secure video teleconferences with team members, including those in Washington D.C. Housed inside the lab was one of the fastest Tflop supercomputers in the world, capable of teraflops, or trillions of calculations per second. Pegasus used every bit of those calculations capabilities.

Since the installation, the lab had been used to aid in many collaborative investigations, from analysis of wiretap audio to enhancement of security camera video. Considered one of the premier criminal forensic labs in the world, more than a few criminals had their fate sealed by work carried out inside their walls, although the lab's very existence was known by very few, the location, by even fewer. Responsible for its operation, and the five technicians usually working around the clock, was Derrick Johnson, a tall, bald, black man, a Londonerry who preferred to work to the music of Led Zeppelin.

"Please have some good news for me DJ," Bryan said as he joined Doctor Parker and the lab's wizard. The two were sitting in front of a workstation looking intently at an image on a thirty-inch flat panel monitor.

"We just may have some good news Bryan. Do you know all the cell phones, iPhones and other electronic devices we ended up with from Harrods?" Shannon began first.

Bryan knew exactly what Shannon was talking about. Two large boxes of phones, cameras, MP3 players, iPhones, laptops, and other electronic media had been collected from just the Harrods crime scene alone. There was also an entire storage room filled with similarly charred electronic devices collected from the other locations.

"I'm with you Shannon, carry on," Bryan nodded.

"DJ take it from here on out," Shannon deferred to the wizard.

"Okay, you're on the air DJ," Bryan said, using the standard pun of the lab.

"Boss." DJ paused, and then looked at his Bryan. "Ye know tha' we've been workin non stop ere for the last week an' so far 'ave come up with very lit-al." DJ stood up from the chair and motioned with his right hand outstretched to a pile of partially melted cell phones. The head of the lab had a graceful elegance about him as he moved, especially considering the fact that he was just a shade less than six and a half feet tall.

"Continue," Bryan said, nodding at a speaker close to his ear. The lab's rock music was playing a little too loud for his taste.

"Let's go en ta the thear-ta room, boss." DJ pointed to a door of a room in the lab that had just been converted into a home theater, complete with the prerequisite theater chair seating. The lab staff would occasionally watch old robbery videos on the sixty-inch screen from the comfort of the black leather recliners.

"Put on the Razor, will yeh?" DJ said to one of his staff as the three entered the theater.

"'Ave a seat ere boss." DJ offered Bryan a recliner in the center. Bryan didn't know why, but DJ had called him "boss' from day one, and it stuck. Bryan really didn't mind.

"As ah was sayin'. We 'adn't come up with a thing, not-a sausage." He paused a moment. "Until we took a look at this." He held up a Motorola Razor, fully opened between his thumb and index finger. DJ handed it to Bryan and continued on with his brief.

"No' mint that's for sure, pretty mucked up when we got it."

Bryan looked carefully at the cell phone. It had been through hell. The plastic casing was charred and the LED glass display was shattered.

"Hmmm, you mean to tell me, you were actually able to get something off of this damn thing?"

"'Ow 'bout bloody thing sir, ya'd beh surprised. Rememba when the Space Shuttle broke up en re-entry?" DJ was speaking of the Columbia mission that had been doomed from launch. Bryan had been a friend of a crewmember since the Gulf War and knew the details of the accident.

""Yeah," Bryan said, folding his arms.

"They'd one special piece o' equipment that's not designed ta beh crash proof, unlike the black boxes en airliners. But et survived disintegration and a fifty mile freefall ento a field somewhere's en Texas," DJ said moving his hand down from above his head for a visual.

"Yep, in fact, I do remember that distinctly. It was eventually recovered weeks later – and point is?" Bryan encouraged his tech forensic genius.

"Da point es dey found da box containin da sensor data dhat confirmed foam damaged ta da tiles at take off, an' caused da Shuttle breakup oen re-entry."

"We have the same thing here?" Bryan held the phone close to his ear.

"Well, yeah, en'a way. The owner of the cell phone an' 'er kid were da closest to da suicide bomba' when 'e blew 'imself up." DJ dimmed the lights in the room and turned on the large screen with a remote control. The three were now looking at a freeze frame from one of six security cameras mounted on walls near the ceiling of the Food Hall. Bryan had watched the security camera video numerous times already, yet it was still distressing to view a week later. DJ pointed a red laser at the screen.

"Ere we 'ave Missus Perkins and 'er little boy enjoying a bite." He circled fuzzy figures sitting at table in the right hand corner of the screen with the bright red dot. She was facing her young son, who was the last figure in full view on the image.

"Now over ere, to Missus Perkins' right, we 'ave Missus Stein, the American woman on 'oliday and 'er kids, God rest their souls." He moved the dot rapidly back and forth over their images.

"Ah 'ave to tell you something boss, they 'ad a real 'orses race to get to that table first - Missus Perkins won. And the prize for 'er victory was a seat closest to the mofo with the bomb." Bryan was unconsciously moving closer to the edge of the leather seat as he listened and followed along.

"Now what Missus Perkins didn't know was that over ere, on the opposite side of the eatin area, was another free table. Way over ere." The red dot moved to far upper left hand corner of the screen.

"This table is ninety feet away from the explosion and everyone in this general vicinity lived," DJ added.

DJ pressed a button on the remote to begin moving the footage forward frame by frame.

"Alright look over ere. We now see a partial of Mista Suicide." Bryan could just make out half of his Hip-Hop clad torso. He looked like any other teenager goofing off.

Shannon chimed in, "This is where we ran into problems trying to identify him before Bryan. His cap is obscuring his face and he can't really be seen clearly from any of the other cameras in the Food Hall." It was an observation that had not escaped Bryan earlier.

DJ rapidly stepped the frames forward until the bright flash of the explosion signaled the end of the security camera footage. The three sat in silence for a moment. Shannon and Bryan having both been to the scene, recalled the horrific images from their memories with vivid detail.

"That's where the Food Hall's images end boss. The camera nearest the explosion didn't make it through the bombin. Didn't matter anyway. The bomber's blown to bits. All you'll see after that is, ...well, you've seen it before, 'adn't you," DJ said sympathetically, shaking his head.

"So where's that leave us now?" Bryan said looking back and forth at both of them. He knew there was a point to the demonstration, and he wanted his team to quickly get to it.

DJ smiled a wide grin, a gap between his top front teeth. "From all of these cell phones, cameras and other rubbish we 'ave ere, we didn't get much. And 'ad Missus Perkins just looked to her right after leaving the queue, she'd probably be alive right this minute, and we still wouldn't 'ave a clue. But she chose the table nearest the wanker instead. Unfortunate for 'er, but not for us." DJ reversed the video frame by frame until just before the blast.

"Cheers Missus Perkins," DJ said smiling and then looking down at his boss, who was now sitting so far forward on the edge of the leather chair, his butt was almost about to slide off.

Bryan's anticipation grew. DJ began to zoom the image in, which as it grew larger became more pixilated and undefined. One thing was becoming clearer to Bryan though, DJ's ranting about black boxes and Space Shuttle explosions were beginning to make sense. Mrs. Perkins was holding something in her hand and it was pointing directly at the bomber. Bryan looked down at the broken device he was holding. There it was right on the face of the broken phone "MEGAPIXEL."

"Jackpot. In 'er 'and is a phone with a camera," DJ said slowly to emphasize his discovery.

"Unfuckin believable," Bryan exclaimed.

"Boss, I think what we 'ave ere might just give you your first clue." DJ manipulated the remote and a new image appeared on the screen.

The picture was extremely sharp, Danny Perkins holding an F-16 model airplane. Bryan remembered the boy. He'd looked at passport photos of all the victims; in fact their photos had been put up on a wall in the situation room as a reminder of the human toll inflicted. The new photo of Danny served to anger Bryan even further.

Bryan remembered how cute the young boy was, "sitcom ready," he thought. Sandy blond hair and large eyes; what would the future have held for the remainder of his life? Judging from the boy's looks and the pedigree, it probably wouldn't have lacked for much. However, it was a future that would never be, cruelly cut short by an act of terror.

"Cute, but what does this photo do for our investigation?" Bryan asked skeptically, masking his feelings of anticipation.

"Well, not a thing actually," DJ said before a slight pause. "That is, if it were just a photo." He hit the play button on the remote.

"Poor Missus Perkins," DJ narrated. "She 'ad evidently just acquired said cellular - the one that you now 'ave in your 'and. And she really 'adn't learned 'ow to use the thing very well yet either. Plus her bloody long nails were really muckin' 'er up. She thought she was making a call, but what she 'ad really done was start the video. And the star was none other than our piss-arse bomber."

The video image buffered slightly, caused when Julie had moved her hand during the video recording. Bryan was watching Danny Perkins eat his pizza and fly his toy plane around the table. The scene captured the pathos of the ultimate event. A few other patrons of the Food Hall could be seen coming in and out of the viewfinder. Suddenly the camera stopped squarely on the face of a man wearing a ball cap pulled down, level with his eyes. It was the bomber. DJ paused the video. Bryan could now see the features of one of the killers for the first time.

"This can't be possible." Their boss was dumbfounded as he looked at the face.

DJ looked down at Bryan Craig and waited for the right moment before switching to a new image.

"Now ya get it, don't ye boss? Well let me elp ya a lit-al bit more. We've enhanced the image just to be sure it's our man. 'Aven't done a faceprint yet, needed to enhance this image first. And ah've been working on it for a couple of 'ours. Yep, we're sure its him alright."

DJ pushed a button on the remote, enlarging the face, which now completely filled the sixty-inch screen. Bryan threw the damaged phone down in anger. All three looked at the familiar face of a bomber, a moment of poignance, if there were one.

"This should cause quite a stir the states. What about verification?" Bryan asked, retrieving the phone from the floor.

"Well, let's see what FaceScan thinks."

DJ sat down at a monitor and entered his password. The Led Zeppelin screensaver dissolved indicating *FaceScan* was ready to go to work. They were again looking at the bomber. He no longer had the familiar beard of the person they recognized, and his complexion looked as though he'd a touch of adult acne, but he was definitely someone they knew; yet they had to be sure. The team needed that all-important legal verification, one that would hold up in a court of law. That meant double checks followed by cross checks, then more double checks again. No big deal to DJ, he lived in a world of tedious follow-up after follow-up. FaceScan mitigated possible errors.

FaceScan was a biometrical facial recognition technology that used proprietary software to compare known features of a person's face with an image, confirm that image as matching, and do so with a reasonably high percentage of confidence. Since the Al-Qaeda attacks, facial recognition software had seen an exponential increase in application at airports, bus terminals, train stations, and many other places heavily frequented by the public. The first large-scale testing of facial recognition occurred *en masse* at the 2000 Super Bowl in Tampa, Florida when an entire stadium of football fans were scanned and analyzed unbeknownst to the ticket holders. That of course had led to complaints of invasion of privacy, violation of constitutional rights, and "Big Brother" watching. All the things that DJ thought were "inconsequential."

"Boss, you 'aven't seen FaceScan in action yet, 'ave you?"

"No. I've read the Alpha and Beta reports - and approved the budget, but..." Bryan stopped mid sentence, searching for a reason why he hadn't tracked the research and development of FaceScan with DJ more closely, after all it had cost over $25 million through the Beta. The expenditure was a significant dent in their operational budget but proved to be very cost effective.

"Don't worry about it boss. You'll see it in action now. If that's our man there on the screen, FaceScan and Jimi will find 'im," DJ said winking at the other two, as if the ghost of Led Zeppelin was the soul of FaceScan.

"Boss let me explain to you the system that you 'ad spent so much on - FaceScan 'as perfected existing technologies to provide a much 'igher accuracy rate than any system developed before it. My software program uses mathematical algorithms that analyze the minute distinguishable characteristics of a person's face. Those are what ah call landmarks."

"For example - a bump on the nose, a mole, or a pock mark – something like that?" Bryan asked.

"Precisely. The FaceScan program creates mathematical relationships between those landmarks. Ah call em nodal points o' nodes for short. The precise positioning of the chin, eyes, nose, ears, are surveyed and measurements taken, to determine the width of the nose, depth of the eye sockets, length of the jaw line, and all that. FaceScan software looks at over three thousand nodes to arrive at a very unique number. It's my code – some call it faceprint. Harrods security is designed for faceprints, just FaceScan does it much better."

Bryan and Shannon looked on in silence as DJ went to work with FaceScan. First scanning the image of the Harrods bomber into the FaceScan hard drive that ran the program, the software analyzed the image, assigning unique numeric values. Then he compared those values to values of the image they suspected as being a match. Moving the cursor to select a new file, he opened it and began to look for a particular bearded face among a page of dozens of suspects.

"There you are you wanker. Abdul-Malik," DJ exclaimed.

He highlighted the file and dragged it over to a screen labeled "Compare." Then FaceScan began do its most important job. DJ reached over and turned up the volume to "The Immigrant Song." Drumming his pencil on the desk, they waited. It was one of his favorite songs. He sang along.

FaceScan completed the analysis in less than a minute, indicated by a high-pitched "ping" sound.

"He's all terrorist, that one," he said as he clapped his hands together. FaceScan had registered a perfect ten out of ten score as a comparison of the three thousand nodes. It was a perfect match. There was no doubt about it. The young man on Mrs. Perkins's camera video, wearing hip-hop clothing, that blew him self up, killing all those people in the Food Hall, was the same guy from the file mug shot wearing an orange jump suit. DJ printed the results and then moved the cursor to close the file that the mug shot came from. The file read "GIRD_SCD." Gitmo Released Detainees – U.S. Supreme Court Decision.

"Roger - that confirms who we're looking for - Islamic terrorists. And partially home grown ones at that," Bryan said, putting his hand on DJ's shoulder. "Tie into the airport databases here, we'll see if we can pinpoint when and where Mister Malik landed back in England."

"Do you want to call Washington yet?" Shannon asked.

"Get me his file first, I'd like to review his associations once more before jumping on the horn with them," Bryan said. "Let's set up a conference call with all local agents in charge. Make it for this afternoon. I want everybody on the same page by the end of the day," he added, hoping the breakthrough was going to lead somewhere.

CHAPTER 9

JUNE 1, 2008
LONDON, ENGLAND

"SERVANT OF THE MASTER. That's the meaning of Abdul-Malik in Arabic," Bryan reminded himself. He'd taken a keen interest in this particular detainee well before the Supreme Court decision. This Malik "servant" however, was not Arabic but British, born in London, the third son of Pakistani immigrants who were both MDs. His given name at birth had been Rafik Zia, yet while growing up in England, was generally called "Rafi" by all who knew him. And by all accounts, was a bright student, and well liked by his fellow classmates. He made straight A's at the Wellingborough School in London.

Standing from his desk chair and stretching while letting out a serious yawn, Bryan looked out the window. It was a clear spring evening in London. If he could see Big Ben, it would be telling him it was almost midnight. Although late, he wanted to review Rafik Zia's file one more time. Splashing some water on his face from the wet bar in his office, a perk for the executive that had the corner space when a corporation took up residency here, he checked his face in the mirror. He felt a little tired, but surprisingly it didn't register on his face yet.

His hair was starting to get too long though, he thought, preferring it to be cut very close on the sides, hiding some of the grey. He opened the file and sat down on the couch for a night of study.

Rafi's father was Pashtun, and from Rawalpindi, when the British Empire still held that part of the world in their hand. It was a remnant of the Empire's imperialism, and the remaining symbol of colonialism. His grandfather had been a proud member of the British Indian Army during World War II. As a doctor who was trained in England, he'd tended to wounded allied soldiers throughout Southwest Asia and the Pacific, and had worked on the medical staff of Lord Mountbatten, the British Empire's last Viceroy of India. With the end of the War came the ultimate independence of India, and finally the separation of Hindus from Muslims. The country of West Pakistan was born, which very soon became simply, Pakistan, literally meaning "the Pure Land."

The new Pakistan found itself in turmoil from the beginning. Britain had always favored the rich and fertile land of the subcontinent of India, which as a result, flourished during the Empire's reign. The North West Frontier region, with an inaccessible, inhospitable mountainous terrain, was largely ignored and tribal people forgotten. Karachi however, because of its North Arabian Sea coastal port, persevered and kept the brand new country on the radar screen of the west; especially that of the United States.

Rafi's grandfather sought the opportunities afforded by life in the West, and when that opportunity presented itself, accepted British citizenship, moving the family to England. He was immediately accepted into society, for a time anyway.

Bryan had studied this Al-Qaeda convert closely. And it was no wonder why. What could possess this seemingly good-natured young man to flip to the other side? He didn't fit the stereotypical "disenfranchised convert" profile. But after closer examination, maybe he possibly did after all.

Rafi's grandfather had begun a general medical practice in London during the early nineteen fifties. He was Islamic in belief, a Sunni Pashtun Muslim, yet adored Viceroy Lord Mountbatten, the overseer of the separation of India and Pakistan. The Pakistani doctor's practice flourished in his adopted home. But they lived an isolated existence, only really accepted in British society as former subjects of the Empire, as Indians who weren't Anglo. Most of his patients were Asians living in London, or the impoverished who couldn't afford to pay their bill. Charity work became the norm, but he didn't mind. Their social interaction with Anglo neighbors however, was superficial, the family becoming reclusive; with the exception of their only son Ishaq, who embraced his adopted country.

Born in Pakistan, yet transplanted to Great Britain when he was just a toddler, Ishaq was impervious to the prejudice that his mother and father faced. An extremely bright student as well and exceptionally handsome, he cut through social morays without ever realizing the racial and cultural boundaries that inhibited his father. Soon he mingled in social circles that his father could never have dreamt. Excepted as one of the "in crowd" among the famous British celebrities, he became a famous doctor before he even completed medical school. His chosen specialization was cardiac surgery, and was considered one of the best to emerge in the later twentieth century.

He'd married another doctor. An attractive French Moroccan, schooled at Johns Hopkins. Not a surgeon, but researcher specializing in comparative study of plagues. Work that took her to third world, disease plagued countries in African and Asia studying contagions such as smallpox. There as a student, she witnessed the horrific effects of the Ebola virus firsthand. It would be her life's work to discover cures for horrific diseases such as that, right up until the very end of her own life. Rafi's parents fell in love after a chance meeting during a London conference on smallpox; his father had been asked by a colleague to fill a vacancy. A chance meeting that became a permanent union.

Everything began to unravel for Rafi the day his parents died, killed in a tragic automobile accident. A freak accident, their car skidded off the highway during a rainstorm. Hitting a tree, the vehicle burst into flames. Both of his parents were dead, burned to death. Rafi was devastated.

For a time he found solace and comfort from the love of his grandparents. Mutual grief had brought them closer for a time. Rafi needed more than shedding tears though, to ease his pain, he needed answers and would do whatever was necessary to understand why his parents had died. For an unknown reason, he believed his answers were in the schools of the Islamists. The Madrasahs.

He left for Pakistan the day he turned twenty. Two years and a month later he was in detention at the Guantanamo Bay U.S. Military Prison, Camp Delta. Special Forces captured him near Kandahar, Afghanistan, along with a number of other suspected militant combatants. Bryan knew the area well, having spent the early days of Enduring Freedom in the mountains of the Konar, Nangarhar, and Nuristan provinces, areas that bordered Pakistan's North West Frontier. It was there that Abdul-Malik was captured.

The ISI of Pakistan first had their way with Abdul-Malik, and interrogation techniques employed by the ISI were not pleasant, yet interrogators could never break him into a confession, or force him to divulge any information whatsoever. Near death, the U.S. Military intervened and sent him to Cuba along with many other detainees, where perhaps a softer approach would be more effective. That was the story of Abdul-Malik that Bryan had known up until the detainees release. The assignment now – find out what turned the detainee into a martyr. That's what Shannon was hired to do, he reasoned.

* * * * *

JUNE 2, 2008

LONDON, ENGLAND

"Bryan Craig?" The soft female voice accompanied two firm knocks on the door. He opened his eyes. Moving an arm resting on his forehead, he saw Shannon's head peaking around the door, now slightly ajar.

"Come in Shannon," Bryan said, feeling somewhat embarrassed to be caught sleeping on his office couch, Abdul Malik's file resting on his chest, some of it on the floor. Shannon's presence still made him a little uneasy at times, reminding him of another woman he'd met several years ago, and who also excelled in a traditionally male occupation.

"I hope I'm not catching you at a bad time, am I?"

"You mean, while catching some z's while on the job? No not at all," he said motioning her to enter with his fingers.

"Bryan, you really should go home for a change. It won't be the end of the world if you sleep in your own bed," Shannon lectured him in a motherly fashion.

He gave her an irritated look and said, "What do ya have?"

"DJ's conclusions are right here," she said, holding up a folder as she entered the office, closing the door.

Bryan got up from the coach and sat behind the desk. Shannon opened the file laying it down facing him. She was smiling; her hands placed in her lap and posture straight. Every bit a professional, she had excelled in her class at the FBI's Quantico academy. Her demeanor was somewhat guarded, yet she managed a sophisticated sense of style, maybe even a little fun, right down to the fashionable narrow rims she was peering through. Not really a clotheshorse, she nevertheless paid close attention to her appearance. Mostly sophisticated skirt suits or pantsuits, she favored Ellen Tracy, St. John, and Theory. Bryan thought her taste on the expensive side, but her family did have money. Her dyed blond hair framed her face perfectly, cut just below ears accented by pearls. High cheekbones, small nose; he thought her lips were on the thin side, and she was pale. "Too pale for even London," he thought. Her eyes were what most people noticed about Shannon though, green irises and unbelievable naturally long eyelashes. But she was all business, apparently too busy for a boyfriend, let alone marriage.

Physical attributes aside, she was part of Pegasus because her skills put her there. Bryan was meticulous in the selection process and Shannon Parker merited the job. She joined FBI three years before. It had been her goal since 9/11, provided she first met personal benchmarks along the way. Psychology degree, check; master's degree psychology, thesis on socio-pathological behavior and terrorism, check; doctorate in psychology, specializing in terrorist profiling, check. She was multi-lingual, Spanish, French, some Hebrew and Arabic. Written numerous papers and one book, "Terrorist Masterminds – the Future of Jihad." The Bureau ensconced her in the beltway, a lecturer on terrorist profiling and personality analysis. He attended one of her courses, thought she might measure up. He asked her for a meeting, he wanted to learn more.

Midwest background, successful father who kept a darker side hidden from his family, Shannon masked the scars well. But Bryan knew better. On the surface, her father, a second-generation physician, local family practice, church going, and civic minded, a deacon, was one of the pillars of the community. He deceived his family and everyone else, finally self-destructing with prostitutes, booze and gambling. Secrets buried away from his family and friends for twenty years, he ended it with a revolver in his garage. Shannon was devastated and while in medical school, switched her focus to Psychology.

"Catastrophic background, but brilliant and earnest, perfect for the job," he thought. Here she was.

Bryan read the name on the photocopy of a Spanish passport. "Hmmm - Eduardo Arias? So Malik arrived here as a Spaniard," he said matter-of-factly.

"Entered England five months ago. Blended right in as a hip Spaniard," she said.

"I take it that he must have vacationed there while growing up in London," Bryan added.

"Not just vacationed there, but studied for a year. Madrid and Seville. Fluent. Had a Castellaño accent."

Bryan looked through the file. The passport photo certainly resembled a young man from Spain. The country did have its Moorish influences, when Muslim conquerors crossed into Iberia from Northern Africa. It was a good cover for a sleeping Al-Qaeda terrorist. Very well planned. Bryan read Shannon's quickly scribbled notes on the folder. He liked her thoroughness. Attention to detail.

"So he came in through..."

She finished his sentence. "Heathrow. Was enrolled as an engineering student at King's College." Shannon pointed to her notes. "He lived in multiple flats throughout the London area. Nothing high-end – simple places. Renters keep to themselves. And he moved twice in six months."

"So our old friend from Gitmo leaves the States two years ago as Abdul-Malik, and then returns to the UK as Eduardo Arias, an engineering student from Spain. Once here, he does a Jekyll Hyde, and then blows him self up killing fifty-two people."

"Apparently so," Shannon said taking in the furnishings of Bryan's office, surprisingly sterile, without even one photo or piece of artwork.

"Yeah, well it makes perfect sense to be a Spaniard while you're planning mayhem," Bryan said. "I asked for a list of Latin American student visas both here and in the States."

"Sounds rather ambitious, wouldn't you say so?"

"I don't think so, that's why I'm focusing on a narrow field - six months before and after his visa was issued. They said they'd have them by tomorrow. I'll match those against students actually enrolled."

"And what afterwards, run FaceScan?"

"That's my plan."

"Good luck with that one."

"You don't think that's worthwhile?"

"Do you have any idea the number of people you're talking about?"

"I've got the numbers right here," she said thumbing through the paperwork.

"Too many to waste your time, and ours. That's how many. I scrapped that program anyway. Not cost effective. We have an easier way."

"Which would be?"

"First, things first. Question all neighbors, relatives, his old school chums again, etcetera. See what slime surfaces."

"I'll get right on it. Anything else?"

"Yeah, and have Madrid run a search there too - we want the following - how long he was in Spain and any contacts there, things like that. See if he had ties with the terrorists involved in the Madrid bombings. What about bank accounts?"

"Two bank accounts and debit cards – Visa and MasterCard. I'm getting ATM transactions now - should have everything within the next hour." Shannon sat back in the chair. Bryan closed the folder looking at her. He thought she needed to get some sun.

"Do you want me to forward this to Mister Bussmann?" She asked holding up the bank info on Malik.

"Right away. He's the critical part of the easy approach. And give him a call. Tell him we're flying in tomorrow morning," Bryan said. "Say, in time for some work and then lunch." Bryan stood up and motioned Shannon towards the door. He was ready to try and catch up on a little sleep again.

"I'll see you this afternoon. Say around fourteen hundred for the daily briefing," she said. Shannon still had the twenty-four hour clock drilled into her brain from Quantico. She was hardcore in many ways, Bryan thought, never backing down, always in your face. It was a nice fit.

"Sounds good."

"I'll send an agent out to follow up with neighbors, we'll get on that right away, and if you need me, I'll either be in the lab, or at the gym. Call my cell." Shannon made it a point to workout on a Stairmaster for an hour each day, and in lieu of that, a power walk, and on weekends, tennis, her favorite sport.

A good day so far, Bryan thought. He'd forward the update to Washington, and to the British Home Secretary's counter-terrorism office. Pegasus was finally getting some traction and they had their first suspect. Follow the money trail. It was up to Gil Bussmann.

CHAPTER 10

JUNE 3, 2008

MÁLAGA, SPAIN

ACCELERATING THROUGH THE CURVE of the on-ramp, he merged onto the highway giving the brand new Peugeot convertible more gas while changing lanes and passing slower traffic. Two young Spanish girls on a light blue Vespa, their long black hair flowing, smiled and waved as they passed. Bryan looked in the rearview mirror. The driver was scrunched down at the handlebars, her face hiding behind the tiny windshield, tan legs together at the knees. She was still smiling.

Gil lived in Málaga, on Spain's Costa del Sol, coast of the sun, and less than an hour away from Marbella. Both coastal cities were considered to be retreats for the wealthy, and residence to an assortment of expatriates, and successful felons, some still on the lam.

Málaga was a port city in Andalucía, an autonomous region of Spain known for bull fighting, fairs, wine, and its Islamic history. Muslims had ruled this part of the Iberian peninsula for eight centuries, finally being forced out by a Catholic monarch the very year that Columbus discovered the new world. While they did rule however, the Muslims left a mark on the land they called Al-Andalus that was very visible to that day. Many conquerors had left remnants of their civilization in Spain, including the Romans, who left bridges and aqueducts, but it was the Muslims that gave the area not only its name, but influenced the very fabric of its culture more so than any other conqueror. Bryan commented on the appearance of the people. "One needs not search far to see the Moorish influence; just have a look around at the people."

"I can see why Malik chose to be a Spaniard – he blended in perfectly," Shannon said, recalling the man's appearance.

Muslim dynasties began with the first conquest of the peninsula and the establishment of the Iberian Emirate in 750 AD, the rule of the Emir of Córdoba. Not quite two hundred years later, in 912, Rahman III, a Shi'ah of the Ummayad dynasty ascended to rule Al-Andalus at the age of twenty-two. In 929 he proclaimed himself the first Caliph of Córdoba, setting a precedent of a Caliphate in Spain lasting until 1031. The period saw the construction of the first magnificent castles and mosques, the most famous being la Mezguita de Córdoba a Moorish mosque built during the Caliphate.

"You've been here before, right?" Bryan asked, as he tried to get his bearings.

"Sure have, in school. I know the area very well, *mi canta España*," she said. "It has such a deep and varied cultural history."

As they rounded a turn near downtown, Shannon pointed out a few famous historical monuments, cultural influences present in Malaga, monuments to art and conquest. "Right over there you have Islamic culture stacked on top of Roman, and Spanish on top of that," she said as they passed the Moorish fortification and a Roman amphitheatre.

"Pretty amazing," Bryan said as he tried to get a glimpse of one of the seven remaining Muslim citadels left in Spain.

"The Islamists know that these are here too. They believe they own them and may well have their sights set on Iberia again," Shannon said.

"So you think that the cells that surfaced here in Spain have that in mind as their goal?" Bryan asked.

"It's possible," she said.

"But it's also why it's a good move on our part to have Gil close by, considering the terrorists seem to be moving through here routinely," Bryan added.

"I've never met Gil before. How exactly did he end up on the Pegasus team?"

"Yeah of course, you've had only the pleasure to see his face on a video conference call. Well my dear Shannon, Gil's probably the most important piece to our little team. By that, I mean when it comes to the financial matters – as in tracing the bad guys and their cash flow." Bryan turned the radio down and continued; "I've known Gil since prep school."

"Born in the States, right?"

"True blue. His father was a brilliant banker. He has two older sisters. One's a doctor, the other writes children's books. A family of over achievers - especially Gil, who had academic scholarships thrown at him from many universities - ended up at Harvard though, majored in Math and Statistics."

"You mean 'Sadistics.' That's what we called it at IU."

"Yeah, well he was a bit of a nerd then."

"I thought you said he's some sort of stud muffin."

"I don't believe you'd ever catch me referring to another guy using those words. I think I said he'd a reputation for chasing women."

"Sorry," She said laughing.

"Money has a way of changing people Shannon. Especially someone like Gil, so he turned himself into what you said."

"So Gil's money turned him into something hot, huh?"

"Can't respond to that. How about not as much of a nerd." Bryan said with a chuckle. "He was a skinny, six foot two non-athlete - thick glasses. But a chip off the old block - also brilliant - Stanford Business School by twenty."

"That's impressive."

"Very, and while still a grad student he was already making big bucks in the financial markets. Actually had a weekly financial newsletter - charged three thousand dollars per subscription. He was already rich from family money and now richer still. Turned fifty thousand from his grandmother into over three million."

"And that's when he got into trouble?"

"Not quite. Every Wall Street firm wanted him. It was the early nineties and the stock markets took off like a rocket ship. The era saw huge new fortunes."

"I wasn't one of those."

"Likewise."

"Well, it didn't last long, many evaporated by 2000," Shannon said.

"How very true. But at the time it seemed everybody was playing stocks. Gil would say he sometimes knew to short a stock, when his bartender bragged about owning it."

"You mentioned before that he made his money using the net. How?" Shannon asked.

"Right, the key was the net, and he's a master. He gleaned information on company summaries, and financials from the net. He also used the net to place orders as well."

"When I was little girl, I can remember my grandfather taking me on occasion to his stockbroker's office in Bloomington. He'd sit for hours watching stock tickers in a room with other clients of the broker," Shannon said.

"How nice," he said with touch of sarcasm.

"I remember once, his broker placed an order for him. He wrote it down on a piece of paper and put it in a pneumatic tube. Like the drive-in at a bank," Shannon said.

"Well by the nineties most investors just went online. It was slow, you know, they used dial-up. No trips to the broker's office though. A trader like Gil had a T-1 for his Internet connection. Twenty-fives times faster than dial-up. Gil took advantage of inherent execution inefficiencies."

"Meaning?" She asked.

"Volume bottlenecks of the early days of trading on the net. Similar to a log jam."

"He did this with his own company?"

"Not initially. Top firms such as Morgan Stanley, JP Morgan, Goldman Sachs and such, all wanted him. Gil had other ideas - opting for a low-key atmosphere - a smaller, second tier trading firm. There he would have autonomy, and avoid scrutiny..."

Shannon jumped in and said, "The scrutiny from people like the feds, wondering about suspicious trading maybe. No doubt top firms had compliance departments that looked at everything. What sort of boiler room did he join?" She was beginning to wonder about the ethics of her Pegasus team member and Bryan's good friend.

"Shannon, it wasn't a boiler room per se. I mean they had real clients with legitimate services. Most accounts were large institutions - pension funds - money managers and the like."

"He was busted ripping off retirement funds?"

"I wouldn't say he was ripping them off. His clients did make large sums after all - we'll just say, he bent the rules."

"Bryan, I'm sure you heard the expression that 'you can't get just a little bit pregnant'," Shannon pointed out.

Bryan explained how it worked. Gil would fill orders for his clients, who would spread around 'big block' orders consisting of thousands of shares at a time to trading houses just like his. His job was to execute the trades at the best prices possible. Most of the techies followed Microsoft's lead and gravitated to the NASDAQ for their public listings, which was where the first real big Internet action was initiated.

"I'm familiar with that Bryan, they use a four letter symbol as opposed to the NYSE which use one, two, or three. And at the New York Stock Exchange they place their orders with an actual person standing at a post. I think they call them specialists," Shannon said.

"How about that - your interests know no boundaries," he said smiling.

"Funny, I've watched CNBC," she replied with a little laugh.

"Anyway, all trades were made using the old auction format, but on NASDAQ the auction's one hundred percent electronic. Gil calculated correctly that bottlenecks would occur. It completely opened a Pandora's box. An inherent arbitrage by being ahead of the fund's trades - it was very cunning."

"I'm afraid you lost me a little on the arbitrage part. There was a disparage in price?" Shannon asked trying to follow the complicated nature of Gil's stock trading.

"Gil made the arbitrage for himself, but because he had the price of the trades in advance. Obviously an advantage that no one else had – and that, as they say is the rub."

"Now he was breaking the law. It's like insider information."

"Make that market manipulation sprinkled with fraud. Not a good mix to say the least. And he was co-mingling the clients accounts with bogus nominee accounts, making sure the winning trades went to him," Bryan said.

"He just did it right there in the open?"

"I said he's cunning - he waited until the end of the day and switched accounts in the confusion of the trading reconciliation, when they matched the buys and sells with client orders."

"Why did it take so long to catch him?" Shannon asked, miffed at the possibility of such fraud.

"Well, they finally got their man, as they say. In only six years they netted more than two hundred million dollars. But he couldn't stop. The trading only became bigger as financial markets moved into the new millennium."

"Obviously regulators had their trades on the radar screen by then," she said.

"Well, it was the stock they targeted; a mortally wounded company already hawked by regulators. Three large short trades brought the house of Gil down. His eight-year run was over."

"Who bailed him out of that mess?"

"Before he was bailed out he had to be indicted, and it took months for the feds to build the case. Well after 9/11 before they had an indictment prepared. At the time I was still on assignment with the Navy and hadn't jumped to a desk yet. I can tell you this - Gil's father's connected – very connected. I think the White House actually had a hand in the deal."

"That was it? No jail time, no fines? The President or someone intervened and your friend just walked," Shannon asked, perturbed at the light sentence.

"No, he paid a fine - twenty million dollars, but not a single day behind bars," Bryan said, looking at Shannon, raising one eyebrow.

"Twenty million dollars – that's it? I thought you said they made a couple hundred million?" She asked still dumbfounded at the favorable treatment Gil received.

"He did, and he kept a good portion, more than seventy million. The catch is that he'd be working for Uncle Sam in its war on terrorism for as long as they said so. They in turn, have loaned him to me. Of course at my request."

"Of course, and you think that special favoritism is worth it I suppose?" Shannon asked, crossing her arms, somewhat irritated.

"I'd say so Shannon. Terrorism requires vast sums of capital to fuel its engines. Money for recruiting, training, housing, and weapons, just like any real army. But they're not a real army, and they finance everything illegally. Pegasus, meaning me and you, needed the expertise of someone that knows how to hide illegal financial activity."

"Seems like putting the fox in the hen house," Shannon said as she looked out the window, shaking her head.

"It was the feds that came up with the idea. They set a precedent for assigning folks with particular skills in deceit to head up securities regulators years ago. You should remember that, you minored in history too, if I'm not mistaken," Bryan said.

"Close, European History to be exact, but I'm familiar with the fact that Joseph P. Kennedy was the first head of the SEC."

"As I said, who better to have enforcing rules than the best of the rule breakers? The practice worked then, why not now? He first got his feet wet by helping the DNI when he was at SOUTHCOM."

"When Admiral Barnes busted Venezuela and Haiti," she said.

"That's right. Now Gil Bussman is our man." Bryan was satisfied that he'd made a succinct point, the winning point.

"Well then, why not make Gil the next Chairman of the SEC?" Shannon countered, smiling.

"Touché."

"How did he end up here in Spain? Seems he should be under house arrest." Or at least wearing an ankle bracelet, she thought.

"Gil chose Málaga because he loves Spain, speaks Spanish and we were on board with his choice. Spain has an extradition treaty with the United States; besides, he's right at home with the characters near by - the best crooks and money launderers in the world," Bryan said.

"Marbella."

"Exactly."

"And an official employee of the Embassy, I suppose," she said.

"With diplomatic immunity, and protection of our in-country FBI folks – with a little help from the company," Bryan added.

Bryan and Shannon pulled up to a new ten story beach condominium. His friend had done well. The units there were priced from one million to fifteen million dollars for the penthouse, Gil's penthouse.

"This is where he lives?" Shannon asked, checking her make-up in the visor mirror. She was irritated at the apparent lack of justice, and couldn't believe one person could be so valuable that a blind eye would be turned to his past crimes. He should be in jail, she believed. She'd need to see some real evidence first hand to prove that Gil was so valuable. Bryan knew her irritation would probably fester more once they entered Gil's home.

The elevator doors opened directly into the private vestibule of the penthouse. Greeted by Gil's long-term housekeeper Inés, a short Spanish woman in her fifties, Bryan kissed her politely on both cheeks as was custom and introduced Shannon.

"¡Buenos días Inés. ¿Cómo estas?" Bryan said.

"Oh, estoy bien, gracias Señor Bryan. ¿Cómo está usted?" Inés responded.

"¡Muy bien!"

"Quiero presentarles Shannon Parker."

"Encantada. Usted parece una modela. Usted es tan hermosa." Inés told Shannon, informing her that she was beautiful enough to be a model.

"Buenas días Inés y gracias, pero no soy una modela," Shannon said, explaining she wasn't a model.

"Don't feed her ego Inés," Bryan said laughing.

"Oh no, no Mister Bryan. Por favor, come with me to Mister Gil." She used "spanglish," now commonplace on the Costa del Sol due to the large number of English speaking residents, mostly British expatriates.

They followed her through the foyer into a ten thousand square foot bachelor pad. Bryan looked around to see if there was some new statue or piece of artwork since his last visit. A grand piano, that's new, he thought. He saw a set of bongo drums, also new, an empty wine bottle on top. Inés tidied up by grabbing the bottle as they passed. With twelve-foot ceilings, panoramic views from the maximum window area possible, and the only private swimming pool, the condo encompassed the building's entire top floor and was the jewel of the Costa del Sol. Tastefully decorated in minimalist style, the furniture resembled displays in a design magazine rather than something to settle comfortably onto for a Sunday afternoon of leisure.

"Well I'll have to give him credit for having fabulous taste," Shannon whispered to Bryan, bewildered at the interior design.

Keeping a few steps behind Inés, they approached the entrance to the pool area. Two young models wearing micro bikinis were lying next to each other on teak chaise lounges. Both were talking on cell phones as they tanned under the hot Spanish sun.

"Just some of his playthings I take it?" Shannon asked sarcastically.

"They're new to me," Bryan said, curious about the women.

As they stepped outside onto the marble deck Gil came into sight. He was kneeling down at the edge of the infinity pool, casually chatting with another young model, whose topless body was silhouetted in the dark blue water as she held the side, slowly frog-kicking. Gil looked up and waved, a wide grin forming on his face. He stood up from his crouch, as the girl pushed off the side and made a few strokes toward the infinity's edge. The motion of her body caused waves to cascade over the side, creating an illusion that the pool was a waterfall pouring into the cerulean blue sky.

Gil skipped a step and jogged over to Bryan and Shannon. Wearing just baggy swimming trunks and sandals, it was obvious that he'd been sticking to his daily workout regimen of weight training and kickboxing. He had the lean cut of a male model fifteen years younger. A far cry from the geek Bryan first met in their youth. Gil had also lost the glasses, having undergone Lasik surgery years ago.

"Hey Brother." They shook with an arm wrestling grip, pulling each other close to bump shoulders and pat the other's back.

"And this must be the indomitable Doctor Shannon Parker," Gil remarked, smile now even wider.

"Nice to meet you Mister Bussmann," Shannon said, extending her hand for a formal shake. His smile was bright white against his dark tan. Too white, she thought.

"The pleasure's all mine," Gil replied, kissing her hand instead. Bryan winced at the sight, certain a friendship was not in the making.

"You're looking a bit worked there Bryan. Need a Red Bull? Or something harder?" Gil asked, perpetual smile intact.

"Red Bull's fine."

"And for you my dear Shannon?"

"The quarto de baño first, and I'll have some sparkling water, please."

"Coming right up and Inés will take you to the servicio. Inés llévela al servicio para la piscina."

Shannon turned and followed Inés as Gil reached into a refrigerator under the poolside bar, grabbed a Red Bull, a Perrier, and a bottle of Fiji water for himself.

"Bryan. My man. So this is our new profiler," Gil commented.

"That would be her."

"How about that Doctor Parker there? Great legs, huh. Where do you recruit – spinning classes?" Gil teased as he watched Shannon walk across the deck to the dressing room.

"Easy there pal, she's damn good - and very smart," Bryan said, as he also looked at her legs. The Stairmaster was paying off.

"She's not really my type, way too vanilla. Ya doin her?"

"You're pure comedy - and no," Bryan said, as he sat down on a cushioned high chair at the bar, glancing over his shoulder at Gil's poolside guests.

"Now those two are my types bro. Couple of wild and hot Russians - sticking around for the summer to keep me entertained, and both available I might add." He handed Bryan the Red Bull, still grinning. Bryan could see that Gil hadn't lost his reckless, wild nature. Some habits were too hard to break.

"You my friend, never cease to amaze. But we've got work to do," Bryan said, wanting to get to the business of Pegasus.

"Roger that. But you need to live a little. Ask anytime, and you shall receive." Gil raised his water bottle, tilting the cap toward the girls who both waived. Their phones still glued to their ears. Bryan made a mental note to check into the girls further.

Opening double doors using a biometric scanner and keypad, the three entered an office off the master bedroom with its own large balcony and a view that faced west along Spain's famous coastline. Gil closed the doors and pushed a button on the wall. Roman blinds lowered from the ceiling, covering the thick hurricane-glass windows. As the ambient light of the tropical sun grew dimmer, it was replaced by an artificial one of plasma.

Gil sat down at his Knoll designer desk. As much known for its artistic design as it is for functionality, the expansive "L" shaped mahogany surface area supported four, twenty-inch flat-panel monitors that lined up side-by-side directly in front of him, and an additional two screens and second keyboard to his right. Bryan recognized the latter as a Bloomberg, the system used by financial institutions all over the world. Jokingly, it was rumored to be able to even count the pocket change of CEOs.

"Doctor Parker, I'm sure that my buddy here has told you the sordid details of my sordid past," Gil began.

"Google offers quite a bit of information as well," Shannon said. "This is a nice witness protection program you've got," she added sarcastically.

"That's great, you've got a real sense of humor. Ready to tango?" Gil said with a mischievous grin.

"Go right ahead," she said.

"Now you're about to find out why I'm here and not in jail." Gil said as he moved the wireless mouse side to side and tapped the space bar on the keypad. The plasma screens came alive. His fingers then went into blurring overdrive, the click of each key being depressed blending into the next, becoming one constant whirl. Shannon, her mouth gaped open, watched in awe.

"Impressed, huh?" Gil said, seeing Shannon's reaction. "I play the piano too."

Shannon looked at Bryan, her mouth still open, understanding what he meant about being "blazing fast" on the keypad.

Within a matter of seconds he had all four screens displaying a series of financial transactions. He stopped the clatter of the keys for a moment and combed his dark hair back with the fingers of both his hands. Resuming his task, he moved the cursor to highlight an area on the far left screen and began a synopsis of his financial forensics.

"I used SWIFT to isolate over six thousand separate international wires of interest – wires that I'm interested in – ones I think are suspicious – and that's out of hundreds of thousands during the seven banking days prior to the Memorial Massacre," he said looking at Shannon, who was now leaning on the desk with both hands so as not to look over his shoulder.

Gil continued, "SWIFT – do you know what that stands for?

"The Society for Worldwide Interbank Telecommunications," Shannon answered.

"That's right. Headquartered in Brussels, the consortium-owned, banking co-op provides secure messaging services, including wires, for over eight thousand financial institutions worldwide. It's been the primary tool for tracking down sources of terrorist financing," Gil said.

Bryan contributed to the explanation, "The Society's been cooperating with the Treasury Department, FBI, and the CIA since 9/11. In the past, the agencies could 'swiftly' track transactions from suspicious accounts at a broker-dealer in, perhaps Berlin – let's say, to disbursement of the proceeds at an ATM in Bali. SWIFT's existence was leaked to the press and its effectiveness compromised, leading to the creation of Gil's program out of the Pegasus budget."

"These are possible terrorist related transactions here?" Shannon asked.

"Yep and nope. What you're looking at are relevant transactions based upon parameters that I input. If I only relied on SWIFT, we'd be hosed." He swiveled his chair around to face Shannon, who was leaning against the desk, arms folded, her back to the Bloomberg. Her skirt now mid thigh, revealed the true definition of her legs, a momentary distraction for Gil, now having second thoughts about whether Shannon was his type or not.

Gil re-caged his brain, getting back to his lesson. "I trim the SWIFT data down to four hundred or so with Pegasus. It's over a half a billion dollars from fifty-five accounts in the States and UK - then after bouncing around the planet a few times landed on just a few that I want to know more about." He opened his bottle of Fiji and took three large swallows.

Gil looked back at Shannon and began to explain the complicated elements of pinning down a terrorist finance scheme.

"Bryan's heard this all before Shannon, but ya see, tracking terrorist's financing is kind of an art now, and involves a thorough knowledge of financial markets and banking nuances. And I'm the master," he said with a laugh. "Especially since terrorists are being tipped off by the well intentioned, but naive media. They really don't realize it's at the expense of national security," Gil said with his head slightly cocked toward Shannon. He then delved into his area of expertise. "Major league bucks freely flow between accounts worldwide virtually anytime fed wires from the States are permitted. The feds can hardly prohibit Morgan Stanley from accepting funds from a bank based in Athens or the Isle of Lucy - simultaneously, US regulators have little or no idea regarding the ownership of the assets held in correspondent accounts at those same institutions," Gil said, also testing Shannon's wit and sense of humor.

"Isle of Lucy? Cute," Shannon said with a slight grin. "Who's covering the accounts then? Is it up to the institutions and secondary jurisdictions?" She asked, shifting her weight against the desk.

"Oh you can sit up there if you want. I'm sure it'll hold a buck twenty," Gil said, moving the wireless keypad out of the way.

"Thanks." She scooted up on the desk, crossing her legs, hands on one knee. Gil was sure he'd been wrong in his judgment now.

"Is it up to the institutions? That's a good question, but not exactly, anti-money laundering efforts have focused on persuading, or should I say - pressuring low-regulation jurisdictions to improve their scrutiny of slacker institutions. But with only a moderate success rate, if any at all."

"I can understand why, I mean, what's in it for them, right?" She was familiar with money laundering, but curious about the international varieties of schemes.

"Well, the incentive for some places would be on the side of fewer restrictions. There's always the greed factor though, and a few will be tempted by riches," Gil said.

"Shannon, the 'money talks and bullshit walks' concept," Bryan offered. "The bad guys pay bribes to avoid governmental oversight. Very typical in developing countries or corrupt governments," Bryan said, thinking the two generally went hand in hand.

"Exacta-mundo brother. And to date any sanctions imposed by rich-countries, or the U.N. haven't been large enough to really stop it, or make the rewards unappealing." Gil took another swallow of his water.

"The areas I tend to scrutinize the most Shannon are 'low regulation shell banks.' The ones established at low costs in easy jurisdictions, like the Channel Islands, Caymans – places that typically have opaque ownership structures."

"You mean where shareholders are designated either as a private corporation or organized through a trustee?" Shannon asked.

"You did your homework - good job. And you're correct again, a shell bank transacts business in high-regulation, on-shore jurisdictions - they use correspondent accounts maintained with very recognized foreign banks. The correspondent bank – in Dubai or Karachi, let's say – knows only that the account holder, or customer, is another bank. There is no way in hell that they can ever know the ultimate beneficiary of the funds in the accounts. That's unless someone else tells them."

"What you're saying is that not just any moron can coordinate these sophisticated networks," Shannon said setting her Perrier bottle on the desk.

"Well, unless you consider lawyers and bankers morons. They both play critical roles in structuring offshore accounts and shell corporations. I might also add that the bankers are critical in organizing the procedures that keeps the money movement outside the reach of government regulators," Gil said.

Bryan and Shannon looked at each other and smiled. "Find the banker," Bryan said to Shannon. "These types of schemes are brilliant for tax avoidance."

"And also great blueprints for desperados wanting to move money around the world for more dangerous purposes, the ones we're after," Gil chimed in. "And don't forget non-financial services."

"What would that be? Gaming?" Shannon guessed correctly.

Gil responded by counting with his fingers, starting with the thumb, "Precisely. One - casinos and bookmakers generate huge amounts of cash that are used to disguise illicit funds transferred all over the place. Two - real estate deals can be used to transfer ownership of assets across borders. And three - shipments and sales of precious metals, or if you want, smuggling large amounts of cash - all are frequently used to evade the scrutiny from formal inter-bank transfers."

"So how do you catch them? Look for foreign real estate developments and deals?" Shannon asked.

"Pretty good guess, but be patient girl. That's why Uncle Sam did a very smart thing by not sending me to the pokey," he said smiling at her. She returned the smile, warming to him.

Gil went on, "I look at terrorist financing just like I would any old money-laundering scheme, only in reverse. Instead of funneling the money down from a bunch of tiny payments starting somewhere to a few bad guys in another place..."

"Drugs for example," Bryan interjected.

"Exactly – the drug model works just like that. But I look for fewer sources, located in under-regulated areas, and connected to a larger number of recipients. If you try that approach with the standard drug-financing scheme – you know, tracing the flow of funds backward from the receiver to the originator of the deposit, well you go nowhere. It does the drug enforcement absolutely no good at all."

"Right, you'd just end up with some street dealer selling crack at a schoolyard," Shannon said, understanding the drug model completely now.

Bryan jumped in as the picture became clearer. "But with terrorist assets, you work in reverse from Malik. When a terrorist or cell of terrorists is identified, then you can trace the transactions back up the chain to the mastermind."

"That's very accurate. Usually it results in finding assets of the financier. Those are the tactics I use, and that's why SWIFT was so important. We definitely need the cooperation of foreign institutions. But now if you really want to screw regulators up, you throw in the Hawala system."

"Yeah, the Asian system that doesn't require promissory notes and bypasses government regulators." Bryan remembered that Hawala was widely used in Pakistan and in the Middle East.

"So how were these accounts set up, and how did you track it?" Shannon asked, now believing that Gil was worth saving after all.

"That's the clever part. Whoever set up the accounts that I'm looking at now did a great job, but they had some help from leaks in the media too. All they had to do was read a newspaper to know what not to do. We'd been looking one way, so they went the other. Everything was legal, by the book. And they used offshore trusts out of the Channel Islands, Bahamas, Caymans, Panama, and a few other favorite safe banking havens of mine."

"Like for your nominee accounts," Bryan said referring to Gil's old days.

"Similar sure, only a little more clever though."

"No way. I thought you were the best." Bryan let out another dig about his buddy's colorful past.

"Hardly on this scale, not even the crooks at Enron ever thought of this. What makes it so clever is they used offshore insurance policies as a conduit to funnel the money into U.S. brokerage accounts, and completely undetected. It doesn't raise any red flags from the IRS or Homeland Security screeners. They also used the real estate scenario that you jumped on right away Shannon."

"Not sure I follow you." Gil had stepped into an area of money laundering that Shannon was unfamiliar with.

"These offshore policies can be titled under trusts of legitimate policy holders, naming employees of foreign real estate development companies as the insured and the trusts as the beneficiaries. They also can use the largest insurers and re-insurers in the world. All very kosher." Gil moved the cursor to the far screen on his right.

"I don't know the account holders yet, what I do know is this…" He moved the cursor to bring up a bright blue, digital outline of the Northern Hemisphere over the black background of the screen. The images were animated with bright yellow lines as he narrated.

"Here's a series of large short-term treasuries purchased exactly two weeks ago. I'm confident that they were paid for by money borrowed from the policies. Don't forget IRS fact number one - money borrowed from an insurance policy is not taxed, and therefore not really scrutinized unless a regulator or agent has a particular reason to do so. The money makes it onshore tax free, and minus any suspicion." Bryan and Shannon both raised their eyebrows, fascinated.

Gil went on. "That's pretty smart stuff alright. Money can end up in these accounts and not picked up by U.S. Patriot Act parameters. From there it can, in theory, be dispersed to a bunch of sociopaths waiting to put it to use for the things they do. It's a premier money laundry operation that actually generates cash profits too."

"I can't wait to hear this one," Bryan stated.

"Remember those offshore insurance policies? Well those policies are invested in a combination of U.S. treasuries and hedge funds that use leverage, plus they guarantee the principal. They can double up on their bets and the policies can never lose a dime. The funds remain intact, while at the same time they are financing global terrorism."

"And you think you know the owner?" Shannon asked, uncrossing her legs, and folding her arms across her chest.

"Well I've used my program to pinpoint where the outbound wires ended up, and the source of the premium payments for the insurance policies. I don't know the account number or name, but I know the bank." Gil picked up the Bloomberg keypad. "Just scoot over a little Shannon."

As the screen brightened, Bryan's eyes focused on three words. Shannon read the words out loud "Bank of Dubai."

"And you're positive on this fact?" Bryan asked, knowing that he was soon going to be taking a trip to the Emirates.

"Five by nines my brother. The recipient of the wires from these U.S. brokerage accounts and source of the offshore premium payments are one in the same. Right here from the Bank of Dubai. Figure the odds, huh Bryan." The sarcasm couldn't have been more blatant. "That's where the suspicious wires from the U.S. landed. I figure we crack that nut, and we'll be able to put these particular terrorists out of business for quite awhile. The bad news is that I'm still working on figuring out who owns the accounts. Dubai's banking laws won't let me run through customer accounts. But I wouldn't be surprised to find out that someone on the coast a little west of us isn't involved also. I've got my Spanish banking contacts looking into it."

"You mean Marbella," Bryan said, agreeing that many Muslims had vacation homes and yachts there, and quite possibly one of the resident money-laundering specialists might have gotten their hands dirty.

"Exactly, I've found a couple of wires that bounced off Spanish banks."

"What's the good news then?" Bryan asked, putting a hand on his friend's shoulder.

"Here's the good news. No, actually make it great news. Thanks to Doctor Parker's call earlier yesterday, I've got more for ya. A whole lot more."

"Meaning?"

"Meaning that I traced the suicide bomber's bank account straight to a wire from an account at the Bank of Dubai - probably not the same account that's linked to the premium payments, but definitely linked to your suicide bomber. There're numerous inbound wires from an account at the Bank of Dubai. Just look right here." Gil highlighted the transactions on the Bloomberg. "I've got over ten in the two months prior to the bombings. A total of one hundred and twelve thousand dollars for Mister Eduardo Arias."

"Who sent the wires?" Bryan asked Gil.

"He had two places that wires came in from. One was this account here." Gil highlighted an entry on his screen.

Shannon read the entry "Banco de Santa Maria."

"And the owner of the Madrid account would be?" Bryan asked open-ended.

"It would be Eduardo Arias, or Abdul-Malik – it's confusing, these terrorists and their multiple aliases. But the name is Eduardo Arias on the account card in Spain. Here's his address in Madrid."

"Right, we've got that address. The Madrid office is checking that out as we speak. Who owns the other account?"

"This guy here. Some Russian. One Leonid Petrov."

Bryan let out an affected laugh at the sound of the name he just heard. "That's absolutely bizarre," he said dismayed.

"You know this guy or something?" Gil asked, draining the last drop from of his Fiji bottle.

"We just came a complete full circle. Yeah, I know this guy."

"Why's it bizarre?" Shannon asked.

"Hmmm - how can I put this? Real piece of shit, this guy – Petrov's committed war crimes as far back as the Soviet Afghan campaign, that's twenty years ago, as well as atrocities in Chechnya. In fact, probably had a hand in murdering scores of civilians - all Muslims. He's hated them ever since the Mujahideen got the best of the Soviets. Has been bent on revenge whenever he could exact it. Why, as far as he's concerned, the only good Muslim's a dead one."

Gil and Shannon watched Bryan as he walked toward the draped window, pulling it to the side several inches. He glimpsed the rich blue of the midday Mediterranean Sea, the bright sunlight outlining his face. He was thinking about the Russian, finishing his thoughts out loud, "Petrov financing fanatical Islamic terrorists would be the equivalent of Nazis wiring funds to Jews. That's why it's bizarre."

CHAPTER 11

JUNE 4, 2008

DUBAI

THE BUSINESSMAN SAT QUIETLY in the lobby of the temporary reception area, his hands folded on a leather briefcase as he waited patiently to be escorted to his client. Occasionally he looked up at the beautiful young receptionist when she answered incoming calls. Obviously Middle Eastern, she was dressed in couture Western fashion, only partially modest, a simple scarf covering her hair, and spoke with a perfectly clipped British accent. Callers wouldn't have a clue to her ethnicity without a visual.

When not admiring the building's staff, he passed the time by watching the video brochure on the monitor built into the wall opposite him. It had been over an hour and he was on the fourth viewing of the fifteen-minute production. He'd literally begun to mouth the script along with the narrator.

"... A vision this bold requires visionaries. Creating the centerpiece for a new world capital attracted the world's most esteemed designers, developers and builders." A female production-talent narrated the commercial. The subject was the world's reining champion of tallest buildings, the Burj al Baaz. At a height of nine hundred and forty meters, more than three thousand eighty-four feet, it soared two hundred stories. The businessman feared that his destination on this day would be somewhere near that top floor. Nearing completion but slightly behind schedule, the skyscraper had just a few floors opened for a limited number of offices and was going though some final touches, including the lobby area where he now sat.

The Euro-Chic voice continued as the video ran through an historical timeline of the ambitious project "...it is not by chance that it is being built in Dubai. In less than thirty years, this city has transformed itself from a regional center to the world's centerpiece, and the world's tallest building will be its global monument." He looked up through the transparent onion shaped dome high above him and could see the concrete and steel sides of the building, covered in glass, shooting endlessly skyward. Never a fan of heights, it made him dizzy.

"*Al Salaam* Mister Petrov. How nice to see you again, my friend."

The sound of his name quickly grounded him back to terra firma. He looked in the direction of the familiar voice to see the slightly built man of medium height. He was immaculately adorned in bright white cotton Thaub, buttoned from his neck to his shoes. He also wore a white schumagg, a scarf-like head cover with a black band to keep it in place. Draping down below narrow shoulders, it framed a thin face punctuated by piercing dark eyes and perfectly shaped, tightly groomed black mustache and goatee.

"*Zzdrast-vet-yah* Wazir," Petrov said, returning the greeting in his native language. Standing up, he added "is there rreason I vaitink ere dis long?" Petrov was obviously irritated.

"I'm very sorry Mister Petrov. The delay was unintentional. Please come with me," Wazir said, knowing this would be the last day he would ever have to deal with the Russian again. He was happy about that.

They shook hands and made their way to the elevators just beyond a collection of contract engineers. The engineers looked and sounded like Americans. Several were huddled over a makeshift table covered with blueprints while a few others were looking up at one of the domes. They appeared to be in disagreement about something. Not a good sign Petrov thought.

"You may go right in sir," a receptionist said.

He could barely hear what the young girl was saying, his ears still acclimating from the rapid ascent to the hundred and tenth floor that took less than thirty seconds, the fastest elevator in the world. From her desk she motioned to large metal double doors. They were gold or gold plate, and ornately inlaid. The pattern resembled the Chechnya Muslim Shield, but the Arabic scripted center had been replaced with a brilliant white mountain two meters in diameter at the base. It appeared to be made of hundreds of perfectly rounded pearls to create the effect of snow, and mother of pearl for the rock. The design split in the middle as the doors opened inward to the office.

"*Al Salaam a' alaykum* welcome to Dubai Mister Petrov. Please be seated." The tall, elegant man patted a red silk covered sofa adjacent to his own as he sat down himself.

"I hope that you are finding your stay here in the Emirates pleasant." The man reached forward to pick up a cup of coffee while speaking, the long sleeves of his white robe touching his knees as he put the cup to his lips.

"*Da*, charmink place." Petrov was lying. From the culturally rich city of St. Petersburg he looked down upon Dubai as an artificial abomination. Epcot Center in Disney World was more authentic, he mused. He extended his hand in greeting. It was ignored.

"I assume your mission has been fruitful for my cause?" Amir Kahn asked speaking softly, but bothering not to look in Petrov's direction.

"Jeas, in fact exactly what you vant." Petrov held up his briefcase.

"Let's have a look." Amir Kahn brushed the white cloth of the schumagg away from his face and dark sunglasses to see his prize. Petrov put the case down by his thigh and opened it, removing a small hand-sized metal box. He placed it on the sofa next to his host.

"Very good work Leonid Petrov. Our business is concluded. Wazir will handle things from here. *Ma'assalama* – go in peace."

"*Dosvi`daniya*," Petrov smiled. He was now going to be a very rich man. Satisfied, he stood up and waited to be shown out by Wazir.

"Mister Petrov, there is something we would like you to see while you are here in the building, if of course you have the time," Wazir said as they waited for the elevator.

"Of course, why not, eh? I think after today, I make time here and there," he said. He should show some gratitude to these people, he decided. They were making him wealthy, yet he still despised them.

"Very good. We're going up to the observation deck," Wazir said as he text-messaged on his cell phone.

"Observation deck? What 'ell es way up derr dhat's important to see?" Visibly irritated, Petrov asked angrily. He detested heights.

"You'll see, Mister Petrov. God be willing, you'll see."

Shoved hard by Wazir as the doors opened at the two hundredth floor, Petrov stumbled forward, falling to his hands and knees, dropping his briefcase. He looked up, stunned, as a man dressed in blue laborer clothing, face covered with a red checkered schumagg, swung a one-meter pipe, connecting flush with Petrov's nose. Blood poured from the gash as he fell backwards, unconscious.

Voices were faint and unintelligible. He didn't speak Pashto. He was now lying on the side of his face when he opened his left eye; the right was already swollen shut. He felt a searing pain up his spine as the man with the pipe swung again, this time striking him on his tailbone.

"Aahhh," Petrov groaned as a third blow landed on a kidney.

"Shut up my friend." Wazir nodded to another man in blue, who grabbed the Russian by his hair and lifted him up to a sitting position. Petrov tried to focus on his attackers; he could barely make out any of the four, including Wazir. Blood was streaming out his nose and splattered across his white dress shirt.

"What you fuckin doink?" Petrov gasped.

"What am I doing, my friend? You pathetic son of a goat, do you see this man here? Do you know who this man is?"

Petrov strained to see through his one open eye, but was unable to make out the man's face, which was now uncovered. He shook his head.

"No? I will introduce you then." Wazir motioned with his hand as he spoke. The man took a half a step forward before kicking Petrov in his sternum. He fell back against unfinished dry wall with a thud.

Barely conscious and now expecting certain death, Petrov managed to ask a question "Vhich stinkink...Muslim dok...dhat I forgot to kill...are you?" He defiantly labored, spitting blood. The man started to kick him again, but was stopped by Wazir.

"This man is Chechen, my friend. He was four years old when he watched as you killed his grandfather, his father, and his brother. Then you and your infidel soldiers raped and killed his mother and his sister. That's who this man is Mister Petrov," Wazir said, and then spat on him.

"Pleast to meet you. *Yob tvoyu mat'*," Petrov replied in partial Russian with a laugh, followed by a cough of blood. His body was becoming numb.

"This man, Mister Petrov, is from Nuristan. His name is Ahmed. He was also four years old when he saw you force the people of his village to all lay down on the ground. Then you drove over them with your tanks," Wazir said with his hand on the shoulder of the man with the pipe.

"Pleast to meet you too. *Ya sru na tvayu mat'*," Petrov saying he defecated on the Nuritani's mother.

The Nuristani leaned over very close to Petrov's face, pulling away the schumagg, allowing the Russian to see his face. Petrov, seeing the man's eyes, became fearful. The Nuristani spoke, "I speak Russian - you dog. *Yob tvoyo mat'*," he said telling Petrov to go fuck his own mother. The Nuristani then swung the pipe, striking the Russian across the face, sending broken teeth, blood and part of his tongue onto the unfinished cement floor. Maybe it would be over quickly from this point on, Petrov hoped.

"You're a liability now Mister Petrov my dear friend, and no longer needed. Now strip or I'll let them do it for you. As Allah is my witness, I promise you will not like that," Wazir said, throwing blue workman's clothing at Petrov's face. He felt his pants being tugged.

A happy couple, they were holding hands and strolling beneath the Burj al Baaz. The middle-aged Germans had gotten used to many things in the Desert city on the coast, but the heat was not one of them. And it was hot, over one hundred ten degrees Fahrenheit, but the official Dubai temperature was ninety-nine as usual.

"Let's step inside somewhere, and have beer, it's too hot," the German said to his wife. He was exhausted and sweating profusely. Looking up toward the sun, he thought about how miserably hot it really was, and at seven o'clock in the evening it was still, too damn hot. Something caught his eye, something blue - very blue. It was flying, he thought. No, or "is that something falling," he said out loud to his wife, changing his mind.

"Come on dear, move here - quickly, *schnell*," he said, tugging his wife off the sidewalk and underneath a nearby shade tree. He put his hand over her eyes, as the blue mass rapidly grew larger, impacting the sidewalk with a crunching thud twenty feet away, bouncing slightly before settling in one spot. The rich dark red pool spread outward from the blue, while at the same time soaking it, turning the blue to indigo.

CHAPTER 12

JUNE 5, 2008

DUBAI

IT HAD BEEN SEVENTEEN years since Bryan Craig was first there, in the days following the end of the Gulf War. Since that time, he'd made numerous trips back and the place never once remained the same. He looked in awe out the window of the helicopter as it raced southwest along the coastline one thousand feet up. He decided one thing was certain; Dubai was no longer a place searching for identity. It had shed the skin of being just another Arab oil-producing machine into something the world had never witnessed before. It was a modern day Babylon. A place where foreign engineering and construction continued round the clock, building higher, bigger, better, and more elaborate. On the heels of high oil prices seemingly unlimited banking credit, there was no such thing as a project too expensive or ambitious. *Was it a dangerous house of cards – a financial powder keg?* On the flight from Madrid, Bryan gave Shannon the rundown on Dubai.

"It's not really a city and not really a country but an Emirate," Bryan explained. "The story of Dubai really began in 1971 when the

United Arab Emirates where formed out of six Trucial Persian Gulf
States. Dubai however, was not even one of the original six."

An Emirate, in the classical sense of the word, is a place on the
coast of either the Persian Gulf or the Gulf of Oman and run by an
Emir, or tribal chief. The Arabic Peninsula is filled with Emirs, also
called Sheikhs, and quite often they would tend to disagree with one
another, as has been the case for centuries. Bryan pointed out that
"Just three generations ago arguments might have been over camels,
or freshwater well rights, now they're over oil rights – and the
disagreements in the past were settled the same way as they are now -
with brute force."

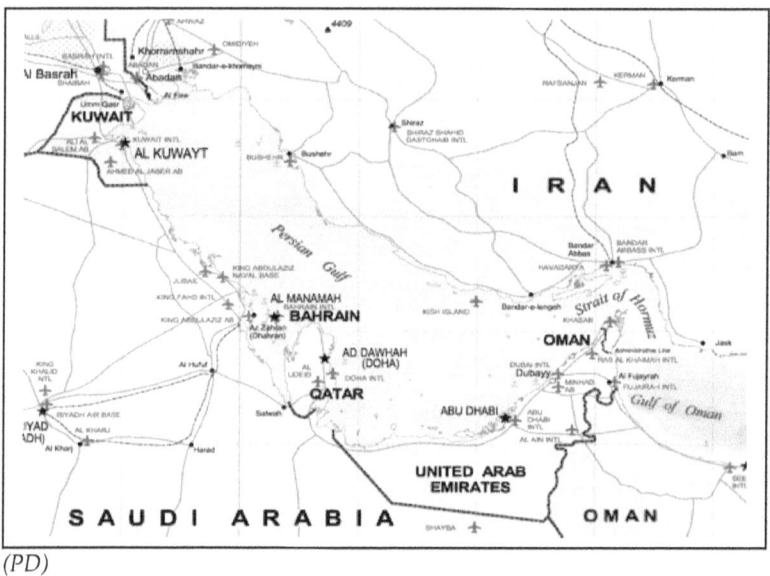

(PD)

Bryan studied the NASA satellite imagery and map of the Persian
Gulf on his computer. He admired this collection of principalities.
The UAE had managed to figure out a way to get their Emirs together
and unite under one flag, more or less. They created a border resulting
in an area slightly smaller than Maine and a government to preside
over a population of almost three million that was loosely based on
the British Parliamentary system.

"It's interesting," Bryan told her. "The UAE has an Executive
Branch, Judicial Branch, and Legislative Branch, just not any real
elections. It also has money, and lots of it. And it's all from oil and

gas that was discovered after the Rolling Stones had already been considered too old to Rock and Roll."

With a Gross National Product rivaling the strongest European economies, the UAE had surged from an impoverished pile of sand to an area that could arguably make the claim of having one the highest standards of living in the world. And the Flagship Emirate was Dubai.

Bryan recalled his first impression of the UAE's seventh member. He'd spent one week in Abu Dhabi, the Capital of the Emirates, as part of a Coalition team negotiating the use of UAE ports. One area of interest was Jabel Ali Port, a brand new facility at a place nobody had ever heard mentioned before. The place was Dubai. "Right next to the port today is *Palm Island*, one of the few man-made objects that can be seen from the Space Shuttle," Bryan said, relaying a Dubai factoid. "The place is kind of modeled after Singapore."

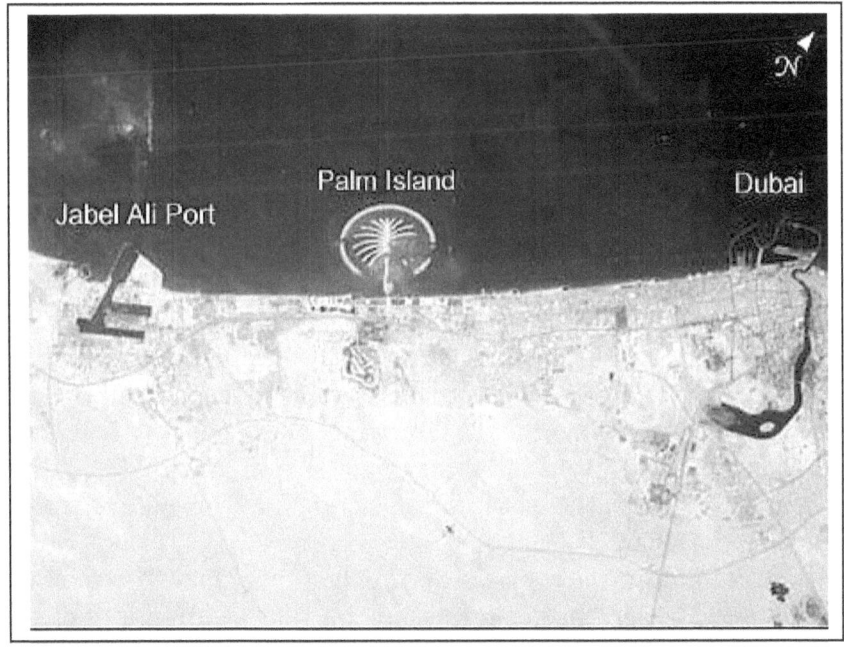

(PD)

Sent to Dubai to investigate the port, he spent a few days in the sweltering heat. It was dry, dusty, extremely hot and no wind. Bryan remembered, "In those days there were just a few high rise buildings scattered along a brand new road that mixed the glass of modern architecture - certainly symbolizing the future, with the dirt and poverty that was rapidly being left behind."

The Emirate's billionaire ruler was the Crown Prince Sheikh Mohammed bin Rashid al-Maktum, affectionately called Sheikh Mo by westerners. "The al-Maktums and extended family call the shots in these parts," Bryan said.

The helicopter flight from Dubai International Airport to the Hotel was short, only five minutes. Below them, Bryan and Shannon saw what had to be the largest collection of construction projects ever conceived. Literally dozens of luxury glass and chrome colored high-rise condominiums, all more than a thousand feet tall. And for every finished structure, two more were under construction, all topped with multiple cranes.

Bryan imagined the city-state as the ultimate facsimile: "Care to go snow skiing, no need to wait for winter and jet to the Alps, simply take the Rolls Royce on a five-minute ride from your beach resort to Dubailand Mountain, the city's indoor alpine skiing facility," he sarcastically thought. "

Whimsically, Bryan added, "And if that's not too outrageous, how 'bout your very own private island a community known as *the World*." It was rumored that rock star Rod Stewart had bought Great Britain for more than thirty million dollars.

Of course the jewel in the eye of Dubai was the twenty-first century's eighth wonder of the world, and tallest building, the Burj al Baaz. Yet, a visitor could never miss the original monument to the Arab nouveau riche, the *Burj al-Arab*, the tallest and only hotel in the world with a "seven-star" ranking. Bryan wasn't sure hotel classifications actually went to seven stars, "But if one did it certainly had to be in Dubai," he stated.

Vacationing in the world's newest hot spot, and "hot spot" was appropriate Bryan reasoned, was not on his list of priorities. The matter of Leonid Petrov was number one. The former Soviet and Russian army officer had ended up dead the day after they discovered Petrov's connection to the Memorial Day attacks. It was more than just a mere coincidence, both Bryan and Shannon reasoned. And he met death in a very unpleasant manner, a journey that took him from three thousand feet to concrete in about twenty seconds, including acceleration to critical velocity of 124 mph.

With his eyebrows raised, Bryan said, "Enough time for the former communist to contemplate many things, depending of course, on whether he was still alive when he took the last big step."

Petrov had links to the Al-Qaeda, Taliban, and many other terrorist organizations. He'd been suspected of dealing weapons to both, and reported to have assisted in some aspects of their training at secret camps located in remote locations of North West Frontier of Pakistan and North East Afghanistan. They now had evidence of Petrov's link to the Bank of Dubai. If they could track all of Petrov's financial transactions, they would be well on their way to finding the source of funds for the suicide bombers, and the master planners themselves.

"There are more people actively involved in this than sociopaths hiding in caves," Shannon commented.

"Or a lone opportunist such as Petrov," Bryan added. He was certain that the coconspirators were more dangerous, more sinister; they operated in the open and mingled freely in the business world.

"Shannon, look there - the Burj al Baaz," Bryan said while pointing to the tallest building in the world. Shannon simply gawked and shook her head in disbelief.

"I read that they're spending two hundred billion a year in Dubai for development. Sounds ambitious for such a small country," Shannon said.

"Ambition - the very essence of their spirit here. And it's not really a country, more of a small city-state actually. Only twenty-five years ago it was nothing more than a dot on a map. A place where sand that's baked to 120° meets the warm bath-like waters of the Persian Gulf," he said looking out the window at the blue water.

"Have you ever heard of the film '*Metropolis*'?" Shannon asked, testing Bryan's knowledge of movie trivia.

"The silent era film about the futuristic city. I haven't seen it, but recall something about it," Bryan answered.

"You said before that the urban planners here used Singapore as their model."

"That's right," Bryan said.

Looking at the amazing glass towers Shannon said, "Well I believe Dubai's more of an equivalent to *Metropolis*." The movie was a favorite "non-talkie" of Shannon's. "I wrote a paper on it for a Political Science. A German film from 1926 – pre-Nazi."

"Set in the future, right?"

"One hundred years in the future to be exact, and a city-state, much like Dubai. Also like Dubai, it was divided between two distinct classes. There were designers and thinkers that planned everything - who lived in towers high above in a world of endless skyscrapers and luxury."

"Yeah, that sounds like Dubai," Bryan said.

"The similarities are remarkable. In Metropolis they also had workers that lived far below in underground communities. Their lives were dedicated to building the city, and sustain the lives of the privileged high above."

"Weren't the workers saved by a woman?" He asked.

"Well, yes in fact, there was an evangelical character named Maria. She took up the case of the workers in hopes of saving them from their dreary plight. The twist came when the antagonist designed a robot that was identical to her. It's known as a Gynoid, or fembot," Shannon said.

"As in a female robot."

"Exactly. It's classic - life imitating art," she said.

"They even have working robots here in Dubai now," Bryan added.

"I only hope that Dubai doesn't have the same plan for their workers when they finish this city as the antagonist had for the workers in the movie."

"Why, what happened in the movie?" Bryan asked.

"In the movie, once the workers had completed the city and were no longer needed they would be eliminated."

The Bell Jet Ranger approached the hotel's helipad high above the waters of the Persian Gulf. Attached to the building's spinnaker shaped, southeast face, the helipad had once been temporarily converted into a tennis court for a match between two tennis stars. Bryan looked at the windsock as the pilot circled to find the most favorable landing angle. The sock indicated twenty knots of wind, which must have given the two tennis aces fits. He was certain that neither had tried very hard to run down shots going near the court's edge, it was a nine hundred foot drop straight down.

They touched down and waited for the Jet Ranger's engines to shut down and rotor blades to come to a complete stop before opening the doors. The warm air hit his face as he exited the craft. He turned and helped Shannon step carefully out the doorway. A helipad attendant grabbed his arm and Shannon's to keep them from straying, while another tended to their bags.

A short stocky balding man wearing a short sleeve golf shirt and khaki slacks was standing at the top of the helipad stairs holding onto a railing. Bryan guessed that the enthusiastic, shoulder-level "thumb's up" signal from the smiling man was meant for the two of them, which he returned at half-mast. It had been a long non-stop flight to Dubai and he was exhausted, desperately needing a "pick me up of something."

"Hey Bry. I'm Kevin Davis. Just call me Kev. I'm your man here in the UAE." He thrust out his hand to shake Bryan's, who was sure that he'd never seen fingers as short and stubby as Kevin's before. Kevin Davis was the CIA's case officer in Dubai, and Bryan's local contact. The CIA man now focused his attention on Shannon, who politely introduced herself.

"Come on crew, let's get inside. I'll buy you both a drink. I've already taken care of the rooms and our Paki man here will take care of your bags."

"Sounds like an idea." Bryan picked up his computer case as Kev gave the man now in charge of the luggage a thumb's up.

"Wait until you see your suites Bry, my man. They're beauties. Whose ass have you been kissin anyway? Or do you have friends in very high places? I was told to put you guys up here in suites we reserve for VIPs. You're going to think you've both died and went straight to heaven." Bryan looked at Shannon, who just shrugged. He was sure his brain was not ready for this 5 foot 7 inch fire-hose of hyperactivity and non-stop chatter. And he hated "Bry," the shortened version of his first name. The drink was a good call.

They entered the Al Muntaha restaurant one floor below the helipad and sat down at a table that offered a remarkable panoramic view of Dubai. The low sun cast a bright pink ambient hue across the horizon as it was refracted from the late afternoon haze of the Arabian

Peninsula. From the "God's eye" vantage Bryan could see the true scope of the seemingly endless construction projects underway. He concluded the glowing haze was actually airborne dust particles from the hundreds of projects.

A helicopter, he assumed the same that they arrived on, began slowly moving into view from his periphery. It hovered for several seconds only twenty-five meters from the window before turning and flying back to the airport. The waiter arrived just as the helicopter became a faint dot and disappeared into the distant haze. Bryan ordered the same as his new friend Kev, cold beer.

"Perrier please. Thank you," Shannon ordered, preferring an alcohol free meeting with the CIA. It was her first on-the-job overseas trip.

Kevin began, "So I understand that my clearance is now compartmented on this now?"

"That's right, need to know only," Bryan said. "Which may include a few additional people from the U.S. and British embassies later on."

"Who would that be?" Kevin asked.

"Don't know yet – and I said it may include."

"Gotcha. So you're Navy then?"

"That's right," Bryan said.

"A Navy SEAL."

"Was."

"But you're not retired, I mean you're a Captain," Kevin noted. "And she's with the FBI, I've seen her lecture," he added pointing at Shannon with a stubby forefinger.

"What's your point?" Bryan asked.

"I don't know, guess I'm just trying ta figure out who the hell you two work for."

"That's on a need to know also."

"Okay, but here's my reason why I think I need ta know – I've got these orders from my boss in Langley – says I need ta march lock step with ya. Why's that? – I mean I've got certain sources – people I've developed relationships with – it's taken me years. So why the hell should I trust you?" Kevin asked, now pointing his stub at Bryan.

Resisting from breaking the man's finger, Bryan answered "Fair enough. You've got your boss in Langley, right?"

"That's right, Bry," Kevin said sipping the beer.

"And he's got his boss in Langley. Oh, and I think the chain of command goes up two more times before you get to the DCIA. Am I still right?"

Looking back and forth at Shannon and Bryan "Yeah."

"I work for the same guy your DCIA reports to, and I report to no one else but him. How's that?"

"Figured as much. You Navy guys are as thick as thieves," Kevin said, sitting back in his chair. " Okay then, I have you both set up to meet with this local banker tomorrow."

"What time's the meeting?"

"We'll meet him at 8 AM. I'll pick you up at seven sharp. Be in front of the valet and look for a black Mercedes sedan. Oh, make sure your cell phone is charged, I'll call when I'm on my way."

"What's the bankers name?"

"Robert Rowley, an expatriate Brit. One of the many here."

"Where?"

"Downtown, near the Burj al Baaz, tower of the falcon – uh, I hate birds – you ever see "The Birds?" Kevin said, shaking his head.

"Let's get back to the banker," Bryan said.

"Bryan?" Shannon looked at him, waiting a nod that he quickly gave.

"Mister Davis."

"Call me Kev, Doc," Kevin interjected, as she nodded, acknowledging the informality. Kevin's habit of shortening names to one-syllable pet names was quickly going to get under her skin, she ascertained. She believed Bryan was already near the boiling point.

"Kevin, thanks for reviewing the file I Emailed to you concerning the questionable account at the Bank of Dubai. And now you believe that this Mister Rowley has some knowledge?"

"He just might," Kevin answered, thinking Shannon was a total rookie and out of her league. He was about to teach her a valuable lesson, he decided.

"Captain Craig and I will certainly be looking for more than that as a response," she said irritated.

"Okay, I'll put it to ya this way then. If he knows something, I'll get it out of him. If he knows where the source of the info came from, but doesn't know it at the time, I'll send him to the source, and we'll know the answer ASAP. One way or another I'll have him singin like a canary. Ya get my drift?" Kevin whistled like a bird and flapped his small fingers for emphasis, proud of himself for out-dueling the analyst, befuddlement to her straightforward questions. He liked intellectual battles between competing intelligence agencies, and he thought he'd just run roughshod right over her. It was ugly, Kevin thought.

Bryan interceded, having heard enough. "That was outstanding Kev – really brave stuff," Bryan said with a slow clap. Leaning forward at the table, Bryan waved Kevin closer with his fingers, lowered his voice and added, "Now, how about this plan – I go into the Bank of Dubai tomorrow and come out with exactly what I want. How's that for a plan, ay?"

"Yeah, sure Bry, but."

"And what floor is his office on?" Bryan said cutting him off.

"The eightieth floor. Why?"

"Tell me Kev, do you know how to play good cop bad cop?

"Huh? I guess, but what's that got to..."

"Well, answer her questions instead of playing games. If not, then when we go to the bank tomorrow, if Rowley doesn't answer her good cop questions, then I'm going to have to play bad cop. Something I really don't think you want ta see."

"I don't know about that – I might like it – watching you dangle Rowley out the window of his eightieth floor office by his shoe laces." Kevin said laughing at the image of the three hundred pound man dancing upside down from one thousand feet above the sidewalk.

"I'm not gonna dangle Rowley - I'm going to dangle you, Kev. Now, do you get my drift?" Bryan said, almost causing Shannon to laugh her Perrier through her nose. Kevin, for his part, just smiled nervously.

"Yeah, sure. Anyway, Doctor Parker – hmmm, I'm sure that we can put the right kind of pressure on him to find out whatever it is ya need. If I can't get him to budge, then I'll bring in the Consul General, Rodgers Christopher."

"Thank you very much Mister Davis," She said holding up her Perrier to toast his new attitude. He tapped her bottle with his glass.

Bryan looked out from the sweeping window to try and find the world's tallest building. He could faintly see the dark silhouette of the Burj al Baaz in the distance through the pink burqa of dust and haze.

"What do you know about the death over there – happened yesterday I think?" Bryan asked preferring that the CIA man name the dead Russian first. It was now time to talk about the obvious. A true test of how willing the CIA man would be to cooperate with his investigation.

"Yeah, ya mean Leonid Petrov, the Ruski that bought the farm. The real reason you're here, right? Well, he went base jumping without a chute," Kevin said motioning downward with his hand and whistling lightly for his classic crash and burn sound effect. He was happy the former commando had decided to shift conversation gears. "He was a real character all right. We've had him on our radar for years. The dude was into everything over here," Kevin added.

"For example, what - drugs, oil, human flesh, weapons?" Bryan asked, already knowing the answers.

"Yep. All of them." Kev sipped his beer.

Bryan had actually been thinking Kev might answer either choice a b c, or d. Not e, all the above. That was a good sign that the short, balding man might just work out after all.

Kevin continued, "He slithered around the fringes of Narco-Terrorism over the last ten years, dealing in everything that he could get his hands on. Mostly from the old Soviet weapons caches."

"No kidding," Bryan answered, wanting Kevin to go on.

"Movin oil, money launderin for drug lords, weapons, prostitution. Even rumored he'd somethin to do with missing enriched uranium. Surprised he ended up around here though."

"How so?" Shannon asked.

"Surprised he plied his trade to Muslims - he wasn't exactly the sharpest tool in the shed, and he was arrogant – a ruthless bastard. But it seems he'd have had enough common sense to not play in their sandbox, if you know what I mean?"

"What exactly do you mean?" She was very interested in the Russian. He was a complete deviant, a classic sociopath, and a good study, she thought.

"He'd been a commander of some Russian tank brigade or somethin over in Chechnya; anyway it got pretty out of hand during the uprisings. Very messy - lots of people were killed - lots of villagers. Ya know I think he did the same stuff in Afghanistan."

"I know Chechnya too well." Bryan knew the story all right and discussed the history in depth with Shannon on the flight to Dubai. The early days of the Soviet Union's break up saw many satellite states seek independence. Russia was determined to maintain control over Chechnya and prevent a Muslim independent republic, so it invaded in ninety-two. Sporadic uprisings continued over the years and eventually got out of control until ninety-nine, when the Russians invaded once more. As for Petrov, he certainly committed crimes in both conflicts, Bryan thought.

"Petrov was one of those bad-ass commanders that got pretty mean with the Muslims. There were stories of executions, things like that. It wasn't pretty. I mean war isn't pretty, but he went way past that – right to the gates of hell. If it had been Bosnia, the bastard would have been brought up on War Crimes."

"Yeah, of course. And you think Chechens had something to do with his death?" Bryan asked fishing for the CIA's take on Petrov's murder.

"Don't really know for sure - you know around here for the most part, the Arabs are what I call 'Jack Muslims.' Kind of like a 'Jack Mormon.' You know - like a guy that grew up in Salt Lake City, which is a very dry kind of place, not supposed ta drink booze, and who is also a Mormon, but drinks anyway. Kind of like me. It's why I had to go to New Orleans for school," Kev said laughing. Bryan and Shannon both smiled faintly.

Kevin continued on with his gossipy story, "These Sunni Muslims around here couldn't give a rat's ass what happened to a few Chechens ten years ago, or if some Danish artist drew cartoons of Mohammed and they were published in a Western newspaper. Couldn't give a damn, I mean, they're really kind of like us here."

"Are you serious?" Shannon asked, perplexed at Kevin's analogy.

"Yeah, absolutely. What I mean is - they're progressive. Sure they're Muslim and some of them pray every day, but they're not fanatical. Hell, here in Dubai they drink from dusk until dawn durin Ramadan, while the rest of the ragheads are fastin for Christ's sake. But over there..." Kevin nodded in the direction of Iran on the other side of the gulf. "Over there you've got millions of hard core Shi'ah Islamists that never forget even the slightest damn insult, let alone the takin land they believe is rightfully Islamic."

"Now come on – are you implying that Leonid Petrov was dealing arms to the Iranians?" Shannon asked, wondering where Kevin was going with his story.

"Not just Iranians, I mean sure, Petrov was sellin weapons to those types - hell, he'd sell to anyone that'd pony up cash and wire it to a Swiss bank account. He was the quintessential opportunist."

"A profiteer?" Shannon added.

"Yeah, a profiteer. But he must have been smokin crack; I mean these fanatic Islamists will even send their own family members in as human bombs. Man, once they're done with ya, you're toast." Kevin leaned in and whispered for emphasis, "Especially if you had tied and blindfolded every male in a village from five to eighty years old, laid them out on a road, then drove tanks over them while they were still alive." Kevin leaned back in his chair after he finished.

"Like I said, he wasn't the sharpest tool - he should've moved to the U.S. instead. I mean our messed up legal system would've helped keep him alive no matter what he did, and he still could've been an arms dealer," Kevin said. "Just mean, and dumb."

"What actually happened?" Bryan asked, angling for details.

"Honestly, don't know the 'official facts' yet," Kevin said, using his small fingers to sarcastically make quote signs. "The locals aren't sayin much. His name and the accident were kept out of the news. Very hush, hush. It's like, the dude showed up in Dubai, and then five hours later ended up in a nosedive onto pavement."

"Nothing more than that?" Becoming agitated with Kevin's seeming evasiveness, Bryan pressed him for more information. "Level with me – tell me what you know. Time, as they say, is of the essence."

"Sure, but strictly off the record – okay? I mean you didn't hear this from me."

"Right, sure – go on."

"A good source at the medical examiner's office told me that Petrov had the livin shit beat out'uv 'im. They'd really never seen anything like it. Blount force trauma, you know like with a pipe," he nervously replied.

"They were able to tell that after he fell three thousand feet?" Shannon quizzed Kevin, imagining it being somewhat difficult to determine the source of other non-puncture wounds, or contusions.

"You can tell a whole bunch from a dead body, lady. He was nearly beaten to death with a metal pipe, kicked, punched, and maybe some other Crusades type of bad shit. Then he was thrown off the building, or maybe forced to jump. But he was definitely alive until he hit the sidewalk. Almost landed on a couple of Krauts. The official cause of death was due to, and I'm quotin here, 'due to the effects of high negative G forces resultin from instantaneous deceleration.' Call it - impact with a planet," he chuckled, finding his description of Petrov's death amusing.

"Now for the eight by ten, Kev. What about leads? Who killed him?" Bryan asked.

"I'm serious when I tell you that I've no idea who, or what group ordered him taken out, but as for leads? Well, I don't know if you can call this a lead or not, but there's one thing I found out that was kind'uv odd. Could mean somethin or maybe nothin," Kevin said, looking at Shannon with a frown.

"Which is?" She motioned with her hand for him to finish.

"It's what the guy had on," Kevin said as he paused to take a sip of his drink, and finishing, "He had on that blue clothing the construction workers wear."

A private butler escorted Bryan and Shannon into adjoining duplex suites on the twenty-second floor. One of the many "seven-star" perks the hotel offered their guests was a butler, each room had its own. Dubai was becoming famous for exploring new boundaries of luxury and their suites were testimonies to that. Each double-story unit was really two suites in one, and both had floor to ceiling windows. The bright combinations of colors on all furniture are what Bryan noted first. Every piece had gold on the upholstery somewhere. The sight conjured up images of Aladdin, flying carpets, and Genies.

As he stood looking out the window at the night skyline of Dubai and its' endless sea of teaming lights, it occurred to him that this Emirate had become a place where fantasy could come true, much like the imaginary places of "Arabian Nights." That is, if someone had enough money to buy it. But also, because of the talk of the blue laborer clothing, he wondered about the hundreds of thousands of Muslim workers, most of them from Pakistan, toiling day and night, in the dust and heat, for the lowest wages imaginable. *What would happen to them when it was over and they were laid off?* Discarded.

Thrown back to the desert. *Where would they go? Who would find them? Would the wealthy upper class of Dubai rescue them and take them in as their own?* Bryan was sure that was the least likely scenario. *Would they want to return to the poverty of Pakistan?* Doubtful. Bryan reasoned it was likely that a sociopath impersonating a Mullah would take advantage of their despair with veils of kindness and compassion. Islamists would be there to lead them to the fanatical elements of their religion and point out the enemies of their faith. A militant guide would convince them to take vengeance against their enemies. *Would one society's instrument to build become another's instrument of hatred to tear it down?* Disturbing possibilities, Bryan recognized, but possibilities he considered to be leaning closer to factual. His thoughts were interrupted by a knock on the door. It was Shannon.

"Welcome to my palace Doctor Parker. Care for a magic carpet ride while you're here?" Bryan motioned with an outstretched arm to the gaudiness that was his suite.

She laughed. "Why thank you Captain Craig. I do declare, how elegant," she answered in her best Scarlet O'Hara impersonation. "I'll pass on the carpet ride, but a drink would be nice. Maybe a glass of wine," she added falling into an over-stuffed chair.

"Coming right up." Bryan found a Napa Valley Pinot Noir stocked in the suite's bar. He poured them each a glass.

Shannon offered a toast and raised her glass to his. "Cheers. May they never actually figure out how to have magic carpet rides here."

"Cheers, a grand example of Americana in Dubai." Bryan took a small sip. "Rather a very convincing grape, easily approachable, a bit of heft - complex flavors - wood, spice, richness, texture – oh, and definitely a long finish, something that can go with a – hmmm – how 'bout a barbecue sandwich." They both laughed hard, equally punchy.

Shannon brought up the subject of Kevin Davis and the CIA. "Do you trust him?"

"Trust him? Hmmm, good question. Don't know the answer to that one just yet." He took another sip and added, "If you think he's bad, just wait until you have to work with the Foreign Service types. Good lord. And what do you think of our Mister Davis?"

"Besides his obvious bird phobia, evasive, boorish, immature, short, bald – everything that attracts me to a man." They both laughed again, and touched wine glasses.

Still laughing, "Honestly, I think he's given us what he knows so far, and it seems that he'll continue to do so. He seems sincere, and I'm sure he understands the gravity of what happened, even though he's insolated here in Dubai."

"Agreed. That's a good observation Shannon. Now we need to pin down the Petrov connection. Why was he wiring money to terrorists? We also need his account information from the bank to nail down the identities of the other bombers. Rowley will at the least have access to that, but it may require – coercion, if you will, to get it out of him. We shouldn't expect to just waltz in and have him turn it over to us."

"Legally - can we obtain the records?"

"Legally, unfortunately not. But, I'll try to cajole him into giving us something tangible at the very least. It's more important that he lead us to the real money in back of the conspiracy, rather than only the names of dead martyrs."

"You're not that concerned?"

"About who the other bombers are? Of course I am. By the same token, we've got to keep our eye on the prize. It's not just about solving a crime; it's also about shutting down an entire sinister operation."

"But your plan is to leave with his account data."

"Oh, I intend on having that in my hands, but what's it really gonna tell us? That Petrov was wiring money? We know that already. So we pick up a few more names. We'll get those anyway too - Gil will certainly track that info down sooner or later."

"What exactly are you looking for?" Shannon asked, resting her head on the seat back. She was longing for a massage.

"The trail that Petrov left. Why he was killed? I think when we've found the answer to those questions – we may actually be on track to find the financial sources. Killing Petrov might have been the mistake we're looking for our prey to make."

"Prey" was an interesting choice of word for Bryan, Shannon thought. She asked, "Why would killing him have been such a bad mistake?"

"You're the Doctor; think about his death for a moment."

"Well, it was definitely very brutal. It appears from Kevin's story that he was tortured, then killed."

"And what's that tell you?"

"Someone either just wanted information, which is doubtful, because he would probably still be alive someplace and still being tortured. An upper floor of the Burj al Baaz would not be my choice as the best place for interrogation."

"Makes perfect sense," Bryan said, rummaging through the remaining wines. He settled on the French Bordeaux.

"It's evident that whoever killed him felt very comfortable with the surroundings - probably knew him. They wanted him to suffer both physically and psychologically. He was beaten severely and in such a personal way – apparently a tremendous amount of physical abuse. Then he was thrown off the building, for what you figured to be a twenty second freefall."

"There's your psychological anguish," Bryan said, uncorking the new bottle.

"They despised the man's very existence," Shannon added.

"Nice deduction Doctor Parker and on track with my thinking. I agree that the killer was very comfortable with the surroundings, maybe even worked there. We don't know what floor yet, but let's assume for the moment, it happened on a floor that was still under construction."

"Paki laborers may have killed him."

"Possible, or someone posing as laborers. And if Paki laborers were there – if they witnessed anything, it's doubtful they would ever report it." After waiting for the wine to breathe, Bryan poured the Bordeaux into his glass and picked up Shannon's empty one.

"Aren't you supposed to use a new glass?" Shannon asked.

"This is French middle country, Shannon – a Medoc – ninety-six Château Latour. This is seventy-five percent Cabernet Sauvignon, it'll kill whatever's left of that mediocre Pinot," Bryan said confidently. "Ninety-six is one of the best vintages for this Grand Vin."

"Didn't know you were such an expert on wine."

"Learned it from Gil. Château Latour is his favorite," Bryan said, checking the legs of the red wine. "He once told me that he hoped it would be the last thing he ever tasted before he met his maker."

Shannon took a sip. "Mm, very nice. Smooth - so what now then?"

"We follow Petrov's path up to the time of his death."

"And you know where that path leads?"

"I know where it'll take us to a point," Bryan said, opening his computer and turning it on. Confirming a solid Internet signal, he logged into the Pegasus secure Virtual Private Network. The Pegasus VPN, like the iPhone's VoIP communications network used encryption that would require a super computer one year to crack a packet of code. Pegasus however, used seven packets each day. He pulled up a display and set the computer on the coffee table so that Shannon could see the screen.

"Pakistan. So you think it's a Pakistani cell, huh? I suppose," Shannon said.

"Right here."

"The North West Frontier and Karachi," she said following the movement of his fingers.

"Chitral District to be exact, and of course Karachi. The ISI has provided information leading us to believe that Petrov was in Karachi and the NWF area just a few weeks ago. He's been there a number of times according to their reports. We still have some ground work to do, beginning with getting the CIA and ISI to give us as much information as possible."

"But you think Pakistani militants are in back of this?"

"Malik was a Paki, and Petrov made the majority of his contacts from that region," Bryan said. "It already adds up."

"Okay, now speaking of Pakistanis, what about the blue work clothes? What's your impression about that sordid detail?"

"It's certainly symbolic, that's for sure."

"Symbolic of what, or whom?"

"Don't have that sorted out just yet - sooner or later, though."

Shannon thought for a moment, as she felt the irritation in her armpit. "Was this really necessary?" She asked as she felt the small nodule under the skin that was the source.

"Just a precaution for us these days, Shannon," Bryan said. His own nano-tracker, the size of the head of a ballpoint pen, had been embedded in his body two years ago.

They finished the bottle of wine, and Shannon politely excused herself to her suite, but doubted if she'd be able to sleep. They were both exhausted and keyed up, the strange mixture of fatigue and wine that often results in insomnia.

Bryan lay back on an overstuffed pillow, hands behind his head. He was looking at his reflection in a gold-framed mirror on the ceiling above. He looked fit, he thought, but wanted to find more time for exercise, maybe some rowing once in awhile when he got back to London. "Once all this business is over I'll get back into a regular regimen again," he promised himself. Laughing at his last thought, he rolled off the bed onto his feet. What a joke that was; this "business" would never be over in his lifetime, he realized.

CHAPTER 13

JUNE 6, 2008

DUBAI

K EVIN HAD BEEN WAITING in the black Mercedes sedan for twenty minutes. He was parked near the valet. The license plates were Diplomatic, a telegraph of sorts Bryan thought, as he and Shannon approached the car and jumped in. Bryan noticed a McDonalds bag on the floor of the front seat. Somehow he wasn't surprised at Kevin's diet.

"Well, good morning Mister Davis, here early are we?" Bryan said, placing his feet on either side of the trash.

"The drive took less time than I thought. Anyway, I like getting here early for the hotel coffee. On my second cup already," Kevin said. "Put the trash here." He reached over, opening the glove compartment, revealing a Walther P5, nine-millimeter handgun.

Bryan made room for the trash and looked between the seats for a place to put his bottle of water. There was a plastic Redskins coffee mug sitting in the car's cup holder.

"I take it they're big fans of football here, huh," Bryan said, smirking.

"No, I took this cup inside to get twice as much for seventy-five dirham a cup," Kev said with a wink. After some quick math Bryan figured that Kev had gone through about $30 worth of UAE java during the short wait.

Crossing the short causeway from the Burj al Arab's manmade island of asphalt and sand, they passed Jumerirah Beach. Bryan could see a dozen or more attendants on both sides of the road readying beach chairs for resort guests. They would be leisurely strolling down to the beach in just a couple of hours.

Kevin maneuvered the car onto Sheikh Zayed Road, Dubai's major expressway. Lined with elegant palm trees, the highway had the feel of any interstate in a major U.S. city at 6:00 AM. Traffic was not congested yet, but quickly developing to what would soon be a snarl. The dissimilarity between the rush hour in Dubai and cities in the U.S.; every other car in Dubai was a Mercedes similar to Kevin's, Bryan observed.

"Anything more about Petrov from the Dubai police?" Bryan asked as they bounced from lane to lane, finding the path of least resistance.

"Nothing's changed from yesterday. They're still keeping a very tight lid on it?" Kevin took a final sip of his twenty-dollar cup of coffee.

"Any reasons why?"

"Could be they're trying to keep bad news out of the spotlight, considering who's arriving in Dubai later today."

"Who?" asked Shannon.

"Four mega rich businessmen from the States, here's the memo." Kevin reached between the front seats, pulled out a brown file folder and passed it back to Shannon. "Look at the top Email inside."

Shannon scanned the piece of paper quickly and then read the names. "Richard Squire, George Lancaster, John Chamberlain, and Tobias Davis. These are all American billionaires," she said, leaning forward between the seats and handing the file to Bryan.

"More than that Shannon," Bryan added. "They're giants in their industries, which includes real estate development, communications, software, and construction. What sorts of deals are they involved with here, Kevin?"

"It's huge, the Burj al Baaz and community - Tower of the Falcon - a massive development. The tower's already the tallest building in the world. Now they're developing the surrounding sand. Supposedly the most expensive community ever planned."

"Watch out," Shannon yelled pointing at the car ahead. Kevin hit the brakes hard, locking them, avoiding a BMW that had just skidded to a complete stop. Bryan looked ahead to see numerous red brake lights.

"Shit, just our luck. Another damned labor demonstration," Kevin said.

After twenty minutes of inching along bumper to bumper, they saw a gathering of men in light blue clothing, demonstrating on both sides of the road, many holding signs over their heads.

"We've had about a half a dozen of these in the last two years - large protests shutting down several of the major construction sites - including Burj al Baaz. Two protests turned into full-blown riots."

"I would imagine developers being rather unhappy about these guys," Bryan remarked. "Dubai's hidden guest workers, Shannon," he added.

He explained that the 'Guest Workers," as the construction laborers from Pakistan and India were called, were paid between fifty to seventy-five dollars per week, depending on the contractor, but one third of that was allocated to the camp canteen for meals. International Humanitarian groups had placed the UAE on a short list of Arabian countries that routinely violated international laws against trafficking in persons and forced labor. The Emirates however, were simply students of the very government that had created the borders for countries of the Arabian Peninsula. The British Empire had, after all had been built on the blood and sweat of hundreds of thousands of Indian and Pakistani workers. The majority of those laborers had actually been indentured servants, working for just a few rupees per week, sometimes forced into outright slavery.

Bryan recalled that that "Slavery had been officially abolished by the Trucial sheikdoms just two years before I was born. Yet there are still many violations and abuses. In fact, I remember a recent report on cable focused on the use of underage camel jockeys for races in Dubai, one being just three years old."

"Yeah, I saw that too," Shannon said. "Many kids had been kidnapped from Pakistan, and sold into slavery as jockeys. The report must have been a major embarrassment to royal members of the Sheikhdom," she added.

"It was. You know that they're owners of triple-crown winners, and travel in the elite circles of U.S. thoroughbred owners. Labor is a very sensitive subject," Bryan said.

"Hence the protests, which is why I gave us an hour to drive just eight miles." Kevin said.

"What company are they protesting against?" Shannon asked.

"I think this one's about Bell and Van Wouter, a U.S. and Dutch partnership. They're one of the contractors building Dubailand." Dubailand was a seventy thousand acre development of entertainment, homes, villas, malls, and of course, luxury high-rise hotels.

"A couple of the workers hung themselves at their camp in protest. I think all they really wanted was official thermostats at their worksite, and a raise of five dollars a week," Bryan said.

"Thermostats and a raise, it's so sad, " Shannon said.

"The official law here Doc, states that laborers shouldn't work when the outside temperature exceeds one hundred degrees. The key words are 'should not work,' as opposed to 'shall not work,'" Kevin said making quotation marks with his fingers, as was his habit. "If they didn't work around here every time the temperature was above a hundred degrees we'd still have nothing in Dubai but sand. I mean it's always above a hundred, usually one-ten and higher. They also want an extra dollar per hour for every hour that the temperature is above a hundred."

"That's all?" Shannon asked amazed that the complaints of poor working conditions were being ignored. Samuel Gompers, the first President of the American Federation of Labor, would've had a field day here, she thought.

"That's it – that's all they wanted," Kevin said.

Slowly, they moved by the sea of blue protesters, all appearing to be from the Indian subcontinent, "either Pakistan or India," Bryan said.

The men looked and sounded very angry. As a psychologist, Shannon thought it interesting to study the way people from the region communicated.

"Something about the people from that part of the world - they seem very theatrical," she said. "A simple discussion could appear to be a quarrel to someone from a different culture."

Sometimes they were very colorful to watch, especially if the conversation became an argument, Shannon recounted seeing two drivers get into it while she was waiting at the JFK airport taxi stand "Both men were frowning and speaking loudly, on the verge of screaming at any second. And both were waving their hands frantically in the air," she said, mimicking the gestures. "One abruptly stopped and started walking away. He took one step, turned around and picked up where he'd just left off, arms flailing once again," she said laughing.

"What were they arguing about?" Kevin asked.

"I assumed by the looks of them – and they were serious – I thought it could have been a Pakistani and an Indian fighting Kashmir. I was completely wrong," she said, slapping the back of Bryan's seat. "Do you know what it was?"

"What?" Kevin asked.

"Guess – go on – just guess. You'll never get it in a million years."

"Cricket," Bryan said, taking a wag at it.

"How the heck did you know that?" Shannon asked, giving Bryan a light punch on the shoulder.

"It's easy, what else could it have been?"

"Well I never would've guessed that. I had to ask my cab driver, who was a Pakistani. And that's what it was alright – Cricket."

The protesting "Guest Workers" had more to be upset over than a Cricket Match though. They were being worked to the point of despair, nearly at the breaking point. The organizers were taking a big chance by voicing their anger in such a public forum however; efforts to organize labor, public protests, and strikes were illegal in Dubai and could result in their "Guest Worker" status being revoked. Violators were often deported.

Bryan pointed out who he thought might be the organizer of the protest. A blue clad man was standing on a makeshift stage of fruit crates, holding a megaphone to his mouth. Whatever he was saying was effective, the crowd repeating each of his rants. Bryan assumed they were chanting the same phrase that was written on all the cardboard signs being displayed, English on one side and Urdu on the other.

THANK YOU FOR WORK.

BUT PLEASE PAY US.

Apparently, it seemed, the majority of those employed in Dubai hailed from two very distinct stations. Of course, there was the manual labor force, predominantly coming from the subcontinent of India, lived in squalor, and were paid miserably low wages. On the flip side were the other "Guest Workers," those from the West, who were paid ridiculously high salaries, and took advantage of Dubai's accoutrements. Certainly worlds apart in status, station, and compensation, all were hired to build and manage Dubai. Bryan was convinced that when the boom went bust, as booms surely always do, the financial separation between the two classes of guest workers could prove to be a hair trigger for something much more frightening than a financial meltdown.

Kevin turned off the highway onto Burj al Baaz Boulevard, the perimeter road of the lagoon and lake complex. It was lined with the other office buildings in various stages of completion, luxury hotels, and address No. 1, the focal point of the complex, the massive tower itself. As they curved around the lake, Bryan looked up at the building. The tower redefined the word "skyscraper," at least as it applied to these manmade objects of glass, steel, and imagination that continued to go skyward. He'd never seen anything like it before. As if some kind of an illusion, it seemed to defy the principle laws of engineering and architecture. Buildings nearby, most nearly a thousand feet tall, some taller, huge structures in their own right, were brought to their knees by the enormity of the Burj al Baaz.

The title of "World's Tallest" had traditionally been bestowed on buildings from America's great cities. The first building to really have the dubious distinction of was New York City's Chrysler Building, a shiny silver monument to Art Deco and American know-how. Completed in nineteen thirty-one, it marked the United States as now being the leader of innovative architecture and engineering design. It was the first building called a skyscraper and the first to reach to the heavens beyond one thousand feet. But it held the record for less than a year, overshadowed by the two hundred foot addition of the observation deck and taller spire on the Empire State Building.

Tallest building rights were held firmly in the grasp of American hands for almost three quarters of a century, and only two more skyscrapers would make the claim of world's tallest, the doomed twin towers of New York's World Trade Center and lastly, Chicago's Sears Tower at five hundred twenty-seven meters. There the record remained, until Malaysia, a country trying to shed its third world nation status, erected the twin Petronas Towers just before the end of the twentieth century. The record would be topped shortly after the dawn of the next millennium as the Taiwanese pushed heights to the five hundred meter mark as well, more than sixteen hundred feet, upon the completion of Taipei 101 in two thousand and four. The building's higher floors make it the tallest. Skyscrapers had become the ultimate symbols of western culture. Symbols, they were the towers of capitalism, cathedrals of commerce, monuments to modernity.

The Burj al Baaz, or Tower of the Falcon, now was the Master to the symbols of mankind's ingenuity, the defining objects that separated civilized man from prehistoric ancestors, and built on a stretch of sand called Dubai; ironical, in that the location was Arabian, the monument however, was distinctly American. Burj al Baaz's architect was Davis, Redding and Morgan LLP, a New York based firm that had been around for seventy years and the architects of some of the grandest structures in the United States. A revolutionary design, the building embodied various aspects of Islamic architecture using Arabic calligraphy etched into the marble exterior of the reinforced concrete as well as into the steel framing. Inside the spaces vaulted upwards from circular domes at the base. A mini-city of its own with eight hundred private condominiums on floors fifty through one hundred and ten, the rest corporate offices and an upscale hotel.

"If they can't be the tallest in the States, why not here?" Bryan pondered. Architecture and its history fascinated him.

"Here we are," Kevin said. He pulled the car into the drive of a smaller eighty-story building directly across a large park and lake from the tower. Getting out, Bryan and Shannon looked skyward to find the blue of the earth's outer skin. Similar to midtown in New York City, they were at the bottom of a forest of skyscrapers. Dubai's buildings however, were newer, taller, and shinier. *Capitalist cathedrals on Islamic sand!*

Entering a security area, they saw an image of a middle-aged woman with thick glasses on a monitor adjacent to the express elevator. She was clearly English, her accent having a Liverpudlian cadence.

"Good morning, the Bank won't be opened for another hour," the face on the screen informed the three.

"Hello Susan, it's me," Kevin said, giving his standard thumb's up at the security camera.

"Oh, yes, of course Mister Davis. Please come right up," the woman said, obviously familiar with Kevin after seeing him clearly.

They entered a glass exterior elevator bound for the eightieth floor, which quickly accelerated to a steady rate. The eighty-floor ascent would take less than a minute. The view as they rose was unobstructed with the exception of the massive steel cross supports that whizzed by every ten stories. Bryan looked down at his feet and through the glass floor watched the ground drop away. From their vantage point, near the heart of Dubai, Bryan and Shannon both got a sense of Dubai's future.

The world's most luxurious, cosmopolitan city was now officially the fastest growing and had been for several years. Bryan recalled seeing an economic report regarding the strain that Dubai had put on the world's crane supply. The report cited several sources, and concluded that up to twenty percent of the world's construction of cranes were being used in Dubai alone. That amounted to almost thirty thousand cranes hauling glass, metal, and concrete slabs to build stadiums, indoor ski slopes, and skyscrapers. Nearly five billion dollars were being spent each week on construction. The proof was in their vista, panning the horizon.

Similar urban quagmires of steel and glass around the world also had a like sense of artificiality. Taipei, Shanghai, and Singapore were three Asian metropolitan landmarks, born out of the century of the skyscraper. They too suffered from the same malady that now befell Dubai, lack of imagination, uninspired architecture, Bryan believed. He recalled an American real estate mogul whose favorite adjective to describe a steel and glass edifice he'd built, "Huge." The mogul's annunciation invariably dropped the h from the word, coming out "uge." Huge is what inspired planners in Dubai, Bryan surmised. And that very same mogul was right in the middle of it.

The elevator quickly and uncomfortably decelerated, stopping at the bank's foyer entrance. Entering the bank with Kevin leading the way, they were immediately greeted by the English woman on the monitor.

"Mister Rowley is expecting you. And you must be Mister Craig and Doctor Parker. Good morning, I'm Susan Thompson. It's a pleasure," she said formally.

"Good morning Ms. Thompson," Bryan said.

"One moment please while I inform Mister Rowley that you're here." She walked to the nearest desk and picked up a phone.

Bryan took in the subtle nuances of the bank. It was a departure from the over-the-top opulence that was prevalent elsewhere in Dubai. There were certain similarities, true; for example the lobby was oversized as everything else was in the city-state. But it lacked the detailing that he'd become accustomed to with interior design there. The ceiling was vaulted, at least forty feet high, with large opaque, concave glass windows as walls that bowed slightly outward. The furniture in the lobby was distinctly modern and expensive, but without the lines to carry someone's attention for more than a moment. He noted there didn't appear to be a teller; customers obviously didn't frequent the bank to cash checks or make deposits in person. And not very many desks, just two, leading Bryan to ask, "How many employees do you have up here?"

"On this floor, just five," she said.

"Only five?"

"The express elevator services just this office - the only one on the floor. Few clients are permitted at this level. Throughout the remainder of the building we have two hundred and fifty employees on five floors."

There were however, an abundance of cameras throughout the large room, covering every possible angle. An ant would have difficulty crawling though the bank without being spotted by security.

Looking directly at the Burj al Baaz through the massive window, the world's tallest building was two hundred fifty meters away, and Bryan could also see downtown Dubai spread out far below, stretching to the horizon. But even at this height, the Burj al Baaz climbed higher still, the top of the tower out of view. Just then he heard the familiar sound of hard leather soles echoing off of marble flooring and looked down a hallway for the source. A very large man with a double-breasted suit was briskly walking towards them. His thin hair was dyed an unnatural black, as well as his beard. The visible portion of his face was pocked, most probably from juvenile acne, Bryan guessed. He was out of breath and laboring for speech by the time he reached the lobby to greet them.

"Oh bloody hell. Good to see you chaps," Rowley said. He was completely out of breath.

Laboring, hyperventilating, trying to find oxygen, he finally spoke again "Pleasure to meet you Mister Craig, and you as well Doctor Parker. I'm Robert Rowley – I sort'uv, err run things around here," he said with an uncomfortable grunt like chuckle. Sweating, he wiped his brow with a handkerchief and tucked it in his pocket.

"Follow me," he said. "We'll go to the conference room for a chat."

They followed him down a dark hallway; the floor only indirectly lit by the spotlights on museum quality paintings hanging on the wall. Originals from Abstract Expressionists of the twentieth century, Bryan recognized the work of Franz Kline, Motherwell, Rothko, Jackson Pollack, and Still. "There's at least a hundred million dollars worth of artwork between the reception area and the conference room," he said to Shannon.

The large Englishman, who Bryan likened to a younger, taller version of Pavarotti, flicked on the lights of the dark conference room; dim ceiling lights that cast unflattering shadows downward on their faces. Rowley motioned for them to sit down at a large rosewood table.

"Mister Craig, it's always a pleasure to have an American in our midst. Where exactly would that be – oh, that's right, I must correct myself, you're military?" Rowley asked.

"You are in fact correct," Bryan said.

"That's right, it's Captain Craig - and I understand you're currently stationed in London," Rowley said.

Bryan nodded, asking "And you're originally from?"

"Ahm fra Newcassel me sel," Rowley said laughing. Looking at Shannon, he translated the accent, "That would be Newcastle, Doctor. Anyway, let me show you both something very exciting."

"Here's our latest endeavor," he said gleefully, adding, "I apologize, but dreams never stop becoming reality in Dubai." He pushed a button on a control panel lying on the table.

Overhead lights dimmed. Lasers, mounted flush in both the ceiling and the walls, flashed on displaying a 3D hologram above the table's surface. The detail was vivid and included a coastline, yachts, and desert golf courses. At the center was the massive tower, the Burj al Baaz, surrounded by smaller buildings as well as acres of development, single-family homes, clubs, soccer fields, and shopping malls.

"You're lookin at Burj al Baaz. The 'Tower of the Master Falcon,' and of course the city complex, communities, malls, and golf courses that goes with it - now called Baazland," he said. Leaning forward and cupping his mouth, he added in a whisper of selective inclusion, "We're even getting very close for an approval by the Sheikhdom for gambling."

Bryan and Shannon exchanged glances, both thinking the same thing - non-financial services deals for laundering dirty money. Rowley had just covered two of Gil's list of three - real estate and gambling.

The complexity of the development was amazing. "How much area does this cover?" Bryan asked as he looked at the three-dimensional image.

"You Mister Craig are gazing upon a perspective from five thousand feet above. The entire development is twice the size of Dubailand. And the tower is one thousand meters. Beautiful isn't it," Rowley said with excitement. "You know we sold out all of the condominiums in ten hours from release. They average seven million dollars U.S."

"A three thousand foot tower. How much taller could they go?" Bryan wondered. *Was this the new Tower of Babylon?*

"Do you see these buildings here?" he moved his hand into the hologram, waving it over a section of images near one of two eighteen-hole golf courses.

"Every one of these skyscrapers is taller than any building outside of Dubai - taller than the Petronas Towers, or Taipei 101. But the Burj al Baaz is one thousand feet higher than all of those. And we'll have the world's best playing tournaments right here beneath these fantastic buildings." He moved the palm of his hand right through the hologram of the golf course, landing it with a thud on the table.

"That's amazing Mister Rowley," Kevin said in deadpan monotone. Bryan sensed that Kevin may have heard the presentation at least once before.

Rowley continued proudly, "We have over sixty thousand homes planned, fifteen acres of park, and two lakes."

"How many slaves do you need for this deal?" Kevin asked with obvious sarcasm.

"Not funny mate," Rowley said looking at Kevin with a cold stare, and then bursting back into his enthusiastic diatribe.

"But if you're asking, I'd 'ave to say about eighty thousand. Anyway, go bugger off, wanker," he laughed and gave Kevin his middle finger.

"How are you financing this little endeavor?" Bryan asked.

"Well mate, just a part, but of course the lead part, will be the Bank of Dubai. The rest of the group is made up of four banks from the UAE, five from the States, um... two Japanese banks, and two from the good ole union jack, and of course our private investors, principally Americans. By the time we're done, it's a fifty billion dollar venture."

The assistant entered the room carrying a tray with a pot of coffee and four coffee cups. "Would you care for anything else Mister Rowley?" She asked.

"Gents? Lady?" They shook their heads. He nodded for her to leave the room.

Rowley pointed to small table. "Sugar and cream there."

"When do you start on Baazland?" Bryan said while pouring the cream into his coffee.

"Of course, the building is nearly finished - we've recently broken ground on Baazland. And we're thanking the Americans for their investments and protection. You know the Sheikhdom likes 'avin the U.S. nuclear carriers close by. It gives em a sense of security from the neighbors over there to the Northeast," Rowley said pointing in the direction of Iran on the hologram. Rowley was correct on another subtle point as well; the United States was providing protection for Dubai, and all on U.S. tax dollars. The UAE spent virtually zero on defense, yet poured tons of money into social programs, such as education. As a percentage of their respective Government's annual budget, the UAE spent ten times more on education. But why would Dubai need a defense budget anyway? "They have the west," Bryan thought.

"The investment that's been made in Dubai and the UAE as a whole is significant Mister Rowley, both by the United States and Great Britain. No doubt we will do what we have to protect our interests here in the Persian Gulf area. I don't believe we're going to fall asleep at the wheel as was done twenty years ago when Iraq decided to invade Kuwait. We don't intend on letting that happen with Iran," Bryan said.

"I'm glad you understand things so well Captain Craig. What can I do for you today anyway? Mister Davis has informed me that you have some specific questions regarding a suspended account?"

"Dubai is a favorite of unscrupulous characters because of the lack of regulatory scrutiny. To be blunt about it – money laundering, drug trafficking, and terrorist financing happens right here in this modern city-state," Bryan said deciding to get right to the point. He felt his Blackberry vibrate against his hip and looked to see the caller. Gil.

"How can the Bank of Dubai help?" Rowley responded as though his hands were tied.

"I need your cooperation where SWIFT leaves off," Bryan said, feeling the phone vibrate again. He looked once more, a text message. He'd check it later.

"If you want the ATM receipts of all of the bank customers, I'm sorry, but I can't do that. Dubai has privacy laws, and something like that would be in direct violation of those laws – well, and I might add - I could lose my job," Rowley said, twiddling his thumbs.

"What about this idea Mister Rowley? Your bank is the correspondent for an account holder that we're very interested in. A Mister Leonid Petrov," Bryan said, opening he door for discourse. Shannon braced herself for verbal fireworks.

"Technically, no longer an account holder at the bank, as I understand Mister Petrov has met with a very untimely end."

"That's very true, but he was a suspect in possible terrorists related activities. We believe that an investigation into his account activity may yield important clues and lead to the capture of other conspirators. I'm here to make a request for copies of his account statements." Bryan couldn't have put it any more succinctly. He waited for Rowley's response. Shannon held he breath.

"Captain Craig, if you will excuse me for just a few moments. Let me check on that matter for you," Rowley said standing up from the table then abruptly leaving the conference room. Bryan and Shannon looked at each other with mutual surprise.

"Interesting, what's he up to?" Bryan asked Kevin, who appeared to be equally stupefied.

"I have no earthly idea."

Bryan used Rowley's absence as an opportunity to check Gil's message. Just three words on the subject line that read: Falcon Holdings Corp. He opened it and quickly read the text, showing it to Shannon after he finished.

```
B — Falcon Holdings Corp. account at
B of D. Big outflows and inflows.
Many shareholders. Don't know who
they are. Maybe the Russian — don't
know. Good luck :)
G
```

Rowley returned to the conference room within ten minutes. Again, he was fighting for breath. Bryan was ready for him but throttled back his eagerness.

"I apologize to everyone here," Rowley said dropping down in the conference chair.

"Here you are Captain Craig," Rowley said, sliding a CD-ROM in a case across the table to Bryan. The case read "Leonid Petrov" written on masking tape across the cover.

"What's this?" Bryan asked.

"It's what you asked for."

"This is Petrov's account information?"

"Everything. In fact two accounts. The passwords are written inside the cover – you can review his accounts online."

"Is that a fact?" Bryan said, as he opened up the case. Rowley wasn't joking, there they were.

"I thought your privacy laws prevented divulging the account information?" Shannon asked.

"What I said before is absolutely correct. For someone that's alive with an active account, or an account holder that has passed away and has a joint account, or tenants in common as you have in the United States. In fact the law also applies to a client of the bank with a living heir. Mister Petrov falls under none of those categories," Rowley said, explaining the ambiguity of the banking rules.

"So if he had a living relative, we wouldn't have that disc," Shannon confirmed.

"Even if he was suspected of possible criminal activity?" Kevin asked.

"Suspected alone won't matter. We'd need an international court order to get the account information without local jurisdictional cooperation," Bryan said.

"You know your international law, don't you Captain Craig," Rowley responded.

"I know a little something. But this disc may prove to be helpful. Thank you," Bryan said.

"You're very welcome – now is there anything else I can do for you before I get back to the business of the bank?" Rowley asked, smugly interlocking his hands.

"Tell me about Falcon Holdings Corp," Bryan said, springing the surprise.

Initially stung, Rowley quickly regained his composure. "Unfortunately, we have come to the fork in the road Captain Craig. The issue of privacy again," he said adamantly.

"Well, to do all of this Dubai needs support of the Great Britain and the U.S.," Bryan said, waving his hand at the hologram. "But we're just a little concerned about money flows recently - especially to your bank through Falcon Holdings Corp – immediately before and after the bombings."

Rowley looked at Kevin. "Falcon Holdings Corp is a client of the bank, but that's all I can share. The privacy laws prevent divulging anymore information," he said.

"Yeah, I know all about the privacy laws. You've informed me already. Do you know the principals of the account? That should be fair game?" Bryan asked.

Fidgeting, Rowley opened his hands. "The structure of the account is a limited partnership with many partners. The UAE doesn't disclose individual partners on public records."

"And the General Partner?" Bryan asked.

"There's no disclosed general partner for this group either."

"What did Leonid Petrov have to do with this group or your bank besides being an account holder?" Bryan asked.

Rowley feigned a grimaced smile. "What do you mean?" His expression changed to that of a kid caught in a lie. His sweat showed through his shirt.

"Exactly what I asked. Was he involved with Falcon Holdings or not? And before you answer remember who's providing the muscle for your development project." Bryan's tone had raised a notch as he fixed his sights on the man from Newcastle.

"I think he's made it kind of clear Bryan. They can't reveal that, or rather they don't know who's involved," Kevin said, sensing the beginning of "Bad Cop" of the "Good Cop – Bad Cop" game.

"You must know something Mister Rowley; I mean he splattered himself within view of your office. Don't play stupid with me, and don't underestimate our determination to find out who was behind the bombings last week," Bryan said, feeling the time to lean hard was now.

"Hey hold on there Bryan," Kevin interjected. "Robert here is just working for the bank. I think we should probably…"

Bryan broke in impatiently. "How about getting to the bottom of international money laundering, conspiring to cover up fraud, and the other shenanigans that the Bank of Dubai may have going on?" Bryan said, testing more hardball tactics.

"Mister Rowley, we're not accusing the bank of being complicit with the attacks or financing terrorism, but we need to look at every suspicious customer," Shannon offered, doing her best good cop.

"And how long do you think you would last Mister Rowley? Petrov was working for someone associated with this bank - I'm convinced of that. Look what happened to him." He was still playing bad cop, but now his anger was starting to well up inside. The jpeg of Danny Perkins had resurfaced in his memory, fueling his commitment to nail the bad guys to the wall. Rowley sat still but was visibly shaken as he nervously looked at Kevin for something; bail, some kind of coaching.

Kevin stood up. "I think we are done here for the time being Robert. We'll get back to you. Let's go Bryan," he said while grabbing Bryan's elbow to leave.

Bryan shook him off. He pointed his finger at the banker. "Think about this as you look out at the view from your office window on the eightieth floor Mister Rowley - and mark my words, I'm going to get to the bottom of this, and there isn't a damn thing that you, the bank, or anyone that you work for can do to stop me. Thank you for the coffee and the tour," Bryan stood up, signaling to Shannon.

The drive back was solemn. Passing the protest area, they noticed the demonstrators had dispersed for the most part, a few stragglers collecting protest signs. Kevin finally chimed in with a synopsis of the meeting. "Interesting good cop, bad cop. What prompted the questions about Falcon Holdings Corp?" he asked.

"Just say a little birdie told me. Do you know something about them?" Replied Bryan.

"They're a major player here - very mysterious, an international consortium. Identities secretive, unless there's a reason for some sort of publicity," Kevin said.

"I suppose that you don't know who the shareholders are either?" Shannon asked.

"Oh I know of a few, and you'll get a chance to see them later today."

"And where will we be seeing these shareholders?" Bryan asked curiously.

"If my information is accurate from the embassy, at least four shareholders as well as Rowley will be at the racetrack this afternoon," Kevin said, taking a drink of the cold hotel coffee. "I'm taking you to a camel race."

"You must be joking," Shannon said. "A camel race?"

Bryan thought for a moment before adding, "It'll be similar to Metropolis – just you wait and see," he told her.

CHAPTER 14

JUNE 6, 2008

DUBAI

WITH EACH PLODDING STEP, amber hooves pushed up fine plumes of brown dust from scorching sand, into the hot afternoon air. Long lashes drooped like blinds over giant eyes, protecting their vision from dust storms. The procession of camels was colorful to say the least. There were fifteen, all *Dromedary*, each having just a single hump. The camels however, were not the long distance carriers of the Bedouin, ships of the desert, legendary for their ability to cross the Arabian Desert in caravans without water. Certainly these fifteen had evolved like all camels, to survive for weeks on end without drinking water or for more than a month without eating. Nature's design made these particular fifteen camels no different from any other, but man's design made them quite unique.

Camels evolved to manage dehydration, steaming sand, and blistering sun better than any mammal ever. The harsh conditions of the desert would overcome a man in no more than a day, two at the very most, but for the camel, no problem. Long legs keeps its body high above the hot sand; a smooth tan coat reflects the oppressive heat of the sun; uniquely shaped red blood cells allows it to keep blood flowing, even after the animal is dehydrated; they can withstand large fluctuations in body temperature, reaching over 106°F without ever breaking a sweat; and it can saturate itself with water beyond the point of any other land mammal due to an unusual osmotic process. The camels in the procession possessed all the characteristics that nature and evolution endeared to them, that was true, including the large eyes and long eyelashes, mouths in constant motion, seemingly always preparing to spit. But these camels would never cross great distances over the scorching desert sand as mere pack animals. They cost more than a million dollars each and were bred for speed, for racing.

The camels weren't just saddled, they were decorated and on display. Each camel and jockey was uniquely and brilliantly colored with gold and red reins, orange and blue, and many other variations. Then there were the camel jockeys. All colors aside, the riders of these ships of the desert were unlike any jockeys the world had ever seen. Robots spirited the camels around the track.

"I've never seen anything quite like these things. Absolutely life-like," Shannon exclaimed.

"Robotic camel jockeys, they were developed by a Swiss company, now everyone's tryin to get into the action. They cost around ten grand each," Bryan explained.

The robots weighed thirty-five pounds, stood two feet tall and were powered by a four hundred megahertz processor. Inside the plastic and aluminum body were shock absorbers to dampen the ride of a camel doing twenty-five miles per hour, plus a box containing a soundboard and microcontrollers. Operators could follow the race in SUVs using a joystick and remote control to manipulate the robotic jockey's arms. The robot could hit the camel with a whip, tighten the reins, even sound effects were programmed for phrases of encouragement blasted from a speaker inside its body. The robots had childlike faces and were designed to be as lifelike as possible so the camels acquiesced to their presence.

"Interesting event that you brought us to Kevin," Bryan said.

"This is utterly fascinating, I think," Shannon added, thrilled at the spectacle.

"I thought you should get a taste of some of the local racing festivities Doc. You know - a little culture and take in a cocktail while you're at it," Kevin said with his usual chuckle, arms and shoulders bouncing up and down.

The sixteen-kilometer racetrack was built on the southeast outskirts of the city. The standard in Dubai had become "design and build it to be the best in the world." The standard bar was being raised higher and again higher. The newest racetrack in the UAE measured up to that standard. The track was state-of-the-art, the camel racetrack of camel racetracks, rivaling the best of any type of arena, stadium, or track in the world, a lavish place with over-the-top personal attention. Built for five thousand spectators, the modern air-conditioned stadium and grandstand facility, with private boxes and a five star restaurant for members. More people can watch. More expatriates betting in private boxes equated to more boxes. Camel racing was catching on. For the nouveau riche of Dubai it was the sport "du jour." En vogue. *Children weren't the jockeys.*

"There's our guy," Kevin said, handing the pint-size binoculars to Bryan.

"Robert Rowley, how nice," Bryan said.

The banker was at the far end of the indoor stadium facility, standing outside a private box speaking with Arab men dressed traditionally in white thaubs and schumaggs.

"Who are the four locals that Rowley's blabbin with?" Bryan asked. They appeared to be engaged in casual pleasantries, discussing aspects of the stadium's design. Bryan likened Rowley to a museum tour guide, his audience turning their heads with each sweep of his hand. Three of the men looked vaguely familiar, even under the head garment, one in particular. The other he didn't recognize.

Kevin took the binoculars and fine-tuned the focus. "Well, let's see here. The two big guys are cousins of the Sheikh. The little guy I don't know. And the medium size guy is the Governor of Bank of Dubai," Kevin said.

"It seems like I've seen the smaller man somewhere before." Bryan asked, still trying to place the one Arab. "Where are the guests of honor?"

Kevin checked his watch. "They should be arriving any minute."

The DJ modified camera phone pulled from his pocket was now in Bryan's hand and ready to go. Although cameras were no longer banned at camel races since the adoption of robotic jockeys, Bryan didn't want to be too obvious. The phone design would conceal his real intention of recording quality digital images of Rowley and his companions. DJ converted the small phone, the same size of an iPhone, into one of the most sophisticated digital cameras in the world with an amazing ten times zoom ratio. Bryan was facing the track ninety degrees off target, zooming in on the Brit's bearded face. Rowley's image appeared on the LED display. To a casual observer, Bryan was dialing numbers on the keypad. Once the image was captured, Bryan sent the digital image attached to an Email for FaceScan.

"Smile for me Mister Rowley," Bryan said as he snapped several of the banker. "Looks like he's really enjoying this event." Rowley was nearly giddy as he entertained the Arab businessmen.

"The Bank of Dubai wouldn't have the approval for any development without the Sheikh's blessing or the blessings of family members - especially a deal this big," Kevin said as he panned the binoculars along the track. "Of course they stand to make tens of billions," he added with a hint of jealousy.

Bryan zoomed in on the smaller Arab man. Younger than the others, he was in his late twenties or early thirties and had a very neatly groomed moustache and goatee. Although wearing sunglasses, their small size didn't obscure much of his face; only his eyes were hidden. Bryan thought he had enough features to capture a descent image for FaceScan. The small camera whirled away, taking a dozen shots. The man turned, Bryan clicked several more, ensuring there were plenty of angles for FaceScan's nodal computations. As if on cue, he removed his sunglasses. Bryan took more. *Who the hell is he?*

Commotion at the bottom of the escalator grabbed the attention of most in the vicinity. "What do we have here?" Bryans said holding the viewfinder of the camera over a railing. "Take a look at the main entrance."

Murmurs came from a small crowd that had formed in the lobby, increasing in their intensity until a minor commotion. Armed security lined the doorway from outside. At the center of the fuss were four American businessmen, leaders in industrial construction, real estate development, software, and telecommunications. They were attention getters as they paraded inside towards escalators. Each was considered to be among the select group of the world's multi-billionaires. The real estate mogul had reached a quasi celebrity status from his many self-promoting appearances on commercial television. Five Arab men in traditional dress and two western diplomats accompanied the billionaires along with a number of aides, and several wired bodyguards. Bryan recognized the diplomats. He pointed them out to Shannon.

"The tall, slender guy's an American, Rodgers Christopher - career foreign services, kind of a real policy wonk, currently posted in the UAE. He's our host here in Dubai," Bryan said.

"The Consul General," Shannon confirmed.

"That's right. He's loaning us some office space while we're in town," Bryan said.

"I've met him before - at a State Department event last year. He'd been the Director for Middle East Development and no doubt very interested in U.S. business development in Dubai," Shannon added.

"You're up ta speed on him alright," Bryan said, wondering if she also knew he was a real prick.

Bryan really didn't care for him, and when he was around the diplomat, he had a hard time containing his irritation. Sometimes it showed. Christopher was often vaunt, known for his haughty, arrogant style of diplomacy. The second diplomat Bryan knew as well, Edward Basingstoke, the genial British Consul General. Both diplomats were seasoned veterans of the Arab peninsula and fluent in Arabic, Farsi, and French, both had a lot at stake in Dubai.

The collection of visitors rode up the escalators, all visibly impressed at the grandeur of the stadium, paying particular attention to the two hundred thousand gallon aquarium that arched over their heads, forming a tunnel for the spectators to ascend and descend through. Built with four-inch thick Plexiglas, the aquarium was filled with thousands of tropical fish, including sharks, rays, and scores of other species. A waterfall staircased between the up and down sides as a divider, a hundred fountains spouting streams of water in three-foot arcs. The group joined Rowley and the four Arab men, proceeding into the Bank of Dubai's private box. The furor over the grand entrance dissipated after the door to the box closed.

"I'd like to have an idea what they're discussing in there," Bryan said.

"Do you think Rowley's playing both sides?" Shannon asked.

"He's a banker, just don't know how greedy yet," Bryan said.

The associations Rowley kept that day impressed Bryan. The banker was a big deal in the business circles of Dubai. No disputing that, he thought. The Burj al Baaz project and its mini-city community were second to none in terms of size and expense, in spite of the low costs of labor. Bryan couldn't imagine what the price tag would be if a similar project where attempted in the States. Chances of a breaking ground would be slim, let alone a completion, costs would be too exorbitant, particularly labor.

Noticing that the seats were filling with spectators, Bryan checked the time. "It's 4:25, the race starts in five minutes. Let's move over to the viewing area by the restaurant," Bryan said, also wanting to see the Bank of Dubai group through the front of the private box. Reaching the restaurant, he realized the box's glass front was tinted. It was impossible to see inside. With the race getting ready to get start, Bryan decided instead to just sit back and watch the robots and their rides.

Race distances varied between four to ten kilometers and could include anywhere from fifteen to seventy camels, possibly more. The running that day was a challenge between just several owners. Bryan and Shannon watched as the camels were led into the starting gate. After a large, multi-strand barrier was lifted, the ten-kilometer race was under way.

"And they're off," Kevin said mimicking a horse race announcer.

"Look at them go," Shannon said. "This is so funny looking. How fast are these guys?" She asked, bemused at the site of the robots precariously bouncing along on top of the camels.

"About twenty-five miles an hour," Kevin said.

"So this is a ten kilometer race – that's about fifteen-minutes," Shannon said after a quick calculation. "I'm betting on number five, what about you Bryan?" she added with a laugh.

He smiled, replying, "You can be certain they're betting in that box." Gambling was illegal by Islamic law, but of course only public betting. Hundreds of thousands, perhaps even millions were being wagered in the private boxes for just this one race alone. Bryan couldn't fathom what the total of the bets must have been.

"You got that right, and drinkin' – probably some of the Arabs too, especially when behind closed doors," Kevin said.

"Camel racing had been part of the culture of the region for centuries. Ships of the desert they call them. It's no longer just a source of transportation anymore," Kevin explained as he looked for a good table. "How 'bout this one?" They sat down with a good view of the finish.

"How long has Rowley been dealing with the U.S. businessmen?" Shannon asked Kevin as they settled down at the table.

"Recently, but all are owners in the tower. With them in Baazland, the money will pour in from now on. It'll seal the deal, so ta speak," Kevin explained.

Bryan could see several advantages for the developers to have the wealthy Americans invest. Future investors wouldn't have a perception of Dubai posing any significant risk, even though it was dead center of the Muslim world. Unrest and terrorism hadn't spilled over into the UAE. In fact several other countries besides the UAE, including Bahrain, Oman, Saudi Arabia, and Kuwait, had remained more or less free of violence. Only Saudi Arabia had sporadic turbulence during the last five years.

The United States, on the other hand, now seemed to be in the sights of the terrorists, all non-military targets. The randomness and the non-tactical value of shopping centers had an unnerving effect on people in general and businessmen in particular. Bryan could see why Dubai presented a very attractive alternative to the United States for big business, big profits.

"What did you say that the Burj al Baaz cost to build again Kevin?"

"I believe that it was just under one billion."

"That's one billion over four years. And they used twenty five hundred Pakistanis on average twenty four seven for those four years."

"Sounds about right Bry."

'Shannon, help me with the math on that, would you?" Bryan asked.

Shannon pulled out her Blackberry to use the calculator. "That eighty-seven, call it eighty eight million man hours. And you said the laborers are paid on average about forty-one cents an hour. So that's thirty six million dollars in labor costs for a billion dollar project," Shannon reported.

"That seems pretty good to me," Kevin said with a nod and his usual thumb's up.

Bryan began to wonder about Kev's ethics. "Do you have any idea what the labor costs would be if the project was done in the

States?"

"Lay it on me," Kevin said, flipping through the restaurant's menu, seemingly distracted from the subject.

"I'll tell you, how about this - in the U.S. unskilled labor gets paid twelve dollars an hour for forty hours of work, then they get paid time and a half beyond that. But let's say that they're paid exactly the way it's done here, without the time and a half. Shannon, what's that work out to?"

"The developer would spend over a billion dollars at the bare minimum on labor alone," Shannon said.

"That's one billion versus thirty six million? I'd say that's nine hundred and sixty-four million reasons the top American real estate developer is in that box sucking it up with the locals," Bryan said.

"Well it sounds like that's just good business to me," Kevin said, waving at a waiter.

"Is this guy for real?" Bryan thought. *Was Kevin ignoring the moral conundrum of the construction business in the UAE?*

"Well, unlike illegal aliens that might end up at a work site in the States, these Pakistani's won't be rounded up and deported, unless of course they protest shitty conditions or missing paychecks," Bryan said.

"And there's no chance an employer will be heavily fined either, let alone face possible jail time for getting caught hiring illegal aliens, or paying less than minimum wage," Shannon pointed out.

"Well, this is the way I look at it – it's a win-win. American companies have a friendly, progressive Muslim country to come into and develop right alongside our Arab buddies - and make a lot of cabbage in the process too. Dubai pays the U.S. and Britain for technology to build the greatest city that's ever been built," Kevin said, rubbing his thumb and forefinger together to emphasize the dollar value of the arrangement.

"Just my point," Shannon quipped sarcastically. They'd ventured onto her turf. She was the expert.

"What's your beef anyway, Doc? These deals here help the economy back home. Companies are lining up for these lucrative deals. Do you want the French, or the Russians, maybe even Chinese in here instead? Besides, with the new waves of terrorism like last week, U.S. companies are nervous – Dubai, on the other hand, looks sweet. I don't know about the Brits, but havin a friend like Dubai is important for American interests," Kevin scoffed.

Of the volumes of dribble that came out of the C.I.A man's mouth, Bryan thought the last statement was a salient one. Great Britain and the U.S. both needed friends in the Muslim world, that was a given. And certainly Dubai was one of the few true Muslim friends the U.S. had in the Middle East. Saudi Arabia, Bahrain, Qatar, Kuwait, and Oman were friends, but uneasy ones. Getting too chummy with the U.S. could lead to reprisals from fanatics, violence, and insurgency. It often did.

"Jihadists are growing in number and threatening the current rule of any progressive Muslim country. Especially those that are friends with the West," Shannon reminded them. "Dubai is taking a leadership role, but always looking over its shoulder."

"Which is the reason so many leaders of the progressive states talk out of both sides of their mouths," Bryan quipped.

"The problem stems from the riches of the oil-based Muslim countries," Shannon said. It was apparent to Shannon that wealth, or lack of it was at the root of the problem. She added, "In progressive, less populated countries such as Kuwait, that are rich from fossil fuels, the wealth is spread out among the entire nation, at least in the form of a stipend of some sort."

"The same could be said of Dubai and the UAE," Kevin countered.

"That's true, but UAE is not demonstrating aggressiveness to other Muslim countries. But in countries that are filled with tens of millions of impoverished people – people feeling oppressed by rulers friendly to the U.S., the Jihad movement is on the march," Shannon asserted.

Bryan knew exactly what countries Shannon was referring to, non-theocracies, generally Sunni. Pakistan came to mind. Islamic extremists had planted the seed for Muslims of the world to expel the infidels, and take back land they believed was rightly theirs. The extremists were operating based upon an ideology and *Sharia*, the Islamic law, frozen in the middle ages. The goals of the new Jihad were to liberate lands from the West, unify their borders, and reestablish the *Caliphate*, an older form of Islamic beliefs born out of the seventh century, a strict and total adherence to Sharia. If possible, establish universal theocratic governments and ultimately, total destruction of the United States.

Shannon explained that, "A caliphate would establish the civil and religious leader, the head of the Muslim community as well as the representative of Allah on the earth. Islamic extremists believe that a caliph would rise up and unite the entire Muslim world with the boundaries predicated on those at the height of the original Islamic Caliphate."

"Talk about an ambitious plan," Kevin said.

"It's complex, yet simple at the same time, complex in fighting the movement, yet simple to understand the ultimate goal. If the land was Islamic before, it must be Islamic again." She reminded them of the scope of the ancient Muslim Empire. "It's massive, and the liberation of that land is the goal of the new Jihadists. Even Spain and parts of France that were ancient Islamic territory would need to be liberated and unified," she said.

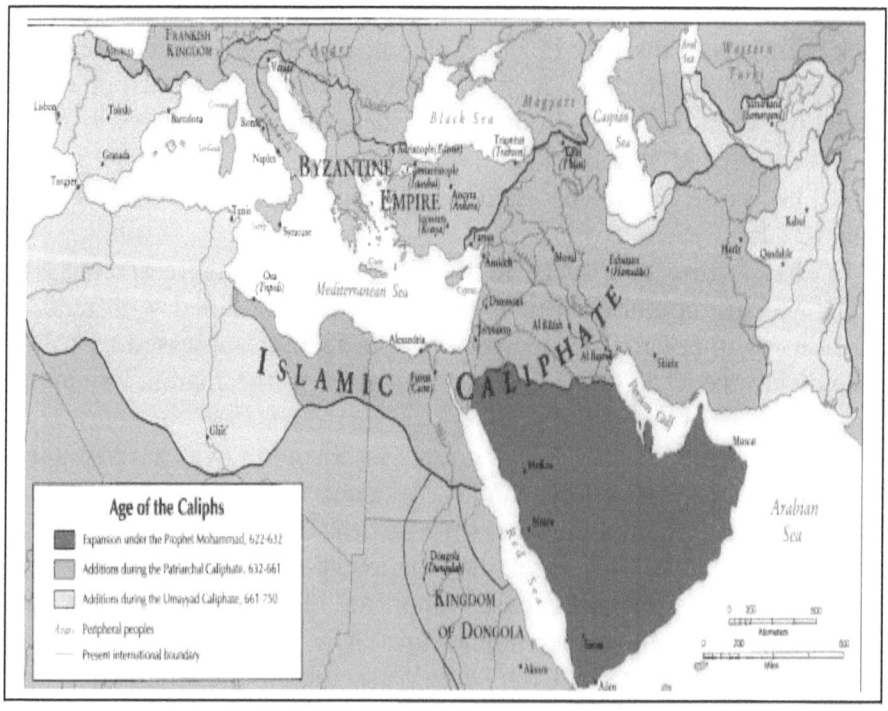

Islamic Empire Caliphate (PD)

Shannon focused most of her studies on understanding the goals of the extremists, the Jihadists, who seemed to operate outside the bounds of the Quran, which was only the start of getting to the bottom of the Memorial Day attacks. Her contribution. She saw the need to grasp what motivated the suicide bombers to blow themselves up in the name of Islam. The money trail is what brought Bryan to Dubai, but he believed a broader perspective had to be kept in mind to solve the crime and nail the conspirators.

"I understand the importance of Dubai as a buffer Kevin. But at what cost to the Pakistanis - the ones that have come here to toil under these extreme-working conditions? Isn't that just another example of 'Robbing Peter to pay Paul?' Aren't we just making enemies to make friends?" Shannon lectured.

"Valid perhaps Doc. But like I said before – if we don't profit from the opportunities, then someone else will. Besides we owe it to the Sheikh after screwing Dubai over on the Port deals a couple of years ago."

Bryan wasn't surprised the subject of the Port fiasco was broached. "I completely get the need to demonstrate good faith as part of our mission. Like cozying up to Dubai on deals such as Baazland - selling technology – those kinds of things, they can go a along way, absolutely. But how about not alienating a whole shit load of other people in the process? You know - do the deals so that they're fair for everyone involved. Kind of like these robot-jockeys," Bryan said.

"That's the attitude Bry. Just like the camel jocks. Now you're starting to get it."

The camels were coming into view from the far turn, approaching the front of the stadium. Just in time as far as Bryan was concerned. He'd had it.

"I've got a meeting with this journalist tonight, you should be there. Oh, maybe you know him, Dylan Sizemore – the Australian news guy that works for CNN," Kevin stated.

"Rings a bell. What's he got?" Bryan said, hiding the relationship.

"Don't know the details, but it has to do with rumors of money launderin' and Swiss banks. We'll soon find out."

"Swiss bank?" Bryan asked, wondering where that came from. He'd check on the validity of the lead with Gil.

"Could be the answer you're lookin for. Maybe even a slam dunk."

"Slam dunk," huh, Bryan thought, cynical over Kevin's choice of words. CIA guys really seemed to love those two words.

"Look, here comes number five," Shannon exclaimed, tugging on Bryan's sleeve. "He's in the lead."

Bryan looked at Shannon dismayed. "You can't really be getting into this," he said sarcastically.

"Oh this is great – look at them go," Shannon replied excitedly.

Number five, with blue colors, was moving out in front of eight, predominately red. "Come on number five, come on five – he's gonna do it. Yes!" Shannon yelled throwing a victorious fist in the air as number five crossed the line first.

CHAPTER 15

JUNE 6, 2008

WASHINGTON, D.C.

TAYLOR P. COX WAS FURIOUS after exiting the closed-door hearing. A Virginian, the fifty-two year old junior Senator was coming up for re-election in the fall. He was popular, unyielding in his advocacy of tough Homeland Security policies and led in the polls by twenty percent over his nearest challenger. A lawyer, he served in the JAG Corps as a reservist during the Gulf War and had a successful career in private practice. He ran for Congress from the Richmond district where he'd grown up, and won. After eight years as a congressman, he jumped into a hotly contested race for the Senate against a four-term incumbent. Campaigning invigorated him; he never shied away from it, in fact he thrived on it. Terrorism and Homeland Security were his forte and he painted his opponent as weak, unsure, waffling. He won that race and was re-elected six years later.

He might not have been known necessarily by name until recently, but his face was distinctive, somehow obviously familiar. He was the prototype of the steely politician, the no-nonsense senator, the assured lawmaker, stentorian leader, Cox looked out of place without his patented pin-stripe suit and power tie. With silvery hair, perfectly trimmed mustache, he swaggered with nonplussed bearing by design, yet aggressive air when it was called for; a take-charge manner that reminded people of the "Obi-wan Kenobi" character from the classic "Star Wars" series. His record was consistent; he was for the Patriot Act, for the Terrorist Surveillance Act, and against a Supreme Court decision that ultimately resulted in the release of more than one hundred Gitmo detainees. He believed that the Court's decision would be looked upon with profound regret one day. He was the newest member of the Senate Select Committee on Intelligence, and on this day during the hearing, his dire prediction had actually come true. The first suicide bomber identified had been a released Gitmo detainee.

Two years before in a vote with many ramifications, the highest Court had decided the President overstepped his authority in conducting the War on Terrorism. The Court ruled the President could not impose Military Tribunals on suspected Al-Qaeda being held at the controversial military detention facility. The detainees lacked the sufficient protections as mandated by the Geneva Convention and by the Code of Military Justice. They were in effect, prisoners of war. Each was a POW by the court's definition. And prisoners of war had the right to see all evidence against them and would also be able to attend all hearings concerning their case, thus possibly compromising secret anti-terrorism operations.

Cox believed the decision was a terrible one. Politics were a sad but necessary reality, he knew that all too well. But those that had irresponsibly put the country in this position had to be purged one way or another and the sooner the better, he believed. Senator Cox was convinced that the preservation of the American way was at stake.

Taylor Cox would pound the pine in session at times, saying, "Keeping information concerning sensitive operations classified is essential for effective conduct of the war against the militant Jihadists. Allowing lawyers for the detainee's access to classified intelligence would jeopardize operative's lives and relations with allies in the war on terror." He would steam over the very thought. "It's a farcical notion," he'd say.

A legislative remedy to keep suspected terrorists behind bars was ultimately passed, but not before a number of detainees had been released to their respective countries of origin where they quickly disappeared. The damage was done. His committee had just been advised that Abdul-Malik was the bomber in London.

"I can't believe that this lunatic was ever released. Look at the evidence. He'd been captured in Afghanistan, for Christ sakes. What was he doing there? I don't believe it was vacation – plus we had video evidence of him training at a camp," Cox fumed at fellow lawmakers. "We had him once - held in Cuba. Then he gets released only to return as a student from Spain to kill a bunch of innocent people. We should've held him at a black site some place, kept him as a ghost prisoner." The Senator was pissed off.

"We didn't have anything on him then Senator. The tapes hadn't been found yet from the camps showing him there," Tom Billings, his legislative aide explained. "And his lawyers had filed a motion for a writ of habeas corpus. Had that been granted, the military would either have to release him or show the evidence."

"I told them over and over that they needed to put some pressure on the court," he said to Billings as he walked into his office. "We have fifteen Senators on just this Intelligence committee alone that knew about this guy, and half of them are going to be scrambling for damage control. Don't forget about the White House; this will put their enemies right in the middle of their sights. They won't wait for a story to get leaked." He picked up his Titleist putter leaning against his desk, an old habit when he was fuming.

Confident the revelation would be leaked sooner rather than later, he needed to formulate a quick action plan. The other side of the aisle would be clearly embarrassed, especially those seeking re-election that had agreed with the court's decision. Liberals leaning further towards rights and freedoms, rather than security and safety were the most vulnerable. A pre-emptive strike on the part of the White House would destroy the other side's chances to circle the wagons. Policies of the Administration regarding the Military Commissions Act and those that supported it would be affirmed, and may even cement the nomination of the party's Presidential candidate early, if not clinch the actual fall election in the end.

"I'm afraid they didn't get a chance to posture," Billings said.

"What?"

"Look at the TV," the aide said, pointing at the television on the office credenza. A reporter was broadcasting live from Dubai.

"Un-mute that," the Senator demanded. The aide did so, dropping the remote on the Senator's desk. Cox listened to what the reporter had to say.

"Again, we have breaking news from Dubai. Authorities have identified at least one of the suicide bombers responsible for last week's attacks on Memorial Day. With us from Dubai is CNN's Dylan Sizemore. Dylan?"

"Thank you Tom. That's correct. Less than an hour ago we received information from a top official that reported a former detainee held at the notorious Guantanamo Bay facility was identified as the terrorist suicide bomber responsible for the attack in London. Officials from Dubai were instrumental in aiding in the investigation. The bomber has been identified as Abdul-Malik, a British citizen of Pakistani descent. Malik was associated with a known Russian weapons dealer..."

Senator Cox pushed the record button on the remote control and turned the volume down. "Who the hell leaked this? Dylan Sizemore knew about this before our committee," Cox said to his aide. "Gina, have Lieutenant Commander Johns come in here," he ordered his secretary.

"He appears to be fingering Pakistan," Billings said referring to Dylan's naming the bomber as a Paki.

"Fingering them and giving us the finger. He doesn't necessarily just blame Pakistan. He did throw in two other friends of ours too, the Lion and the Bear." He thought for a moment and added, "We need to get to the bottom of this fast. Check our sources at the White House, State Department, hell everyone. I want to know who knows what. I smell a rat with this one - maybe someone from the E-ring at the Pentagon, possibly a friend of yours commander," he said as Johns entered the office and Billings fielded a phone call on his cell.

"Senator, it's Jim Simons," Billings said, putting the phone on mute.

"Crap – tell him I'll call him later," the Senator said. "Simons and his evangelical hoard need to wait. I can't take lectures from the religious right about the millions of fanatical Islamist Nazis at this point."

"Islamic fascists sir," Billings corrected.

"Just splittin hairs, isn't it," Cox said, leaning on his desk, looking at a picture of his family, his wife and two teenage boys. He was leery of having a conversation with any Christian organization until he got to the bottom of things.

"Before we address our religious constituency," he began slowly, quickly firing up with intensity, " I want to make damn sure we known who we're dealing with. I don't want to listen to Simons – you know, telling me over and over again about all the Islamic rallies here and in the UK, calling for death to America and Great Britain. I already fuckin' know about it – everybody does – it's all over Arab television and now here on cable. God damn it – just flip on fuckin' Al Jazeerah News – I think it's on channel thirty eight." Cox picked up the remote control from the desk and theatrically began flipping channels.

"Those jackasses takin' advantage of obvious freedoms of speech are known entities. They put their bearded faces on TV for Christ's sake. Where's the surprise? What I want to do is nail the sons of bitches to the wall. Virginians, all believers of free speech mind you, don't want a bunch of hate mongers, who are callin for the destruction of the United States, holdin rallies on our soil."

"Sir, what about the report from DNI," Lieutenant Commander Johns said, referring to paper sent to the committee addressing the need for more proactive measures against suspected terrorists organizations and nations supporting them.

"The report from the DNI, huh – shut the fuckin' door Tom," the Senator said, corralling his long-term aide Tom Billings and his military aide, Lieutenant Commander Rick Johns.

"You guys ready?" the Senator said to his two advisors.

"Sir?" the Lieutenant Commander said, unsure what the Senator was asking. After many years with Cox, Tom Billings was used to the Senator's occasional flamboyant ranting. The Navy man wasn't.

"Get down here with me and pray," Cox said, dropping to his knees on a Persian carpet in the office. Billings, ready for theatrics, stood still as the Navy officer racked his brain.

"Get down here, damn it – I mean that's our only choice, right? Oh, I'm sorry, maybe the fuckin' carpet's pointin' the wrong way," he said, standing up, licking his thumb and holding it out as a compass.

"Which way to Mecca?" Cox asked, grabbing the carpet as if to turn it. "Aren't you guys gonna join me, or what?"

"Sir, let's call a meeting with the DNI, see what he says," the senior aide said. The DNI correctly suspected that the recommendations would get bogged down in a quagmire of partisan politics. It was rumored that the DNI used non-appropriated funds to create a special team to carry out exactly what he recommended in his report. Johns was hand picked by the Senator because he was close to the DNI.

"Good thinking Tom – glad you're here for me," Cox said, bemused at the obvious. "Let's hear from the Navy guy," the Senator said, putting the junior officer on the spot. "You're an Academy guy, right – what's your idea?"

The military aide's brain went into overdrive. He was on the hot seat but had been there before. Just six months on the Senator's staff, he'd been tested virtually every day. Cox depended on him. "Have Tom call DCIA for a meeting and then cancel later in the day – tell them it's not necessary. Tell Homeland that you've got a meeting with the DNI to discuss the bombings," Lieutenant Commander Johns said, not sure where he was going with his idea.

"Then what?" Cox asked

"One last call," Johns said, ready to pull the rabbit out of the hat. "Call the DNI's office – say you want to talk about Greek mythology."

Cox realized the devious logic, and immediately understood why the Navy man had been his choice as a military aide. Just seven years before, as a Lieutenant, John's had been Admiral Barnes' aide when Barnes was commanding a Task Force. It was a good plan.

"They'll cross check each other, both knowing I cancelled the meetings. But kept one with the Jack Rabbit Barnes. We'll pressure them into bringing us in the loop," Cox said.

"Exactly sir," the Navy aide said, now feeling the warmth.

"What've we got to lose? Let's try it."

One of the things that caught the Senator's attention was the fact that the suicide bomber was Pakistani. Pakistan was a fair-weather friend of the United States, and the Senator believed that in the past they had helped a great deal in rounding up Al-Qaeda hiding throughout their rugged country, but fell short with the Taliban. Cities such as Karachi and Islamabad were overcrowded and terrorists could easily blend into the population, as well as easily come and go across the border with Afghanistan. However, Pakistan officials had stepped up to the plate for the U.S. for the most part.

Pakistani intelligence had played crucial roles in nabbing a number of the top planners of Al-Qaeda, and the Senator was happy that Pakistan was playing ball. The Government of Pakistan had also done the U.S. a big favor by turning a blind eye to the Special Ops missions that routinely went over the Afghan border into northern Pakistan chasing Taliban that the Pakistanis wouldn't touch. The officials who'd condoned those missions did so at great political and personal risk and would immediately be ousted at the very least if their complicity were made public. Many in Pakistan had a disdain for the United States. The leadership there was under constant threat of assassination by radicals. The Senator reasoned that there was something very important about the Pakistani connection to the bombings.

Senator Cox had an in depth knowledge of Pakistan and the region. He firmly believed it was vital to have a complete picture, because without understanding the history and the culture, decisions where subject to chance. "Might as well throw darts at a board," the Senator said. "Cause if you know what the hell your talkin about, gross missteps are gonna be made in foreign policy and intelligence matters, severely handicapping us in the war on terror."

The Islamic Republic of Pakistan as a nation was very young, but as a civilization, the people there had a past as rich and diverse as any the world had seen. The south Asian country was the size of the states of California, Oregon, and Washington combined. Split by the Indus River, it had its beginnings near the top of the world in the mountains of Tibet and ended in a fertile delta at the Arabian Sea.

The first evidence of man in a region that would one day become modern Pakistan came with the discovery of two hundred thousand year old stone tools in the Punjab province. One of mankind's earliest cultures, the Mehrgarh, built farming settlements in the Indus valley nine thousand years ago. They grew wheat and raised livestock such as goat and cattle. Invaders would eventually discover this place and attempt to add it to their empires. Over the centuries the armies of ancient Persia, Alexander the Great, the Huns, the Afghans, the Turks, Mongolia, Arabs, and finally Britain would all occupy the land. Each would leave its own indelible mark woven into the fabric of the modern Pakistani culture, but the two most profound influences came from the Islamic and British Empires.

The British East India Company had established trade rights granted by Queen Elizabeth I with India. As business boomed, the company expanded in the subcontinent, ultimately monopolizing on most trade. What had been a joint stock company engaged in commercial trade would later become the rulers of India as British forces arrived in the 1700's to back the Empire's interests. The future Pakistan was incorporated into British India in the late nineteenth century and later partitioned from India following World War Two. Hindu East Pakistan, which borders India to the east, would come to be known as Bangladesh, and the Islamic West Pakistan would later become just Pakistan.

Having been born in Pakistan, his parents both missionaries, Tom Billings was an expert on the country. He briefed the Senator on its state of affairs and political climate. "Modern Pakistan has one hundred and sixty four million people; ninety seven percent of those are Muslim. The other three percent are Hindu, Christian, and various tribal faiths. The country is both impoverished and a nuclear power. The United States had always taken a keen liking to Pakistan, mostly because of the country's proximity to areas of interest to the U.S., particularly Pakistan's border with the Soviet Union."

"It's always been a great buffer," Cox added.

"Yes sir, in fact after Great Britain's exit and Pakistan's independence, the United States became the only country from the West to set up a military presence in the North West Frontier."

"The Cold War was on and the U.S. had the Soviet Union to worry about," Cox said.

"That's right Senator, and the hills of the lower North West Frontier was an ideal spot to build a runway for the U2 reconnaissance aircraft."

For agreeing to let the CIA build facilities and an airfield for U2 fights in the North West Frontier, the new Pakistan came out pretty good. Pakistan was the first country outside of the United States to have the modern F-4 Phantom fighters in their Air Force. "Even back then they were an impoverished people with a modern military," the Senator said.

Pakistan would soon play a major role in geopolitical events just twenty years later, and again it was because of a border with another country, and a crippling conflict. Afghanistan was the country and the conflict involved the United States and Great Britain's old nemesis, the Soviet Union. The Soviets, not paying very close attention to history, had decided to invade the rugged country. Not such a good idea, it turned out. The past had shown that foreign invaders never fared very well when they attempted to impose their doctrines on the fiercely independent Afghans. The Soviets wanted the Afghans to give communism a try. It failed, and that failure was pivotal in the eventual collapse of the superpower. It was Pakistan though, that played a key role in smuggling weapons from the CIA to the Mujahideen militiamen. The Soviets were finally defeated, and the President of Pakistan, a shrewd military man that governed the country under martial law, got what he wanted - brand new F-16 fighters from the United States.

The Senator summarized Billings' brief, "So over the years what we've got is consistency at least. Pakistan is an impoverished country with a high infant mortality rate, a literacy rate less than fifty percent, a country with high risk of infectious disease but has a military that could scare the hell out of most others, especially India."

"And now they have nukes," Lieutenant Commander Johns said.

The Senator stood up from his chair. "And now they have nukes," he concurred disconcertingly.

The driving force for Pakistan was their neighbor India. A nuclear power for more than thirty years, India possessed a thermonuclear arsenal with individual weapons having yields many times greater than the bomb detonated over Hiroshima. Now Pakistan too had entered the nuclear club because of the efforts of one man, Doctor Abdul Qadeer Khan. AQ Khan, an Indian by birth, was as industrious as he was brilliant and headed up Pakistan's nuclear program. Kahn had managed to smuggle secret blue prints for a uranium enrichment centrifuge from his former employer in the Netherlands, URENCO. With blue prints in hand, all Kahn needed to do was acquire components such as the steel rotor tubes required for the centrifuge. And he managed to do just that. Kahn and his team were successful in producing enriched uranium and Pakistan tested its first nuclear device in 1998, making AQ Kahn both a national hero, and icon of the Islamic world. Kahn's success for Pakistan made the powers in the west nervous for sure, but what he did next would down right scare the living hell out of them. A fear that persists to this day because of fallout that is still unknown. *"What crazed radical Islamist already has a weapon, just waiting for an adequate delivery method and the opportune time?" all in the Western powers wondered.*

Following the events of 9/11 and Enduring Freedom came the invasion of Iraq and the search for Weapons of Mass Destruction. The monitoring of existing nuclear programs was intensified to prevent continued proliferation of nuclear weapons, particularly by rogue nations such as Iran, Libya, or North Korea. Suspicions of possible proliferation at the hands of Kahn were confirmed when a ship was intercepted with parts for a Uranium Centrifuge. The ship was embarked for Libya and the parts had originated from AQ Kahn's lab in Pakistan. Intelligence officials from Pakistan investigated and came to the conclusion that AQ Kahn Research Laboratories was a major supplier for a nuclear black market that was based out of Dubai. Whether it was the illegal trade in slaves, camel jockeys, opium, or arms, it seemed two countries were always mentioned in the same sentence, Pakistan and Dubai. "What was the connection? Who was the link?" The Senator wanted to know the answers.

Senator Cox's next moves would be crucial. His criticism of the Supreme Court for placing interpretation of law ahead of the safety of the American people had been justified. His visibility in the Senate had just been increased enormously, and very soon, so would his national name recognition. He needed to be as well informed and briefed on the events of the weeks to come as was possible. Therefore it was imperative that he remained in close contact with those on the cutting edge of the investigation. With a little help from those in the know, he could dragoon his way into the center of the storm, and the junior Senator from Virginia would soon become one of the most powerful political forces in Washington.

"Gina," the Senator barked to his secretary. "Get hold of our media friends. Tell em I want to go on record this afternoon with a statement."

"Right away," his right arm of fifteen years said. She'd been with him since his days of private practice as well.

"I'll put together some talking points," his aide said.

"Good, let's be proactive on this one from here on out," Cox said. "And Gina, have Tom call for meeting with Admiral Barnes.

CHAPTER 16

YAWNING, HE DARED NOT close his eyes for fear of going into a nightlong coma, so instead he breezed through the NSA file one more time. They'd a couple of hours to kill before dinner, and although he was familiar with the digital dossier, he felt it was prudent to review a few of the material details of Kevin Davis' CIA career once again. Shannon had also made some comments on the file, and he enjoyed reading her psychological profiles.

Kevin Davis was born and raised in Salt Lake City and attended Tulane University graduating with a Psychology degree in 1983.

"That would make him forty-seven. A few years older than me," he murmured while chewing an ice cube from a club soda on the rocks.

Bryan scrolled the data on the laptop back a few pages, verifying the birth date. He made average grades and was in ROTC, receiving his commission in the Air Force. The ice cubes rattled in the glass as he shook the drink to chill it faster.

"Let's see how your tours went Mister Davis," Bryan wondered as he slurred through the ice in his mouth while perusing a few of

Kevin's Fitness Reports from the Air Force. Everything looked copasetic so far. Kevin had gone straight into intelligence and ended up in both Greece and Turkey during the Gulf War.

Stationed in Athens and Incirlik Air Base, Turkey as an Intel Officer responsible for reconnaissance and attack briefings, he had the requisite clearances and was given excellent marks on all of his Fitness Reports. Bryan read one Commanding Officer's comments, thinking how much it was right on the mark, "Captain Davis is an outstanding officer and often livens up the painful downtime of a wartime atmosphere with an unexpected quip or sarcastic remark, usually followed by a 'thumb's up' sign."

He laughed at the NSA investigator's added comments that "Captain Davis was called 'Tom' by Navy pilots because of his continual use of the largest digit, especially when pointing to a mission target on a map, and also for the shape of his body."

Bryan read the file further.

"Hired by the CIA in early ninety-three and sent to the "Farm" at Camp Peary outside of Williamsburg, Virginia, followed by a junior analyst job at headquarters in Langley, Virginia in ninety-four. Landed in the Middle East three years later." Bryan looked for specific locations.

"Cyprus, Kuwait, Karachi, and the UAE. Back to Langley for a year with some language skills - Arabic, Farsi, Urdu."

Bryan believed he was reviewing the record of a CIA man that had been on course for consistent promotion. He'd managed to get through assignments without "stepping on his crank," and had a knack for avoiding implication in intelligence snafus such as Iraq. He hadn't been damaged professionally; it appeared on the surface, by the U.S., Ports of Dubai controversy but had been in Dubai for seven years, which would have put him there at the time of the public relations disaster.

At the center of that controversy was Ports of Dubai International, owned via a holding company by the government of Dubai. PDI therefore, was essentially state-owned and had purchased British Ports & Stevedore LTD, also known as BPS, which just happened to own the contracts for the management of stevedore operations at nine major U.S. Ports on the East Coast, as well as additional operations at twelve other minor ports. The nine major ports were located in New York, Maine, two in New Jersey, Philadelphia, Maryland, Delaware,

Louisiana, and Virginia. The transfer of the management contracts from **BPS** to **PDI** had been approved by executive branch of the government and had the support of the President.

Everything fell apart after a junior Senator from New York was alerted to the pending deal by a New York company about to become an unwilling partner with the Dubai owned parent. The Senator in turn contacted the press and the story erupted into the mainstream media as yet another example of botched foreign policy.

That an Arab country was actually even being considered was unimaginable to average Americans when they first heard of the proposed arrangement. Opponents played into the public's fears, fanning the flames of xenophobia, painting a picture of terrorists minding the U.S. ports. The ports were in turn, off loading container ships from Iran, and of course, like a modern version of the Trojan Horse, the containers could be filled with more terrorists, or worse yet something nuclear like a dirty bomb. Bryan sarcastically thought that, "Terrorists would have an easier time smugglin in WMD by hiding them in bales of pot, which seemed to have no problems getting across U.S. borders or through U.S. ports."

The subterfuge worked, the problem was that the real story couldn't be further from the truth. In fact, foreign companies were already managing over eighty percent of U.S. ports, and the actual security of the ports themselves still fell squarely under the control of the United States. It was clearly an example of negative fallout from 9/11 that had adverse foreign policy ramifications. Bryan thought it unfortunate. The administration though, had no doubt erred in not making the deal public beforehand. Once in the hands of the media, the arrangement became analogous to turning over ship building contracts to the Japanese on December the eighth, 1941.

The bad press resulted in some bruised egos and was an embarrassment for the State Department, CIA, and White House, but the situation also made for some strange bedfellows as it united foes from both sides of the aisle, both in favor and in opposition. It was clear that PDI lost out though. After the deal had been completely derailed by both a House and Senate vote, PDI announced their intent to sell the rights to a U.S. owned company. Billions of dollars were lost due to the failure of the deal. Kevin Davis had been in the UAE during the debacle, and for that matter, so had Rodgers Christopher.

"Shannon, you realize that both Davis and Christopher were here during the ports fiasco," Bryan said as Shannon entered his suite.

"That, I do. They both seemed to have survived it though. Other than that, did you find anything else interesting in there?" she asked as she looked over his shoulder at the computer.

"I'm not sure – probably not," Bryan said. "It couldn't have helped either one of their careers though," he added, getting back to PDI.

"Yes, no doubt."

"Come to think of it, both have apparently hit a plateau," he pressed further for her input on the ports issue. There was something there, he believed. He couldn't pin down what it was though.

"Well, while you've been dissecting that file, Dylan Sizemore just finished a report on the news about Malik and Petrov," she said. "No surprises there, but are you expecting anything to come of it?"

"I don't know," he said, hardly paying attention, still focused on PDI.

They entered the rooftop bar with Kevin at 9:30 PM on the nose. The bar was at the top of the Madinat Jumeirah, Arabian Resort of Dubai. A massive resort cut right into the desert less than a mile south of the Burj al Arab. The architecture reminded Bryan of the Alhambra in Granada, Spain. Built in the fourteenth century out of bearing masonry, the Alhambra is a masterpiece of symmetrical terrace designs and intricate geometric patterns. It seemed to Bryan that the architects of the Jumeirah had the Alhambra in mind when they designed the oasis.

The beach resort combined two hotels and over two dozen courtyard houses, complete with a giant beachfront pool, ancient style wind towers and domes, and meandering waterways lined with magnificently landscaped gardens. If that weren't enough, the resort also had its own health club and spa, arena, outdoor amphitheater, retail plaza, cafés, restaurants, and water taxis. And virtually every corner of the resort had a fantastic view of the Burj al Arab, as if linking the fantasies of modern Dubai with the symbolic splendor of old Arabia.

Looking left and right, Bryan saw who was waiting for them, Dylan Sizemore, and the two diplomats, Rodgers Christopher and Edward Basingstoke.

"You didn't tell me that this was a diplomatic event," Bryan said to Kevin.

"Last minute party crashers. Both are friends of Size. I really didn't have much of a choice."

One glance at Christopher's attire and Bryan knew it was going to be a memorable evening. Dylan dressed casually as he normally did, wearing a lightweight sports jacket. The British Consul General, a slender man about six feet tall, classic angular features of aristocrats, slightly thinning hair, could have just stepped off the golf course. But Christopher, his thick sandy blond hair, becoming gray, was slicked back. He had on expensive slacks, probably Zanella, Bryan thought, and a collared shirt, blue double-breasted blazer, brass buttons.

Bryan nudged Shannon. "Look what he's wearing," he said out of the corner of his mouth.

She did so and almost laughed. On his feet were red "Palm Beaches," monogrammed shoes with faux-suede piping, no socks. "Oh my god, and an ascot," she said.

The three waiting stood up from their seats on a large sofa, extended pleasantries, and plopped back down again. After several minutes of superfluous conversation, Rodgers Christopher kicked things off by attacking Shannon's theories. "I've read some of your pieces on the psychology of terrorism, doctor. Interesting stuff, but do you really believe that it's the goal of the Muslims to take over the Mediterranean from Spain to the Middle East?" Rodgers Christopher asked flatly.

"I believe we had this conversation before," Shannon remarked, recalling the State Department event.

"I think you're right. Are your opinions still the same?"

"As I said before, that's not exactly what I wrote, I made the assertion that Islamists are bent on the establishment of a new caliphate and believe that it should include all lands previously Islamic, which would include Spain," Shannon corrected.

"I see, but you don't actually believe that the West, or for that matter, the progressive Arab nations would just stand by and let that happen, do you?" Christopher asked.

"I think that fundamentalist regimes believe that the progressive Arab state governments can be overthrown, ultimately uniting the Muslim world under Islamic theocracies," Shannon said.

"Yes, excellent premise indeed Doctor, I think we've heard that one bandied about more than once," the British Consul General said. "However, both the UK and the U.S. have considerable investment here, as well as in the rest of the peninsula to allow for that, whether you consider oil or not."

"It's a matter of us being on our guard, Rodgers," Bryan said.

"You think we're not prepared here on the front of the Islamic world?" Christopher asked.

"Had we been on our guard before, I wouldn't be here for business – I'd probably be skiing, wouldn't I?" Bryan said.

"Right, how brilliant – and funny," Basingstoke said. "Anyway, always nice to have the FBI and a Navy man around, isn't it? I already feel safer."

"She's top notch, Mister Consul General," Bryan said.

"Yes, I've read some of yer work as well. In fact, I reference it quite often. Excellent conclusions actually, very good," Dylan commented. "Perhaps we might 'have the opportunity to compare notes while you're here?"

Dylan Sizemore had lost the longer blond locks, now favoring a stylish close cropped look, his hard charging journalistic style complimented by rugged physical characteristics. The quintessential Western journalist who thrived on reporting from the most hazardous locations, he was either putting himself in peril for a story or elbowing up to a smoky bar for shots of some hard liquor. Many journalists, wanting to make their own name for hard core reporting in war zones, used his record as their inspiration. His reporting from Iraq was legendary. Bryan had been right in his prediction many years ago; Dylan was a star newsman.

At great personal risk, he'd been the only Western journalist that managed to infiltrate and speak directly to a few of the most ruthless terrorist leaders. Following strict protocol, he'd been carted around blindfolded, transferred between multiple vehicles, to numerous secret locations. After twenty-four hours, he arrived at a small house, for what was an unprecedented two-hour interview with the leader of a ruthless splinter group operating in Afghanistan. "He seemed polite initially, but I could tell he'd 'ave my head on a platta if he thought it would do him any good," Dylan would say. After finishing the interview, he was forced to repeat the same blindfolded journey on the return. He was dumped off near the most hazardous areas of fighting in Kandahar. His final report, carried by virtually every major news organization was lauded as death defying.

"I'd welcome getting together and compare notes, if we have the time - that was quite piece you did on Al-Qaeda two years ago."

"Thanks Doctor," he said matter-of-factly.

They sat down on the Moroccan style sofa at the far corner of the Rooftop terrace, with a spectacular view of the Burj al Arab framed by the black Arabian night sky. The waitress walked off with the drink orders, and the business at hand got underway.

"Dylan has developed some sources that may be worth something," Basingstoke said.

"Is that so?" Bryan asked looking in the direction of the two Consul Generals. Rodgers Christopher was now reclining in the large cushions of the sofa, legs crossed and sipping his Chardonnay. It was typical of his Prima Donna affectation.

"Right Bryan. Just some rumblings about a Russian and Swiss bank accounts, could be tied to this Malik fellow. I understand that you're here as some kind of investigator?" Dylan said.

"That's right Dylan – but I don't believe everybody here's cleared for this conversation," Bryan said looking at Kevin.

"Bryan, I referred Dylan to Kevin. I was made aware of the Dubai interest from our State Department. My clearance is good, and of course Dylan has been working with us for years. Just doing my part to help," Rodgers said with hubris, still sitting back in the sofa.

"Alright. Fair enough, but I'm afraid that this is going to be a one-way, information-sharing conversation. If Dylan has something concrete, then let's have it."

"I'd say I'd have to agree with Captain Craig. These are delicate matters," Consul General Basingstoke said.

"Not a problem, don't wanna git in the way of UK and USA diplomatic issues. I've a Dubai functionary that believes the financing source you're interested in comes from accounts in Switzerland."

"And you have a name?" Shannon asked.

"Not yet."

"How about the name of a bank?" Bryan asked.

"Working on that one as well."

"Well isn't this meeting premature then?" Bryan said, gazing at Kevin.

"Your financial man can focus on that area and use whatever programs you have to nail down the bad guys," Christopher said cavalierly.

Angrily, Bryan stood up. "I'm sorry, but I believe the meeting is adjourned," he said.

"Oh damn Captain Craig, please Bryan. Please, sit back down. Dylan, would you please excuse us?" Basingstoke said.

"No problem fellas. As I said, don't wanna get in the middle of your business. But if you need my input Bryan, here's my card. Jest give me a call, ay," Dylan said with a wink, handing Bryan the card and exiting the terrace area. Bryan noticed a note on the back "Meet me in Trilogy."

"What exactly do you believe your role should be in our investigation?" Bryan asked Christopher.

"Just trying to help you guys out," Rodgers replied smugly, taking another sip of wine.

"How? By speaking so freely to an outside source? Have you ever heard the expression 'Bead Window' – as in classified information?'" Bryan asked rhetorically.

"He's reliable for Christ sake. And he'll keep things quiet," Rodgers Christopher said.

"I suppose the report from Dylan is evidence of that, but I'm not referring to Dylan," Bryan said as a matter of fact. "Unlike others, the idea is for him to provide information for us, which we'll gladly review."

"Look, the UK and the United States have a large number of investments here - billions of dollars have gone into this region, and we can't afford to have a rogue counter-terrorism investigator running around screwing up deals," Christopher said, taking another sip of wine.

"I might remind you that Britain and the U.S. collectively have almost five hundred dead civilians at the hands of terrorists that could have their source of funding from right here under your nose. Or perhaps you're suffering from a bit of myopia? You know – can't see the forest for the trees," Bryan retorted incredulously, looking at Shannon, who thought it best to play the role of quiet observer for the time being.

Rodgers dismissed Bryan's comment with an imperious wave of his hand, and sat forward out of the shadows, setting his glass of wine on the large wooden cocktail table. Basingstoke, relying on diplomacy, intervened before the tension ignited in the hot evening air.

"Please gentleman, please - Rodgers bea with him, I understand that Captain Craig has been on the go non-stop for better than two weeks. The British..."

Cutting Basingstoke off, Bryan said, "Please, no excuses for me, but my team - who they are and what they do, is classified. I'm not going into it here."

"What do you expect from us Captain Craig?" Basingstoke asked.

"The U.S. and British Embassies have been given instructions to aid in our investigation – without interference. I don't believe I can be any clearer than that sir," Bryan said.

"You're out of line Craig," Christopher said.

"No Mister Christopher, you're out of line."

"Look, I'm already putting out your fires. You threatened an employee of the Bank of Dubai. I believe you insinuated that he would be tossed off a skyscraper," Christopher said.

"I think that Rowley knows more than he's telling us, let's just put it that way. And I'll use hardball tactics whenever necessary," Bryan said dismissively. He couldn't believe Rodgers Christopher's gall.

"Well, how about not creating an international incident in the process of your discovery? Think you can handle that Captain?" Christopher said.

"Before we have war over this, please let's take a step back," Basingstoke pleaded. "Doctor, you're developing the psychological profile and working with forensics to tie everything together. Am I correct on that?" He asked Shannon, delicately attempting to ease the tensions.

"Yes sir, that's a fairly accurate statement," she said.

"And you believe somewhere behind all of this is someone who fancies themselves as the next caliph," Basingstoke said.

"Potentially, only because of the sophisticated nature of the attacks, their coordination across two continents and the amount of money it would take to plan and effectively carry that out," she responded."

"Mister Consul General, all arrows first point to the Bank of Dubai, and we also believe there is a significant Pakistani connection," Bryan said.

"And I take it that you would prefer it that we give you free rein for your investigation?" The British Consul General asked.

"I'm requesting that you help, rather than hinder," Bryan said.

Christopher cocked his index finger as if at a lectern. "Well you can't run roughshod over bankers here - bankers in the middle of sensitive business negotiations with the United States. I'm not going to tolerate that. If you don't get in line, I'm going to go through State to have some restraint placed on your operations here? I do have that ability, and don't kid yourself into thinking otherwise," he warned.

Bryan knew a veiled threat when he heard one. "We have a dead Russian that I've confirmed as having ties with Al-Qaeda and Taliban. Petrov was also connected to the Bank of Dubai and your friend Rowley. I think that it would be in your best interest, and the interest of the State Department to be damn sure that everything is clean before four billionaires commit to a business deal with Rowley and his syndicate. If it turns out that Falcon Holdings is laundering money and financing terrorists, you're going to have one hell of a scandal on your hands. You can also kiss that ambassadorship goodbye too."

Christopher stared blankly at Bryan, searching for a retort. Nothing came up. Clearly the meeting was over as far as Bryan was concerned.

"Folks, if you'll excuse me, I think that I can cab it back to the hotel."

Sending Shannon back solo, Bryan nonchalantly eased into the hotel's disco to find Dylan. A stiff drink would work wonders too, he thought. He was about to order when Dylan surprised him.

"You two get along just great don't you," he said lighting up a cigarette, whiskey on the rocks in hand.

"Yeah, we're best buddies. Can't ya tell?" Bryan replied sarcastically.

Dylan took a big drag and exhaled. "You ex-SEALs are all the same mate. You never trust the ass-kissers, and they in turn think you're going to undermine their careers."

"You think you've got us wired, don't you Dylan?"

"Call it how I see em. But if I ave to take sides, I'll go with the guy that gives me a rare scoop, rather than the guy that's always givin me the run aroun'."

"That's very kind of you my friend."

Bryan ordered his drink, "Grey Goose tonic, lemon twist."

"Put that on mine mate and I'll have another," Dylan said as he jiggled his empty and tossed a credit card down on the bar.

"Thanks, what's on your mind, I mean - I've got to believe it's more than a ridiculous Swiss bank account for us to meet like this?"

"Word has it that ya met up with Petrov before. Is that true?"

"Petrov? When was that supposed to have happened?" He paused while picking up his drink, a grin on his face.

"In Pakistan, North West Frontier – about the time I met meh wife, ya know back in the good old days chasin Al-Qaeda with your SEAL teams."

"You know that we don't chase anybody, Dylan - we catch 'em and kill 'em. Chasin's for monkeys, and anyway, we never went into Pakistan," Bryan said coolly, taking a tiny sip of the stiff drink. "I've got to keep your ass out of that business."

"Quick, catch those monkeys bein catapulted from me ass." Dylan turned and acted as though he'd just captured one of the imaginary primates by the tail. "Don't worry about me, I can take care of myself."

"Funny – alright, just what are you lookin for Dylan?"

"I want the Prince Rehman story, ...an I'll give ya somethin in return." Dylan took a puff of his cigarette and waited for Bryan's response.

"What Prince Rehman story?"

"Well I happen ta know your followin Petrov, and he was in Chitral," Dylan said.

"And?"

"That's where you're goin then, and you can't operate in Chitral without sitting down with Rehman."

"Not bad investigative work, my old friend," Bryan said noting his friend's knack for getting the scoop. "You give me what you have and I'll take it under advisement. How about that?" Bryan knew that Dylan was aware of his protocol, and Dylan could count on Bryan for something worthwhile as a result.

"Fair enough my American friend. Let's start off with the Swiss account."

"Wild goose chase, huh?"

"Well let's just say I had my sources check into its validity. Just some cursory checking, mind you, but it doesn't show anything promisin up to this point. Still checkin though."

"Who are the sources?"

"Oh come on mate. What do you take me for? Someone who'll jest kiss and tell?" Dylan put out his cigarette and knocked back the remainder of his first drink, then started on the second. "That's good stuff, put 'air on yer chest," he said with a grimace before continuing. "It appears Rowley's the key, whether he's a knowing or unknowing participant is unclear."

"Rowley. You don't say, I guess my hunch about that guy wasn't too far off base then," Bryan said.

"Be careful Bryan. You don't want to ruffle too many feathers round here."

"Yeah too many falcon feathers," Bryan said with his glass near his mouth, partially muffling his words.

"Some sort of inside joke?"

"Not an inside joke, but since we're on the subject, what do you know about falcons?"

"As in falconry, the plane, or the buildin?"

"The one with feathers."

"Well it's an art for nobleman, and in the case of the Arabian Desert and Sheikhs, someone who practices falconry is regarded with great respect and considered a leader. I think the sport has probably been around for several thousand years or more. I've seen the Sheikh's family even practice it from horseback and on camel. What's your curiosity with falcons, other than the new development? Is there a connection to the bombins?"

"I don't know, just curious as to the significance, the development using the name – that's all."

Bryan ordered another drink and continued, "So now I have a deceased arms dealer that worked with Taliban and Al-Qaeda. Let me tell you Dylan, Petrov was all over the North West Frontier doing his deals – that's why I'll need to see Rehman - I also have a definite link between Petrov and the Bank of Dubai. Then there's Rowley – he could very well be a dupe and not know a damn thing, or he could be right in the middle of a conspiracy."

"I've got to ask the million dollar question – what are you going to do when you catch your man?"

"Good question. We want the deranged planners that are hiding in caves for sure, but we've got to nail the money behind the scenes," Bryan said.

"It'll give me a good story."

"Anything short of that, then we've failed. I've gotta have a face to put on a wanted poster."

"And I need a face for breakin news," Dylan said looking forlornly at his drink.

"We need it for the healing process, so I've gotta catch the bad guys, then we'll all feel vindicated."

"Or is it revenge mate?"

"Yeah, revenge – exactly. And what will we do when we catch them you ask? Freeze accounts - most certainly, you know, put the moneymen out of business. But once I have my man, my job's over. The politicians can decide what to do with him after that," Bryan said.

Bryan wasn't sure what his marching orders would be once they actually had a name for the hunt. It could very well be a mission for Task Force Blue. That remained to be seen. What worried him was the seeming endlessness of the funding. Terrorism was being bolstered by rogue states, such as Iran and Syria. Those countries however, were reticent to openly fund terrorists organizations bent on attacking the United States. They may privately cheer terrorist acts against the U.S., but they were very much aware of the wrath that would be exacted on them should a direct link be made following an attack. Therefore, they left that sort of messy business to individual backers. But when the source was put out of business, there was always another waiting in the wings.

"Getting back to the Burj Falcon project, no doubt that Rowley's your man, an you're absolutely correct about a definite Paki connection, an not jest with the Burj al Baaz development."

"What's the connection?"

"It's better that I show you, rather than tell you. What are your plans in the mornin, say aroun' 5:00 AM?"

"Hope to still be sleeping, but considering I'm days behind on Emails and have a million unanswered messages on my cell phone - what do you have in mind?" Bryan was sure that Dylan was getting ready to surprise him.

"We're goin to take a little field trip in the mornin Bryan. You remember field trips don't ya?"

"My favorite thing to do in fifth grade. Where are we going?"

"The very place that the powers that be don't want you to see - the Paki labor camps."

The day had truly felt like one of the longest of Bryan's life, and he couldn't wait to lie down on the king-size bed of his suite. Bryan unwrapped one of the chocolates that came with his late room service meal of pasta and smoked salmon. He sipped on a 1950 Barros port wine after eating the chocolate.

"What a mismatch," he thought as he read the wrapper. "Hershey, PA."

Bryan sat down on the bed and looked at the clock. It was midnight. He called the front desk for a 4:30 wake up call and set his phone alarm for back up. Un-wrapping the other chocolate, he popped it in his mouth.

"Hershey, PA," he said slowly, enjoying the bedtime treat.

"Pennsylvania." Bryan rubbed his whiskers as he thought about the State and the bombing in Philadelphia. He wondered how far Philadelphia was from Hershey, and how that chocolate got all the way from there to Dubai.

"Well, no doubt my little friend you jumped on a boat and were shipped from there to here - they need too many of you to put you and your chocolate buddies on a plane," he said, zoning out.

"Shipped from Philadelphia down the Delaware River through Delaware Bay, out to the Atlantic and finally here to Dubai. That's a long boat ride... Shipped," Bryan said out loud. He thought for a moment as he took a sip of bottled water. He was tired, and needed sleep. Just go to bed, he thought. "You're losing it."

Head on the pillow, lights out, he shut his eyes. He tossed and turned, but sleep wouldn't come. An hour had gone by and the same puzzle kept drifting back into his thoughts. He turned on all the lights in the room from the bedside table and clicked on the bedroom TV. Getting out of bed, he went to the safe and removed his notebook computer, plugged it in, and booted the power on.

There they were; the states that had ports to be managed by PDI. He hastily scribbled each State down in a column on the hotel's stationary. The first heading he labeled "Port Deal - State." He made a heading for a second column, yet to be filled in, labeled "City." Then he made a third column labeled "Bombing."

Next he filled in the "City" space with the cities that had ports to be turned over to PDI as part of the deal. The first State and city were New York. He put a dash under "Bombing," and completed the rest. He stared at the three columns blankly, and then looked up at the ceiling.

"Unbelievable," he said quietly. He glanced back down at the pad and began rapidly putting check marks along the last column.

"Shannon, come over here. I've got somethin to show you," Bryan said. Hanging up the phone he looked at the list again. This was more than just a coincidence. Shannon arrived five minutes later, wide-awake as well.

"Shannon, look at that list," Bryan said, handing the paper to her.

She began reading from Bryan's writing out loud, "Port Deal – state - New York...you think that the port deal falling through and the bombings are linked somehow?" She asked not quite ready to accept the connection just yet.

"It can't be that much of a coincidence."

"But what about New York, which hasn't been bombed, and London which was? London's not a U.S. port."

"New York I don't know. Maybe somethin happened, or the bomber got cold feet. But London's obvious – here, give me the sheet," he said holding his hand out. He wrote something at the bottom and gave it back to her, which she read.

"British Ports & Stevedore are headquartered one block from Harrods," Bryan said. "The attacks were pay back."

Port Deal – State	City	Bombing
New York	NYC	-
Maine	Portland	✓
New Jersey	Camden	✓
"	Newark	✓
Pennsylvania	Philly	✓
Maryland	Baltimore	✓

Delaware	Wilmington	✓
Louisiana	New Orleans	✓
Virginia	Newport News	✓

Owner - British Ports & Stevedore Ltd. - London

"This puts a new wrinkle into my profile, but I'll agree, you've really made a connection here."

"We've got to find out what happened in New York and if someone's standing by to attack," Bryan said. The revelation was an eye-opener. How could he have missed this before? There it was right before his eyes, nine out of ten. Planned, or a coincidence? The answer to that question was obvious. Bryan checked the signal for the Internet and pulled out his iPhone.

CHAPTER 17

JUNE 6, 2008
NEW YORK CITY, NEW YORK

WHEN THE CALL CAME in, post attack counterterrorism procedures had been in effect for two weeks. The FBI, CIA, and all federal and local law enforcement agencies had been on the highest possible alert. The NSA, coordinating with the FBI, had also been busy, gathering high value data that included video surveillance, Internet surveillance, telephone records, and just about every other minutia of cyber information possible. Homeland Security had lowered the risk assessment for citizens though, from Severe to High in the last twelve hours. Bryan could only presume it had more to due with easing Americans' fears, and less to due with an actual threat, which he knew to be imminent. He now was directing a concentrated focus on New York City. It must have been in the plan and had not been carried out. The only way to be sure was through an intensive search using many assets. They had to catch the bomber before he blew himself up and a hundred or more people, and Bryan was positive he was out there.

Bryan's guidelines had been very specific, but the investigators had a lot of information to work with. They wouldn't be looking in small town Americana; this was New York City. With the threat of a remaining attack still looming, they had to pull out all stops and direct as many resources of the NSA and FBI as possible to find their man. That meant redirecting a few of the NSA's supercomputers to aid in performing much of the analysis.

"We're looking for a former detainee, who's probably a Pakistani - and maybe stupid enough to still be wearing Hip Hop clothing," Bryan advised.

"My gosh Bryan, there are hundreds of thousands of Pakis in the city. Which taxi cab do we start with?" Shannon was flabbergasted at the complexity of the task at hand.

"Oh, and that information is only a hunch. But a qualified hunch though," Bryan said.

The failure or success of catching the suicide bomber was the onus of DJ initially, at least in developing a narrower field to search. FaceScan roared into action. He made detailed FaceScan analysis of eighteen former Gitmo detainees, all Pakistani, which were interfaced with video surveillance systems throughout New York City and its surrounding five boroughs of roughly sixteen million people. It was a daunting task, but they had the help of the NSA.

Not on par with London's "Ring of Steel," Manhattan's streets had over eight thousand security video cameras at street intersections, on the corners of buildings, on doorways, alcoves, rooftops, and above garage doors. That amounted to tremendous horsepower for video surveillance. The problem was that eighty-five percent of the systems were private. Only twelve hundred surveillance cameras were under direct control of DJ back in London. Parameters were further defined.

Presuming the bomber would follow the same modus operandi, the Pegasus team honed in on malls, shopping centers, schools, banks and their ATM machines. Banks were easy to coordinate with to gain access to ATM video cameras. The bomb making material could readily be purchased so they also needed access to point-of-sale cameras from as many of the city's drug stores as possible. Federal agents had over two million hours of digitally recorded information already obtained for New York, but at the time had no idea who they were looking for. DJ interfaced FaceScan with the power of the NSA's Fort Meade supercomputers and waited to see what would pop up.

Determining the identity of the suspect was the first step; next they'd have to find him. They didn't even know if he would still be in the United States, if in fact he existed at all. DJ wasn't necessarily skeptical; it was just that a huge amount of resources in the way of microprocessors had suddenly been shifted to one task alone, based upon a hunch. DJ turned up the volume on Led Zeppelin.

"DJ, ya ever get tired of them?" Ian Davis, his lab technician asked.

"'Ow old are ye boy?"

"Twenty-eight. Why?"

"Well let me expand the horizons of yer twenty-eight years with the sound of the greatest guitarist that 'as ever uttered a note." DJ commenced an air guitar riff of "Whole Lotta Love" to Ian's amusement.

"Yer a crazy bloke DJ. Ye must 'ave overdosed on drugs or somethin," Ian said with a chuckle.

"Why would ya say that? I can assure you that I never OD'd," DJ insisted.

They both laughed and DJ got back to his work, graphically interchanging images of former detainees with various fashions and hairstyles. On the large monitor was a man in a watch cap with a moustache, then the same man without the moustache; then a goatee, and so forth.

"How many different combinations do you have?"

"Aye've one undred and eight possibilities. Aye enter one image, an' FaceScan will coordinate with NSA's supercomputer to search through all images recorded during specified date fields and match the face regardless of facial hair or clothing. For the cop on the beat, we'll reduce it down ta only two. If of course, we ever 'ave a need to pass around flyers to the cops."

Bryan deduced that a single suicide bomber had failed to carry out his mission. He'd also deduced that the bomber was probably no longer in communication with his network, isolated and most likely waiting for the right opportunity to complete the mission. There was the alternative possibility that he had second thoughts or obtained a conscience, but that possibility was the less likely of the two. History would indicate that suicide Jihadists were a very determined and motivated bunch, with very little regard for human life, including their own. If New York were in the plan, he would try to carry it out until he was physically unable to do so. The Pegasus team had to go with the probability that New York was in fact in the plan. They had to find him, stop him, and catch him alive, if at all possible.

"Ian, we ave a hit," DJ said. FaceScan had been pouring through the databases for three hours and on the monitor was an image of a young man in Hip Hop clothing. He was standing in front of a bank ATM withdrawing money. The video was grainy, out of focus and buffering. He looked Hispanic, but also could have been African-American or Arabic too. From all appearances, he could have been just getting some quick cash for a fun night out on the town. The man's face was a match for one of the Gitmo detainees though. The parameters had been very specific. FaceScan was using probabilities with ninety percent accuracy. FaceScan's batting average though was one thousand percent. It had never erred yet.

"Let's see who we ave ere. Whas your name little fellah?" DJ said as he highlighted "Search Target" and pressed enter.

The program searched through the database to uncover the match. After a few seconds, a detainee's mug shot in the familiar orange jump suit appeared adjacent to the ATM image.

"An ere you are."

"This is the guy we're looking for?' the technician asked.

"Apparently so, but now we need ta git some info off the ATM. We'll want the address, date and time."

Without warning, the FaceScan program lit up with a second hit.

"Uh oh, let's not Kum Bay Ya just yet, seems we've got more than one bloody winner."

The monitor now was running a video of a young man boarding the subway. The target turned his head slightly and at that precise moment, FaceScan stopped the video, initiating a series of enlargements, each followed by a sharpening of the pixilated face.

'Here we 'ave number two."

"They look the same," the technician commented.

"Fortunately FaceScan doesn't suffer from your myopia mate. And it looks like it ain't finished yet either." The program was running again and had found yet one more match, the final pairing and the only photo of a man not wearing Hip Hop clothing. He was in his late twenties or early thirties and was dressed in preppy fashions, polo shirt and a New York Yankees baseball cap.

"Now mate, what we'll do is correlate the images with detainee photos and see what sort of information that we came up with about these persons of interest."

"DJ. Persons of interest?" Roger was ready to find the former detainees and take them down immediately himself.

"Are you certain that they have committed a crime yet? Perhaps other than being in the U.S. illegally. I mean after all, they were set free by the government." It was a tiny ribbing that DJ gave the technician, but it was enough to almost set him off. Roger decided not to voice his opinion. In his mind they were all terrorists and he would just as well rather "Snag em, tag em, and bag em."

DJ had been right on one point, and Bryan emphasized that very notion. The former detainees were only suspects, but prime suspects, and wanted for questioning. Standard procedures would be in place; extreme caution, use of force when necessary, use of deadly force when in self defense, or if the suspect was in the process of committing a deadly act. And they needed to move expeditiously.

An additional concern was to keep the information as close quarters as possible. A leak would give a reason for the Mayor of New York to raise their alert level and possibly cause a panic, not to mention a media circus. It was a fine line that they had to walk, at least for the next twenty-four hours. DJ finished the identification process of the three former detainees.

Kahlid Mujab
Bank of America ATM
126 Delancey St
New York City
05/22/08
10:22 Hours

Rashid Nasim
Lexington Ave Subway
05/25/08
08:30 Hours

Hanif Zar Wali
W New York Hotel
541 Lexington Ave
New York City

05/ 30/ 08
21:12 Hours

With new information that they now had on the suspects, the Pegasus team, again with the help of the FBI and the NSA, would try to sniff out the suspects; where they lived, worked or aliases. DJ began with Mujab, who used a bank ATM. The time and date help to pinpoint the account number of the transaction. Chances were that if he were a terrorist, the ATM card number would either be a fake, or stolen, but at least they had a name and some address. With any luck, they would find the whereabouts of one, which could lead them to others. DJ and the technician patiently waited for FaceScan to do its thing.

It was early morning and the sun was just beginning to rise. Bryan was looking out the window of the hotel as his cell phone rang. It was DJ.

"Mornin boss – aye've got some answers for ya," DJ said. "Aye got three matches an aye've forwarded everthin ta the FBI. They're workin to find the two o the blokes now."

"I thought you said there were three," Bryan said.

"Yeh, aye did say that, but one of em doesn't make sense," DJ said. "'is name's 'anif Zar Wali."

"Zar Wali's dead," Bryan exclaimed, waking up Shannon, who was curled up on the sofa under a blanket.

"Aye told ya it wouldn't make a bit o' sense. But another thing - aye thought the bloke looked familiar when aye saw his mug shot an aye was right - e was at yer bloody camel race." Bryan checked his Email for the JPEGs.

"Are you sure?" Bryan asked, in disbelief.

'Look et the next JPEG boss, aye pu' a beard on 'im. Maybe ye'll recognize 'im now?"

DJ was right it was the same man; they matched. Bryan was looking at a ghost.

"Yeah, of course. I'll be damned - that's why I thought the son of a bitch looked familiar," Bryan said. "Well it's a certainty that Hanif Zar Wali's dead, so who's the look-a-like?"

"'It's my conclusion boss. Has ta be his identical twin. It's the only possible conclusion, aye mean FaceScan es always right."

"And he's associated with Rowley, no doubt about that," Bryan said. "Shannon, dig up everything you can on Mister Mohammed. Let's see if we can link these two. Thanks DJ."

"Ya got it, boss. Cheers," DJ said, hanging up.

The news was disconcerting to a degree, calling for more unanswered questions. The first thing was to investigate Hanif Zar Wali's twin, bring him in for questioning if possible.

"Obviously we want to keep this quiet," Shannon said.

"Yeah, I don't want Rowley suspicious."

"Tell me more about Hanif Zar Wali," Shannon asked, now fully awake.

Bryan delved into story of Hanif Zar Wali for Shannon. "He was picked up in the early days of Enduring Freedom - same time frame as Abdul-Malik."

"Afghanistan?"

"Northeast, in the foothills of the Hindu Kush. He and Malik both were thought to have been at a camp that we took out. They may have been two of the only survivors."

"Right, now I remember something about that – Hanif Zar Wali died in the infirmary at Gitmo. It was thought initially that his death may have been caused by abusive tactics of the CIA or military interrogators," Shannon said, now vividly recalling the details. "That caused a stir."

"Yeah, until they figured that he'd suffered a concussion when he was first captured in battle and had a brain aneurism waiting to pop. The NIS got involved – JAG was lookin into possible charges against a Navy SEAL," Bryan said as his thoughts went back to Afghanistan seven years before. "During a hearing in front of the investigators, it was asked how the militant was apprehended, you know – what sort of force was used."

"They were in a combat area, aren't you supposed to use force?" Shannon asked.

"It was a Marine Corps JAG with a bug up his ass, fishing for anything – he was standin there demanding, 'What did you do to subdue him?' The reply was that Zar Wali had been hit," Bryan said with a short chuckle.

"Did you say the SEAL responded that he hit him?"

"Yeah, that's what he said, but the SEAL's counsel, a Marine Captain, jumped up and said 'Well I believe that it's already been stated, under oath, that poor Mister Zar Wali was found asleep in back of an outhouse and was apprehended after having been given a butt-strike.'"

"What's a butt-strike?" Shannon asked.

"Same thing the Major wanted to know. And the Marine Captain went on to describe it as a 'Method of delivering a good ole shoein' when your fists are full of rifle and a boot's also otherwise occupied – as in the case of the Navy SEAL, who had his boot on the combatant's throat, one fist full of his rifle and the other full of his gun,'" Bryan said, now laughing.

"What?"

Still laughing, Bryan continued, "The Marine Captain, a Southern guy from Alabama, was just makin a fool of the investigator, then said 'A butt-strike is just a good ole fashioned shoein' with the rifle. You simply bring the non-shooty end of the implement into contact with the head, balls or other interestin' part of whoever is in one's bad-graces at the time.' Case closed."

"Maybe his twin doesn't think the case is closed though," Shannon said.

"Getting revenge, a new caliphate, to reclaim old territory – what's the common ground?" Bryan asked.

"You just answered your own question Bryan. It's all common to fanatical Islamists."

"Fanatical was the best way to describe Hanif Zar Wali," Bryan said. "Maybe this twin is just as fanatical."

"Weren't tapes recovered from the camp?"

"Videos of both Malik and Hanif training along with other recruits. More accurately, it was Hanif that was actually conducting the training. He'd been a hard core terrorist with plenty of training, a member of the Pakistani army, and assignments that included cross training with U.S. Special forces prior to 9/11."

"And he was a double agent?"

"He looked and played the part of the best of the best Pakistani soldier, but was really working for the other side. Very intelligent and highly skilled, he would've been extremely valuable if we'd been able to keep him alive. Strange event happened though."

"What's that?" Shannon asked.

"Before goin' to Gitmo, he'd been detained at a Pakistani facility and they had an uprising there – a few other detainees escaped – a guard was killed, and when order was restored they found Zar Wali unconscious. He'd been perfectly fine prior to that," Bryan said, stopping for a moment. "He came to, but was never quite the same – in and out of consciousness all the way to Gitmo. Doctors said he was delusional and died very shortly after arriving of a ruptured brain aneurism."

"Maybe that was a good thing. At least he wouldn't have been released. Think about how much worse it could have been now," Shannon said.

"Oh, he never would have been released. Trust my face on that one, Shannon," Bryan assured her.

"Just curious about one thing that you never mentioned though," Shannon said.

"What's that?"

"Did you know the Navy SEAL, I mean did he work for you?" Shannon asked carnestly.

"Why, do you want to do a profile on him?"

"Just might, you know, you never can tell," she said with a wry smile from the corner of her mouth. "So did you know him?"

"You can say that."

"Who was he?"

Bryan looked at her coldly, unblinking, emotionless. "I was the Navy SEAL."

CHAPTER 18

JUNE 7, 2008

DUBAI

A CHAIN-LINKED FENCE SURROUNDED the temporary compound of shelters. Pulling up to the security gate, a uniformed guard looked inside the car, Dylan produced the necessary identification. A metal black and white barrier raised and they drove in the length of the dirt driveway. Passing their car going in the opposite direction were four buses filled with workers on their way to a job site in the city. The men in the bus stared blankly out the windows, seeing nothing, and nothing was there for them. They parked the car on a dirt lot at the end of three rows of dormitories, got out walked towards the barracks.

The labor camp conditions were deplorable. Bryan understood why Dylan had insisted that he should see it for himself. The camp evoked an undercurrent of despair that coursed throughout. Haggard men of all ages, dressed in blue work uniforms, were either busy washing clothes in rusted metal tubs, huddled together discoursing in small groups, or if they were lucky, making a meal or if very lucky, smoking a cigarette. It was that bad.

The facility that housed several hundred Pakistani laborers had a dark cloud of depression hanging over it. The blue and white prefabricated shelters that the laborers lived in were austere and grim. Made of plywood and aluminum siding, six workers slept in each thirty square foot, windowless room, connected to one another by hot, airless corridors. Without enough space inside, their belongings were kept in personal crates outside the shelters, exposing everything they owned to the elements of the Arabian Desert, notably the endless sand combined with heat. Then there was the scourge that always followed man in squalor. Rats lived under the shelters and sewage ran out, the product of twenty-five men that shared each bathroom. Stoves used for cooking the worker's one daily meal were makeshift, improvised out of whatever materials may be found lying around the facility, such as coals, and metal gratings, which combined with a shallow hole made a stove or grill.

Dylan guided Bryan slowly through the private-labor camp, pointing out numerous infractions of Dubai's Migratory Labor Laws. As they passed through the doorway of one dormitory, a large rat popped out from the top of a garbage drum that was overflowing with refuse and suddenly scurried under the shelter.

It was just 8:00 AM, yet the temperature was already ninety degrees Fahrenheit and would reach one hundred fifteen for the high temperature by the end of the day. Inside the dormitories of the camp, temperatures would stay above one hundred degrees 24/7. It was a sweltering existence, and there was nowhere for a construction worker to ever escape Dubai's unbelievable heat.

"How are you sahr?" A Pakistani inside the oven of a shelter greeted them in English.

"How long have you been living here?" Bryan asked the man, who was smiling at him. He looked to be in his fifties, but could have been much younger. Two of his upper teeth were missing, and his shirt was soaked with perspiration.

"Two years." He held up two fingers as he spoke. A second younger man joined them and answered as well.

"I have been here two years too. Are you a journalist?"

Bryan looked at Dylan and decided to roll with the ploy

"Yes we are. Do you mind answering a few questions?"

"No I don't mind," said the younger man, also smiling.

"What's your name and where ya from?" Dylan began the questioning.

"My name is Gabir. He is my uncle, Baqar. We are both from Karachi."

"Tell us about your work, why don't ya," Dylan suggested.

"We both were working at the Burj Arabia. We are now finished with our jobs, but we have not been paid for six months of work."

"You haven't been paid for six months? Who hired you?" Bryan asked.

Dylan spoke for the two laborers. "Bisilah Construction hired all of the workers here, but has since ceased to exist. The same with their sponsors – poof, jest like that - vanished into the desert sands along with the money that's owed them. Took their work visas es well," he said, snapping his fingers.

"Is this true?" Brian asked the older man.

"Yes, it is true. Bisilah in Karachi hired us. We were promised eight hundred fifty dirham per month and had to pay ten thousand dirham each to come to Dubai," he said, brushing flies away from his face.

Bryan did the math. Workers paid a sponsor twenty seven hundred dollars for Dubai visas as laborers, approximately what they would earn in a year there if they were ever paid. Bryan shook his head in disgust.

"And how long was your contract for?"

"We were to work on the Burj Arabia for two years and then at the World for two years. When we came here, our pay was reduced to five hundred dirham each month, and they only paid us for one year and a half."

"Mate, the bastards completely reneged on the deal. Paid em a total of twenty-four undred dollars, but took in twenty-seven undred from these blokes, and another ten thousand from the developers. These slums they're livin in were built for nothin essentially – and because the employer was a limited liability company and is now gone, these bastards here don't have a legal status in Dubai. So they're stuck here without money, or means to get back home."

"Do you have any authorities looking into your situation?" Bryan asked.

"No but there is a meeting after prayer tonight. We will discuss it then I am told," the older man said. At that, the younger man began to angrily castigate the older one in Urdu, a classical diatribe.

"Thank you," Bryan said to the two men. He grabbed Dylan by the arm to move along.

"I picked up on that, anything you heard?" Dylan asked.

"My Urdu is a little rusty, but the nephew's not happy with his uncle. They'd been told not to discuss it," Bryans said. "How many more are there here in Dubai with similar stories?" Bryan further asked.

"Fortunately, the employers are not all exactly like that one. Laborers all have to pay work visa fees as they did, and the wages generally suck. The living conditions are the same in most of the camps too - the difference being the majority of the employers do actually pay their workers. Probably only five percent screw 'em - but there's somethin like eight hundred thousand workers here in the Emirates. That means about forty thousand are gettin' the ultimate shaft," Dylan said.

"So the employers concoct some fabricated story about the job and the pay to lure them here. Once here, they work their ass off all day, then get to live in these shit holes, piled on top of each other without electricity or running water. Please tell me it doesn't get any worse," Bryan said.

"But it does, mate. Last year over one hundred workers committed suicide rather than go back to Pakistan to face their family without the promised riches they should've received in Dubai. They're humiliated for needin to borrow against future wages, jest to have enough money to eat. Not to mention almost all of the workers are sendin half their pay back home to their wives and family. Here's another nice statistic – jest over one thousand workers were killed on the job last year in Dubai, but wrongful death suits never occur - not allowed."

"These projects aren't helping the workers at all. In fact they're aiding and abetting their despair, fueling a desperate predicament. What about Dubai's laws or that of the UAE as a whole?"

"Foreign labor makes up about ninety percent of Dubai's work force. For construction, you might as well call it one hundred percent. But let me tell you about the laws that Dubai has on the books. The law doesn't grant workers the right to organize unions or to strike - both illegal," Dylan explained.

Dylan continued to say that, "Any worker can seek redress through the courts, but none can afford a lawyer to take the case, and there are thousands of cases, but no such thing as a class action suit."

"Class action is also illegal, I take it," Bryan said.

"That's a fact, and I might add that so is forced or compulsory labor, the problem though – some dishonest staffing agents brought the miserable blokes to Dubai under conditions that approach indentured servitude – but no one can do a damn thing about it."

Bryan shook his head. "With such strong barriers against collective action and a government that has little motivation to protect non-national workers desperate for income, it's not surprising that exploitation of these poor Pakistanis continues." He thought for a moment and then asked, "Dubai's Ministry of Labor just does nothing about it? And what about the World Bank? Doesn't this fall under their bailiwick?"

"The World Bank's been notified about the conditions. I even sent a letter to 'em. Nothin's ever done. They couldn't care less, it seems - and the government agency responsible for tracking these employers – no way. The labor population has grown too fast for em to even keep up. They've eighty employees responsible for over two hundred thousand companies throughout the UAE. The workers are provided with a toll free hotline, and the camps are also randomly inspected – but most fail the mandatory requirements such as one man in a thirty square foot room, not six, one bathroom for ten men, not twenty-five. But as I said, the officials are over worked and under staffed. The majority of the problems simply slip through cracks in the system," Dylan said, pulling out a pack of cigarettes.

Most of what Dylan was saying Bryan was familiar with. He had already heard and read about over the last few years many times, but seeing the circumstances firsthand, the impact of the words became very real. He couldn't help but wonder what the worker's circumstance would be when the Dubai building boom failed. It was already rumored that an economic calamity was percolating and Sheik Mo was considering a moratorium on further construction.

Dylan lit a cigarette, inhaled and continued, "The UAE Labor Minister is posed with a dilemma – if he stands up for the rights of the workers an ensures that the laws are enforced, there's a fear that it could have an impact on the economic growth of the Emirates - so the result's jest lip service. 'Go speak with your supervisor if you have complaints.' We know that'll get the workers absolutely nowhere."

"Dylan, I need to ask you for a few favors," Bryan said, putting his hand oh the man's shoulder.

"Go ahead mate, ask away," Dylan responded, preparing himself for a whopper.

"I need for you to bring me out here tonight, that's one."

"Not a problem at all, mate," Dylan said, adding, "That's only one though, what's the other?"

"I need to stop by an electronics store, and a drug store, and I need a blue workman's uniform," Bryan said coolly.

"That's more than a few, but I'll see what I can do."

"We're gonna find out what's going on at that meeting tonight."

Shannon was busy looking over her notes, finally adjusting to the temporary surroundings of the Consul General's office on the twenty-first floor of the World Trade building in downtown Dubai. The State Department, at Bryan's request, provided one small interior office with phone in the SCIF. The *Sensitive Compartmented Information Facility* in the Consul General spaces was a secure area used for intelligence briefs. Usually simply configured, it was an enclosed work location in a trailer, truck, or in this case, a building, where confidential, secret, top secret, or compartmented information could be discussed. Within the SCIF, Shannon and Bryan had secure access to all Pegasus databases, and certain NSA computers using the SCIF's own system. There were no windows, and Shannon was able to really concentrate on her work. She was deep in thought and startled as Bryan burst in the room.

"Let me pose a hypothetical to you Shannon?"

"Feel free, I'm dying to know," she said closing her notebook.

"If I were a Jihadist mastermind and wanted to recruit an army of suicide bombers, martyrs, the best place to recruit are the slums, where the impoverished live in a world of despair. And bonus points if there happens to be some ethnic group, long-standing enemy, or Israeli bombs landing on their villages, killing a younger sister, or parent, maybe a grandmother. I mean that's where the Hamas and Hezbollah have traditionally recruited suicide bombers. Isn't it?"

"No question," Shannon said.

"If I'm a Sunni and want to blow up Shi'ah – same game plan."

"Again, agree with you every step of the way," she said nodding.

"So misery, despair, desperation, and vengeance are the principle ingredients necessary to motivate a man, or a woman for that matter, to blow themselves up in the name of a just cause."

"Just cause, in their brainwashed mind," she interjected.

"No doubt, and at the end of the road, in their mind, is eternal peace, salvation, martyrdom, money to the family, and maybe seventy-two virgins - and of course, what better places to recruit than right here in the miserable camps. They're penniless, despondent, and possibly suicidal anyway. If one hundred committed suicide by hanging themselves, then a smart terrorist scout simply directs that potential suicide to commit the act with a bunch of explosives strapped to his body."

"Now Captain Craig, I think you've got it," she said, standing up from her chair, stretching her arms over her head.

Bryan got it all right, and he believed it was much more sinister than terrorists lying in wait. He wanted Shannon to fill in the rest of revelation.

"Shannon, you don't think it's a simple case of terrorists taking advantage of the situation, do you."

"No, I don't Bryan, not at all. I think that it's by design, as you've concluded," she said.

"We need the proof though. If we can get that, we just might be able to put some of these fringe fanatical groups out of business permanently.'" Bryan said.

Bryan picked up a tennis ball sitting on a bookshelf. Bouncing it on the floor several times while he thought, he said, "Shannon, here's what the scenario looks like as I put this together. The bank accounts are being used to create employers and recruiting companies with the plan of having them go bankrupt, but not to abscond with the cash, but to use the money to fund terrorism plots."

"And a banker along with Petrov could've set that up," she threw in.

"Right, plus the suicide bombers are pre-funding their own deaths, in some cases years ahead. They're taking loans against pay and giving to the terrorists," Bryan said. "The camps are built with the intent of fueling the Jihad with recruits from Pakistan. It's just a 'Farm System' for Suicide Bombers and terrorists in general."

Shannon nodded in agreement, stating "That's what I think is going on here too. Some fundamental group is bribing workers using the worker's own money. You know, pulling them aside and telling them that they'll send over twenty thousand dirham if they carry out such and such a mission. Maybe they actually even send the money, but the amounts we're talking about are huge, hundreds of millions per year, easily. Without even investing a dime."

"Well you can bet your last dollar they aren't just letting the money sit around idle, I can assure you of that." Bryan was recalling Gil's offshore insurance scenario to move money around.

The scheme was brilliant in its simplicity, yet diabolical in its purpose. At the center of the organization would have to be someone with a great deal of power and influence over many aspects of government in the UAE, and Dubai in particular. He'd have to be well connected with characters such as Rowley, who moved with ease in the world of finance, as well as weapons suppliers like Petrov. Resources such as those could allow for such a person to have an army of terrorists to send anywhere he wanted. If he needed to impress on an Islamic point, or spark some trouble in regions such as Iraq, or Lebanon – off they'd go to stir the pot of insurrection, anarchy, sectarian attacks, whatever was needed. *Who could this person possibly be, Bryan wondered?*

CHAPTER 19

JUNE 7, 2008

DUBAI

CALLING TO THE FAITHFUL, the *muezzin* announced the evening prayer from the mosque's minaret, his voice amplified by loudspeakers. Chosen for his vocal qualities and melodic delivery, the muezzin began the chant of the adhan, a call *"Allah Akbar, Allah Akbar, Allah Akbar, Allah Akbar,"* his voice resonated that God is the greatest. *"Hayya 'alas-salat, hayya 'alas-salat,"* he chanted telling the Muslims of Dubai who could hear him to make haste towards prayer.

A middle-aged man maneuvered his wheelchair toward a balcony that faced Mecca. "Sika, please come with me to pray for *Maghrib,"* he said. *Maghrib* is the sunset prayer, one of five obligatory daily prayers that all Muslims of the Sunni faith should perform.

"It will be my privilege to join you in prayer Mullah Afzar." Amir followed the man that before had been his teacher, still that, and much more. They went outside to the expansive wrap around balcony that served as the home's prayer hall. It faced Dubai's largest mosque and lined up perfectly on a plumb line to the *Kaaba* in Mecca, the small cube made of granite and covered with black silk cloth decorated by gold embroidery; the holiest earthly thing in Islam. Tradition held the belief that the *Kaaba* was built by Abraham and was the principle destination of the *Hajj*, the pilgrimage made by nearly four million Muslims each year.

Amir's personal pilgrimage to Mecca was memorable as any Muslim's first pilgrimage would be. The *Hajj*, as the pilgrimage is called, is a requirement as part of the five pillars of the Islamic faith, and occurs on *Dhu al-Hijjah*, the final month of the year according to the Islamic Calendar. He was twenty-one when his eyes saw Islam's sacred mosque for the first time. Known as the *Haram Sharif*, the mosque had evolved over the centuries to what it was today: a modern place of worship for the Islamic faithful, holding up to a million people at a time, complete with the conveniences of any twenty-first century, three story building; air conditioning, bathrooms, elevators, and escalators.

Islam's holiest of all holy places was not immune to the evil acts of terrorism, including kidnapping and murder. Nearly thirty years before, just one month before the invasion of Afghanistan by the Soviet Union, the sacred mosque was the scene of a terrorist attack by fundamentalist Sunnis from Nadj, Saudi Arabia. Two hundred extremists armed to the teeth were led by a militant who believed the Saud family, the rulers of Saudi Arabia, had become too westernized, too patronizing of the United States and its oil companies. In the militant's eyes, and those of his Wahhabi Sunni followers, the Saudi government, and the Al Sauds were illegitimate corrupt rulers. Their plan called for a siege of the Grand Mosque.

The siege lasted two weeks. In the end, French counter-terrorism commandos and Jordanian paramilitary forces retook the Grand Mosque in a bloody assault. Over three hundred worshippers that had been held hostage were killed during the ensuing battle. The surviving rebel and their leader, were rounded up and beheaded during a live public execution, one that was televised. Amir and Afzar were both Sunnis, and each ashamed at the desecration of the *Kaaba*. Amir knew there was a better way. *Let this be a lesson!* "A lesson that religion is a powerful thing that can take men to great heights. Where they can accomplish wondrous things. Or cause them to follow a misguided path, resulting in horrible acts," Amir said.

Similarities between Christian and Islamic faiths seemed to be more pervasive than the differences. Both are monotheistic religions, believing in one God. Moral codes, commandments, and basic concepts of religious practices are so closely related that from an outside observer it would be difficult to distinguish between the two. The Old Testament and the teachings of the Quran are nearly the same. One God, one evil figure (Satan), covenants, omnipotence of God, judgment day, freewill, the spirit or soul, miracles, transgressions, Adam and Eve, Moses and the children of Israel, and Jesus Christ born to the virgin Mary are like basic concepts. Faith, human rights, parents, society's laws, suicide, and homosexuality are like moral codes. Prayer, congregational worship, and charity are like practices. The Quran affirms the Biblical prophets including Abraham, Solomon, and Jesus Christ. The major difference being that Islam believes the final prophet to be Mohammed and Islam doesn't believe in the trinity of the 'Father, Son, and Holy Ghost" as one entity. Since Jesus was unable to transcribe his teachings, and his philosophies were instead passed down through the ages with dozens of recensions, the Bible is considered "corrupted" by Islam. Essentially, Christians had lost the word of God as dictated to Jesus by Gabriel because *"they don't follow the prophet Mohammed."*

Mullah Afzar believed that the differences between the two worlds were becoming impossible to bridge, unless of course, fundamentalists on both sides of the fence could agree with each other. Amir was beginning to agree with his mentor. Just within the Islamic faith alone, the gap between Sunnis and Shi'ah, and extremists from any two secular beliefs were virtually insurmountable. *How could fundamentalist Christians and Islamists ever agree on anything but to wipe each other out?*

Amir recognized the likelihood of mutually assured destruction if more than one half of the world's population failed to bridge those very subtle differences. The world's Christian population was more than that of Islam, two billion versus one and a half billion, but Islam was the fastest growing of the two, and it was a member of the nuclear club. An all out nuclear war between the two people would wreak unimaginable permanent damage to civilization. But Islam had to gain its status back and be respected, Amir lamented.

The teacher and his pupil faced Mecca and waited for the prompt of the *muezzin* again, signaling to begin prayer. Mullah Afzar, who was paralyzed from the waist down, remained in his wheelchair, as Amir stood next to him. The view from the balcony gave them a magnificent vantage from one hundred and ten stories above the desert. The mosque's minaret was one mile away to the west and far below them. The prayer was called for. They both raised their hands and spoke simultaneously, first the phrase that "God is greatest," and then recited the first chapter of the Quran.

"In the name of God, the beneficent, the merciful. Praise be to God, Lord of the worlds, the beneficent, the merciful, master of the Day of Judgment. You alone do we worship, and you we ask for help; show us the straight path. The path of those you bestowed favor upon, not anger upon, and not of those who go astray." Amir dropped into a prostrate position, and then placed his nose, hands, and knees on the carpet. In Mecca, when done in congregation, one million worshippers bowing to the floor simultaneously, sounded like an enormous clap of thunder.

They then began the second part of their prayer. "All glorification is for God. All acts of good deeds and worship are for Him. Peace and the mercy and blessings of God are upon you, O Prophet. Peace is upon us and all of God's righteous servants. I bear witness that there is no god but God, and I bear witness that Muhammad is His Servant and Messenger. O God, exalt Muhammad and the family of Muhammad as you exalted Abraham and the family of Abraham. Verily you are full of praise and majesty. O God, bless Muhammad and the family of Muhammad as you blessed Abraham and the family of Abraham. Verily, you are full of praise and majesty."

Amir and Afzar completed the prayer as per their Sunni tradition, with each turning to their right and left and saying "Peace be on you and the mercy of God."

"Sika, you've been distant lately." Afzar noted as they came back inside their home. It was a vast space, occupying one half of the floor. The main living area walls were the color of sun-dried clay, with a faint reddish hue and elaborately ornamented with intricate stucco patterns and inlaid tiles. There were large arches at the ceiling were dominated by intricate tiled mosaics. The room had nine elongated windows modeled from the Alhambra, three per façade, each rimmed with inscriptions and interwoven with gold flowers and leaves. The flooring was predominantly white marble. At the center of the room was one-half scale facsimile of the Patio of Lions fountain, and a pool that ran the length of the room, five feet wide and fifty feet in both directions from the fountain. It too had ten waterspouts running down the length of both sides of the pool. Twenty-foot high marble columns dotted the five thousand square foot space. Plants and trees were placed throughout, giving it the feel of an outside garden.

"I fear world events Mullah Afzar. My plans may need to be accelerated," Amir said.

"World events are always a concern Sika, but you have the wisdom and the resources to make events work for the best." Afzar called him Sika from the time that he was a boy.

Amir sat down on the large sofa and motioned to an attendant standing close to the cage containing his favorite falcon. The bird stepped onto the man's gloved hand. He brought it to Amir. Removing the falcon's hood, Amir gave it a small piece of meat, which it immediately devoured.

"Afzar, do you believe that the Islamic world can be responsible with the possession of nuclear weapons? For this is my concern - if Shi'ah want to kill Sunni in secular attacks, and they have a small nuclear device, wouldn't they use it? Would a Mullah such as you stop Sunni fundamentalists from doing the same? How do we protect Muslims from Muslims? The West must have confidence in our ability to manage our own kind before they will trust us. We must be cautious before we pounce and claim what is rightfully Islamic."

"Perhaps they'll never trust us. That's something that we must always be prepared for. We alone must be responsible for our destiny and can't be dependent on what the West wants for us. Your people know of you Sika, and they are waiting for you to lead them. Your own destiny will be fulfilled; I will see to it. And now with the Islamic world in a state of confusion, the people need the leadership you possess. God willing, perhaps the time is right, and not a day should be wasted. But you should be the one with the power to make the difference. Islam cannot survive by being too close to the United States or so fundamental, that we ignore progress," Mullah Afzar said.

"I understand. When will you be leaving?" Amir asked.

"I will leave for Pakistan tomorrow," Mullah Afzar said.

"Will Shamema be ready?"

"She will be acceptant," Afzar said nodding his head.

"And her grandfather?"

"That is in your hands, Amir."

Staying one step ahead of government officials, international inspectors, human rights activists and the multitudes of other watchdog groups were challenges the shapers of Dubai faced routinely. And building on the scale of the visionaries was a monumental enterprise. Titanic construction operations needed hordes of laborers desperate for work. And they needed hundreds of thousands of them. The Dubai projects were larger than a hundred Great Pyramids of Giza, and would require ten times as many workers as Pharaoh Cheop used. Four thousand five hundred years separated the gargantuan efforts, yet conditions for the workman had few differences.

Baazland was going to pose immense challenges. No development had ever been conceived that had a greater vision, and none would need a greater preponderance of unskilled manpower; the manpower that came from the ghettos of Pakistan and India. Impoverished men of desperate circumstance willing to toil under the scalding sun of the Arabian desert; twelve hours a day under one hundred and ten degree heat, for the equivalent of thirty-five dollars a week. These were human resources that were kept behind the scenes. Hidden by the high walls of labor encampments. Hidden from the view of the American investors and their State Department officials. Of course, they all knew too well about the severe working conditions that existed, but the grandeur of Dubai induced myopia. And once out of sight, then out of mind. For now, Amir reasoned, the ends justify the means, but that wouldn't always be the case.

Skillful deception was needed, much like the illusionist. The Sheikhs and their family members, as well as other Emir's in the UAE had been wrong to allow the use of Pakistani children as camel jockeys.

"How much more indiscreet and foolish could these slave traders have been?" Amir would often ask rhetorically of the Sheikhs.

The jockeys had been kidnapped or sold by their parents, more than seven thousand in all since the end of the Gulf War. They'd been beaten and nearly starved into compliance in many instances. Without their parents to protect them and unable to speak Arabic, the young boys became the slave-jockeys of the UAE's multi-billion dollar camel industry. Spectators from the West most certainly found the races interesting, if not a bit absurd. Human rights organizations took notice too, immediately hoisting the penalty flags of human trafficking and child slavery. Embarrassed by the folly, the UAE replaced children with remote controlled robots as jockeys.

The predicament for the Pakistani laborers, the workers pledged to shape Dubai's skyline, was not very different from that of the camel jockeys. Investment groups would envision a new project of massive proportions. The syndicate would hire architects and construction companies from the United States or Europe to build their vision. Agents were then enlisted to recruit and sponsor the unskilled labor for specific projects. The Pakistanis would say goodbye to their families and board ships or planes for the short trip to Dubai, and upon arriving in the Emirate, their passports and work visas would be confiscated by their agents. That was by design. *They can't get away.*

Improvements should be made for the people who built Dubai, Amir believed. He would be the one to do it. Baazland would be the place from where changes would commence. The workers, the Pakistanis, would be brought into the fold first. They would be pledged to him. Baazland would be built, and it would be his.

Was he a modern day conqueror? Amir was sure if there were to be conquests, he'd start with Dubai, a launching pad. The pioneers of Dubai would be absorbed, taken over, just as corporations in Las Vegas bought out native Nevadans. Mullah Afzar told him "Conquest is your nature, Sika - and leadership in your blood." Dubai needed a leader, Amir thought, and so did Pakistan. In fact the entire Muslim world needed a leader, one that would guide them to prosperity, not secular Islamists bent on mutual paths to condemnation. Timing was everything and the Islamic world at the brink. The stage was set for a new reign. Amir would have what should be his.

Amir Kahn was born in the land of warlords and insurgents, the Kom nation of Nuristan. Destitute and considered inconsequential by Afghanistan's government, the sixty thousand inhabitants of Nuristan had barely advanced beyond the nineteenth century. Like Chitral, their neighbors to the east, Nuristan was remote and mountainous, without roads and only few rocky trails connecting tiny villages. Dardic, an Indo-European language spoken by the people of the region, had many dialects, most being unintelligible with another. The people who lived there were constantly in need. They didn't prosper growing opium as some Afghans to the south had. The ground was simply too rocky. They instead were artisans, much like the Kalasha, experts in wood crafting and ceramics. Nuristanis were also independent to a fault. Fierce defense of their homeland had in fact kicked out all invaders and as a consequence, had unfortunately limited progress as well.

The Soviet Red Army was the most recent invasion force that learned first hand the determination of this unique clan. Amir was too young to remember the day in December, the twenty-fifth day of a Christian year, nineteen seventy-nine. It was a day of significance for Christians. It was also the day the Soviet Union entered Afghanistan uninvited.

The Soviet Union and Kabul had been friends since the People's Democratic Party, a Marxist regime, had taken power in a bloody coup the year before. The Soviets in fact already had over four hundred advisors in the country's capital. One day the Red Army's advisors suggested that the Afghan tank battalion should stand down in order to conduct crucial maintenance on their Soviet made tanks. Three days later, on Christmas Day, the Soviets flew into the Airport at Kabul and took over, in the process killing their former friend, and President of Afghanistan.

The first resistance of any significance came from the Nuristanis. The Soviets had already captured Kabul, but the scope of their influence literally ended at the city limits. Nuristani warlords, living up to their reputation, called for a Jihad against the invaders. Mujahideen forces, often on horseback, assembled in the Nuristan Province. One Mujahideen General, Ahmed Shah Massoud, a charismatic former engineering student, became known as the Lion of Panjshir for his bravery in facing down the world's second superpower. His leadership of the guerilla warfare attracted more than just men; he attracted the attention also a particular fair-haired twelve-year old. Amir Sayyid (Zah-hîd) found himself in the middle of the guerilla fighting that would ultimately claim the lives of so many Soviet conscripts, more than fourteen thousand. The youngster would learn how to fire a Russian made AK-47 and become a hero after he shot down a Soviet Hind helicopter, and the first to do so with a burst of small arms fire. The act would earn him the highest praise from even the Lion of Panjshir himself.

The steep terrain of the northern Afghan provinces, the western edge of the Hindu Kush, provided ideal hiding places for guerilla fighters when ambushing Soviet troops and convoys. The Soviet Generals countered with the introduction of the Mi-24 Hind gunship, sending in more than five hundred of the lethal helicopters. The Hind packed a punch, as it had a cannon on the nose and also carried stations for launching unguided missiles. Hinds killed many Nuristani warriors and civilians.

Amir and fellow young rebels had little in the way of effective weapons to combat the mighty Hind, at least not before the CIA was able to provide weapons through Pakistan. A few warlords had obtained SA-7 shoulder fired surface to air missiles, and had some occasional successes. Small arms fire was completely ineffective on the Mi-24; until the day that a twelve-year old showed everyone how to do it.

A heavily armored Hind had been on patrol along the mountain valleys searching for bands of guerillas such as Amir's. The Mujahideen surprised the helicopter and attacked with their Ak-47s from below, but doing no damage and unfortunately drawing the Hind's attention to their location. With their cover blown, the guerillas scrambled for cover. The Hind turned around to counter the guerilla ambush. The Mi-24 raked the side of the cliff with its machine gun on the first pass, blasting rock and dirt in all directions. The guerillas flattened themselves in back of what little cover could be found for protection from the killing machine.

Several Mujahideen perished on the initial firing run. The men, including Amir, stood up in defiance, bravely firing their small arms at the "flying crocodile." The helicopter returned for a second pass, the results nearly the same as the first. With five men down, Amir was determined to get the Soviets when they came back again, or die trying. He was certain it would return. The Soviet pilot didn't disappoint.

The attack helicopter, with a crew of three, turned and began to make the third firing run on the Mujahideen guerillas; the pilot convinced that he could finish off all of the Afghans on the next pass. He bore down on them once more, with the Hind's cannon firing quick bursts. Coughing incendiary rounds. Puffing death.

Amir bravely stood his ground and aimed his weapon at the attacker, targeting the large red star on the fuselage. Leading the Hind slightly he guided his rounds into the star. Suddenly, to his and his comrades surprise and delight, the flying machine began to sputter, pouring thick black smoke from the beneath its tail section. The pilot, noting that he was rapidly loosing oil pressure, began flying off in retreat, hoping to find a suitable place to put the helicopter down before it auto-rotated, crashing with a seized engine. The pilot's efforts were futile.

The victorious warriors heard the crash just after the Hind disappeared around the corner of a narrow valley wall. Rejoicing in celebration, the six remaining Mujahideen clambered down the steep rocky sides to reach the crash site. What they found was two of the crew dead, and the pilot injured. After careful examination of the tail section they discovered the oil tank was directly below the red star. To kill the flying crocodile, simply aim at the star. *How convenient is this?*

Amir was the conqueror and rightfully jubilant, but his interest was on the craft itself. Only recently had he ever seen something other than an insect or bird fly under its own power. *How could something like this fly?*

He had asked the others, but no one there knew the answer. Few had ever seen a flying crocodile up close before that day. Amir wanted to know what it was like to fly the contraption and was upset at the others for killing the one Russian survivor, who had the answers to his questions. He vowed that one day he would pilot a machine like the one he had shot down. Word quickly spread to other tribes and warlords. Amir had become well known among the resistance.

The young Amir, whose only family had been killed in the first days of the conflict, was also an orphan, but would soon come under the watchful eye of an educated, caring man from Pakistan, who'd come to see the Afghan conflict first hand. Once convinced that it was a worthy enough cause he decided to stay and help the hundreds of thousands of people that were being displaced by the conflict. The border towns of Pakistan became flooded with the war's refugees. Amir was one of those refugees, his village had been bombed to rubble by the Soviets. It was at one of those camps that Amir, after being wounded, would end up.

Cramped, dirty and either very cold or very hot; that was the nature of most of the refugee camps along the border. Amir had been asked to guide a young, six year old girl to one of those camps for safety. With fair complexion and light green eyes as some Pashtun people, she was the sister of triplets, whose village had been destroyed by the Soviets, killing her mother and grandfather and most of the villagers. Her father was presumed dead, or fighting somewhere else in the country. The young girl was left without the means to keep her brothers alive. Amir now fourteen years old, led the way, seeing to it that the girl and her brothers, who were only four years old, were brought safely to a camp. One of the boys had been injured, struck in the head by debris after an explosion, and another had eyes like Amir's, blue.

The Pakistani left behind a wife and baby daughter, but this young boy, who so bravely took charge, reminded him of his own people, and he took a special interest in him. His light brown hair and fair complexion made the boy stand out. Surprisingly, he was already a linguist, able to read and write Urdu, Arabic, Pashto, and Farsi. Amir explained that foreign Mujahideen had been his tutors at various camps. It was evident to the Pakistani that the boy was an extremely fast learner. He was an exceptional talent, if not outright brilliant.

The Pakistani, who had many years of formal education, would spend hour after hour with Amir teaching him English, mathematics, philosophy, and history. Amir's thirst for knowledge was ignited and his desire to learn, insatiable. The teacher called his pupil Sika, short for Sikandar, which was Urdu for "extremely skilled." The Pakistani told Amir about the people from Chitral and the history of the North West Frontier. He told Amir about Alexander the Great, taught him some Greek, whereupon Amir named the young light-eyed Afghan girl Despoina. He spoke of the British Empire. After much cajoling, Amir agreed with his tutor to leave Afghanistan, away from the conflict, and begin formal studies.

The teacher however, would go back to Afghanistan and continue his mission to help the needy, and at times when absolutely necessary, to take up the fight against the Soviet invaders. Before he left, he made arrangement with British missionaries living in Islamabad to receive the boy, and it would be in Islamabad that Amir would attend school for the first time in his life. But before the two parted company, the Paki gave a special gift to Amir. It was a very beautiful ring with a white mountain in the center. He told Amir that the ring was meant to be his. His teacher said goodbye. Arriving in Islamabad, the fourteen year old introduced himself as Amir Sika Kahn.

Amir's mind was a sponge. He was a prodigy with an aptitude for most every subject he delved into. Completing his studies at the University level by his eighteenth birthday. Islamic culture fascinated Amir, yet he wasn't drawn to extremist notions early on. He did however, respect the Afghan people's struggle against the Soviet occupation; after all he was a Nuristani and a Pashtun. In some ways though, the struggle was to the disadvantage of Afghanis and themselves. The Soviets had opened new schools; and would've educated the entire land, but at what costs? Amir believed that capitalism was necessary, and looked upon certain fundamental elements of Islamic law as being repressive and limiting for the development of a nation, but the underlying moralities he wholeheartedly believed in and followed.

Upon returning to Pakistan he ventured to the North West Frontier, the home of his teacher. Amir wanted to finally meet his teacher's family and return the ring to its rightful heir. And he desired to at last see the places that his teacher had spoken of. There was the fort at Chitral where British and Gurkhas had fought against Amir's ancestors, the Nuristanis, but mostly, he wanted to see the people that looked so like him.

Amir was still very young, only twenty, but a man now, and a very tall one at that, standing six feet four inches. He entered the village of the Kalash Kafirs one evening. They were amazed at his height. Especially for someone who must be one of their own, after all he spoke their language perfectly. The Kalasha also noticed his ring. It was a ring of their ruler in Chitral. *Was this young man an heir? Had he come to Chitral to lead his people?*

"Look for a small structure in the middle of the village. It will have a sign," his teacher said. Amir found it, and entered, searching under the wooden idol where he was told the book would be. There it was. Holding a candle, he sat down to look.

"Look inside the cover Sika," his teacher said.

"There you will find something very important. It may be your destiny that you find. Once you understand, you must put it back."

Amir Kahn did just that. He opened the old book, marveling at the history that was represented on only four pages of guest entries. His hand felt the slightly raised area on the inside of the registry's back cover.

"There it is Amir," he said thinking of Afzar Kahn.

He took out his knife and cut very carefully to open the cover and remove what was hiding there. Something was metallic. His knife grazed it as he skillfully slid the sharp blade along the object's line. The sound and feel of metal touching metal was unmistakable. He continued with the delicate surgery.

There was something metal, as he had deduced. Tin. A journal was there too, hidden for a hundred years. After removing both he put the book down and held the flickering flame of the candle close. He looked at the tin carefully, and then he read the journal. Amir understood.

ABOVE: *Tirich Mir. At 25,230 feet, it is the highest peak of the high Hindu Kush, and 33ʳᵈ highest in the world. The summit was first reached in 1950 by a Norwegian expedition. The peak is overlooking the valley of Chitral Town. (John Jackson)*

RIGHT: *Lake Saif ul Maluk – Hindu Kush, one of the many glacier and cirque fed lakes of the high Hindu Kush. (PD)*

BOTTOM RIGHT: *White Gyrfalcon (PD)*

TOP: *Only survivor Dr. Brydon following massacre at Gandamak arrives at Jalalabad on the 13th of January 1842. 12,000 camp followers and 4,500 British were wiped out in the retreat from Kabul during the 1st Anglo-Afghan Wars. (PD)*

ABOVE: *1st of September 1880. The 92nd Highlanders storming Sahibdad in the battle of Baba Wali during the 2nd Anglo-Afghan War. (PD)*

RIGHT: *"Save Me From My Friends."* Cartoon from 1878 London Times depicting the "Great Game" between the British Empire and expansionism of Russia. (PD)

BELOW RIGHT: Rudyard Kipling (PD)

BELOW LEFT: Amir Abdur Rahman Kahn – King of Afghanistan 1880 – 1901. (PD)

BOTTOM: Queen Victoria awarding the Afghan War Medal to Bobbie the dog, survivor of the Battle of Maiwand, and other members of the 66th Foot at Osborne House (PD)

"SAVE ME FROM MY FRIENDS!"

TOP: *USS Sacramento & Carl Vinson – 2001 Enduring Freedom (US Navy)*
RIGHT: *An F-14D armed with JDAM & Sidewinders flying on a mission to Afghanistan targets in 2001. (US Navy)*

BOTTOM LEFT: *Special Forces in the Hindu Kush (US Navy)*
BOTTOM RIGHT: *MQ-1 Predator Drone armed with Hellfire missiles. (PD-GOV)*

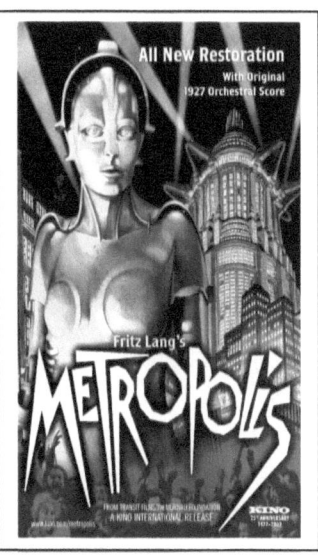

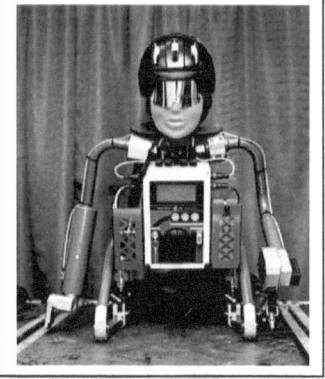

TOP LEFT: *The Burj Al Arab. The tallest hotel in the world at over 1000 feet, and the only "seven star" rating. (AP)*

LEFT: *Toddler Camel Jockey – Dubai in the background (ANSAR Burney)*
TOP RIGHT: *"Fembot" robot of Metropolis. Movie poster for the re-release of the 1927 Fritz Lang classic. (PD)*
ABOVE: *Dubai's robots - camel jockeys, the future of the Dubai camel industry. (AP)*

ABOVE: *Cultures over 2000 years. A Roman amphitheater, Muslim and Spanish fort at the Alcazaba – Málaga, Spain (Manfred Werner)*

RIGHT: *La Mezquita de Córdoba, the 8th century design took two hundred years to complete. The mosque is one of 1000 built by the Caliphs in Córdoba. It was the most magnificent and the only not facing Mecca. (PD)*

BOTTOM RIGHT: *The Patio of Lions at the Alhambra – Grenada, Spain - built between 1248 and 1354. It is a classic example of intricate, Islamic design. (PD)*

TOP: *Evening prayer in Mecca at the sacred mosque. The holiest site for all Muslims is a modern facility that can hold up to one million worshippers.* (AP)

LEFT: *Sheikh preparing falcon for flight - circa 1890's. A millennia old symbol of Arab nobility.* (PD-old)

TOP: *Mujahideen on horseback preparing to attack Soviet positions and tanks – 1986 (AP)*
BOTTOM: *19th century Afghan tribal warriors before the battle of Baba Wali - 1880 (PD-old)*

TOP LEFT: *SEALs on the move (US Navy)*

MIDDLE: *Kalash village in the Hindu Kush. (PD)*

BOTTOM   LEFT: *Kalash pagan idol (PD)*

BOTTOM   RIGHT: *A majestic   peregrine falcon. (PD)*

ABOVE: *Blue-eyed Kalash children whose appearances   are remarkably similar to Europeans. (Alphabet Book)*

RIGHT: *The colorful - Kalash girl (Alphabet Book)*

CHAPTER 20

JUNE 7, 2008

DUBAI

WITH THE HEADLIGHTS OFF, the Ford Mustang pulled up alongside the fence. The camp was quarter of a mile off in the dark, the lights of the compound just visible as they looked into the desert night on the outskirts of the city.

"What do you think?" Bryan asked as he admired his spray-on tan and blackened hair. He'd even applied a small amount of make-up under his eyes for a tired appearance.

"Actually mate, not half bad. At least you don't look orange, but I wouldn't jump on the next bus with em for a ride to a work site, that's for sure." Dylan said.

"Don't intend on getting that close. As soon as evening prayer is over give me thirty minutes and meet me back here. We've got the radios just in case, but don't call me unless you hear two mike clicks – then reply with two clicks and wait for me to call you back. Got that?" Bryan said, holding up the "work-site issued radio."

"Two clicks from you, and then two from me – then you talk," Dylan repeated.

"Perfect," Bryan said. He rolled out of the car and ran to the fence line. Dylan pulled away when Bryan got thru the fence with wire cutters. He lay motionless on the sand for a few moments, scanning the compound buildings with small night vision binoculars. It looked clear from his position to the barracks, he started moving.

The quarter mile hike was not that bad. The sand was thick, but at least flat, and the moon partially waxed. "It's a cake walk," he thought. Inconspicuously, he made his way through the camp, keeping his head down. The *Isha'a* evening prayer had been called, Bryan eased in with other laborers as the mass of blue uniforms lined up to enter a makeshift, open area mosque. Bryan lagged to avoid being spotted by the old Pakistani man or his son. He kept a watchful eye out for the two.

Taking a position at the rear of two hundred plus men, Bryan followed along with the prayer's exercises. All laborers appeared very pious, stern. Their religion was all they really had. At the conclusion of prayer, he nondescriptly began milling about near groups of others, coughing now and then to feign illness, scaring workers to keep their distance. Illness was the very last thing a worker wanted to contract at the camp, medical attention was limited, and a sick day would result in termination.

A man in white thaub and schumagg approached a group of workers. All were smiling as they talked, extending thanks and praising Allah. The stranger's face was obscured. Bryan needed to get closer. He shadowed the group to a pre-fabricated barracks. The men entered. Bryan couldn't, it was too well lit. He stayed out of site, hiding around the corner of the building. More laborers followed the ones before. Soon the fifteen by thirty foot room was filled. Bryan was under an open window. He could hear inside.

Speaking in Pashto. "Salaam Wazir," workers said to the man as they arrived. He would politely return the greeting, saying "May God be with you always." *Who is Wazir?*

The session quickly began with the man named Wazir immediately taking control of his captive audience. Bryan still couldn't see the man's face. He moved to the other end of the small building, under a second window closer to the speaker. Alternating between Pashto and Arabic, Wazir's sermon was delivered with forceful conviction, a tone not unlike a Bible belt evangelist. Cleary full of fear and hate, as was expected, the west and the builders of

Dubai were painted with broad strokes as being evil, corrupt, and filled with sin. The United States and Great Britain were the enemies of Islam.

"The infidels have taken your money, stolen your land, desecrating Islam, desecrating Allah," the speaker said.

"God be willing, a new caliph is coming to free everyone and help you be saved from the infidels," Bryan heard Wazir rant. He needed to get a good look at the guy though, he thought.

"You will be asked to carry out Allah's will," the man said. "And you must be prepared to do what is asked." Bryan could only imagine what the man called Wazir meant.

"God has willed a Jihad," Wazir declared. Bryan grimaced at the word. Wazir then spoke something, "Yoorish Shaheed – Jihad - Yoorish Shaheed." *Yoorish Shaheed? Are they an invasion of martyrs?*

"Dubai is a city that is filled with infidels that must be purged. It is your city, - Yoorish Shaheed," Wazir said, adding, "You built Dubai and now we are giving you new jobs here to begin right away. Your families are being fed and provided for - Yoorish Shaheed." *Who is this sociopath?*

Bryan looked around for something to stand on. He needed to get a glimpse inside the window. He found a fruit crate near a dumpster, and though a bit weathered, it appeared solid enough to hold his weight. Placing it on the sand underneath the window, he gave it a little test before putting all one hundred and eighty-five pounds on the wood. Bryan had just enough of a boost to see the inside. The room was packed. Maybe fifty men crammed into the small room. There was a space between two men inside the room, their backs to the window. He could see the speaker.

"It's Zar Wali's fuckin twin," Bryan said to himself, just before the box gave way. Crashing into side of the building with his elbow, he bounced off the pre-fabricated siding, landing with a thud on the hard packed sand below the window, the Walkie-Talkie landing in back of a garbage can. Wazir motioned to two men near the window. Nothing was there.

Searching the area below the window, Wazir's men found the small Walkie-Talkie. "We found this," a laborer said giving the device to him.

Wazir pushed the talk button, and hearing nothing, pushed it again. Someone responded with two clicks, and Wazir repeated the exercise.

"Bryan?" A voice said, but there wasn't a reply.

"Bryan?" The voice said again as Wazir listened.

"Barely got out of there," Bryan said as he jumped in the car with Dylan. "Let's go – quick," he added, shutting the door.

"What'd ya find out mate?" Dylan said as he put the car in drive and punched it.

"Enough, and you'll have one hell of a story soon. Left the damn Walkie-Talkie back there though," Bryan said, slapping the dash.

"I'm afraid I figured that one out," Dylan said.

Looking at Dylan, Bryan shook his head "It's a Madrasah. They've got a damn conveyor belt of future terrorists, a fuckin farm league – and no end in sight."

"Our suspicions were right."

"I'd say so, and a ghost is runnin the brainwashing," Bryan said. "It was a real love fest between him and the workers."

"Who's the ghost?" Dylan asked.

"If I didn't know better, I'd say it's Hanif Zar Wali - with a neatly trimmed goatee, not the full bearded face he had when I last saw him," Bryan said, taking a sip from a bottle of water. "Same guy with Rowley at the racetrack, and with our U.S. business delegation," Bryan said, still catching his breath after the quarter mile in the sand.

"Are you sayin' that ya think he's not dead."

"No, no – of course Hanif Zar Wali's dead. This guy is his identical twin according to DJ."

"And this one's runnin' the show here?"

"I don't think he's necessarily the head honcho, just the front man."

The Mustang roared towards town. Bryan looked at Dylan and shook his head. "This could be big Dylan. You've got to promise me that you'll keep a lid on this until I say so - got it."

"You're on mate."

* * * * *

JUNE 7, 2008

NEW YORK CITY

The tip came from someone unknown, anonymous. Local authorities put two and two together, deciding it might be wise to coordinate with the FBI. It was a good decision.

"They're just very strange. Come and go from the building - always in Hip-Hop clothes, just like the bombers had on," a female voice said over the phone, a routine call since the bombings. Local detectives followed up.

The borough was Brooklyn, and agents quickly identified the top floor residence of an old walk-up as being the temporary quarters of Kahlid Mujab and Rashid Nasim, the two wanted terrorist suspects and former detainees at Gitmo. The building was placed under immediate surveillance, but only silence came from the residence, nothing stirred inside for hours. It was early evening. Time was not on the side of the counter-terrorism agents. They needed to move on the suspects soon. The special agent in charge waited for the go ahead, and when it came, they gathered for an assault.

Prepared for resistance, a team of seven fully armed FBI agents wearing body armor made their way up the three flights of steps. No decorum, no announcement, only surprise. *Ram in the door and go in.* Signaling the two-man battering ram team to get ready, the lead agent crouched down low, and slid the tiny micro-lens under the door. The hand-held monitor showed the room clear, no booby-trap on the door. Slowly he tested the knob; it was unlocked. He eased it open. He knew what was somewhere inside.

The sound of electrical fans and flies was accompanied by a smell of recent death, hitting their nostrils hard, as they cautiously entered the warm, dark room. Nothing was moving in the stark area, just an occasional fly illuminated by a streetlight peaking through cheap curtains.

The bedroom door was partially open. They had the right suspects, and body armor would not have protected them from what the two dead men in the room had in mind. Surveying the small, two-room efficiency, the evidence was all there; peroxide, acetone, electronic devices for detonation, bolts, ball bearings, and an assortment of other bomb making equipment.

By a partially opened window in the bedroom, Kahlid Mujab laid dead on a bed. Next to the bed was Rashid Nasim, sitting in a chair, slumped over, dead as well.

"Good God, look at their face's," an agent said when he entered the bedroom.

The lead agent held a handkerchief over his nose and mouth. "Don't touch anything. Everybody out – let's seal this apartment and evacuate the building," he said. "And someone needs to call the CDC."

"What do we got here?" He was asked.

"If I didn't know any better, I'd say these two had smallpox."

* * * * *

JUNE 8, 2008

DUBAI

It was early in the morning and Bryan was back in the Consulate SCIF with Shannon, now at a conference table in the small briefing room with a view of the one television. Their only company was the duty officer. A Marine Sergeant. He'd been passing the time playing solitaire on a game-boy. When he got bored with that, he read a book, or studied for his Staff Sergeant exam. Now he was glued to the TV. It was on CNN and the breaking news story was about a possible smallpox epidemic.

Bryan stood up; he was ready to lay everything out. "What we have so far is this – the attacks were coordinated and carried out in cities connected to PDI," Bryan said.

"That fits a revenge profile," Shannon said as she took notes.

"Revenge for screwing over Dubai – a 'Muslim' country," Bryan said making quote marks in the air. "But I'm not convinced it's the only reason, a singular reason – maybe more of a bitch slap."

"You mean as in why go to so much trouble over a progressive Jack Muslim country?"

"That's right – there something more – just what the hell is it?"

"Extremists have certainly carried out revenge attacks many times in the past," she noted.

"Doubtful that Islamists are pissed that Dubai didn't get the deal," Bryan said, trying to piece the puzzle together. "If it had been Saudi Arabia, the home of Mecca – okay, that makes sense. We'll come back to that.

"Then we have this latest revelation about smallpox," Shannon added.

"It explains Abdul-Malik's complexion on the cell phone video, that's for sure – but we know that an actual epidemic would be virtually impossible to start," Bryan said.

"But the fear factor is off the scale. I can hear the alarm bells going off in Washington and London right this minute," Shannon said, looking at the latest of five secure communiqués from the FBI.

```
C O N F I D E N T I A L

From: Steve Tanzler,
Sent: Tuesday June 7, 2008 22:45 PM
To:    Bryan Craig, Captain USN
Subject: CDC/ smallpox issue

Sir,

We've been in continual contact with a
local lab at the CDC, all hospitals here
and in London. Smallpox confirmed on
deceased suspects, but appears all
smallpox contained. Two patients possibly
contracted virus, but are not showing
symptoms as yet. Doctors believe they
won't. Any questions, please contact me
ASAP.

V/R
Steve Tanzler
Federal Bureau of Investigation

Counter-Terrorism
```

"So that's strictly to induce fear, rather than start an epidemic?" Shannon asked.

"Not strictly to induce fear, but it would be fine with the planners if they created a small epidemic anyway. Malik would have known that," Bryan said.

"That's right, his mother was a researcher, specialized in the study of contagions," Shannon said. "Malik was studying to be a doctor - knew how the spread of smallpox worked."

"And Petrov knew where to get Petri dishes of old Soviet stockpiles. I believe Petrov could be the supplier, but he would have kept his distance. The wires to Malik's account were too obvious – it links directly to the bombers and I can't see him being that stupid."

"And the Pakistani workers – the staffing company?" Shannon queried.

"There I would expect to find evidence of his involvement, his finger prints all over the scam. On the surface, it would look above board. He wouldn't have cared less to what happened to hires after he collected," Bryan said.

"So long as he was making money."

"So long as he makes money - that's right," Bryan said nodding in agreement. "Then, as Kevin pointed out, once they figured out all of Petrov's angles and got what they needed, he could be eliminated. Whoever 'they' is."

"Much like the workers in Metropolis?"

"Not much of a stretch, is it," Bryan said smiling from the corner.

"And what about the construction workers?"

"You mean, are they expendable too, I'd ask you that question," Bryan said deflecting back to the psychologist. "The age old question of the ends justifying the means."

"If the laborers are the Yoorish Shaheed, then the answer is yes. Martyrs are the great soldiers in a Jihad."

"And for the mastermind, everyone wins," Bryan said.

"That's right, the martyr believes he has ascended to heaven in a glorious way."

"And it's one step closer for the fanatics," Bryan added. "Well, we need Gil to nail down those accounts for us. Which brings us to the last part of the equation - this Wazir. Shannon, find out what makes this guy tick from a profiler's perspective."

"See if he's willing to sacrifice thousands to carry out their plans," Shannon said.

"That's right – and if in fact Zar Wali had a twin. We'll need whatever Gitmo and ISI had on Hanif before he died."

"Could be another case for revenge," Shannon observed.

"Could be, " Bryan said.

"Lot of dots still to connect, just like the PDI link," Shannon said. "I still think it was more of a slap in the face than revenge, but the real story comes from Wazir and whatever connection he had with Petrov. I've got to figure out a way to flush him out. We need something concrete rather than just conjecture."

"You need physical evidence."

"A video tape, a witness, or someone from the inside coming forward – or maybe somebody to make a mistake."

"Do you have a plan," Shannon asked.

Bryan thought of Dylan. "I've an idea."

CHAPTER 21

JUNE 8, 2008

WASHINGTON, D.C.

THE SENATOR GOT WORD as most everyone else in the United States and the UK had, from a "Breaking News" story on cable: "Terrorist plotters used smallpox with explosives - outbreaks are occurring at hospitals treating the survivors of the Memorial Day attacks," the reporter said.

"What the hell's goin on here?" He demanded to know from Homeland Security. "I've got people comin down with smallpox – how the hell did you folks fuck this away. We'll be lucky if we don't have a national panic on our hands."

But they did, as citizens from both affected countries clamored for more information, calling emergency rooms, elected officials, police offices, even their local clergy. The scare was working as planned, anger turning into panic and fear, terror in some cases.

Cox hung up the phone in a huff. "Son of a bitch at Homeland says there's nothing to worry about," Cox said to Tom Billings. "Says that it's been contained and bein treated at the hospitals where the folks are already inpatients. Only have three others with the disease so far. What the hell do they know? Do me a favor and find out from somebody, maybe at the White House or CDC, if we have a full blown epidemic on our hands right now or not, will ya?"

He fumed for a minute before ripping into Billings more. "And what the hell happened to being proactive on this? Why am I finding out from some jackass on television, like everyone else? We're lookin like incompetent morons."

Cox listened to the White House Official and a CDC doctor on a conference call with two other Senators from the Intelligence committee. They were told that symptoms first begin to appear between twelve to fourteen days after being exposed to someone with the virus, and humans are the only known creatures susceptible to the disease. Transmission occurs by direct deposit of infected cells orally, or through mucus membranes, and alveoli of the lungs, but can also be disbursed via fine particle aerosols, such as through a cough. Initial symptoms would be high fever, severe headaches, backache, and general malaise. One to two days later, a rash appears that tends to "erupt," as the doctor put it, "Into vesicles, pustules, and finally severe scab lesions, deeply embedded in the dermis. But in this strain of smallpox, which has a mortality of greater than ninety-eight percent, we have the same severe prodromal symptoms, and toxemia, only a hemorrhagic rash without pustular stage."

Plain old English would be nice, Senator Cox thought. *What does that mean?*

"Well that sounds all fine an dandy, but what the hell are you prepared to say to the American people? Are we out of the woods on this or not?" Cox asked Doctor Becker from the CDC, the expert providing the medical analysis.

"Senator, the first thing we're trying to do is avoid an epidemic by controlling the contagion, and the way we're doing that is by isolating those few known cases that we do have, and they're not in the contagious phase yet, by the way. And we've also quarantined those that have come in contact with the infected patients," the doctor told them.

"Who's at risk? I mean, I've been to see some of the people that were injured," came the question by the Senator from Maine, obviously concerned for her safety, and that of staff and family of victims.

"The risk is with people that have come into contact with a patient that's already developed a fever, and those that were exposed to the initial spread at each bombing site," the doctor said.

"Excuse me doctor, I want to emphasize that the method of delivery, you know – strapping a bomb onto someone that's contagious, has a very low percentage of being effective, if at all," the White House official pointed out.

"We're going to screen family members, those that have cared for the injured survivors, lab personnel, and virtually anyone that has entered a room where there's a possibility of exposure. And it's correct that it would be very difficult to get an efficient aerosol effect by blowing apart an infected person, but it's not been ruled out," the doctor added.

"Thought that we already had several bombin survivors infected now," Cox stated.

"Could've been from direct contact, we just don't know," the doctor said.

"What about the vaccine?" Came the question from the Senator from Louisiana.

"We're looking into that right now, but at the moment just don't see a need yet. We'll have the vaccine ready though, just in case, and we're talking with Homeland, the FBI, and National Safety Council should we need to go that route," the official from the White House said.

"So the vaccine stockpile will be made available?" Cox asked.

"It will be if we need it. Just be sure that we're handling it here. We're coordinating with state and local officials should we need to mobilize CDC personnel, but at the moment it looks like it's going to be contained," the White House man said.

"Well hold a Goddamn press conference then," Cox said angrily. "And tell the American people that." He hung up the phone when his secretary came in with a rap on the door.

"Come on in Gina,"

"Senator, your car's waiting to take you to 'Meet the Press,'" she announced.

"Damn, I'd like to get a little more poop on this for those guys. Well, let's get going," he said signaling to Tom Billings.

CHAPTER 22

TRACING A FINANCIAL TRANSACTION that seemed untraceable was an obsession for Gil, the more complicated and difficult, the better. He loved solving puzzles, and that's all the job really was. It was a puzzle that had a solution.

He was always a "brain" when it came to solving logic problems, crossword puzzles, brain teasers, paradoxes, or just about anything where the answer is based on rationale, logic, math, or a combination of the three. As a kid he destroyed the Rubik's Cube, solving it in less than thirty seconds. And as a kid he'd marveled at the use of the encryption machine "Purple" that cracked Japanese codes and enabled U.S. Naval Intelligence to intercept a message resulting in the downing of the plane carrying Japan's top naval commander, Admiral Yamamoto. He wondered if today's media would have spilled the beans on the Navy code breakers of World War Two, as they had with SWIFT. It was just a speed bump for him though. He could always figure out the solution.

To solve the puzzles, he had to get into the mind of the creator; he wanted to know what made the mastermind of the financial transactions tick. He was meticulous in his approach.

"What was his motivation? What were his goals, both in terms of the money, and his ideology?" These were the questions Gil asked. He also assumed the money person was a man, considering they were dealing with Islamic Terrorist organizations, but he would keep in mind the possibility that it could also be a woman, just very unlikely.

With the current problem, the person, or persons tried to cover their money flow using multiple offshore insurance policies and directed to a Dubai Bank and a holding company with an unknown number of individual shareholders of unknown identities. It was a complexity that had been relatively easy to uncover. Although the actual shareholder identities were more difficult, financial transparency was advertised not emphasized in Dubai, or at its International Finance Centre, their central bank. Gil managed to clear the muddied waters anyway.

He'd narrowed the field down even more however, to three banks moving funds from the Bank of Dubai. One a Swiss bank, and the other two, banks in Karachi, Pakistan. Yet questions stilled remained. *Who were the owners of those accounts, and where did those funds originate prior to the Bank of Dubai?*

Gil took a break. He'd worked nonstop for hours, now stopping to ponder the puzzle, as the Pegasus program he dubbed "Fuchsia" in deference to the World War Two code breakers, searched hundreds of thousands of transactions at the Swiss and Pakistani banks. It was 4:00 PM Sunday and the weekly political news programs from the States were on. Maybe he would take in some current events, as if he wasn't already on the cutting edge. He called for Inés.

She popped her head into his office. "Sí?

"Inés. Por favor, me gustaría un expreso doblé." What better way to take the edge off than by going right over it?

"Oh, Sí Mister Gil."

He eased back in his chair, put his feet up on the desk and switched the channel to "Meet the Press." The host, Tim Russert was just weighing into the guests with his typical bulldog approach.

"Our issue this Sunday: global terrorism. It's been two weeks since America's cities and London were viciously attacked by suicide bombers and now it appears they used smallpox, making the attacks that much more horrific; a recent Time and Newsweek poll shows eighty two percent of all Americans fear a new attack is imminent and a similar poll by the Washington Post indicates sixty percent believe our country's Homeland Security is failing. What went wrong? Has America's War on Terrorism failed? With us two members of the Senate Select Committee on Intelligence, Senator Taylor Cox, Republican from Virginia and Senator John Morgan III, Democrat from Kentucky. Good morning Senators."

Russert kicked it off with a video clip showing the aftermath of the attacks at various locations. "This was the scene just two weeks ago on Memorial Day. Destruction and many people killed as they shopped. Killed by suicide bombers. Was it Al-Qaeda, or homegrown sympathetic cells?" Russert directed his first question at Senator Cox.

"Would you authorize the use of torture if you thought it could have prevented the attacks that occurred - for example; water-boarding let's say?" Russert asked.

"Good morning Tim. First of all let me say that the bombings were deplorable, appalling tragedies of unbelievable proportion, with a devastating human toll - and we're doing everything we can to track down the planners and bring them to justice. Now with regard to torture, well I think that's a good question, and one that you've got to ask of the victim's families and the American people. You know, I find it interesting Tim - that the question of torture is continually asked of politicians by the media. Maybe the media should direct the question to the public instead," Cox said.

"So you would authorize it?" Russert pressed with quintessential determination.

"Unusually unique circumstances sometimes require an appropriate response and I'll ask you this Tim - if your wife, or your children were held as hostages, with a deadline to be executed, and some person is in custody that may know where they are, would you say that it's okay to pour some water down the person's mouth if it might save your family?" Cox responded, hitting a solid triple, he believed.

"So you would authorize it. Fair enough," Russert said, with a smile. "But Senator, what do know about the possibility of a smallpox epidemic as a result of the attacks?"

"As for smallpox, we've been in direct discussions with the hospitals treating the injured, and with the CDC and it looks as though the contagion was limited only to the two terrorists that were found dead." No need to talk about the two probable infected patients if it were contained now, Cox reasoned. "But this has been a wake up call."

"Senator, what went wrong? Are our efforts failing in fighting terrorism and is terrorism on our shores to stay?"

"What went wrong, you ask? Well, I can tell you that it is not policy related, and not so much a failure of intelligence as it's been a gross failure of the interpretation of law."

"You're referring to the Supreme Court decision of two and a half years ago?"

"That's right Tim. I pointed it out back then that Supreme Court got it wrong. We've got to give our intelligence community the ability to effectively interrogate suspects without giving up sensitive information. We don't want to use extraordinary rendition for interrogation, particularly when the suspect is known to be a member of a terrorist cell."

"By extraordinary rendition you mean the practice of sending terrorist suspects or detainees to countries other than the United States to be interrogated outside our judicial system. Is that morally right? Isn't that just torture by proxy?"

"Tim, we've just had almost five hundred Americans and British citizens killed by terrorists. At least one bomber was released from that very judicial system that is supposed to protect our citizens, not aid terrorists."

"Senator Morgan, is that right? Have we put the law ahead of America's safety? Is the United States Military now being forced to use other governments to carry out interrogation tactics outside of our judicial process?"

"Morning Tim. No I don't believe so. But it has been a failure of intelligence, we lost track of a suspected terrorist that was one of the suicide bombers. But we've got to stay within the bounds of our laws of Military Justice."

Russert chimed in. "You're referring to Abdul-Malik, who had been a detainee at Gitmo. He was the first attacker identified. What do we know about him or any of the other bombers Senator Morgan?"

"Well, not much Tim. We've identified one bomber, and the two found yesterday were also detainees, the remaining we're still looking into."

Cox saw an opportunity while his colleague was asleep at the wheel. "Tim, I have to disagree with my good friend, but in fact we do know quite a bit about Malik, and more than likely we'll see that the others will prove to be cut of the same mold. Malik was captured in Afghanistan and had been a detainee because of his connection with terrorist cells. We know that he disappeared into the North West Frontier of Pakistan, where he was no doubt retrained for his martyr mission there. We also know that he was a Pakistani that came under the influence of extremists. And as far as the failure of intelligence is concerned, you can go all the way back to over thirty years ago when the focus shifted from human intelligence to intelligence gathered by means such as satellites or signal intercepts. We need both."

"So you believe that we need more effort placed on intelligence operatives on the ground infiltrating the Al-Qaeda and possibly other terrorist cells."

"More than that Tim. First we need people that can speak the language, and not just one language. There are more than twenty different dialects of Arabic alone. Then of course there's Farsi, Pashto, Urdu, and the numerous dialects for those."

"Senator Morgan?"

"I'll say that I have to agree with my good friend Senator Cox on that point, but what I'm most afraid of now is the impact that continued terrorist attacks, and the threat of more attacks, is having on our economy. We have more construction projects going on overseas now than we do here in the United States and that's because people are afraid. We have got to do a better job with the intelligence on the ground and ease people's fears and the risks to businesses."

Cox chimed in again before his fellow Senator could steal his thunder, and he wanted to move the discussion to being proactive, finding bad guys and taking them out.

"Tim, if I may - and first, I agree with Senator Morgan to a certain extent. We do in fact have the stock markets at their lowest levels in four years. Even though the Federal Reserve has taken emergency measures by lowering interest rates, we are still looking at a real possibility of slipping into a recession. But let's talk about what the intelligence community is doing right and how our legal system and liberal judges are doing everything they can to impede our hard working agents in the field. If we get everyone on the same page, we can defeat the terrorists and get the confidence in our economy again."

Senator Cox was thinking of what to do to be proactive, stay ahead of the curve for a change. And then he had an idea. Cox employed a tactic that he'd used for years, "What if I were to tell you that I've an advance report here..."

He held up a piece of paper that was actually his flight itinerary. It was a deceptive, but valuable ploy; however, rule number one of talk show bullshit: always be prepared to support your facts with a document, even if it's blank. Something he'd learned from years as a trial lawyer. To an audience, such as a jury, or in this case the viewer and media, he now appeared privy to information his opponent wasn't.

"...That I've a report indicating our Intelligence Officers at the CIA and other agencies employing counter-terrorism agents, have made significant strides in regaining the lost human resources on the ground in Islamic countries, and our friends in countries such as Saudi Arabia, Pakistan and the United Arab Emirates are providing us a great deal of help as we speak in tracking down, and eliminating the people responsible for those attacks. We have to do three things Tim."

He knew that he'd just said absolutely nothing, but seemed like he had. For emphasis he then held up fingers to correspond with his coming count. "One – put Americans, and that means all Americans, ahead of the terrorists. If a person is an unlawful combatant - then our courts shouldn't categorize him as a prisoner of war. He certainly isn't under the Geneva Convention. Two – we have got to prosecute those that contribute to serious leaks for political gain. For example, I can't tell you how far we were set back by the leaks regarding the use of SWIFT as means of tracing dubious financial transactions." He briefly looked at his fellow guest to see if the last statement got any negative reaction. There was none. That was good.

He'd wave the flag. "And three – Patriotism. We've got to pull together as Americans, and that includes the judges who interpret the constitution, Tim. We've got to pull together and regain our sense of patriotism. If we'd done that before, Abdul-Malik would never have been released. And it's that very same sense of duty to our country that'll keep American businesses on shore, rather than taking flight overseas."

He'd said a mouthful, but believed it came out very

"Reaganesque," and "Morgan never had a chance to butt in," he thought, bemused. Taylor Cox knew his political stock just had a big spike.

Gil changed the station to another Sunday morning talk show. The host, a former top official himself, was introducing a top White House advisor. The guest, who was on the President's Council of Economic Advisors, was being asked, "What impact the attacks had, and would continue to have on the economy."

The host stated that, "I have a statistic here that indicates almost twenty-five percent of the world's construction cranes are being used in Dubai, yet here in the U.S. housing starts and new home sales are forecast to drop to their lowest levels in over three years and there is a very real possibility that things could get worse. What steps are being taken now to get our economy back on track, in spite of the ever increasing real fear of terrorism?"

Gil clicked off the television. It was the same questions and responses over and over again. The discussion on "Meet the Press" had been helpful though. He knew Senator Cox as an acquaintance through his contact with Bryan, and had met with the Senator during a closed-door briefing regarding SWIFT after the program was leaked to the press. He trusted the Senator's judgment regarding the failure of Human Intelligence. "He's probably right," Gil thought.

"Human Intelligence. That's the place where I'll zero in on," Gil decided. He stopped the Pegasus program for the Swiss bank trace, and focused on the two Karachi banks.

"Maybe this is a bit of a guess," he believed, but to Gil's way of thinking, it was a logical guess.

Gil's *Fuchsia* program discovered two banks in Pakistan that received money originating from the Bank of Dubai, and specifically from the Falcon Holdings Company. Tracing it backwards Gil could see an outflow of funds from the United States in the days just prior to the attacks. That money had landed in the U.S. undetected as loans from offshore insurance contracts legally established at multiple locations, all very legit. It was brilliant, he thought. But it would have to have a third party involved to write the contracts. Since they were offshore though, it could be anybody. They wouldn't even need an insurance license.

"Someone had really done his or her homework," he thought, admiring the ruse.

The insurance contracts were taken out on dozens of individuals. Key-employee policies on executives of companies associated with the Bank of Dubai and Falcon Holdings. The insurance contracts were probably made without the insured party's knowledge, he concluded. The premiums were funded from who knows where, but again, since they were made offshore, there was minimal scrutiny.

Gil now directed his attention on the suspicious accounts in Karachi. There were two banks he pinpointed:

Islamic Faysal Investment Bank LTD.
Shaheen Complex,
M.R. Kayani Road, Saddar

Crescent Bank of Pakistan
Shaheen Complex,
Doctor Ziauddin Ahmed Road, Saddar

The job now was to trace the accounts from those particular banks. Nail down the owners of the accounts and find the use of funds. SWIFT came in handy at this point: to trace wire transfers, checks written, and even ATM usage from the accounts. He began to go to work solving the problem.

CHAPTER 23

JUNE 8, 2008

ISLAMABAD, PAKISTAN

E LATED TO BE BACK at work, Shamema had returned from a ten-day vacation to Malaysia five days short. She had been told by everyone to try and relax. "You need to get away from this for awhile Shamema," her friends said. Her grandfather suggested that she return to Chitral for the summer, to leave the hustle and bustle of Islamabad and Karachi. It was all to no avail. Work was all encompassing and the totality of her life now.

Born in Chitral, she'd moved to Islamabad as a child, living with relatives. The capital was better suited for schooling, and later, for her job as a lobbyist, social worker, psychiatrist, and doctor. A dilettante of sorts, though professionally trained only as a lawyer. She did whatever was required and became whomever it was that that the helpless needed. And Pakistan was a country very much in need.

After graduating with a degree from Quaid-i-Azam College of Law in Lahore, Shamema had gone to work as a public defender in Islamabad. And an idealist at that, who studied documents from the democracies, her two favorites being the Declaration of Independence and the United States Constitution. The legal system in Pakistan however, was in shambles after the latest military coup.

The Army's Chief of Staff had recently overthrown the elected civilian government of Pakistan, and promptly suspended her country's Constitution, disbanded its Parliament, and abolished all national and provincial assemblies. Military commanders imposed martial law, instituted a Provisional Constitution and swore in a General as Pakistan's President. The military had taken complete control of the judiciary system, which immediately made Shamema's job increasingly difficult. She'd been disconsolate after the coup until she found her calling.

Shamema became one of Pakistan's leading young advocates for Human rights, condemning "honor killings," the practice of killing a wife or daughter for causing loss of face due to adultery, and other forms of severe discrimination against women; an advocate for religious minorities, who were often the recipients of prejudices and discriminated against by Islam; an advocate for children who were victims and abused, or sold into slavery; and an advocate for human rights in the fight against forced labor and human trafficking.

Shamema's efforts to protect children from slavery had largely been successful, particularly her fight to save the very young from being sold to Camel Jockey farms. International pressure, particularly from organizations such as the Ansar Burney Trust had resulted in countries such as the United Arab Emirates to abolish the practice of using children under the age of sixteen. Now her focus was on Human Trafficking.

One of the most horrendous crimes, Human Trafficking included indentured servitude or slavery and had been in existence nearly as long as mankind itself. Shamema believed that no country in the world was victimized by that evil more than Pakistan. Hundreds of thousands of people were lured every year with false promises of a better life, only to be imprisoned or forced into labor camps, prostitution, and now more recently, seduced by recruiters in Karachi with promises of jobs and high pay for work as laborers in Dubai.

Organizations such as Shamema's were generally always in need of funding, and as the world's population grew, so did the number of victims, therefore a need for even more money. It was a never-ending problem for the people she helped, who were almost always indigent. Shamema and her staff provided hope to the hopeless for free. The organization had never received any financial support from the government of Pakistan and operated on a thin budget provided by donations from public entities or individuals.

It was already late, and the day had flown by. She wasn't tired though and would continue to work well past midnight, calling judges, companies, celebrities, all in the hopes of helping people and aiding her cause. She painstakingly opened mail.

"A bill," she said, carefully putting the paper into the inbox labeled the same. She opened another envelope.

"Another bill." The stack was outgrowing the inbox labeled "donations," five fold.

Jamil, her equally hard working young assistant opened a hand-addressed envelope and exclaimed after reading the name on the check and the amount. "Look Shamema, our favorite American actress has come through for us again. Here's a check for twenty thousand dollars. I'm going to rent her action movie again to celebrate." He placed the check into the donation inbox.

"What's the name of her movie again Jamil?" Shamema asked.

"I can't believe you don't know the name of the movie Shamema. When was the last time you even saw a movie?"

"When the stack on the left is above the stack on the right, then I'll celebrate with a movie. But we've over fifty thousand dollars in bills and now twenty three thousand dollars in donations. Looks like I'll be calling on the phone all night."

The two had worked for almost an hour longer as Shamema's distress continued to grow, bills for medicine, legal documents, and other incidentals continuing to pile up. Donations were generally five or ten dollars, and there were probably at least a hundred envelopes with checks. The problem was that the mail had stacked up for more than three weeks. Sunday night was the designated "mail night" for their office of two. As she reached for the next piece of mail at the top, her hand half way, she froze.

"Jamil - look." They both stared at the long white envelope that was addressed in English with a unique Apple Chancery font, and then looked at each other. Shamema smiled, quickly picked up the envelope and carefully opened it with a letter opener. A single check was inside.

Holding the check, facing her employee, "Oh my goodness Jamil. It's more than could ever be expected. Look at this."

Jamil's mouth gaped open momentarily before he could finally speak. He read the amount out loud twice. "One million dollars, one million dollars - that's twice the amount from last year." He jumped out of his chair.

"And again it's anonymous. The same bank though. There are instructions with the donation as before." She held up a piece of paper that accompanied the check.

"Who is responsible for this Shamema?"

"I don't know, but God be willing, one day we will find out."

CHAPTER 24

JUNE 8, 2008

DUBAI

A FORCE OF HABIT, he preferred letting the diplomats do most of the talking, interjecting a salient point now and then, or when asked a direct question. Bryan listened as the ambassadors to the UAE from the United States and Great Britain debated the future and past of Dubai. Lord Stephens was agreeable in most cases with A. Rodney Evans, a State Department wiz kid who became Ambassador at forty-two, but diverged from their accord on the subject of the terrorist threat to Dubai.

"It will happen sooner, rather than later I'm afraid," Lord Stephens said as he sipped his Champagne.

"You think so," Ambassador Evans replied, as he too tasted the Dom Pérignon.

"That I do," the British Lord said. Turning to face the beach, he took a long draw on his cigar, the ash giving way slightly, breaking apart and flittering to the marble pool deck of the beachfront palace.

The property was set off the main road and wound lazily passed rows of palm trees to a modern estate, principally built of marble. The architect created a futuristic home using the circle as the theme, the largest being in the center, with bubbles every 90°, and twenty foot ceilings. The pool was shaped in a circle as well, and twenty-five meters by walkway to a private beach, lagoon, and island. Bryan noticed that the island also had a quest house, dock, and ski boat. The designer didn't leave out any detail, including vents surrounding the pool, some above ground, some ground level, for outside air conditioning. Guests could wander the deck through mist fifteen degrees cooler than the normal air temperature. The gala hosted by the Governor of the Bank of Dubai was in honor of the American billionaires investing in the Baazland, and attended by the who's who of Dubai, including the Sheikh himself, and a number of famous personalities.

Lord Stephens tapped the remaining ash off as he questioned Bryan, "Captain Craig, what are your thoughts on those chaps over there?" He pointed out at the darkness of the Persian Gulf.

"Be prepared," Bryan said without hesitation.

"For what Captain Craig?" the American Ambassador asked.

"The threat isn't just from millions of Iranians, or Shi'ah majority in Iraq," Bryan stated, deferring with a nod to Shannon, who had joined them moments before.

"Captain Craig's right, Mister Ambassador, the threat's also internal," Shannon said with conviction.

"Internal?" Ambassador Evans asked.

"How many guest workers are here in Dubai wearing blue uniforms?" She asked.

"Well, throughout the UAE, there must be more than two million," Lord Stephens calculated.

"They're the threat as well," she said.

Shannon went on to explain in depth, the psychological impact of devoting one's life to projects for someone else's benefit, especially if there is a perception of a miscarriage of justice.

"Regarding pay and the like," the British Ambassador said.

"Pay, working and living conditions," Bryan said.

"You think there a chance of a rebellion?" Ambassador Stephens asked.

"I'm sure you're a student of history Mister Ambassador. How many times did the British Empire see rebellions?" Bryan asked rhetorically.

"I'll grant you that Captain Craig, however, those were colonies of the British Empire and the people were rebelling from British rule. Completely different matter here," Lord Stephens emphasized.

"In what way?" Ambassador Evans asked.

"The Pakis are guest worker's. This is not their sand," Stephens said, waving his cigar-clad hand along the dark coastline.

"Are you really sure about that sir?" Shannon said with a slight smirk.

"Please Doctor, give us a little insight then," the young American Ambassador said. "You're the professional on the subject."

Without revealing their own discovery at the worker camp, and delving further into the plight of the workers, Shannon conveyed the conclusion that, "It's possible the workers believe this to be their rightful land. At least rightfully Islamic."

"It already is Islamic. This sand belongs to that fella standing right over there, Doctor," Ambassador Evans said, referring to the Sheikh.

The distinction between progressive Islamic countries such as Kuwait, Bahrain, and the UAE, and fundamental Islamic nations such as Iran, was well known among the diplomats, and therein became the basis for the greatest debates. Islamists viewed the leadership of the progressive Islamic countries as puppets of the United States and Great Britain, not as a true Islamic land devoted to the teachings of Mohammed and the doctrine of the Quran. In their eyes, those friends of the West had betrayed the Islamic world, had let infidels soil the land, and deserved to be punished, and the land returned. The debate centered on the definition of an Islamic country; "Can the country be defined as Islamic, yet still carry on practices considered 'Jack Muslim?'" Bryan asked.

"That's a damn good question," Evans said, as the British Ambassador led Shannon off to the corner of the pool for some one on one. "What do you consider an Islamic state, Captain?"

"What do I consider an Islamic state, hmmm, well I guess I'm as guilty as anyone in pointing at the Middle East and sayin 'Hey that's a Jewish country, and all the rest are Muslim,'" Bryan said.

"Meaning?" Evans asked.

"I don't distinguish between being fundamental or progressive as much as I do threatening or non-threatening."

"You consider Iran to be threatening?"

"Do you?" Bryan said, preferring to let the Ambassador answer his own questions.

"Why yes, I do. Now, obviously you would consider Dubai, and the UAE as a whole to be non-threatening."

"Potentially threatening."

Laughing, Evans winked as he admonished the counter-terrorism professional, "Oh, you're quite good Captain Craig. Very diplomatic response."

"It's my job."

"That it is. I forget that you've the knack for politics. You had the opportunity to watch from the inside, didn't you," Evans said, obviously referring to Bryan's father. He took a draw on his cigar, adding, "I'll grant you this much - from your perspective, they all should be potentially threatening, shouldn't they?"

"That's correct sir, " Bryan said, noticing Rodgers Christopher in apparent deep conversation with Consul General Basingstoke before seeing Bryan with the Ambassador. Christopher looked as though he was trying to signal Bryan, without drawing the attention of his boss.

"So Captain, you think this nasty smallpox business is over with then?"

"I think we've dodged that bullet, but here's where the preparation comes in again," Bryan said, ignoring the General Consul's hand signals.

"Something worse than a biological attack, I take it,"

"The delivery system for smallpox, or other biological agents such as anthrax is critical, but even if just a few people die, it tends to scare the hell out of people more than a bombing," Bryan said.

"And what about a dirty bomb?"

"Anything with the words 'nuclear,' or 'radiation' associated with 'weapons,' is the scariest of them all," Bryan said emphatically.

Bryan then suddenly spotted Rowley working the room, and to his amazement, Wazir, both engaged in conversation with the host, and with a very tall man dressed formally Arabic, yet wearing tinted glasses.

"Mister Ambassador, do you know the shorter man that the British banker's speaking with?"

"No, but I've seen him before on occasion, yet haven't had the pleasure to meet the man. The tall man's a very mysterious one, and I'm surprised to see him out and about. His name is Amir Kahn.

Somewhat of a Sultan I believe, and when I've seen him, the shorter man was usually with him."

"Do you know much about this Sultan?"

"That he's very wealthy, or rather by his handlers appears to be so."

"Is there a file on him?"

"Come on Captain Craig, of course there's a file on the dude somewhere. There's one on everyone, including you and me," Evans said with a smile and slightly bemused. "Let's go and take the opportunity to meet the Sultan now, after all – that's why I'm here," the Ambassador finished, referring to his diplomatic assign.

Gregarious as ever, Rowley seemed to have already forgotten about the tongue-lashing he'd received from Bryan only days before. The big Brit enthusiastically made the introductions.

"You said your first name was Bryan, is that correct?" Wazir asked.

"That's correct – Bryan," he said feeling as though he were looking at an apparition.

"Bryan, I see," Wazir said curiously.

"Strange that this guy asked twice about my first name," Bryan thought. It struck him that Wazir may have known about his little visit to the camp somehow. Bryan's thoughts were shelved as he was introduced to Amir Kahn.

"*Marhaban*, Captain Craig, I am Amir Sika Kahn. *Kaifa haloka*," He shook Bryan's hand firmly as he welcomed him in Arabic.

"His hand is strong, and he's got two inches on me, six-four I think," Bryan concluded to himself.

"*Ana bekhair, shokran. Wa ant?*" Bryan thanked Amir and asked how he was as well.

"Your Arabic is excellent Captain Craig," Amir said. "Where did you learn it?"

"*Shokran, ahtaaju an atadarraba 'ala al Arabia,*" Bryan said, thanking the Amir, but stating he needed to practice more. Bryan didn't want to get into the where's and why's of his linguistics.

"Very good again Captain, I'm quite impressed," he said in Arabic.

Amir Kahn seemed extremely at ease for someone presumed to be shy, and avoiding public scrutiny, Bryan thought. "Were you in the military Captain Craig," he asked Bryan, again in Arabic.

"Navy, active duty."

"Very good, what brings you to Dubai?"

"Some embassy work. Umm, for Ambassador Evans," Bryan said, as the Ambassador looked on, nodding in agreement. Ambassador Evans was also fluent in Arabic.

"Nothing to do with the terrorist attacks then?" Amir asked, catching Bryan and the Ambassador off guard.

"In fact yes," Bryan said, looking intently at Rowley.

"If there is anything that I can do to help, please let Mister Rowley know," Amir said, leaning to Wazir after being tapped on the shoulder. "I'm sorry gentleman, but my business associate informs me that we have some other matters that I should attend to. I must speak to some of the other guests before we leave."

"Pleasure was mine, *tosbeho, ma'a salama,*" Bryan saying good night and good buy.

Pausing before he moved on, "Thank you Captain Craig. Your talent with Arabic intrigues me very much. What else do you know of Arab culture? Do you know falconry?"

Interesting how that should come up, Bryan thought. "I know something about it, but have never been," he said.

"Good, we will go tomorrow then. I will pick you up at the heliport at two tomorrow afternoon."

"I'm sure that will work, but which heliport?"

"The one at your hotel of course, the Burj al Arab."

"And you know that I'm staying there?" Bryan asked in Arabic.

"I know everything that goes on in Dubai, Captain Craig. *Ma'a salama,*" Amir said, also in Arabic, as he removed his sunshades and shook Bryan's hand goodbye.

The sight startled Bryan; shockingly Amir Kahn's eyes were bright blue, his complexion was evidently light, and judging by his eyebrows, his hair light brown as well. Bryan was dismayed by his appearance and also very impressed with the man's intellect, somewhat taken aback by the man's deft control of the conversation, blunt and intuitive. Generally Bryan controlled conversations, and asked the questions, not the case this time. Exuding confidence, displaying no fear whatsoever, the man was someone to be reckoned with. *Is this our mastermind?*

"Excellent Arabic, Captain Craig. Impressive," the Ambassador said.

"Arabic, and Urdu are the basic requirements for a man in my position," Bryan said. "I'd like that file on Amir Sika Kahn before tomorrow afternoon, if you could help me with that sir."

"I bet you would. I'll see what I can do before your falconry adventure tomorrow. I'll fly you over to the Embassy in the morning," the Ambassador said. "You know what Sika means then, since you have such an adept knowledge of language," he added. Bryan's hesitation led to the answer, "It's short for Sikandar..."

Bryan stopped him in mid sentence, "Sikandar, that's Urdu for extremely skilled. A word derived from Alexander the Great and bestowed rarely, only for leaders." *The ultimate leader?*

"You do know Urdu, and I'm afraid that's precisely what it means."

"Mister Ambassador, there's something I think I need to brace you for," Bryan said with concern.

"Please, go ahead. What's up?"

"Keep this extremely confidential, it's classified, but we have good reason to believe that CNN will be running a story within the next few days regarding the construction contracts here in Dubai. It's not a very flattering picture."

"Labor?"

"I believe so," Bryan said with a wince.

"Well, that's not too shocking. We've had those in the past. It's a continual sore spot, and Dubai's labor agencies are trying their best to get companies to comply with the labor laws. You know, pay and so forth."

"I'm afraid the story actually has to do with terrorism, not just labor problems."

"In what way?"

"Rumblings that some staffing companies were created in Karachi specifically to hire workers that could be turned into terrorists – an assembly line of Islamic martyrs."

"I see. You obviously mean a planned assembly line."

"That's what the story's gonna be."

"You know quite a bit about this in advance, Captain Craig."

"That I do, sir."

"I see," the Ambassador said, puffing on his cigar and looking in the darkness towards Iran.

CHAPTER 25

JUNE 9, 2008

U.S. EMBASSY, ABU DHABI

A SHORT HELICOPTER FLIGHT from Dubai, Abu Dhabi was the Emirate responsible for the wealth of the UAE and its federal capital. Another rich Arab oil state, the Emirate spearheaded the effort to unite the Arab Emirates into a progressive collection of tribes under one flag. On the Persian Gulf, the city is an island the shape of the letter "T," and boasted a population in excess of one million, the majority of which were foreigners. The recent wealth due to oil, and its exploding population resulted in many typical urban planning problems, such as congested highways, and some unusual ones; mail delivery to the Post Office only. Poorly designated streets and addresses make driving a nightmare, further complicating the traffic problems. Planners of Dubai were very cognizant of the problems with their neighbor to the south, avoiding Abu Dhabi's pitfalls.

Bold and new, the U.S. Embassy compound in Abu Dhabi was completed only five years before, and was a landmark for architectural innovation. Contrasting with the vast desert encompassing the landscape, the building took advantage of nature to improve its energy efficiency and aesthetically pleasing qualities.

Light shelving on the building's facades minimized direct sunlight, but amplified indirect light. Rainfall drained down the building and from landscaped surroundings into a dry *wadi* garden, transforming it into temporal greenery. The building was where Ambassador Evans "hangs his hat," as Bryan put it.

"Please have a seat," the Ambassador said, motioning to the comfortable looking contemporary sofa for guests.

Sitting down in a chair adjacent to Shannon and Bryan, the Ambassador started, "Messy business we're faced with now, and I appreciate your incredible efforts at getting to the bottom of this, but first of all what more can you tell me about this controversial news piece from CNN?"

Searching for the right words, Bryan's eyes wandered around the Ambassador's large office. He noticed the standard displays of photographs with foreign dignitaries, the Secretary of State, and with several U.S. Presidents, but obviously most important to the Ambassador were the framed, standard golfing photos on the first tee box. The foursome shot, and there were at least a dozen around the room, some with Tiger Woods and other top professional golfers, and others photos with famous movie stars who were also avid golfers.

"A good source, and I can't disclose the person's name, has indicated that there's a story dealing in the mass brainwashing of Paki laborers."

Evans smiled. "Let me see if I can guess who that source might be - how about Dylan Sizemore for my first guess?"

"Revealing my sources would jeopardize lives, Mister Ambassador."

"But the belief is that some organization, Al-Qaeda let's say, is deliberately creating a miserable atmosphere for the sole purpose of brainwashing Muslims into being terrorists," the Ambassador offered.

"It doesn't necessarily have to be Al-Qaeda sir," Shannon said. "But they are creating an environment to foster that type of Jihadist soldier."

"And I might add, Mister Ambassador, that it requires minimal training," Bryan said.

"In other words, they don't have to build camps to train them, just get the bomb to them and send them off someplace," the Ambassador said.

"Exactly the way the Japanese did it, and the way the terrorists were trained on 9/11. Just enough training as required to carry out the mission," Bryan noted.

Shannon added, "No need to storm a cockpit, overpower a crew, and pilot a plane – they just need to know how to drive a car."

"Whatever you need Captain Craig, we'll see if we can't find it."

"Who's your prime candidate now for being at the heart of this – let's call it a 'probable' scenario?" Bryan asked.

"Amir Sika Kahn seems to fit the profile," she said. "He's purportedly the principle investor in the Burj al Baaz development, according to the notes in the Embassy file. Very mysterious man," Shannon said, walking to the computer and tapping the space bar.

"What profile's that? The coming of the next supreme caliph," Bryan asked seriously.

"Not a caliph, as in what the Shi-ah would want, but a Sultan type of ruler, with a résumé to boot. He has stature, money, power, and experience in a Jihad. He was a Mujahideen at the age of twelve. He's only forty-one now. He could be the answer for the Islamic world and possibly a nightmare for the west. A Saladin for the twenty first century," she said.

A present-day Saladin was clearly a "nightmare scenario" that the United States, the UK, and especially Israel would dread the most. Sultan Saladin was a twelfth century Kurdish Sunni Muslim that united the Islamic world during the Crusades. Born in Tikrit and educated in Damascus, Saladin amassed an army of two hundred thousand, and then set out to consolidate power throughout the Muslim world. He unified all of Islam from Syria, down the Mediterranean coast of modern Lebanon and Israel, the west coast of the Arabian Peninsula, and all of Egypt; his last goal was the retaking of Jerusalem.

Saladin accomplished that goal, yet mercifully did not slaughter the Christians as they had done to the Muslims when Christians had first captured the Holy City a century before. Would a twenty first century version of Saladin demonstrate the same sort of chivalry, or would he revenge the slaughter of tens of thousands at the hands of the Crusaders under the auspiciousness of religion, not to mention the perceived unevenness of today's conflicts. How significant were several hundred victims of a terrorist bombing compared to the massacre of the entire Muslim population of Jerusalem? A new Saladin with a unified Islamic world and the combination of oil and nuclear weapons could bring the West to the same sort of stalemate that the twelfth century Saladin accomplished against King Richard I of England.

"What else can you tell me about Amir Sika Kahn?" *How dangerous was this man?*

"He's believed to have been born and raised for a time in Afghanistan. He's a Sunni Muslim. He was one of the younger guerillas fighting the Soviets, only a boy. He was educated in Pakistan and England and is trained as a physicist. One of the scarier aspects of Amir Kahn's professional life in Pakistan was his association with AQ Kahn. He worked with Kahn's team as a researcher during the development of Pakistan's nuclear program. The point there is that he may know how to build a bomb. Also known as a brilliant investor, with an estimated net worth likely in the upper eight figures, perhaps higher - and very camera shy, I might add. He always wears some sort of headdress, and there aren't any known photos of him without sunshades or dark tinted glasses, that I know of."

Most non-Islamic, Western countries could perceive Amir Kahn as very dangerous. His shadowy movements would make it difficult to track him as well, and evidently he had the money to go anywhere he wanted, at anytime. So he'd have the combination of being both dangerous and aloof, adding to myth. At the moment, there wasn't proof that Kahn had done anything wrong and the Holding Company he controlled was in the eleventh hour of one of the biggest business deals in history with four of the most powerful businessmen from the United States. Was this man really affiliated with Al-Qaeda, or did he have his own agenda? Was he in fact a terrorist, willing to risk all in the name of Allah? Certainly Saladin defined the Arabic word for chivalry, "futuwah." *Could it be possible that Kahn was cut from the same mold?*

"His name has never come up with any briefing that I've been involved with. I'll check with the CIA. Whose report is that, Shannon?"

Shannon searched the file to find an author. There it was. "Rodgers Christopher," she said, blinking in disbelief. "Now why wouldn't he have mentioned this?"

"Good question. Anything on Wazir?"

"Sure is," she said, skimming a few paragraphs from the file. "Complete opposite personality as Hanif."

Reading from the computer screen it was evident that Wazir was an academic, whereas Hanif had early on become a devout follower of fundamental Islamic clerics. Many Pashtun in Pakistan sympathized with, even supported the Taliban and the Al-Qaeda. Hanif did as a youth, but Wazir appeared to be indifferent.

"So Hanif joined the Pakistani Army while Wazir continued his studies - and it looks as though he was studying medicine in Lahore. Interesting transgression for twins" Bryan said.

"No doubt," Shannon said. "Look here Bryan - Wazir and Hanif both studied in Spain for more than a year. The same school, and the dates match with Abdul-Malik."

"The first confirmation of contact between Wazir and Abdul-Malik, " Bryan said. "Unless he's somewhere on the training camp video with Hanif – let's have DJ check those old tapes again."

CHAPTER 26

JUNE 9, 2008

DUBAI

PARTNERNING WITH ITS MASTER, the falcon is similar to a prizefighter, but the fight was always one sided, the outcome equally predictable. The keeper pulls off the bird's hood like a corner man tends to a pugilist, removing his robe before a bout. Both were fighters, the jab a commonality, yet the falcon's contest was predation, its punch was with talons. *Falco peregrinus* is a perfectly designed hunting machine, a raptor so lethal that the deadliest supersonic fighters in the world are named after it, the Raptor and Falcon. With keen eyesight, hooked beak, sharp talons, and world record setting speed of two hundred and forty two miles per hour in a stoop, the falcon is an air superiority fighter as well; in the animal kingdom. Perfected by nature fifty million years ago, the hunter hasn't changed much since then, only adding more species to the genus, thirty-seven at last count. Easy to admire, man decided to harness the creature several thousand years ago, team up with it, a partnership. "To be manned," as falconers say.

What's not to admire about the falcon when it's studied while going about its business? "Absolutely everything," was what falconers also said. And when two falcons are spotted flying together, there's no such thing as casual observation, the larger female flying upside down to receive food midair from its lifetime mate. It's a study of aerial flight so incredible, the pair seemingly defying the laws of aerodynamics and gravity. Observers have a hard time believing their own eyes.

Bryan looked on as Amir Kahn, an experienced falconer, instructed the keeper as he now prepared a juvenile Gyrfalcon for its first free flight, the grand finale and culmination of intensive training and preparation. The Gyrfalcon, also called the "King's falcon," is the largest falcon of all, with a wingspan of four and a half feet, and weighing the same number in pounds. But this bird was much smaller when she first began her training, now almost full grown.

As the host piloted his Jet Ranger helicopter to the desert earlier, Bryan learned from Amir that the bird was captive bred. She had been brought to the point of free flight after a number of critical introductory steps. First, the young bird needed to bond with man, and in doing so she would become dependent on man. Only by man would she be fed and given water. She began to trust him, and then his glove, where she took her meals, small morsels at first, then larger over time. A repetitive process, only for those with extended patience.

Mutual respect developed as she grew, especially a raptor her size, and within time she was eating from a garnish, but still taking food from the glove. Now the falconer backed further and further away, until she leapt to the glove, finally flying to it. A creance was next, tethered to the bird, but lightweight, allowing her to fly twenty-five meters to the glove and her meal. When she flew the length of the creance, and returned to the food, she was ready. The keeper, the maintainer of the hunter, was attaching a narrow wire to her tail feather.

"Your insurance policy Sultan?" Bryan asked Amir in all earnestness.

"One can never tell Captain."

The transmitter served the party well that day. After successfully hitting the lure twice, the keeper removed the creance. Amir sent the young female on her first, unrestrained flight. The Sultan laughed hard as she kept on going, tracked by a four-wheel drive and two keepers.

"That is the result sometimes Captain. You believe they are ready for their mission, but they have other ideas. The desert is a big place, and she's confused. She'll come around soon," Amir said. He signaled another keeper standing by a second Range Rover. Reaching into the vehicle, its engine turning to provide air-conditioning, he produced the Sultan's favorite bird, his prized Peregrine.

"I'm sometimes called 'master,' as in 'master falconer,' but it's he that's the true master," Amir said as he removed the belled hood from the perched falcon. "He's the master of the sum of the sky."

The falcon looked alert and intense as it perched on the Sultan's glove, stretching its wings a full one meter several times. Mesmerized by the bird's eyes, its attentive gaze, Bryan felt a thrill anticipating what was to come.

"Today we are practicing my champion," Amir said as he released the falcon into the air. Bryan noticed that the flacon wasn't wired for telemetry as it began a rapid ascent above the desert.

"He staying close by," Bryan said as he observed the falcon pump it wings accelerating away from them, and then stop flapping, straighten the wings, and glide back.

"That's because he knows his game is coming from me," Amir Kahn said. He blew a whistle signaling the bird, and on cue, the falcon climbed higher. The keeper released a doomed skylark, which was immediately targeted by the falcon. Turning hard, pulling twenty-nine G's, the master of the airways dove, striking and killing the small passerine bird on the first pass.

"That my dear Captain is a marvel of flight, wouldn't you say?" the Sultan asked jubilantly. "*Baaz*, you are the greatest champion."

"The bird's name is *Baaz?*" Bryan asked curiously.

"Yes, of course you already know that the word means *Falcon* in many Muslim languages," Amir said, coaxing the falcon back to his glove for a treat. "Look closely here Captain Craig, if the light is just right, his eyes have a slight blue hue, don't they?"

Bryan looked carefully at the bird, and Amir was in fact right. "That must be very rare," Bryan said.

"No one can seem to explain it. I believe it is what's called a 'Freak of Nature,' isn't it?" the Sultan said, as he placed the belled hood over the falcon's head.

"Maybe it's symbolic, Sultan Kahn," Bryan said with a touch of sarcasm.

"Perhaps."

"I wouldn't know about that, but let's talk about the development – Burj al Baaz and the city that's going up all around it," Bryan said, wanting to get to the heart of the laborer issues. Was the Sultan complicit with organizing a new terrorist cell, Bryan wondered?

"What is that you'd like to know, Captain?"

"What labor force are you using?"

"Pakistanis, as always – perhaps some Indian labor too. But, needless to say, all from the Indian subcontinent."

"And is there a particular reason Amir?"

"Reliability."

"In what way?"

"If you're implying that my intent is something other than building a fine city and magnificent building, well then please be direct with me. I won't mince words with my answer."

"There's a history of fellowship, if you will, between Sheikhs from Dubai, or the UAE and known terrorists. It's happened before, what's to prevent the same kind of collaboration?"

"Yes, you're referring to the infamous Al-Qaeda hunting trip and their guests, family members of the Sheikh," Amir said, recalling yet another example of attention-getting missteps.

"We wouldn't want to see you get mixed up in a similar situation, unknowingly or otherwise. That could cause embarrassment for yourself, and Dubai," Bryan said, using every bit of diplomatic skills he had. He was on a slippery slope, and knew it.

"The embarrassment would be more pronounced with your American investors, and the State Department – would it not Captain?" Amir said rhetorically.

Potentially, another Dubai Ports deal blowing up in everybody's faces, Bryan thought. "I'm just thinking of everyone's interest going forward." Bryan answered.

"Are you a religious man?" Amir asked, startling Bryan with the question.

He thought for a moment, and then carefully answered. "I have been," Bryan said.

"Perhaps only when convenient," Amir replied. "Or is it something in your past that has shaken your faith?"

Recalling his mother's devout adherence to Catholicism, and their many Saturday evenings at Mass, Bryan realized his faith remained, but his spirituality had faded. "Nothing in my past has shaken my faith – let's just say I don't go to an official church anymore," Bryan answered, wondering where Amir was going with his questions.

"I'm happy to hear that your faith remains Captain – that much is important, in fact, in the end it's all that really matters – especially for a Catholic."

"And you know about the Catholic Church?" Bryan asked.

"I know about all religions, especially those that share the same prophets," Amir said. "And our faiths are influenced by the same forces and believe in similar conclusions. The workers from Pakistan are all apart of the same flock."

"Are they true believers, or just sheep being prepared for the slaughter?" Bryan asked.

Amir put his hand on Bryan's shoulder as he answered. "Captain Craig, they are no more sheep than you – but they are finding their faith, which has been lost, or should I say faded?" Bryan felt a chill as Amir squeezed his shoulder with his large hand and spoke. "The Muslim faith and Christianity believe in the second coming of their Profits. Many believe that Mohammed and Jesus will rise together. What do you believe Captain?"

Bryan shook his head. "I don't know."

Standing squarely in front of Bryan, Amir smiled as he spoke, "Perhaps they will rise together as one."

Bryan was speechless.

"Let's go back now, shall we Bryan?" the Sultan said, motioning to the helicopter. He used Bryan's given name for the first time.

CHAPTER 27

JUNE 9, 2008

MADRID, SPAIN

A DARK HAIRED MAN with a neatly trimmed moustache and goatee boarded a commuter passenger plane and departed from Madrid International Airport. The destination was Malaga. He purchased a round trip ticket, and hand carried his luggage onto the plane, a hang-up bag and computer case. Airport inspectors checked him thoroughly, and after searching every square inch of his bags for bomb residue, weapons, knives, or anything that could be deemed as dangerous contraband, allowed him entry into the gate area. Airports had been on high alert for the past two weeks and had relaxed some restrictions, but were still very vigilant.

The passport read Martin Luis de la Vega from Madrid, Spain. He was neatly dressed in lightweight khaki slacks and blue sports blazer with a white open collared shirt. Mister de la Vega was very polite and spoke English with a distinct British/ Spanish accent, as many aristocratic Spaniards were known to have. His flight was uneventful, arrived in Malaga on time, and after deplaning, he stepped into a waiting car for the short drive to the beach. It was late, almost 11:00 PM, but not by Spanish standards. He would have plenty of time to do what needed to be done, and he had all night to do it.

* * * * *

Gil moved easily through the crowd. It was after midnight. At last he could take a break from Pegasus. He had been working nonstop for two weeks with very little rest or relaxation. And this was Costa del Sol. The Russian girls were here somewhere inside the club. He pulled his phone out of his back pocket.

"Hey, I just got here. Where are you guys? I'm at the bar by the pool. Call me right back." He hung up the phone and began a survey of the scene.

Restaurante Toni Dalli was the place to be. It had been around for about twenty years, which was very unusual in a town known for trends. Established clubs didn't stay around very long. It was all about the here and now and what was new. But Toni Dalli's was an Italian restaurant made famous by famous people, all dined there when in Marbella, and helped to develop the restaurant's "in vogue" reputation. Celebrities flocked there and so did the beautiful girls that gravitated to the celebs. He liked that. Gil was in fact somewhat of a celebrity himself, and used that notoriety to his benefit.

"In my experience, power, money and influence always attract the opposite sex. It's something that I've always exploited - with good results," was something Gil sometimes joked about, but firmly believed and practiced to great perfection.

While he waited to hear from the girls, he looked around the pool area to locate some new targets of opportunity. Gil felt it was always a good idea to keep his options open. Gil sipped a glass of chardonnay as he took in the June night. The club was beginning to fill up. And a bit more crowded than usual, as if people, mostly Brits, were finally coming out of their shells and socializing again; trying to forget the bombings and move on with their lives. In Spain, one usually lived for the moment anyway, and the moment of the bombings was already two weeks behind their self-absorbed lives. That was almost a lifetime in pop culture.

"Gil. How are you?"

Gil felt a tap on the shoulder at the same time he heard the familiar voice. He turned to see his friend from Spain.

"Martin. ¿Qué pasa hombre? When did you get into town?" Gil asked. They happily shook each other's hand.

"I just arrived about an hour ago. I'm here for a little business and of course some fun too."

"Well my friend, you picked a good night. As you can see, people are finally out again. For awhile things were pretty somber though, especially here since this city has so many Brits."

"I'm happy to see that the healing process is underway for you Americans and British, but very sorry that such a terrible thing had to happen again. Sometimes the world just seems to be going mad. We've been living through it in España for many, many years now, as you well know. The Madrid train bombings only a few years ago, and we have had ongoing problems with the Basque socialists ETA for decades. Only recently have they agreed to a cessation."

Recalling Spain's experience with terrorism, Gil replied, "I agree whole heartedly with you Martin, it does appear the world's going mad. If there's any place on this earth that remains unscathed from this disease I'd like to know - I'll move there in a heartbeat. I guess I shouldn't be very surprised at the similarity between the bombings and those in Madrid, coordinated multiple bombings is their modus operandi these days. When does it all end? When the world self-destructs? God help us if these crazy fucks get hold of a nuke."

How could anyone forget Madrid's train bombings, Gil thought? The work of an Islamic fundamentalist group with some ties to Al-Qaeda; it had been a coordinated attack very similar to the Memorial Day bombings. Ten explosions using improvised explosive devices had occurred in series at the peak of Madrid's morning rush hour. The attacks were devastating, killing one hundred and ninety two people and injuring over two thousand. As a consequence of the attacks, the Prime Minister of Spain lost his reelection bid, which had occurred only three days after the bombings. Spain then quickly announced the withdrawal of its troops from Iraq.

"People in Spain are nervous too. But nothing has happened again since we left Iraq," Martin said.

"Well, Americans are finally starting to get back to normal. You can't let the fear of an attack ruin your life. It's best to live life as fully as possible."

"Viva Yo," Martin said. "Live for yourself."

"Exactly, after all, you're going die anyway, so my best advice is to drink up, and drink up often - so let me buy you a drink," Gil said as he smiled. He was happy to see his new friend. He hadn't known him for very long, but the Spaniard seemed like a very genuine person.

After a laid back evening of moderate drinking, Gil invited his Spanish friend to join him back at his home for a nightcap. He spoke with the girls and learned that his two Russian houseguests had taken a detour during the course of the evening. Apologizing, they said they'd rendezvous with him and Martin at the condo.

It was obvious to Gil that Martin amused them both, remembering the Spaniard from a previous trip, and recalling his charisma and ability to keep the party alive. Gil also found Martin's company refreshing. The Spaniard was erudite, always ready with intelligent, introspective conversation on virtually any topic. Martin was also a banker, and had been the source of very worthwhile investment information from time to time. "There's nothing better than a qualified tip," Gil reasoned.

Gil pulled into the garage at 2:20 AM, Martin riding in the passenger seat. Taking the elevator up to the penthouse, they entered the condominium. It was dark and quiet. Inés was probably asleep, Gil thought.

Entering the kitchen, Gil turned a corner to the doorway of his private wine cellar. Offering three hundred square feet of refrigeration, it was designed to store the finest wines a connoisseur could need. Always a perfectionist, Gil maintained his stock at exactly fifty-five degrees Fahrenheit and sixty-five percent relative humidity. The cellar's racking preserved more than four hundred bottles of the world's finest vintages in perfect conditions. He moved his index finger across the best before finally stopping on a special vintage.

"Martin, how about a Bordeaux?" Gil asked, offering a bottle of a fifty-nine Château Latour.

"Muy bien my friend. What's the occasion?"

"Let's just say it was a great day, and nice to have some good company as well. I've finally earned my keep, put it that way." Gil had cracked the problem, something he would only be able to share with Bryan once he was able to have a secure conversation with him. It would be in the morning. He uncorked the wine and let it breath, then carefully poured the bottle into a crystal decanter.

"This is a twenty-five rating out of twenty-five my friend. To quote the experts – 'Intense wine. No aging necessary. Unbelievable nose of blackberries, truffles and cedar. A definition that is off the map.' How's that for a perfect description?" Gil poured a glass for each of them. He was whore for the finest life had to offer.

"Are you hungry?" Gil asked.

"Well, in fact yes. I really didn't eat anything on the plane, or at the bar. Perhaps some cheese and ham as before?" Martin remembered that Inés usually prepared something as a late night snack when Gil went out for the evening.

"You bet. Let me check the fridge." As Gil turned, Martin took advantage of the opportunity.

They walked outside to the pool area. It was a beautiful night. The stars were out. They sat down at the bar and continued to converse on numerous topics. Martin looked closely at Gil. He could see that he was becoming slightly unsteady.

"Where are the girls?" Martin asked.

"I don't know," Gil said, wondering the same thing. It was strange.

"Let me call them for a little encouragement," Martin said.

"Good idea." Gil handed his cell phone to Martin after starting the call. Martin began speaking; his back turned from Gil. *That's curious!*

"They're downstairs by the pool. Let's wave at them from the balcony," Martin said encouragingly.

"Sure, let's go." Gil said, standing up and then stumbling slightly. *What's wrong with me?*

Gil's footing was unsure, a staggering gate, as he negotiated the length of the pool deck, dumbfounded that he was feeling that messed up so quickly. It must have been the lack of sleep and lack of food, he figured. But he wasn't hungry. Gil's brain cells had been rendered useless so rapidly, that the judgment and reason necessary for rational conclusions were seriously impaired. He'd been drugged, a realization he would never make. All decisions he was making from that point forward would be the wrong ones.

They reached the railing and looked down to the pool area on the beach. Gil's blurred vision incapable of clearly recognizing the girls, ten stories below. Leaning over the rail, he waved at them as he yelled down "Hola, venga aqui – por favor." Swaying, looking at Martin, he slurred, "I told them to come up – Oh, you know that, you're Spanish – that's right." He thought that he saw them wave back. He looked down again. They were gone.

"Where'd they go? Must be on their way up here, yeah that's it," Gil said tongue-tied.

"Are you feeling alright Gil?" Martin asked, seemingly concerned.

"¿Cómo es usted que se siente? ¿Está usted bien?"

Is Martin speaking in Spanish? He wasn't sure. Reasoning was crippled - the drug sucking valuable oxygen from his brain's gray matter. He was somewhat woozy and now worried he'd embarrass himself in front of his guest. He tried concentrating on Martin's words, but Gil's mind was becoming more confused with each passing second.

Martin felt it appropriate to wait just a little longer; he genuinely cared for Gil, and wanted it to be as painless for his American friend as possible. He could see that Gil was close to being beyond help, beyond hope. Gil's brilliant mind was fighting to regain control. But it was a losing proposition. A wave of fear came over him, then instantly passed. *Am I feeling better?*

Gil was now reaching a state of total drug induced euphoria. He was very happy and completely at ease, but something wasn't right, yet he couldn't fight it, no matter how hard he tried. A twilight zone enveloped his entire being and quickly gave way to a sudden onset of drowsiness. He tried to move; take a step towards the stairs leading back to the pool and inside the condo, but coordination had evacuated his body. He was completely lethargic. Trapped by intoxication.

Martin continued to talk. Gil looked in his direction but was unable to understand anything he was saying. The Spaniard's face was out of focus, distorted. He concentrated with what intensity he had remaining, trying to maintain his composure, but he couldn't. Images were dissolving before his eyes.

Facing the pool, he braced his spine against the balcony and gripped the railing with both hands trying to steady his failing body. No longer able to hold his head up, it fell back on his shoulders. Gil saw the stars. He was in the initial stages of a panic, yet strangely complacent. *Something's very wrong!*

Martin snapped his fingers in front of Gil's face. "Gil? Are you okay?" He could see that Gil was almost incapacitated and needing assistance. There was no discernable response. Now was the time to finish his mission.

Martin crouched down in front of Gil and grabbed both of the taller man's ankles with a firm, solid grip. He breathed in hard and then sprang up using the power of kinetic energy stored in his legs. Exploding with a strong underhand motion of his arms and shoulders, he exhaled and released Gil's legs at rail level.

CHAPTER 28

JUNE 10, 2008

DUBAI

DESPONDENT AS HE WAS, Bryan kept his emotions in check. Workers from the condo's landscaping service found Gil's body early that morning, just after seven. At first they thought that he was passed out or maybe asleep. They had no idea that he had just fallen ten floors. The landing area was freshly mulched shrubbery that had just been watered by the automatic sprinkler system. It was very soft, but not soft enough to save his life. Lying face up, his hands were resting by his side and his eyes were closed. He looked great, as if he was just relaxing some in the bushes and could jump up at any second. But his body was broken. The news of Gil's death came from the CIA.

"DCIA has instructed you to report only to me?" Bryan asked.

"That's what I've been told sir – gave me your number," the CIA man in Spain said.

"Everything stays in house then – tell me what happened."

"We were the first on the scene and have already swept the residence. Spanish police are there now. His housekeeper was drugged. The legal attaché is coordinating with the Spanish authorities to contain all evidence under FBI jurisdiction. He was killed around 3 AM," the agent said into his Blackberry as he looked over the balcony down at the crime scene. The coroner was in the process of having the body removed. He winced at the thought of the long drop.

"How's Inés?" Bryan asked.

"The housekeeper? She'll be okay, one hell of a headache though. Never heard a damn thing. Was probably out when he got home. Guardia Seville had a real hard time waking her up. Their crime scene people are all over the place right now dusting everything, including his balcony where I am. So far it's all clean."

"Well, you know what to do. This is a diplomatic matter now," Bryan said, referring to Gil's status as an official Embassy employee.

"Yeah, roger that, I've already done it. The coroner has the body right now. They'll store it for us, but won't touch it. Legal will make the arrangements to have him flown back to the States," the CIA man said.

"He was pushed?" A rhetorical question, Bryan knew.

"I'd say so, we've got the place sealed right now. We'll bag everything later - the computer, building security video, everything. Spanish homicide is going through the rest of the building as we speak – looking for anyone who heard or saw anything. The graveyard shift security guard said he thought Gil might've had someone else in the car with him - he's not one hundred percent certain. Gil parked in the garage rather than valet, and went up the service elevator to his condo. The security camera was disabled."

"Security camera disabled?"

"Management said the one in the garage had been out for about a week."

"What about the cameras in his apartment?" Bryan asked knowing Gil's cameras were Internet based, and fed into Pegasus.

"They look like they were disabled too," the CIA man said.

Bryan thought about the Russian girls. "What about Gil's house guests?" Bryan was convinced that the Russians must have something to do with his death.

"We're on that one - probably responsible for the housekeeper's hangover. She had coffee with the two of them yesterday afternoon, and was out like a light right afterwards. Both are on an Iberia flight to Madrid. Should be landing any minute. We'll grab them when they deplane."

"What's their itinerary from there?"

"None that we can tell of so far," the CIA man said.

"Don't arrest them just yet. Keep an eye on them for a few days and I want everything they say or do recorded and videoed. Phone calls, everything – even when they take a crap. We'll see where they lead us after they think things have cooled off." Bryan added, "Now if they lay too low, have Guardia Civil run them in. I've a hunch that these two were pretty chummy with Petrov, and with him out of the way they could prove to be very useful. They're apt to make mistakes."

"Roger that."

"Get the old security video from the entire building and whatever electronic equipment that's in Gil's condo, the computers, cell phones – send it all to Thames House – put it to my attention. Also, find out where Gil was last night. Check Toni Dali's – it was Monday night - that's his favorite spot on a Monday."

"We got it all under control Captain Craig. The Guardia Civil has his car right now. I think they were planning on taking it downtown. I'll have our lab collaborate with them. Anything that's electronic I'll send to London."

"Get the car from them too – get it over to the embassy in Madrid. Drive there yourself if you have to."

"What about forensics?"

"Have the team from Madrid go through it before you take it over the mountains, but I doubt they'll find anything they can use. Check Airport security video for anything suspicious as well. My hunch though, is that the killer's long gone by now." Micromanaging wasn't a usual trait of his, but Bryan was taking Gil's death very personally.

"You got it sir."

Bryan was sure that Gil's death had been planned days ago. He was taken out now because he was getting close. The financial forensics man had to be eliminated immediately. Gil's death had urgency written all over it. The details were in the accounts that Gil had been looking at, or new ones he found. Accounts that Bryan didn't know. *What were the new accounts?*

Bryan was going to miss his friend a great deal. They went back a long way. And he was convinced that Gil must have cracked the accounts' mystery, or he wouldn't have been out on the town. He was predictable like that, similar to a boxer in training, no booze or "broads" until the after the fight. Bryan noted Gil tried contacting him twice, but followed strict protocol by not leaving voicemails with confidential information. If Gil had uncovered something that was important to the mission, DJ would find it somewhere in the Pegasus central computer.

"Anything else we can do for you over here Captain Craig?" the CIA man asked.

Kill the bastard that did this! "Don't lose those Russians - and I'll be in touch."

The CIA man, now roaming the pool area, admiring the views and the lavish lifestyle that Gil had so enjoyed, said, "Ferrari, multi-million dollar penthouse, plenty of women, avoid the Russian ones though - great job this guy had."

"He had a propensity for living large, that's for sure," Bryan said.

"He worked for you did he?"

"Yes he did."

"So then how do I get to work for you like this guy did?"

"Learn how to electronically steal hundreds of millions of dollars without getting caught and the job's yours."

CHAPTER 29

JUNE 10, 2008

DUBAI

S TARING AT THE EMAIL, Rodgers Christopher felt the anger well up inside. He looked out the window of his twenty-first floor office in the Dubai World Trade Center and wondered what to do next. The 39-story office tower where the Consulate General's office was located was ancient by Dubai's standards, almost thirty years old, but had been the centerpiece of the city-state's transformation. With the largest exhibit hall and convention center in the Middle East, the DWTC had been host to events that included representatives of the International Monetary Fund and World Bank symposium.

It was afternoon over Dubai, and the city was operating at full RPM. The immediate view from the Consul General's office offered an excellent perspective of the complexities of building construction surrounding the DWTC. Four skyscrapers were rising within two blocks of the tower, construction cranes in constant motion. Within just a few weeks, all views from his corner office would be completely obscured. It upset him. Another thing pissed him off too; he was being jerked around by the likes of Bryan Craig.

The American Consul General wasn't used to being out dueled by an operations type. Especially one with an unknown title, office, or agency, and carte blanche to do whatever he wanted. He was furious actually. Rising stars normally came out ahead. At least he had been a rising star. He had worked very hard too. Put his butt on the line, he thought. Over the last few years, to smooth over the bad feelings following the PDI fiasco, he made promises, granted special favors. Yet Bryan Craig had managed to circumvent his very authority, and on his own turf. Rodgers Christopher was not going to be made a fool of.

"Mary Anne, get Kevin Davis on the phone – no better yet, tell him to get his ass over here to the consulate ASAP," Rodgers barked over the intercom to his assistant, then he read the email again.

Arriving thirty minutes later, Kevin presented his ID. It wasn't needed, the Marine Guards recognized him. He'd been there numerous times over the last few months, a routine visitor. Given his "Visitor" pass, he entered the reception area of Rodgers Christopher's office.

Perhaps the most unique furnishings in Dubai, the offices were decorated in traditional early American motif, highlighted by inlaid mahogany coffee and side tables, and a rosewood sideboard from the early nineteenth century. The sofa was a figurative, shaped like a crest with carved scroll arms, guarded by two identical antique armchairs made of tiger maple. Of course there were the three portraits, the President of The United States, the Secretary of State, and the U.S. Ambassador to the United Arab Emirates. Kevin always felt a sense of "little Americana" whenever he came to the U.S. Consulate.

Kevin sat down on the antique sofa and waited to be called into Rodgers' office. It was just one of his many affectations, and an obvious one at that; calling for a person post haste, only to have them sit around. *Hurry up and wait!*

A television sitting on an eighteenth century antique library table was turned to CNN International News. Kevin thought he'd spend the wasted time catching up on the news. A reporter was narrating a story on the Middle East. It looked like Dubai, or the UAE at the very least. Kevin couldn't be sure what the reporter was saying, if the story was positive or negative. The volume of the television was turned down too low. The reporter came into view; Dylan Sizemore. Kevin quickly turned up the volume with a remote. His jaw dropped when he heard Dylan's report.

"...in spite of the tremendous resources that the government of the United Arab Emirates has today, there are those that are still suffering: The workers that toil under the oppressiveness of not just the hot Arab sun, but also the oppressiveness of the developers of the massive construction projects that these men in blue give their lives to. Accidents are routine here, as one would expect considering the conditions under which they are forced to work. Just two weeks ago, an accident resulted in the death of six laborers. They were killed at Dubai Mall when a crane toppled over." The story cut to the images of the construction site. Kevin turned the volume back down as Mary Anne came out of Rodgers Christopher's office.

As Kevin stepped in the office, he saw Rodgers Christopher sitting with his feet resting on the massive desk in the center of the office. He had a T.V. remote control in his hand. It was pointed directly at the HD flat panel plasma built into the wall. The expression on his face was priceless, Kevin thought. His face was so red, Kevin thought that he literally looked as though he was about to crap his pants.

"Have you seen this damn thing? It's your buddy Dylan Sizemore doing a report for CNN. He's crucifying Dubai." Rodgers said belligerently.

"Not the whole thing. Only a portion outside in..." Kevin replied, suddenly interrupted by Rodgers.

Christopher turned up the volume. "Well goddamn it Kevin. Just listen to this dribble. First the reports about the jockeys, then the ports fiasco, and now this - he's railing the Ministry of Labor – and now insinuating there's some sort of terrorist farm here. You didn't know this was coming?" He turned the TV off, and slammed the remote on his desktop.

Startled, Kevin pointed at the TV, anxious to hear the report. "Well turn it back on."

"Fuck him – what do you know about it?"

"Well I haven't spoken to him about..." Kevin was interrupted again.

"Is that so. Well do you have anything brilliant to say about this?" Rodgers asked, handing the printout of the Email to Kevin, who read it quietly.

CONFIDENTIAL

From: Ambassador Evans
Sent: Tuesday June 10, 2008 6:44 AM
To: Consul General - Dubai
Subject: Bryan Craig, Captain USN

Rodgers,

I have reports indicating that Bryan Craig
has run into a few small diplomatic
glitches while on assignment in Dubai. As
you are aware, his mission to the UAE is
of the utmost importance. He is to be
given every courtesy and available asset
he needs from the embassy and our staff.
Please do not interfere in the slightest
with his investigation. He is operating on
the highest authority and is of vital
national interest.

V/R
The Honorable A. Rodney Evans
U.S. Ambassador
Unite Arab Emirates

Kevin was worried now. Things were starting to get out of hand.
"What do you want me to say? I can't do anything about this," Kevin
grumbled, slapping the Email with the back of his hand. "I think he's
cleared straight from the White House. He's not the kind of guy you
want to fuck with Rodgers," Kevin added, covering.

"That's not the right answer," Rodgers seethed through clenched,
snow-white teeth.

The Consul General stood up from the chair of his oversized
mahogany desk; the kind that could be found in a high-powered
CEO's office on Wall Street who belied omnipotence. The room also
had matching mahogany paneled walls, covered with copies of
Romanticism artists of early nineteenth century America. His favorite
of that period was "The Solitary Tree," an oil by David Friedrich.
Symbolic, in light of his impression of himself, Kevin thought.

Rodgers Christopher cherished his eighteenth and nineteenth century American art though, more than any other collectibles in his possession. Over the years he had managed to obtain a few originals at auctions here and there. A few originals were not enough though. Rodgers wanted it all, wealth, power, and the benefits.

Peering out the window, with the obscured views that now irritated him, his hands behind his back, the he counseled Kevin in a lowered voice, "I know that you don't intend on making the CIA your life's work, do you Kevin?"

"Depends on who's asking."

"Let's just say that I am. How would you like to – well, like to make the jump from intelligence to diplomacy - finally get respect from the leaders and rulers of countries? Actually be a part of the magic of a place like Dubai. Not just running from one assignment to another, as dictated by eggheads at Langley. Sort of what's happening to you right now?" He looked from the window at Kevin, who had now sat down in a chair facing Rodgers' desk. "Wouldn't you agree with that observation Kevin?"

Humility was not a strong suite of Rodgers, and Kevin could predict that the one-way conversation would quickly degenerate. Rodgers Christopher had a bad habit of bullying when given the opportunity to do so. Kevin had been around assholes like him too long to take the bait, but he was very interested in where Rodgers was going with his sudden generosity.

"I'm satisfied with my career as it stands. I don't want to stay here forever, of course, but so far so good. What's your point? Are you offering me an ambassadorship ahead of you?" Kevin said wryly, baiting the Consul General.

"Here's my point, Mister Davis. You're responsible for Craig while he's here."

"Not exactly true. He's on his own, and ultimately we work for the same person. That goes for you too, I might add. Anyway, you have the Email here from the Ambassador - that should confirm the fact that he's beyond your control, or mine. If he wants to stir things up around here, he's going to get away with it. At least until someone way above you fires his ass," Kevin said as he held up the Email.

"Well, you do have some say so in who he sees and where he goes while he's here don't you? I can't emphasize this enough – don't let him interfere with the Baazland project. There's way too much

American investment riding on that deal, as well as our relationship with the UAE. As the Dubai goes, so goes the interest of the United States in the Arab world. It's that big - and one must keep in mind a perspective that takes into account the future of Arab-American relations. Thinking small doesn't work here Kevin."

Kevin could hear the pontificating. It pounded his head and nauseated him. Never before had he met someone with such an overbearing, inflated ego. Now he was trying to browbeat him to take some extra measures regarding Bryan Craig.

Rodgers Christopher added, "And, as I said – you should consider your own future. I can make things happen to ensure that you won't have to rely on just a Civil Service pension fifteen years from now."

"Meaning what exactly?" Kevin asked thinking now was the time to throw a line out and see what he could catch.

"Let's just say that Baazland might have room for a certain Company man that cooperates with the best interests of the State Department, which means the best interest of the United States."

"So, does that mean you're offering me a job with the Bank of Dubai?" Sarcasm was getting the best of him again.

"Don't be a wise ass. I'm saying that your career - from what I can tell, is dead end. You're still stuck here as a mid-grade case officer, after what - eight years or more. You're not going anywhere back at Langley. And what about your family? Aren't you concerned about college for your two daughters? What are they now, twelve and fourteen?"

"What exactly are you offering Rodgers?"

"I've gone to great lengths to help Craig, and he doesn't even realize it. The Swiss accounts are real. My sources are telling me that. That's where the money trail goes, and it's the best trail he's got now that his financial whiz is dead."

What sources are those? "What do you mean that his financial whiz is dead?" Kevin asked taken aback.

"Haven't heard yet huh? Gil Bussmann, the operator that Craig used. You know, the guy that was going to be indicted by the SEC. Craig saved his ass and put him to work on some special project he's got cooking. The guy lived like a king in Spain."

"What do you mean he ended up dead?"

"Happened just last night - at his high-rise in Malaga. He fell from his penthouse balcony. With his death, they don't have a superstar to track down the accounts of the terrorism financiers. I've gone to great lengths, and pulled in favors to help him out. Instead, he's blown me off."

"Let's get back to the Bussmann death – how did it happen?"

Rodgers moved over from the window and sat on the corner of his desk directly in front of Kevin. "Really don't really know what happened to him exactly. I heard about his death from the Embassy in Madrid a couple of hours ago – another good source I've got."

"What source is that?" Kevin asked, now very concerned.

"Kevin, I've been in this business a long time – I've got friends everywhere," he said, putting his hand on Kevin's shoulder. "So let's play ball, okay? Now do I have your word that you'll help me get Craig to work with me here? Keep him off Rowley's back and away from the Bank of Dubai and their clients?"

Kevin was being stroked and kicked simultaneously. "Yeah – sure Rodgers. You've got my word." Kevin said. The Consul General's time was coming, and Kevin thought it would be fun to watch him fall. But he was also very worried.

CHAPTER 30

BRYAN LIKED THE MOUNTAINS. It was good to be back. He'd been to the Hindu Kush many times in the past, and it was a place that never left him, the sight and particularly the smell of these mountains and her valleys. In the warm months it had a kind of sweet aroma that he liked. He could smell it in the helicopter as they flew. He was in familiar territory and it felt right.

Returning to the North West Frontier was therapy for him. A battery recharge not too different than a vacation to the Amalfi coast, or the Greek Islands would be for anyone else that lived and worked in London. The Hindu Kush wasn't at the top of the list of requested vacation packages for most, and for damn good reasons. Wars had a way of keeping tourists away. But Bryan was wired a little different and needed a solid gut check every now and then. Here he could compartmentalize Gil's murder. The Hindu Kush beckoned him.

"RPG in the air. Low two o'clock," the Black Hawk pilot calmly announced over the intercom system, his tone only barely elevated.

Bryan look out the open door of the craft to see the flame of the shoulder fired rocket exactly where Staff Sergeant Horvath had called it. Corkscrewing, it was beginning to arc downward after just a couple of seconds of travel. The small rocket was obviously going to miss the helicopter low and aft. Accompanying the RPG were automatic small arms fire from AK-47s, tracers visible as a few rounds tickled the fuselage. A second and third corkscrew followed the first. The door gunner returned fire with Black Hawk's multi-barreled machine gun, shearing branches off trees from where the RPGs were launched.

Their cover blown, three Taliban militiamen carrying launchers and Kalashnikovs darted out from behind a tree at the base of a small hill. Wood provided zero protection. They were about two hundred feet below and now behind the flight. The lives of the militants were dependent on reaching safe cover near a collection of car size boulders that dotted the hillside. The boulders were fifty meters away. Odds were they wouldn't make it, but their consolation would be a complete understanding of the nature of the Islamist afterlife.

"Dash two, you got those guys?" Horvath asked over the radio. The call was for his wingman in the escort AH-64 Apache Helicopter, flying at the same altitude, with five hundred feet of separation, and on a four o'clock bearing from the lead Black Hawk.

"Roger, One," dash Two radioed as he trained his fuselage-mounted thirty-millimeter Chain Gun on the three, soon to be history, Taliban.

The gun coughed out five rounds as he squeezed a half second burst, leaving very little that was recognizable as human once the dust had settled. Neither helicopter wavered even one degree from flight heading during the ten-second encounter. Bryan checked the disposition of the three SEALs riding along with him. Their demeanors were calm; none budged even the slightest. One so relaxed, his eyes were closed, as if to say, "I'm resting now – conserving energy. Once this thing lands, then I go to work." Bryan thought he detected faint smiles beneath the heavy beards covering their faces.

"Yeah, it's good to be back," he thought.

The district of Chitral in the Hindu Kush awaited the flight, along with the rest of the SEAL team and a long-term coalition guide named Raza.

"It'll be nice to see that good-natured Pashtun again," Bryan said to himself.

The district was on the Pakistani side of the porous border with Afghanistan, approximately two hundred miles northeast of Bagram Airbase, their departure point. The Airbase was forty-seven miles north of Kabul, and had been secured by the Northern Alliance from the Taliban in the early days of Operation Enduring Freedom. By spring of the following year, the U.S. Air Force had moved in heavy construction equipment with C-17 transport aircraft. A total revamping ensued, and after almost two years Bagram had been turned into the primary base of operations for the coalition forces, supporting over seven thousand troops. It was the best staging area for operations like the one Bryan and the SEAL team would be undertaking over the next few days. The elite squad escorting him was an element of the Joint Special Operations Command and Task Force Blue. Only several years before the same team had pinpointed the location of one of the world's most brutal terrorists, leading to his demise by two five hundred pound presents from an F-16.

As they flew up a valley and got closer to the Paki border, the terrain became rugged, almost inhospitable. That's where the pockets of Taliban would take potshots at U.S. helicopters, but usually with similar results as moments before. Soon the hills turned into mountains. They were nearing their destination. He checked his watch. They'd been airborne for an hour.

"Staff Sergeant Horvath, what's our ETA – about twenty minutes?"

"Right on the nose sir," the pilot told him.

The flight had taken them along a track that over flew Jalalabad, Asmar, and the remnants of the compound destroyed by a cruise missile and Navy warplanes almost seven years before. He remembered it well.

"Same Goddamn camp," he mumbled to himself as they passed it by. The compound had been rebuilt, and changed hands twice since that time. It pissed him off.

"Captain Craig, we're here," Horvath announced as the Black Hawk touched down on a flat creek bed. Bryan grabbed his rifle and jumped out of the chopper. The four other members of the team were there waiting at the LZ.

They were standing in a small valley between hills that rose fast, becoming very large and steep. The valley was about one hundred meters wide and had a small stream flowing through the center of it. The elevation and the somewhat level area on the bank made it a good place for a landing zone. There were just a few large boulders. Flat areas with low elevation, meaning less than ten thousand feet above sea level, were almost nonexistent in Chitral.

"Captain Craig, good to see you again – set your gear down here sir – we'll inventory and cut Horvath's flight loose," the SEAL team Commanding Officer said. "Alright Hotshot, Turk, Proton - let's get a gear check and get the hell out a here. Capisce?"

The muscular man dishing out the orders was veteran Navy SEAL Lieutenant Timothy Thomas, affectionately known as T Squared, or sometimes also called simply *"el tee."* He'd just been frocked to Lieutenant Commander and hadn't pinned on new rank yet. The men were enjoying the shorter version address while they still had the chance.

"Roger that Lieutenant. Good to see you too," Bryan said. Thomas was a good man, and had been here with him as far back as Enduring Freedom. "Déjà vu, all over again – wouldn't ya say," Bryan added with a slap on the Lieutenant's back.

"You got that right sir."

Bryan laid his rifle down and began going through a mental checklist of every item he'd brought. He felt comfortable with the equipment and weapons. It was akin to riding a bike, sort of, he thought. As a SEAL he'd been through all the intensive training, with annual refreshers along the way, and he kept up to speed with the rifle and the pistol, practicing at an English shooting range on a routine basis. Skeet shooting with a few of his English country gentleman buddies kept his rifle skills honed too, but there was nothing like the real thing.

He looked at his weapons today. A mental checklist followed. "Heckler & Koch Mk23 .45 caliber handgun and four clips - twelve rounds each." He felt it with his right hand to be sure it was in its holster and attached to his belt.

"Combat knife to slice an' dice, right next door" he noted while his hand was there on the belt.

Lying next to his backpack was his new favorite weapon, the M8 Lightweight Combat Assault Rifle. Made of ultra-light composite material, the replacement to the M4 was twenty percent lighter, weighing just six pounds, and fired 5.56mm ammo. He'd a total of seven magazines in his vest. "Two hundred and forty rounds should do the trick."

As for the remainder of the gear in, or on his tactical vest, he'd a canteen, three protein bars, Bic lighter, Night-Ops illumination light, two signal flares, night goggles, radio, handheld GPS, PRC-148 radio, and aspirin. Everything combined, weighed less than thirty pounds.

The rest of the seven SEAL Team members were outfitted pretty much the same as Bryan, with the exception of two men with very different rifles. Turk was carrying the M60 general-purpose machine gun. The fearsome automatic rifle fired 7.62 millimeter rounds, capable of laying down fire suppression on targets from a distance of fifteen hundred meters. But Cowboy had the weapon that really scared the hell out of the enemy. The Barrett M107 semi-automatic fifty caliber, interdiction sniper rifle, had a maximum effective range of more than two thousand meters. Capable of piercing the armor of a personnel carrier, it could cut a man in half before the sound ever reached the target. Used as a sniper rifle, a verified kill had been made from a mile and a half.

Lieutenant Thomas waited to see the thumbs up from the team, and then sent Horvath and his flight on their way. The Black Hawk and his escort Apache lifted off. The drop off had taken less than a minute. The "whop, whop, whop" of the helicopters soon faded.

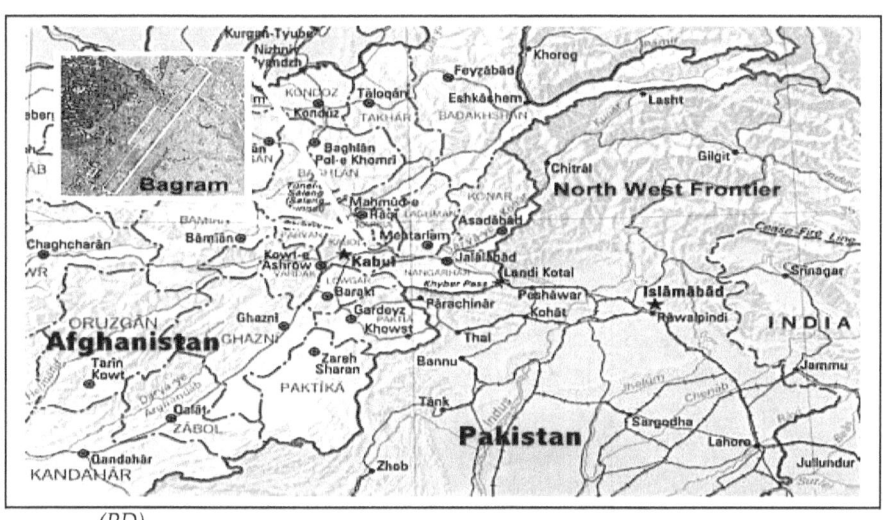

(PD)

The Lieutenant spoke up. "Okay, gather round - brief." The men formed a semi-circle. The SEAL commander and his team had been brought in for Bryan with little advanced warning. Thomas pulled out a waterproof map of the area and placed it on top of a boulder that met him chest high.

"Captain Craig here needs to meet with one particular Chitrali top dog. Prince Rehman and a squad are north of our location; maybe ten clicks at the most, and on the move. We need to link up the Captain with Rehman so he can do whatever it is that he has to do, then get 'im back here and go home. Sound good?" *KISS - he loved being back!*

"Now, and this is the important part - we've got unknown numbers of Taliban between us and Rehman. There are hundreds throughout the area - possibly more than a thousand. They've been skirmishing with Rehman's militia." He scanned his team to make all understood.

"Our job is to get Captain Craig and Rehman together for a sit down. Raza will be the interpreter as usual." The Lieutenant looked over to a boulder two hundred feet up the hill. There the bearded Pashtun man sat patiently.

"Our job is not, I repeat not… to seek out and engage the Taliban. The ROE on this mission is to engage when, and only when engaged upon. Now that's not because we're suddenly friends with these guys, but time is of the essence. Is that right sir?"

"That's affirm, Lieutenant." Bryan saw Turk smile and wink at Proton.

"So we don't want to be screwing around all day trying to pop Taliban. If they get in our way though, then we'll handle them like SEALs. Understood?" Everyone nodded.

"One last thing, this mission is about what happened back home on Memorial Day, so enough said." He looked at Bryan again for acknowledgement. Bryan nodded.

"So let's be successful, let's be Americans, let's be soldiers, but most of all … let's be SEALs. Hooh Yaw."

The rest of the team repeated the SEAL greeting. "Hooh Yaw."

"All right then, let's roll."

As they grabbed their gear and began walking toward Raza, Bryan knew what the wink was for; he'd heard it many times before.

Proton started with a nice tenor. *"Day–oh I say-day-ay-ay-oh."*

Day light come an we droppin the bomb." Turk chimed in with a nice baritone on chorus.

"Run mister Taliban – we know where you're hidin'"
"We kick your ass an we want come home."
"Day–oh I say-day-ay-ay-oh."
"We kick your ass an we want come home."

SEALs, standing for Sea, Air, and Land, are U.S. Navy Special Operations teams that carry out missions considered to be beyond the capability of the conventional military. The team had all been through the same training, and could operate across a broad spectrum of areas, which included maritime, desert, arctic, and mountainous. They were masters of the universe in many mission areas; expert marksmen; where it's said that a SEAL could draw a smiley face on a target from fifty feet with a handgun; skydivers, conducting night jumps from twenty thousand feet and parachuting into the sea where they would scuba to a target area; and of course, skilled in hand-to-hand combat. *Silent killers!*

As if attending a perpetual costume ball, Navy SEALs dressed to blend into their environment, and the team with Bryan that day looked very different than their counterparts elsewhere in the world. They had the same weapons, maybe even the same tactical vests, or perhaps the tan T6 tactical boot, but it ended there. Five were wearing Pakols, a traditional wool hat of the indigenous tribal men, and two had on tan baseball caps, both backwards. Shades were optional, but in the mountains everyone wore them. Bryan opted for the tribal look, complete with the native wool Chapan tunic coat over his vest. A two-day old beard had sprouted.

They trekked along the steep terrain in echelon, professional mercenaries on their mission. Proton led the way, staying twenty meters ahead of the team. As point man he was the eyes and ears. Behind him was the commanding officer. "El-tee" carried the CAR-15 assault rifle with grenade launcher. Bryan, just a few paces in back of Thomas, hung close to the team commander so the two could talk. Scattered from there over the next twenty meters, Turk with the M60, Cowboy and his fifty cal, Hotshot who had the URC-112 SATCOM radio, and Doc the corpsman. Cleaning up at anchor position, Senior Chief "Sinbad" Sailor, the senior non commissioned officer and eighteen-year veteran of the SEALs. Raza was a floater, sometimes he was in sight, and then suddenly he'd vanish. It was just before 8 am, with any luck they would rendezvous the Prince and his two-dozen men sometime later that night.

Prince Rehman ul Mulk was the leader of the tribes throughout Chitral. The capital of the district, also Chitral, was in a large valley forty kilometers from their position. Many of the villages were virtually inaccessible by vehicles from the south. The mountain passes between Chitral and the rest of Pakistan were on the average above eight thousand feet and usually impassible for anything other than mules. A four-wheel drive jeep could make it through less than ten percent of the passes, and only in the summer. Being so remote, the people were largely untouched by civilization. They preferred it that way.

Officials in Islamabad really had no idea how many people lived in this district of the North West Frontier Province. The unofficial census counted two hundred thousand scattered throughout in tiny mountainous villages. An official census of the area was impossible. And the people were very different from any other in Pakistan, consisting of many different tribes, languages and beliefs. A few villages had even managed to resist conversion to Islam, Christianity, Hinduism, or Buddhism, maintaining unique religions of their own. The Kalash were idol worshippers, a religion very similar to the ancient pagan beliefs of the Greeks, praying to deities that closely resembled the twelve Gods of Mount Olympus.

Of the fourteen different languages spoken in the area, none had evolved into written form, and the illiteracy rate in the mountains was above ninety percent. Lacking reading and writing skills, and with the region always in conflict, it came as no surprise that the major industry was now gun making. Boys would become young apprentices of the trade when they were just four years old. Masters before they were teens.

Needless to say, the government of Pakistan had absolutely zero control over the people of the "Badlands." Bryan thought it ironical that a nuclear power would have peoples that were living in a time Daniel Boone would have considered primitive.

They'd trekked now steadily for four hours along the steep grade of the hillside and could see snow capped mountain peaks of the high Hindu Kush in the far distance. Raza, who had disappeared two hours before, was now in sight again, jogging toward the team. Reaching them he began conferring with Thomas, a mini-meeting lasting for at least a minute.

"Probably just found us the only whore house," Cowboy said. The rest started laughing. Cowboy was the comedian in the team. Every team had one.

Thomas slapped the Pashtun on the back and turned, waving the men in close. "All right listen up people. Raza's made contact with a couple of Rehman's men. Almost had his throat cut in the process, but he looks A-okay though." Lieutenant Thomas smiled and put his arm around the smaller man, squeezing his shoulder. "We're two kilometers from a Kalash village. Raza's set up a prelim powwow with a couple of the Prince's men. They want to establish some ground rules for the big sit-down with Rehman."

Contact so quickly. "A very good sign," Bryan thought. Word made it to Rehman from the ISI faster than he'd expected. The Prince knew he was coming and was obviously very interested in meeting. *Would the talks bear fruit?* Bryan was hoping that he'd soon learn the true nature of what Petrov had going on, and who else was involved. The stakes were growing higher. With Gil now gone, Bryan had lost one very important asset. He wanted payback. *Revenge?*

CHAPTER 31

JUNE 11, 2008

NORTH WEST FRONTIER, PAKISTAN

CAUTIOUSLY APPROACHING THE VILLAGE from the west, the team was on high alert for any possible Taliban ambush. It could be initiated from the rocks above them, or from a ridge on the opposite side. The village, like so many others was tucked into the edge of a small valley five to eight hundred feet below the mountaintops. Bryan peered up a nearly vertical rock wall.

The first signs of humans actually came in the form of livestock. The flatter trail they had been on for the last kilometer had turned into a narrow rocky path where a dozen domesticated goats and sheep were milling about, tails perpetually wagging.

After negotiating a rickety wooden plank bridge that crossed fast mountain creek, Bryan could see the village ahead. They came in walking uphill, hugging the path, which was very steep, at least a fifteen-degree grade. The village of less than fifty stone and wooden structures was expertly built on the sharp slope.

"Senior Chief, hang with this guy. Cowboy, jump on the rooftop and follow us in," the Lieutenant ordered, pointing to a man squatting in front of the first shed that marked the entrance to the village. He was cleaning something that looked very similar to a musket. He'd hardly given the team a second glance.

Villages such as this one had many transients that simply passed straight through. Strangers were never a real concern unless they started trouble, but since many villages were armed to the teeth, the possibility of having about two hundred guns pointed at them was enough of a reason not to start any trouble. Cowboy clambered up to the first house. Once on top, he'd walk the adjoining roofs, covering both sides of the road as the team moved into the center of the village.

"Proton, take the SATCOM and go up to the top of town, " Thomas ordered. They didn't want any surprises from either end of the village. "Looks pacified but err on the side of being prepared," the team was taught. *Be prepared!*

As the troupe eased into the village, Bryan thought about the culture and the many influences that the people of the Hindu Kush had seen. Most tribes in the North West Frontier were suspicious of foreigners, and with good cause. Invasion and conquest was generally the purpose of strangers to the region. The mixture of pagan and now Islamic people were mountain folk that lived in an irregular geographical area of narrow gorges, twisted valleys, highlighted by steep torrents of rivers pouring down ravines. In the distance of course, were the ever-present Tirich Mir and numerous glaciers. All drained into a major valley near the town of Chitral. If the rugged and hostile landscape were not enough, consider the altitude.

The region, which split parts of Afghanistan and Pakistan, was located in the northeast of modern day Afghanistan, bordering the North West Frontier to the east, and approximately five thousand square miles, the majority above ten thousand feet elevation. The high altitudes and jagged landscape of both regions limit trees, vegetation, and animals, to only the most hardy. In lower elevations, thickets of wild vines and shrubs line numerous streams that run down the mountainous slopes. Various fruit trees grew near most villages, apricot and apple, giving the villagers another supplement for an all round diet. As the slopes rose to higher elevations, pine and cedar forests give way to juniper and cedar, gradually thinning to only small birch here and there, or a willow patch. Life ceases above five thousand meters with the exception of moss, sparse flowers, grass, but always the ever-present rocks. During winter months, all was blanketed in deep snow. "White and more white, covered by white," Bryan recalled.

Animals of the land were typical of what would be expected in high mountains. Wild goat, sheep, bear, and leopards, all make their home in the Hindu Kush. While trekking across a ridge earlier in the day, Bryan, skirting a high ridge next to Thomas, spotted a rare animal, shy and seldom seen. "Look over there, Tim," Bryan said quietly.

"Isn't that an Ibex?" Thomas replied, his voice low.

"That's right – how amazing is that?" Bryan whispered, as they both knelt behind a boulder to avoid being spotted.

A regal species of wild goat, the Himalayan Ibex lives in high altitudes at elevations up to five thousand meters. An endangered animal, at first glance it appears to be completely unsuited for a life surrounded by steep rocky cliffs. A fairly large cousin of the Ram, weighing as much as two hundred and twenty five pounds, it stood more than one meter at the shoulder. With a thick and wooly, dark brown coat that shed completely in late spring, the dorsal was light, almost white.

It was a magnificent and spectacular mountain animal. What made it magnificent were its horns. Massive ridged horns that curved back one meter, three quarters of a complete arc, and then tapered to slender points. What made it spectacular was its ability to leap great distances from narrow rocky ledge to ledge, displaying uncanny agility. "People have a harder time walking on a marble floor," Thomas said, astonished at the site of the Ibex's leaps and bounds.

"*Capra sibirica hemalayanus.* That's the Latin classification. Third time I've seen the slammer," Bryan had said as he leaned on his rifle, and searched for a bottle of water in his vest. He was referring to the male's battle tactics when fighting challengers for a potential female mate. The males square off, charging into each other with such force that the clacking sound of the horns slamming together can be heard over a mile away.

"Like the falcon, it's the altitude that gives this guy the advantage," Bryan said.

"How so?"

"If they were down low in the valley, they'd be just another goat or a sheep, happily wagging their little fuckin tails and blissfully waiting to be sheared, milked, or slaughtered. But up here, they're slammers. Masters of their realm, just like a falcon," Bryan said taking a sip and passing the bottled water to the Lieutenant. "Speaking of falcons, did you ever hear the story about one that made its nest in the Tower of London?"

"That's right, you live there. No, I haven't."

"Well, interestingly enough a falcon-hawk made its home there for a while."

"No shit. It must have made life miserable for the fuckin pigeons," Thomas said, thinking of the dirty birds with disdain.

"The tower ravens actually, which is why the nest was finally removed," Bryan corrected.

"Right, the superstition of the tower ravens. Yeah, I've heard about that from some Brits back at Bagram. Falcons always seek a high place to nest, like the Ibex – altitude serves it best," Thomas said with a wink.

"Nice rhyme Lieutenant."

"Thank you sir."

"Have you been in this area before?" Bryan asked feeling a bit cautious - it had been a few years since he'd been in the field.

"A few times – very close by to where we are right now in fact," Thomas answered. "Had a little firefight with some Taliban just about a month ago. And you might be interested - got some help from Rehman's men."

"That is interesting," Bryan said, feeling encouraged.

Bryan was very familiar with the indigenous people here. Their customs and life style had remained virtually unchanged for centuries. Some clans were all about the fight, most however were very peaceful. Not a sticking point with the Taliban, slavery was still commonplace, although not as advertised as in years before. The trade in human beings was broken down based upon skill levels. Yet, much to the displeasure of the surrounding hardcore Muslims, the pagan villagers were blatant adulterers and tended to drink alcohol. That didn't sit well with the Taliban, who if they had their way, would take slaves of their own – the youth, and convert them into instruments of Islam. Deadly instruments, Bryan considered.

The village was active, Kalash Kafir women scurrying about, busily preparing the midday meal. Reputed for having an exotic appearance, and deservingly so, their light brown hair was parted or multiply braided in the middle and framed a face accentuated with high cheekbones, light brown eyes, narrow nose, and somber mouth. Sometimes they wore magnificent headdresses of colorful plumes or other features. Their ears were always adorned in silver, or for women of higher status, gold. Each was dressed in a traditional black goat hair robe embellished with layers of multi-colored necklaces, and tiger cowry shells of marine animals found in the East Indies. How the shells found their way to the Hindu Kush was still a mystery. Kalash Kafir villagers, *Kafir* meaning infidel, had never been out of the mountains, let alone seen a beach or an ocean. They just didn't know. The women always had them.

The Kalash Kafir men were master woodcraftsmen, a skill passed down for more than two thousand years. For centuries their carvings had been works of art, dedicated to the creation of intricate wooden idols to their deities, and carved out of the indigenous cherry or oak. They had always been a very kind people, peaceful, but now continually harassed by the fundamental Muslims of the Province, particularly Islamists, who were intolerant of their love of wine, open affection for the opposite sex, and particularly the woodcarvings to gods. But as hostilities spilled over into Pakistan from northern Afghanistan, some warlords saw other uses for their skills with wood: the making of rifle stocks. Artisans were being induced to apply their skills to weapons of war under threats of attack. Violence and fanaticism was spreading and impinging on the culture of the Kalash Kafir.

Kalash craftsmanship was in high demand in the lower North West Frontier of Pakistan. Carved from a hard wood, the finished product was carried by pack animals down the mountain and through passes to Peshawar where they were fitted with barrels and sold. The artists carved intricate designs into the wood while sitting on the porch for better light, while young apprentices, with their keen eyesight could stay inside, sanding and polishing the wood to perfection.

Every square inch of a home was dedicated to their industry. Finished rifle stocks were lined up side-by-side, leaning against inlaid wood walls. Now and then a gun shot was heard when a new design was fit with a temporary barrel, tested and fired. Civilization had snuck up on these people in the form of conflict.

The team made their way into the center of the village. There they began to draw the attention Bryan expected, as the artisans noticed the unusual weapons the SEALs carried. They pointed and murmured their approval. Wide smiles formed on their wrinkled faces.

Several barefoot boys, perhaps four or five years old, sprinted towards the men for a closer look. They liked what they saw. Their light eyes widened, mouths forming smiles as they marveled in astonishment, touching the alien composite material with delight.

"Don't touch my weapon," Hotshot barked at the boys, shooing them away.

"Just keep your eyes and ears open," Thomas said. He whistled and yelled, "Cowboy?"

"Yo el-tee. Everything good from up here." He was crouched on a rooftop, the Barrett in carry position.

Thomas pointed at the guide. "Raza, keep those kids away from the weapons."

Raza yelled out something in Urdu, and then in Pashto, but only got blank stares from the boys. "They don't speak Urdu or Pashto, I think only Kalash, but it's a strange dialect."

"Well, figure it out or just shake your finger at em."

The team must have looked very unusual to the boys in spite of their futuristic firearms. The Kafir men were strong, as most mountain people, but didn't look anything like SEALs, who when not practicing for operations, lived in the gym. Turk being the tallest at six-five was also the strongest and could bench three hundred and fifteen pounds, twenty-five times. The boys' fascination soon moved from the weapon to Turk's tattooed biceps.

Two tribal men approached Raza and began talking with him. Bryan could tell by the Kalashnikovs and ammo belts draped over their shoulders that they weren't rifle-stock salesmen. The group followed the two inside a house on a corner of the village where the rock path turned forty-five degrees.

The largest shelter in the village, it was the only one with a tin roof. There was also a sign on the front of the structure written in Urdu. Since the villagers were predominantly illiterate the sign would have been meant for visitors, travelers wanting to stay the night. Bryan got a chuckle from the one tie to the world beyond the village; a motel for guests. *Who had stayed here?* Passing through the "motel lobby," a small room with a low ceiling, they sat down in an adjacent larger space, completely covered in ornately woven wool rugs. Even the walls were covered. It was there that Bryan saw her for the first time.

A young woman was sitting on the floor in a seiza position, her buttocks resting on her feet and toes pointed back. Her posture was straight, and her shoulders square. Delicate hands were at rest on her thighs, palms partially turned to the ceiling. *What a vision!* Bryan couldn't believe how extraordinary she was. She was wearing a brightly colored outfit similar to that worn by Muslim women to cover their body, with the exception of the face and hands. Called a Sharqyat, it conformed to the Quranic codes of modesty for women. But the beauty Bryan now saw, departed from the fundamentalist guidelines of women's dress. The blouse, which came to her knees, was made of wool, with a variety of colored patterns, from pink, to garnet, and decorated with embroidery and small beads in random arrangements. Her pants were black and also made of wool. Instead of an under-scarf, and shawl, she opted for a white silk shawl only, dark brown hair peeking out from the sides. Although the women of the area were known for their exotic appearances, perfectly applied make-up accented her natural beauty. She was far more beautiful, and her eyes were blue. *Baby blue!* He was instantly mesmerized.

Raza introduced her. "This is Shamema. She is the granddaughter of Prince Rehman. She speaks English very, very good."

Bodyguards of sorts, the Kafir men sat cross-legged on either side of Shamema, weapons in their laps. Bryan took center position sitting across from the hostess, flanked by Thomas on his right, and Raza on his left. *Don't out number the other party!* The remaining team was outside, Turk still entertaining the children, now numbering five, the others keeping a vigilant eye.

"Captain Craig, I am pleased to meet you," she said slowly, but with surprising annunciation, and a hint of aristocratic influences. "You have been expected."

Expected? "Thank you for welcoming us to Chitral and to this village. Where did you learn to speak English?" Bryan asked politely.

"In Pakistan, of course, and England where I have studied as well. Besides the languages and most dialects here, I also speak French, Greek, Arabic, and Farsi," she said smiling, visibly embarrassing Bryan.

She then went on. "I am here at the request of my grandfather, who apologizes for not meeting with you in this place." She turned and spoke with the two Kafirs.

Raza understood this particular dialect and whispered in Bryan's ear. "She's telling them something about you, sahr."

"What?" Bryan asked.

"And she also wants to show you something."

"What?"

"It's a book, sahr."

"Please Captain Craig, my grandfather wishes that you sign this book as a friend, one at peace with his people." She handed Bryan an old leather bound book. The title was faded, but legible. *Registry?*

Bryan pointed the cover in the direction of the Lieutenant. "It's a hotel guest book," Bryan said to Thomas.

"That it is sir."

Holding the book gingerly, he carefully opened it. The inside of the cover revealed the book was bound in London in 1890, and the binding glue had started to decay. Bryan didn't want to cause any further damage. There was a thin cloth glued to the inside back cover not part of the original biding. It covered something shaped square, the size of a three by five. Lightly running his fingers over the shape, he could feel something hard. He wondered what it was. He turned the pages back to the front and scanned the entries. Reading the first three, Bryan was astonished.

Captain John Graham Robinson
Royal Engineer Corps
Twenty Eight July Eighteen Hundred Ninety Two

Rudyard Kipling
Lahore, British India
Twenty Eight July Eighteen Hundred Ninety Two

Captain Algernon Durand, C.B., C.I.E
Military Secretary Viceroy of India
Ten September Eighteen Hundred Ninety Eight

"Who was this? " He held the book up pointing to the first name so that Shamema could read the entry.

"The British officer, Captain Robinson - our first guest along with

Mister Kipling."

"Rudyard Kipling, impressive," Bryan said. Thomas and Raza both leaned over to see the historical signature.

"Captain Robinson presented the book as a gift to Aman ul Mulk II, my ancestor who was the Mehtar when Chitral was still an independent district." Mehtar was Persian for "Mighty," and the title given to the ruler, or King in Chitral.

"That was during the time the Durand line was made. Isn't that right?" Bryan commented, noting the dates of the entries.

"You are correct, and your knowledge of our history is impressive Captain Craig," she said smiling with approval. Her teeth were perfectly white. "It was only a few years later that Captain Robinson was unfortunately killed fighting the Nuristan Afghans. His grave is in Chitral," she added.

"Along with a number of other British soldiers," Bryan said.

Shamema nodded in agreement, her smile disappearing. "There was conflict then - as now."

Bryan knew the story. The Nuristanis were an Afghan tribe, and the subject of the Rudyard Kipling short story "Man Who Would Be King." Bryan guessed the British Captain had been killed in one of the many skirmishes that occurred along the Durand line of the North West Frontier of India at the time. The British Government of India had drawn brand new, contentious boundaries, as they did throughout the old empire. The line tended to anger most warlords affected. The Nuristanis took the lead in doing what Afghan warriors love most, killing invaders. "He must have bought the farm in one of the battles near Chitral," Bryan thought.

A relative of the Foreign Secretary of the British Indian Government, Sir Mortimer Durand, made the second entry. Sir Mortimer authored the dividing line that separated British India and Afghanistan. It was a blatant example of gerrymandering, and a line questioned ever since, Afghanistan considering it illegitimate.

Bryan started to turn the page, but two additional entries at the bottom got his immediate attention.

"Lieutenant Thomas, look at these." He handed the book to the Lieutenant with his index finger marking the spot.

Thomas read the entries.

Lieutenant General Arthur MacArthur Jr.

United States Commander Department of the Pacific
Twenty Four July Nineteen Hundred and Six

Second Lieutenant Douglas MacArthur
United States Army Engineers Philippines
Twenty Four July Nineteen Hundred and Six

He looked at Bryan. "I'll be damned," he said.
"Looks like we're in good company here," Bryan said.
Bryan took the book and found an appropriate place to sign.

Captain Bryan Craig
United States Navy
Eleven June Two Thousand and Eight

He handed the registry to Shamema. "That was an honor, thank you."

"You may thank my grandfather in person when you see him," she said smiling. She became serious and began, "My grandfather is Rehman ul Mulk and Prince of Chitral. He is very interested in speaking with you."

Why the interest with me? "What does he want to talk about?" Bryan asked.

Shamema's eyes narrowed "My grandfather wanted to meet with you here, but to do so would endanger the people of this village. And it is because of the Taliban. They have become very cruel, and now responsible for many atrocities throughout Chitral."

Neither Bryan nor Lieutenant Thomas was surprised at what they were hearing. The Taliban had been raiding livestock, robbing travelers, stealing weapons, and had been a general scourge to the indigenous people of Chitral for the last seven years. Shamema continued. "The Taliban have forced their ways on to peaceful people, for example, the people in this village. The Taliban consider the Kalasha people to be infidels. They brutalize these people every chance they have."

"And the government can't help?"

She opened her arms. "The government would like to help. Islamabad believes in ethnic tolerance, and will not force people such as these to convert to Islam. They are doing much in the lower lying areas of Pakistan where they have shut down dangerous Madrasahs training very young children to hate infidels. But the mountains make it very difficult to stop the Taliban here. The Taliban do not believe in the same intolerance and have kidnapped, even killed some of these Kalash Kafirs." Putting her hands on her lap and tilting her head, she added, "Here, we appreciate what the Americans have done for us, when the government cannot - but I know that many people in Pakistan do not have the same feelings as my grandfather and I have. That is unfortunate."

Bryan understood. He recalled that many of the Muslims in Pakistan considered the outlaw terrorists and Taliban in the same light as Americans had their own outlaws in the Wild West. They were sympathetic folk heroes, romanticized icons, a common theme for the poor and oppressed. Most Muslims in Pakistan hated the United States, and glorified the terrorists that indiscriminately killed Americans. Children in many Pashtun villages had fallen under the influence of the Taliban or other Jihadists, who were bent on destroying the west. The innocents were being taught from a very early age that America was evil. "They're bloody Robin Hood and we're the Sheriff of Nottingham," Bryan recalled a counter-terrorism man from British Military Intelligence, MI6 once saying.

The Taliban were a collection of Sunni Islamist Pashtuns from Afghanistan and the North West Frontier of Pakistan that had come into power in the aftermath of the Soviet occupation of Afghanistan. Unlike the Kalash Kafir, the Taliban, were not fair-haired, with light eyes, but instead they were dark skinned, with heavy eyebrows and low foreheads. With a reputation as plunderers, assassins, and opportunists, they lived by the gun and died by the gun. Fighting was a way of life, seeking revenge and killing was sport.

The Taliban came into power by pure chance. The Democratic Republic of Afghanistan had been overthrown which led to competing warlords vying for control of the country. The Taliban were able to organize a military force and ultimately impose its rule on Afghanistan. The fanatical organization reminded Bryan of *the Mob*. The Taliban became the head family in a country filled with smaller families, AKA warlords. The Godfather was a self-proclaimed cleric who had never completed the required Quranic studies to hold the title of Mullah. Disputes between families were a given, murders and assassinations commonplace.

As for the terrorists on the run from Coalition Special Ops teams, in the past a roadblock of honor and tradition stood in the way. Tribal elders held fast in harboring terrorist fugitives, protecting them from Coalition forces. Pashtun and Kafirs would give their lives before violating the code. But the Taliban overstepped their welcome when they turned into thugs, targeting the very people that hid them. The mountain tribes wanted the marauders out. Armed conflict between the natives and the unwanted "guests" was unavoidable.

Prior to 9/11 the Taliban had been recognized as a legitimate government by Pakistan, the UAE, and Saudi Arabia, the only countries to do so. All three were progressive Muslim countries and very friendly to the United States. Afghanistan under the Taliban was an Islamic State. A theocracy. *Was it a payoff to the Mob?* But the reign of the Taliban was one highlighted by severe Human Rights violations, cruel discrimination of women, and absolute intolerance of all religious practices other than strict interpretation the Quran. As oppressive as the Taliban were, surprisingly enough to Bryan, Saudi Arabia provided funding to the Taliban during their rule. However, as a strong opponent of Shi'ah Islamists, the relationship between the Taliban and Iran rapidly deteriorated and came near to the brink of all out war when the Taliban seized Iran's consulate and summarily executed all of the Iranian diplomats.

Dismayed, Bryan couldn't help but wonder at the never ending conflicts that continued to brew between Shi'ah and Sunni fundamentalists. Both believed in uniting the Islamic world, yet their disagreements were rooted in thirteen hundred years of history. Both believed in the same five pillars of Islam, but categorized in a different order. The discrepancies were enough to start a feud that had lasted for more than a thousand years. Recalling Shannon's story "No wonder that a couple of Paki taxi cab drivers would almost come to blows over some triviality. These people can be as passionate as they are stubborn." The Taliban added barbarism to the equation.

Once in power, the Taliban instituted very strict Islamic law, Sharia resulting in punishments that included beatings, amputations, and stoning. In addition they banned television, radio, music, sports, or any form of imagery, including photography. All citizens were required by Islamic law to comply with traditional dress, men grew beards and women were required to keep their bodies completely covered under the codes of modesty. Bryan read the scriptures that Islamists literally adhered to in enforcing women's dress codes.

> " Say to the believing women that they should lower their gaze and guard their modesty; that they should not display their beauty and ornaments except what must ordinarily appear thereof. " [Quran: 24.31]
> " Say to the believing man that they should lower their gaze and guard their modesty; that will make for greater purity for them, and God is well acquainted with all they do. " [Quran: 24.30]

Strict interpretation of the first led to simple guidelines for modest Islamic women to follow:

> 1. Clothing must cover the entire body. Only the hands and eyes may remain visible.
> 2. The material must not be so thin that one can see through it.
> 3. The clothing must hang loose so that the shape and form of the body is not apparent.
> 4. The female clothing must not resemble the man's clothing.
> 5. The design of the clothing must not resemble the clothing of the non-believing women.
> 6. The design must not consist of bold designs that attract attention.
> 7. Clothing should not be worn for the sole purpose of gaining reputation or increasing one's status in society.

Strict interpretation of the second meant that men could look at a woman once, but not twice, for in doing so would encourage lustful thoughts from the woman. Failing that, Taliban women would be severely beaten, or worse. Men got a pass.

Besides their oppression of women, religious intolerance, and other Human Rights violations, including encouraging the persecution of minority groups, the Taliban harbored Al-Qaeda. That was their real crime. The two radical Islamic organizations had formed a cabal of sorts. In fact, the Taliban gave the okay for the Al-Qaeda to operate terrorist training camps; a state supported haven for terrorists. The

Taliban had also taken the surprising measure of integrating Al-Qaeda militants with their army.

Following 9/11, the United States made five demands of the Taliban controlled Afghanistan and failing those demands, the Taliban faced possible military action from NATO and the United States. The demands were easy to understand. Bryan remembered the words from the President's speech to Congress by heart.

> *"By aiding and abetting murder, the Taliban regime is committing murder. And tonight the United States of America makes the following demands on the Taliban:*
> *-- Deliver to United States authorities all of the leaders of Al-Qaeda who hide in your land.*
> *-- Release all foreign nationals, including American citizens you have unjustly imprisoned.*
> *-- Protect foreign journalists, diplomats and aid workers in your country.*
> *-- Close immediately and permanently every terrorist training camp in Afghanistan. And hand over every terrorist and every person and their support structure to appropriate authorities.*
> *-- Give the United States full access to terrorist training camps, so we can make sure they are no longer operating.*
> *These demands are not open to negotiation or discussion."*

Insular in their attitudes to the leadership of democracies, the Taliban rejected the ultimatum. Clearly understanding the implication of the demands, the UAE and Saudi Arabia no longer recognized the Taliban as a legitimate government. The two Arab countries were correct in their assessment. *A new sheriff was in town!* Never an empty threat, military operations commenced the following month. Rabbit Barnes was the Joint Task Force Commander and Bryan had his Special Ops. *Oust the Taliban and wipe out Yoorish Shaheed!* The Taliban were forced out of Kabul and Kandahar, ultimately taking refuge in the mountains with their terrorist stepchildren.

"Now we have an even greater problem," Shamema said, holding back tears. "The Taliban have allowed a new, even more evil group of

Islamists to hide with them in the mountains of the Hindu Kush. They are independent of any Al-Qaeda, and much more sinister. They have been kidnapping young boys from throughout the district and training them in new Madrasahs. There they are being taught to kill in the name of Allah by killing themselves. They are all Pakistanis and are called Yoorish Shaheed."

Yoorish Shaheed! Bryan felt a chill when he heard the words again. Religious schools run by sociopaths teaching the illiterate children to blow themselves up in the name of God. And the movement was tied directly to Wazir and Petrov. The dots were being connected at last. *The money?*

"How are the schools paid for? It can't be just the Taliban," Bryan asked.

"I am certain that it is illegal activities. The government has found that it is impossible to control because of the many secret passes and tunnels through the Hindu Kush. The opium smuggled from Afghanistan is much greater than ever before, and the Taliban and Yoorish Shaheed are paid to protect the shipments and farmers growing poppy," Shamema answered.

Bryan thought about the laborers. "What about human trafficking?"

"They are committed to that too, I am certain of. I know of a Russian – a very brutal man, who bought young children from their fathers. The children were used as jockeys for camel races in Arabia and the Emirates," she said.

"Is his name Leonid Petrov?" Bryan asked.

"I believe that is his name. My grandfather will verify that for you."

Petrov again. The trail was becoming warmer. "Would this same Russian be involved in the manual labor businesses for construction in Dubai? The businesses defrauding Pakistanis."

"We know he helped build labor staffing businesses. Those same businesses literally stole money from workers. It destroyed many families," Shamema said, her beautiful face becoming distraught.

"How do you know all of this Shamema?" Bryan asked curiously.

Her voice quivered. "My life is dedicated to stopping such things. I build shelters for the homeless displaced from natural disasters. We lobby the government to enforce laws against human trafficking. We seek to protect women who are victims of violence and honor abuses by their husbands. Helping people who are suffering is my business."

Shamema was passionate. They were both on common ground, similar missions. What separated Bryan from Shamema would be their dissimilar courses of action, but not their mutual determination to succeed in saving people and preventing further suffering. Shamema was inherently kind. Nonviolence and peace were her approach. Death would be in Bryan's wake.

"We're here to help you Shamema, but it's important that I meet with your grandfather as soon as possible. Can these men take us to him?" Bryan asked, gesturing towards the fierce Kafirs.

"Yes, of course. He is up in the mountains - at a lake." She smiled at Bryan. "These two will take you to him."

They stood up. She was tall, perhaps five foot eight, maybe an inch more. She shook Bryan's hand. "Thank you," she said.

Lieutenant Thomas stopped Bryan after they stepped outside.

"Captain Craig, just what exactly is our mission up here besides getting you and Rehman together? I didn't plan on sweeping these mountains for Taliban or the Yoorish Shaheed, which must be some faction of Al-Qaeda. I don't mind sir; we can adapt, we're SEALs. I'd just like to plan a tiny bit, or at least let me have the eight by ten photo to study, not the wallet size."

Bryan put his sunglasses on and placed his hand on the SEAL's shoulder. "Here's the eight by ten glossy – get me up to Rehman. The meeting is a must. The Russian she mentioned was murdered last week. He was working with the Yoorish Shaheed and they're the ones responsible for the Memorial Day bombings," Bryan said emphatically.

"Are we going to be active in seeking out the Taliban and these Yoorish Shaheed guys, or is the ROE to fire after being fired upon?"

"If we run into them on the ground, and I'm very confident that we will, we'll engage them. Is that clear?" He'd essentially just bumped up the Rules of Engagement one notch.

"What's your intent with Rehman?"

"I want him to fully understand that we're on his side. That he needs to look at us as his ally. It's important that we establish credibility with him as a friend, not just up here to get what we want, and then take off for good."

"I've met with him on a sit down before, and we really didn't get anywhere," Thomas said, thinking about the Special Ops team that operated for five years searching for key Taliban and Al-Qaeda leadership.

"Times have changed Tim. The Taliban, Al-Qaeda and now the Yoorish Shaheed have been responsible for crimes against Rehman's people and evidently he's completely fed up with them. We'll do what it takes to help him where the Pakistani government can't. It's in our best interest."

"Captain Craig, I think you've just given me the eight by ten."

The Lieutenant radioed Sinbad and Cowboy to move up to the center of town. The team was on the go again. Doc pried Turk away from the children, who were being curled three at a time while they hung from his forearms. Rendezvousing with Proton at the edge of town, the team followed the two Kafirs.

Giving the village one last glance as the team moved on, Bryan thought about the people there, the simplicity of their lives and their link to the vastly different world of Dubai, with its massive towers stretching to the limits of man's engineering skills. The people of the Hindu Kush still stood taller. In echelon once again, they marched on. Turning to the north, they climbed further up into the mountains.

CHAPTER 32

JUNE 11, 2008
NORTH WEST FRONTIER, PAKISTAN

A DRAMATIC ALPINE SUNSET, the conditions were just right. Bright pink ribbons of cirrus accented grey jagged rock jutting high out of a massive, meandering glacier. The warmth of the sun now absent, the temperature rapidly fell to freezing. The air was fresh, clean and sweet, a smell that could be tasted. They were many miles from any sources of air pollution. A narrow crescent moon was looming, and the sky was clear. Stars of the Milky Way illuminated everything to a horizon of endless mountain peaks. Tirich Mir was in the distance, the white top glowing in the night.

Bryan could also easily see everyone in the party, the echelon stretching down the slope. "That could be a problem," he thought. The Taliban would also have very little trouble spotting them. On the top of ice, some losing their footing on the slick surface, Bryan followed a white slide with his eyes, far down the descending pitch, to a reflection of the moon and stars. The glacier's cirque was a guidepost to a magnificent lake below, the dark, still waters a mirror for the heavens above. There they found a Prince of Chitral.

The bivouac Rehman chose was on the embankment of a glacial lake fed by many icy cirques. Lakes such as this were numerous in the Hindu Kush Mountains, a foreboding range that provides a northern barrier to the Indian subcontinent along with their neighbors, the Himalayas. Barren for the most part, trees and stubby brush sprinkled sporadically across the steep rocky slopes, the range has always been inhospitable.

Hindu Kush is Persian, meaning "Slayer of Hindus." So named to memorialize the tens of thousands of Indus captives that died of exposure in the frigid mountains while being marched to central Asian slave markets. Beginning near Kabul, the mountains stretch west to east 966 kilometers, gradually rising to 7,705 meters, the pinnacle being Tirich Mir and western shoulder of the 8,850 meter Mount Everest of the Himalayas.

Tirich Mir, with tremendous vertical relief over the terrain in every direction, was the center of the High Hindu Kush in the North West Frontier of Pakistan, a place known as the Chitral District. It was an excellent place for Rehman to regroup, reflect, and to pray. He was a Muslim and felt closer to God the higher he climbed the steep mountains. The cliffs were safe as well. Access to the area was difficult, few natural passes and high elevations making transit somewhat dangerous. Over the centuries, industrious engineers put man's ingenuity to use, boring a network of tunnels, and constructing mountain paths, yet the trek could only be made on foot in most cases, or occasionally with pack animals. Needless to say, the numerous systems of caves, tunnels, and mountain passes created a porous border between Afghanistan and Pakistan for those industrious and brave enough to attempt it, a border virtually impossible to patrol, or seal.

Rehman's militia was a combined force of one thousand. They were all recruited from numerous tribes throughout Chitral, the majority being Sunni Muslims from the Kho tribe, as well as other tribes including non-Muslims such as the Kafir Kalash. Prince Rehman and a compliment of his militia, thirty men, were gathered in front of a fire midway up the slope of a steep hill, forty-five degree grade, overlooking the lake. The hill was the northwest quadrant, recessed in a kind of bowl. Bracketed by cirques, the encampment, the only somewhat level spot on the slope, was accessible via two ways; a narrow path from the south, with a hundred foot drop to the cirque if a step in error, or by coming up the steep grade, slick with moss. Partially surrounded by yet another collection of boulders, the largest the size of a small house, the encampment gave them the only high ground with cover for a radius of two hundred meters. Close by however, only one kilometer to the north of their position was another hill, with a similar outcropping of rocks and boulders. The hill was lower, but not by much, a potential problem should an attack come from the Taliban. Access to that area could be gained by scaling a rocky ridge from the bank, a path that was hidden from their view. East of the ridge was a sheer drop to the other cirque. They would need to be vigilant. *Be prepared!*

The Kalash Kafir escorts entered the encampment with Raza and ahead of the team. Bryan and the Lieutenant arrived immediately afterward, signaled all clear, and then joined by the remainder of the team. The Prince was seated with his legs crossed on a small rug about twenty feet from the fire. Four men flanked him on either side. All had a Russian manufactured AK-47 in their lap and several belts of the Kalashnikov's 7.62-millimeter ammo crisscrossing their torsos. The Prince's men were well armed; Bryan could see several RPG launchers and rockets neatly laid out in back near the largest boulder.

The standard rule of thumb for a sit down was equal numbers on both sides. Etiquette would have to be forsaken during this gathering however; it was imperative to keep a few members of the team on perimeter, protecting the camp. Bryan, the Lieutenant, and Raza, would again be doing the talking. Bryan took the position in the middle across from Rehman. Everyone had their weapons locked and loaded, the radio volume up.

The Prince looked to be a man in his mid seventies, and appeared to be very fit. Rehman's face was stern and had a well-worn, deeply etched look of a man that had spent seven decades in the dry mountain air and sun. The deeply carved crow's feet merged with facial lines overrun by a massive grey beard that began at his cheekbones, ending in a thick point at his sternum. There was no doubt that the man Bryan was looking at was the grandfather of the beautiful young woman he had met earlier that day. His eyes were an intense light blue just like Shamema's.

"Thank you for agreeing to see us sir. I'm Captain Bryan Craig."

Rehman nodded. He was drinking a cup of Chai, an Afghan green milk tea. Holding up his cup, he offered them some. Bryan thanked him, and enjoyed the spicy brew made with ginger and peppercorn. Bryan would have preferred it more with sweetener.

Raza translated to Rehman in Khowar, the official language of Chitral. Rehman began to speak.

"He says that he is pleased to meet you and he thanks you for coming here to the lake. It is a great honor for him." Raza was now translating in unison with the leader of Chitral.

"The honor is mine," Bryan said modestly. He inherently respected the old man.

"He thanks you for taking up their cause. The Taliban and what they represent are not good for the people of Chitral. They are thieves of everything. They kidnap children from the villages and sell them as slaves. They are poison in the name of Allah."

"How many Taliban are hiding in the mountains?" Bryan asked.

Rehman held his right hand in the air as he spoke, moving it slowly, methodically, panning it across the mountains. A deliberate and effective affectation, Bryan thought.

"He says thousands," Raza interpreted. "They are everywhere and with many Al-Qaeda and Yoorish Shaheed."

"There's a typical lie. He must want us here real bad," Thomas said from the corner of his mouth to Bryan.

"Let's just say exaggeration and keep it at that," Bryan whispered back. "Ask him how often they're engaging the enemy?"

"Every day. The Taliban are hi-jacking caravans of supplies, food, and medicines. They are kidnapping children for ransom or taking them to the Yoorish Shaheed. They are murdering at random." Raza paused for several moments and continued. "They are forcing villagers to transport Khash-khash down the mountains to Peshawar."

Khash-khash was poppy. Bryan decided the talk of opium was a nice segue. "Was the Russian, Leonid Petrov helping the Taliban?"

Rehman's voice raised before Raza could interpret. "Yes – Petrov helped terrorize the villagers. He intimidated them into helping them, but never out of their own free will."

"Tell him Petrov's dead, Raza," Bryan said.

"Good, the Russian was a goat, and deserved to be slaughtered," Rehman suddenly spoke in perfect English, alarming them.

"You speak English – you fooled me," Bryan said.

"I may have surprised you Captain Craig, but fool you? I doubt that. You don't appear to be a man easily fooled," Rehman said with wry smile. "And you are right, I was exaggerating. The Taliban have a thousand strong here."

"Shit – busted," Thomas said under his breath, grimacing.

"One thousand, huh. Thank you for the verification Prince Rehman," Bryan said. "Now as for Petrov – yes he's dead, and he was an important part of the crimes committed not just against you, but the bombings in London and the United States. I'm here to find out who Petrov was working with. I want to know the people ultimately responsible."

Rehman stared at Bryan, not speaking. The Prince was stoic, his eyes unflinching. The old man reached into his thick wool Chapan tunic, removing something. He began speaking in his native tongue of Khowar again. "Is he playing with me?" Bryan wondered.

Confused, Raza continued on with his interpretation. "He says that his people are very strong, very proud and very noble. They are a very diverse people and need strong leadership to keep them united, as well as protect them. His ancestors were leaders such as that."

Was he offended? "Prince Rehman, are we asking you to violate your code?" Bryan asked, concerned.

Rehman stood up. The old man was very tall, at least six foot four. He handed Bryan the object he pulled from his coat. It was a very old tintype, protected by a laminated coating, but badly damaged. Bryan took out a penlight, giving the metal cursory once over. Twelve men were in the picture, one elder man of importance in the center, others gathered around him. Several faces were indiscernible. They could've been the same Chitralis sitting on the hill now, Bryan thought. The clothing was the same, and the only real difference being the men in the photo were holding Enfield rifles, not Kalashnikovs. The central focus of the portrait must have been the great King, and Rehman's great grandfather, Bryan guessed. He had a falcon perched on his right hand.

"Is this the Mehtar Aman?" Bryan asked.

"The greatest ruler of Chitral before darkness fell on our land," Rehman said, shaking his bearded head. "He was a very honorable man and a Muslim - very devout, yet tolerant of those who were not."

Curious about the falcon, "The Mehtar practiced falconry?" Bryan inquired as he gave the tintype back to Rehman.

"The falcon is the symbol of a ruler - and one of his best weapons. Certainly his most clever weapon when used correctly. It is a symbol of leadership. These are the traditions that should be honored and respected," Rehman said as he tapped the tin with his forefinger. "Do you have such traditions with your family, Captain Craig?" Rehman asked.

Bryan thought for a moment about his father. There was little doubt that Rehman, Mehtar Aman and Bryan's father held similar traditions of duty and honor. Bryan responded, "Yes Prince Rehman, my father was a great warrior and I hope to live up to his name one day myself."

"I understand that you are here to help the people of Pakistan and catch the evil that has attacked your people. And I want to help. But it is a difficult undertaking for me and requires great sacrifice," Rehman said.

Sacrifice what - the code of honor? "I'm here to find the people responsible for the bombings, and responsible for enslaving Pakistanis – leading them down the wrong path. I'm here to help save them," Bryan said, feeling a sense of pleading.

"At the end of your journey you will accomplish both. Failing one, you will fail both," Rehman said, sage-like.

Lieutenant Thomas looked at Bryan with a perplexed expression. Neither one of them really understood what Rehman was getting at. Thomas thinking, "I've seen this guy in a movie before – only a quarter the size and five hundred years older."

"Are you referring to what Petrov was doing here? Who was Petrov the agent of? Was it a man called Wazir?" Bryan asked.

"Of course Petrov. But he was only just a puppet - used to cause pain to the people of Chitral. Wazir was but one of three, and a puppet too."

Bryan could sense that he was getting close to solving the riddle, but he needed to be very respectful. He feared offending Rehman. The sit down would be over if he pushed too hard. But the Prince seemed to be on a role now. He was obviously agitated and staring to rant. Maybe the best approach now would be to let him continue on and see where it would lead.

"Respectfully Prince Rehman, who was their leader?"

Gradually a story began to unfold, one that explained the entirety of what Rehman believed was happening in the North West Frontier, and what could be corroborated by the Bank accounts in both Karachi and Dubai. As Rehman explained, "Wazir had come to Pakistan and to Chitral at the request of an acquaintance of my dead son, killed many years ago. Wazir had said that he was here to help the people of Chitral and the people of Pakistan, but he would need safe passage through the mountains, and would require safe haven from time to time." Rehman paused and asked for water from one of his aides.

Bryan sensed a certain discomfort in the old man's voice. Rehman tentativeness was an indication that he was hiding something. "When did you realize that Wazir had deceived you?" Bryan asked.

"It was the Russian," Rehman answered. "I learned that he was responsible for killing many Muslims in the past – both in Afghanistan and Pakistan - an evil man, conspiring to send young Pakistanis to their deaths with Yoorish Shaheed. I could not allow that. I banished him and Wazir. They could never be seen with our people ever again. Disobeying that order would mean their death. They did not deserve our honor," Rehman added, very angered.

Rehman described the events that occurred after his decision to withdraw support. "Petrov and Wazir were transporting opium from Afghanistan - a scheme designed to enrich Petrov and finance other terrorist related enterprises. Khash-khash is strictly forbidden," Rehman said.

"What did you do about it?" Bryan asked Rehman in Urdu.

Rehman became stern. "They paid the Taliban to take arms against me," Rehman said. "The Taliban attacked us and I declared a war against them. You see Captain, we have a mutual enemy - and I know to whom Wazir and the Yoorish Shaheed pay their allegiance," Rehman added.

"Who? Is it the Sultan Amir Sika Kahn?" Bryan asked. The words sparked an emotion in Rehman, one that Bryan had not yet seen that night – sadness. The old man's shoulders drooped, his head hung down momentarily, followed by a forlorn expression. For an instant he was trancelike, suddenly snapping out of it. Bryan looked on as Rehman lifted his right arm in the air, bent at the elbow. He turned his hand so that Bryan could see a ring on his little finger, but said nothing.

Rehman pointed at the photograph of his great grandfather. "Aman knew of the problems that would come from outside the

Hindu Kush. The people of the three valleys, Birir, Bumburet, and Rambur – the Kalash Kafir – they never knew of violence and murder – that is until the poison of the Yoorish Shaheed." Rehman put his hand on the Kafir's shoulder to his left. "This man was forced to learn war." Rehman was cut short.

Bryan first felt the tiny projectile's wake turbulence with the fine hairs on the skin of his ear lobe, followed by the shrill sound of the bullet's whistle after it had passed. The bullet's impact point was the forehead of the Kafir Rehman was speaking of. The man's posture stiffened slightly as his Pakol hat flew from his head, landing on the RPG launchers at the base of a boulder. He was already dead as his body crumpled in a heap.

What followed was noise and a maelstrom of automatic weapons fire from a ridgeline on a hill about two hundred meters away. The 7.62-millimeter Kalashnikov rounds ricocheted between the boulders with the rapid sound of a drum roll. It was the kind of unexpected event that Bryan had expected, but didn't care for.

The first seconds were chaotic as the bright streaks of fire from AK-47 tracers danced with sparks created by rounds bouncing off boulders. Bryan saw Rehman start to stand up, then shrink back to his knees as he let out a grunt. He was holding the tintype in both hands as he fell forward onto the carpet. Bryan leapt on him, providing a human blanket of protection for the wounded leader. The firefight was on.

The SEAL team had already begun returning fire as Rehman's men scrambled to retrieve their launchers. They had the advantage of good position on the enemy, most certainly Taliban. The SEALs were protected for the most part, behind the boulders, and on the high ground with great look down. Night-vision goggles gave them excellent situational awareness, and yet another advantage over the enemy.

Thomas radioed Turk to move along the ridgeline high above them, taking a flanking position seventy-five meters to the east of the enemy fire. He would be right on the edge of a cliff, with the cirque three hundred feet below. Suppression fire from Turk's M60 would deceive the Taliban into thinking that there were a dozen combatants shooting at them from above. And that was the idea. The big man began a crouching run toward an ideal clumping of rocks. There, he set up the counter attack, and radioed, "I'm in position."

Proton, Sinbad and Hotshot took flanking positions just to the south of the camp. The plan was to funnel the Taliban down the slope from their position, where the three SEALs would cut them down. In the meantime, Cowboy had already climbed to a point near the top of the hill, high above everyone. From his natural "bell tower," he could take aim on any enemy attempting to flee to the backside of the hill or over the ridge. The attacker would suffer the devastating consequences of being in the crosshairs of his Barrett .50 cal. The Taliban couldn't go left, couldn't go right, and couldn't go up. They were doomed. *Yoorish Shaheed?*

The flash of an exploding rocket illuminated the enemy's ridge. Turban heads were as bright as actors on a stage lit by klieg lights. Several Taliban either trying to evacuate, or gain better position, ran into serious problems. As they scurried across the ridge, they were mowed down by the M60, their bodies falling a hundred feet onto the icy slide feeding the lake. Other attackers, dissuaded by the M60, ran opposite direction, firing their weapons erratically as they scrambled, now putting them into positions directly opposite Rehman's men.

Two of Rehman's militiamen were working as a team effectively deploying an RPG-7. Squatting next to a footlocker filled with fragmentation tipped rockets, a militiaman was tossing rockets to another manning the thirty-seven inch launcher, who'd load and fire. A bright plum would corkscrew to the enemy position, and explode in fiery sparks. The Taliban were pinned, the only way out was down the slope to the lakebed and low ground, a death sentence. With zero options, they dug in, opening up their own automatic weapons fire and RPGs.

Bryan, staying with Rehman, heard the sound of the battle as it echoed throughout the mountains: the whoosh of the rocket-propelled grenades, the unmistakable roar of Turk's M60 above the pops of Kalashnikovs, the M4s, and the Barrett. He could feel Rehman's body heave up and down, as the Prince strained to breathe. He was alive, but badly wounded, Rehman's Chapan tunic already soaked with warm blood. Bryan felt the Prince's pulse, it was throbbing, but getting weaker.

Bryan saw the medical corpsman checking for signs of life from the first man hit. "Doc. Help me move Rehman to better cover," Bryan hollered.

They dragged Rehman carefully by the leading edges of the rug under an overhang, in the shadows and protected from the line of fire. He'd be safer there, but Bryan was concerned for the old man. Rehman, still clutching the tin with his right hand, was coughing blood, which began to soak his fine white beard. Bryan could now see the ring on his little finger. Even in the shadows its brilliance was apparent. Doc got busy looking for the wound as the intense firefight raged around them. Crouching, Bryan popped a magazine into the M8 Lightweight Combat Assault Rifle, and sighted an enemy combatant in the green display of the night vision scope. "Pop-pop."

"That's one more down," he said as the dead Taliban joined his comrades at the bottom of the cirque.

The Lieutenant's plan had worked, plus he had help from Rehman's fierce militia, who were blasting the Taliban from a closer position, now less than twenty five meters from the enemy. Their numbers decimated, only two remaining, they got as close to the cirque as they could, and jumped the twenty feet onto the ice. They were wet, but alive. Thomas called a ceasefire and assessment.

The fact the Taliban had attacked with lower numbers from an inferior position left little doubt that by design, it was a suicide mission, or at least one that could never have resulted in a victory of any kind. Had the goal been assassination? Could the SEAL team have unwittingly led the Taliban right to the Chitrali leader, handing them a regional leader doing everything possible to rid his land of his enemy? Bryan presumed it was assassination as he conferred with Doc on Rehman's condition.

"Here's the entry wound sir. He's hit in the chest. It's bad," Doc said now applying gauze to the wound.

"Will he live?" Bryan asked.

Doc looked up at Bryan, narrowed his eyes and shook his head. "Not unless we can get a Medevac for him ASAP." Doc turned Rehman slightly, eliciting a heavy sigh from him. "Shit, I'm still trying to find a fuckin exit wound Captain Craig - it tore him up inside. He's already lost a lot of blood," Doc warned.

"Keep 'im alive Doc," Bryan said adamantly, closing his eyes, rubbing the bridge of his nose. "Can you do anything for him until morning?" Bryan finally asked, knowing a helicopter would be available.

"Morning? I don't know if I can give him five minutes sir," Doc hushed. "I can give him some morphine though. Try to make him comfortable."

Suitable consolation? "Alright - well do that, if that's all you can do," Bryan said, setting his rifle down, kneeling by Rehman's side.

Doc cut Rehman's pant leg open at the thigh, inserting a morphine Syrette into his leg. A Kafir militiaman yanked the Syrette out before the painkiller was squeezed into Rehman's bloodstream. He was one of the men in the village with them earlier. The other was dead. The emotionless fighter shook his head as he moved Doc's hand aside.

Rehman tried to speak, his words barely audible. Raza's ears were close, and he heard what Rehman asked. "He says he wants to be moved to the light. He wants to see the lake and Tirich Mir."

Picking him up from the shadows, they gently moved him near the slope. They propped him up to view the mountains. He was looking beyond the lake, over the tops of the peaks. Rehman could see Tirich Mir.

The end couldn't have been more sublime. He had cared for his people as best he could, preserving the edicts and tenets of his forefathers from a thousand years before. He had also brought his people closer to the modern age, encouraging education and literacy. But there was something more that he could still do. He motioned for Bryan to come closer.

Bryan called out to the interpreter. "Raza. Get over here. I need to understand everything he says."

Bryan Craig knelt close to the mortally wounded man, looking into his light blue eyes, so common of his family. Rehman's men and the SEAL team also gathered close to the fallen leader, the campfire still burning, illuminating their saddened faces. The Kafir knelt behind Rehman to support his wounded body, helping him to sit upright. Bryan leaned close to hear the dying man's words.

"Captain Craig, listen carefully to me."

Rehman pulled Bryan in close with his right hand, laboring, but Bryan could feel he was determined to communicate something. Bryan gripped his hand as he did with his closest friends. The man's hands were unusually large, his grip still strong. Bryan felt the old tintype now pressed in his palm.

"Go to Dubai - Captain Craig," Rehman said. He coughed a small amount of blood onto his beard, red droplets glistening under the light of the stars.

He struggled. "Go to Dubai..." Rehman grimaced in pain, coughing.

"Get him some water." Bryan took a canteen from Thomas and held it to Rehman's lips.

Rehman could barely manage the words. "Falcon - the tower." Rehman coughed, a gurgled hack.

He pulled Bryan in close to his face, the grip tightening. Their hands were now resting on Rehman's face, his ring touching his lips.

"Find your falcon," he whispered in Bryan's ear.

Rehman looked in Bryan's eyes as he kissed the white center of his ring, shaped like a mountain.

His hand began to lower as the life ebbed away. Rehman squeezed again, this time with a force that surprised him. Bryan looked into the man's eyes as he shuddered and started slipping away into eternity. For the moment though, his pupils were still small and intense with life, just inches away. They spoke volumes; things that his voice could no longer say; the history of his people; their culture over thousands of years. He squeezed Bryan's hand one final time. It was crushing. Gradually his pupils dilated, and the once strong grip lightened. His large hand went limp as life exhaled from his lips in a fog, condensing in the cold night air.

Rehman's militia gathered around his body, some crying. Bryan felt a touch on his shoulder. It was Thomas. "Captain Craig, we've flushed out most of what's left. Rehman's men took out the enemy along the ridgeline, with the exception of two that we let get away."

The plan of the day was to follow the stray bees back to the hive. "Who'd you send to track em?" Bryan asked.

"Proton and Raza are tracking the two. Once the hive is pinpointed, they'll coordinate with home plate to take it out - then join us back at the pickup point.

"Okay. Let's get some a rest then. Check the dead for anything that's high value," Bryan said.

Thinking of Rehman, he searched for the meaning of his dying words. Who was the falcon, he wondered? Was it Amir Kahn?

CHAPTER 33

JUNE 11, 2008
NORTH WEST FRONTIER, PAKISTAN

THE SUN SHONE BRILLIANTLY on the mountain lake, its light turning the flat surface of the deep water into a magnificent mirror, reflecting the snowy peaks and glaciers. The lake itself was dark and mysterious, the true bottom having never been found. On that morning, the lake became even darker as death had collected on its bank, and on one of its hills. Taliban were lying motionless, face down at water's edge, having paid the ultimate price. And on the hill was Rehman.

They'd waited until daybreak before moving off the lake and down the mountain to the valley. Rehman's men had wrapped his body and the body of the fallen Kafir fighter in blankets, securing them with rope onto makeshift wooden litters to carry up and down the slopes. Wishing to prepare the villagers for the arrival of Rehman well in advance, a courier bearing only the bad news of his death had left before sunrise. The village would need to make preparations for both Rehman and the dead Kafir. Bryan thought of Shamema, and wondered how she'd grieve for her grandfather, but for some reason, certain that she'd show strength.

Although they'd just lost their leader to a Taliban bullet, the grieving from the militia was over and it was already back to business as usual. Bryan could see several Chitrali militiamen on the opposite hill where the Taliban had fallen the night before. Rehman's warriors were picking through the dead enemy, fourteen in all, for weapons and anything salvageable. Their remains would be left on the mountain, and in the water for whatever nature had in mind. The SEALs had already checked each of the Taliban for possible items of interest. None were found. With nothing more to accomplish at the lake, they started down; it was 6:00 am.

As Bryan humped his way down the mountain, he looked at the ancient tintype of the old Mehtar and his men, the one tangible thing that Rehman had given him before he died. "Was there some sort of significance to the photo?" he wondered. "Or, maybe there was nothing to it at all, other than sentimental value?"

Looking at the tintype closer he tried to analyze it as best he could. The Mehtar was sitting in the center of the photograph. There was a Flacon on his right arm. The rest of the photo was difficult to make out because of the poor quality, but it looked as though there were eleven other men. Of the individuals he could see, he noted they bore a striking resemblance to Rehman, confirming their link by blood. Bryan wanted to have the tintype enhanced, if for any reason, perhaps as simply a present to Shamema, a sentimental keepsake of her grandfather. "This is definitely a job for DJ," he thought. He'd have it scanned and Emailed as soon as they landed at Bagram.

The mood of the village had swung one hundred and eighty degrees from the morning before. Oddly enough it was festive. The Kalash Kafir had gathered in a large group, waiting for the fallen men to arrive. They were singing and playing drums, rattling shells, even flutes, and dancing. Rehman's body would make a temporary stop there for ceremonial purposes, before continuing on to a place where many of his ancestors had been laid to rest. Bryan learned the other man killed, whose name was Aziz, was considered a very important man in the village, with two wives, and five sons. He'd been a master wood craftsman, of course, in the art of rifle stock design. Aziz's funeral would be a celebration, a reason to get drunk on wine for those pagans that had never converted to Islam.

Aziz's chestnut coffin was already prepared and waiting for him, and it was the custom of these mountain people to bury their dead above ground, the coffins secured against the walls of cliffs or on top of stone supports. His fellow villagers were dressed in traditional festival attire, the men wearing Salwar Kameez; the Salwar, or loose trousers with vertical red and yellow stripes, and Kameez, a long sleeve turquoise shirt. The women were dressed in their standard brightly embroidered black goat hair robes and ornate headdresses. As part of the ceremony, a goat would be slaughtered, and the family and friends would view the body. The coffin would then be covered and taken to a sacred place outside of the village, where he was laid to rest. A forty-eight hour celebration of dance and drum beating would follow. Not a tear would be shed.

Shamema was standing near her grandfather's body, which had been bathed, and rewrapped, in a plain cloth as per the Islamic burial ritual. His body was then placed on a cattle cart and covered with a blanket of ornate Kalash embroidery. An image of a mountain was embroidered into the cloth covering him. She was speaking with a villager and holding a satchel that Bryan assumed must have been for some of Rehman's personal affects.

"I'm sorry for your loss Shamema. He was an extraordinary man."

"Thank you for your kind words," she said with a kind smile.

"Where will his body be taken?" Bryan asked.

"My grandfather has a special place where he has always wished to be placed. In Chitral, which is not very far from here. Perhaps two days."

"Your grandfather had a ring with a mountain in the center just like the one that's on the blanket covering him." Bryan asked, noting the similarity between the ring and the blanket.

"That's the Kalasha gift to my grandfather. It will be removed before he's buried. The mountain is Tirich Mir, the highest in the Hindu Kush, and the home of the deities that the Kalasha Black-Robed Kafirs worship. Legend has it that Alexander first came to the Hindu Kush to see the mountain and the people are his descendants," she explained.

"We saw the mountain from our camp. It was one of the last things your grandfather's eyes saw," Bryan said. "Your grandfather also had a photo in his hand. This is it here - an old tintype." Bryan showed her the picture of what he presumed was her great, great grandfather. Shamema was surprised.

"Yes, this is Mehtar Aman. The book you signed was his. I've never seen this picture before. You said that my grandfather gave this to you?" Shamema studied the old photo curiously as Bryan held it.

"Yes, he did. Just before he died. Do you have any idea of the significance of the photo, or who any of the other men in the picture may be?" Bryan asked.

"This is surely a very important heirloom of my family. I can remember hearing rumors of the existence of such a portrait, but as I said, I've never known it to be true. This must be the only photograph of the Mehtar's stepbrother and of Afzal, one of his sons. Afzal considered himself the next in line as Mehtar of Chitral."

Setting the satchel down on the dirt road by the cart, she took the photo from Bryan, moving it closer and at different angles to get the best perspective. "This was a time of terrible strife and betrayal," she said.

"What happened exactly?" Bryan asked.

"Mehtar Aman had agreed in principle with the new Durand line but died before signing the agreement - I believe in the late summer of eighteen ninety two. He had a very long reign – for thirty five years."

"And he died soon after the registry was given to him," Bryan said.

"Only one month later," she confirmed. Pointing at the photo she added, "The young man sitting on his right is Afzal. The Mehtar's son and heir would always be on his right for anything official such as portrait or this photograph. And the other young man sitting on the left could be Aman's younger stepbrother. He betrayed Aman and had killed Afzal in an act of terrible deceit."

The story was fascinating. Bryan encouraged her to continue.

"The Mehtar had agreed to sign the British agreement for the new Durand borders with Afghanistan but as I said, he died shortly afterwards. His son, this man here, Afzal, proclaimed himself ruler during the absence of his elder brother. Initially he was in agreement with Prince Shir, the stepbrother, who was opposed to the border."

"Why were they opposed to it?" Bryan asked.

"It was divisive - splitting many tribes in two – one being in Afghanistan and the other in British India."

"But Afzal went along with the line in the end?"

"He did. He changed his mind when he realized his uncle had

been conspiring with the Afghan ruler in Kabul. Their plan was to forcibly convert Kafir to Islam as had happened in Kafiristan."

"How were they being forced?"

"Shir was being paid by Afghan King and using Russians to kidnap young boys from the district. They were taken to Kabul."

"Let me guess Shamema – they were brainwashed into Islamic fanatics," Bryan said.

"That's absolutely correct, how did you know that?" She asked.

"Lucky guess, let's just say," Bryan said. "Please go on."

"Shir opposed the new British border. Shir instead wanted to consolidate the kingdom of Nuristan with Chitral. He conspired with warlords of Nuristan, who were newly converted to Islam and against the British rule. They and vowed to kill all British soldiers that were on Nuristani land so they plotted to overthrow Afzal."

Bryan remembered that there had been a General Issa of Nuristan that had been the first to take arms against the Soviets following their invasion into Afghanistan. He'd called for a Jihad against the Soviet Union encouraging the remaining Muslim tribes in Afghanistan to follow his lead. Unfortunately he was assassinated early in the conflict. "These Nuristanis are the ancestors of the people who first rose up against the communists?" Bryan asked.

"Yes, these are the very same people.

"What happened to his son Afzal?"

"Afzal, who was the new Mehtar, was killed by his step-uncle, Shir. He then proclaimed himself Mehtar and did not recognize the British drawn border."

"Afzal was killed by his uncle, what happened to Shir after that?"

"Please, first let me tell you how Afzal was murdered by Shir. Afzal took a wife, a beautiful young girl from a place near Kashmir. She was an exotic beauty, with enchanting bright blue eyes."

"Similar to your eyes," Bryan said, not being able to resist.

She smiled, and continued, "The ceremony was a beautiful event, and Afzal invited officers from the British garrison to attend the wedding. Shir invited the Nuristan leaders as well, claiming they'd finally agreed with the new border made by the British. There were hundreds of guests and Afzal was married in a ceremony full of flowers and pageantry. The bride and groom left for their wedding chamber to consummate their union. During the night, Shir, along with several Nuristanis slipped into their chamber surprising Mehtar Afzal and his bride. Afzal tried valiantly to fend off Shir's attack, but was overwhelmed by the Nuristanis. Shir killed Afzal by stabbing him with a dagger. He then kidnapped the widowed bride. The Nuristanis captured the nine British officers and their men, holding them hostage at the Fort."

"And Shir was now the new Mehtar with Afzal's wife as his queen?"

"Yes, but there was a battle at Fort Chitral first. The British soon learned of that their officers were being held hostage at the fort. A Gurkha managed to escape. The senior officer being held, Captain Robinson, had given him a message for the British. Five hundred British soldiers and Gurkha Rifles arrived the next day to take back the fort from the Nuristanis, who now numbered more than one hundred men." She looked at the photograph once more.

"The same Captain Robinson in the guest registry?" Bryan asked.

"He was the same man. He was an honored guest of the Mehtar at the wedding."

"And that's when Robinson was killed?"

"When the British and the Gurkhas recaptured the fort, they found all nine officers dead."

"Shir and the bride – what about them?"

"Shir managed to escape and tried to rule Chitral, but lasted only one month before he was forced to flee to Nuristan, taking the girl with him." She paused, and held the photo for Bryan to see. "There is something unusual about the photo you brought from my grandfather."

"What is it?" Bryan looked down at the tintype of the men from more than a century before.

"This picture is backwards," she said.

"This is tintype, Shamema. The process created a negative that was captured on a piece of metal. In this case a piece of tin to make the contrast correct, but it also meant the portrait would be a mirror image."

"I see – well in that case, the man on Aman's right is obscured by this bad scratch over his face," she said. "And the man that you can clearly see is Shir, the stepbrother. That would make sense because Shir would not have looked very similar to the rest. Can you see that he appears to be darker? Afzal would have had a very light complexion and blue eyes. Shir was said to be a like typical Red-Kom from Nuristan, with dark eyes," she said.

"Okay, please go on." Bryan registered the information, but wanted her to finish the story.

"Shir fled with the remaining Nuristanis back to Afghanistan. The Nuristani force strengthened to three thousand men and laid siege to the fort led by Shir himself. The British, along with the Gurkha Rifles, defended the fort for two months when the British Indian Army commanded by General Low finally aided them, defeating the Nuristanis."

"Shir remained in Afghanistan?"

"That's right, he couldn't come back to Chitral, and he'd married Afzal's widow. They had a son almost immediately and their only child. Angry because of the defeat at Fort Chitral, the Nuristan Red-Koms killed Shir. They never trusted him and believed that he would probably betray the Afghans as he had betrayed the Mehtar of Chitral."

"What happened to the son?"

'The Afghans accepted Shir's only son as one of their own, and he was unusual, having blue eyes. The Nuristanis believe, as we do, that people with blue eyes are descended from the Greeks. I've heard of a boy that was a hero during the Soviet war who also had blue eyes. He may have been descended from Shir."

Bryan ran the numbers in his head. If Shir's son was born around eighteen ninety-two, that was a hundred and fourteen years ago, or about six generations of descendants. That could be a lot of blue eyes, he thought.

"Who became the Mehtar after Shir?" Bryan asked.

"It was a terrible time for several years. With Afzal dead and Shir in hiding, Nizam became the new Mehtar at the same time that British India took control of Chitral. Unfortunately, Nizam's rule was very short – Amir ul Mulk, his own brother, murdered him."

"Uncles killing nephews and brothers killing brothers," Bryan said, shaking his head in disbelief.

"It didn't end there I'm afraid. Amir ul Mulk, fearing the British for some reason, fled. I think they may have given him an ultimatum to either abdicate or be killed. Shuja, the youngest son, who was very popular with the British, and had been close to Captain Robinson, became the Mehtar."

"I've heard his name before," Bryan said, recalling the last official Mehtar of Chitral.

"He ruled the State of Chitral for forty-one years and his sons served bravely in the British Army during both World Wars."

"You've never mentioned your father. Why?"

"It's been a long time since he was here. I never really knew him."

"What happened to him?" Bryan asked.

"My grandfather said that he was killed fighting with the Mujahideen in nineteen eighty."

"In Afghanistan?"

"As a young man my father joined the Jihad against the Soviet occupation. He became a Mujahideen. It was there that he was lost in the fighting, his body never returned to Chitral. I have a picture of him with me – he's holding me - I was only two years old. It was the day he left," she said sadly, opening a locket on a chain around her neck. A very handsome young man was holding her. The photo was in color, and Bryan could see where Shamema got her eyes.

"And what about you Shamema? Where will you be going now?"

"My grandfather will be buried tomorrow. Afterwards I'll leave for Islamabad."

"Islamabad? What takes you there?"

"I said that my work is to help the people of my country, well I'm an attorney and an advocate for the Pakistani Human Rights League, a non-profit, non-political, and non-governmental organization," she said frankly.

"Human rights?" Bryan asked.

"As we spoke of yesterday, there are so many Pakistanis suffering from so many things, including the violation of their civil rights. We are part of a network that desperately seeks equality and better treatment for all the people of Pakistan, and without discrimination. We want to help the people here in Chitral and the millions that are suffering elsewhere in my country." Shamema put her hand on her grandfather's body as a tear rolled down her cheek. "He, in his own way, tried to do his part. I must now do mine."

"Shamema, what happened in Chitral more than one hundred years ago is happening again, today - you may already be aware of that, but they aren't stopping at simply making Pakistani men fanatics, they're turning them into terrorists."

"That happened before as well. Some fanatics became martyrs."

"Shamema, I believe your grandfather was killed because," Bryan stopped to weigh his next words.

Shamema finished his sentence, "Because of Yoorish Shaheed?"

"I believe that may be who wanted him dead," Bryan said.

"'Yes, it's sad that he may have died helping to ensure his people had their civil liberties and freedoms. In a way, he too is a martyr then. But from his sacrifice and death, I will raise awareness," she said with courage.

They said goodbye. He had to get back to Bagram, and then to Dubai as quickly as possible. Bryan found Thomas, who with the Senior Chief, were by the old motel watching the start of the funeral parade with fascination and disbelief. "Was our mission a success Captain Craig? Did you find what you came for?" Thomas asked, as snapped a few photos of the procession with a tiny digital camera.

Bryan looked at the SEAL commander as he tucked the tintype in the pocket of his combat vest. "I'm one step closer."

CHAPTER 34

THE PREDATOR GAINED ALTITUDE, surveying the mountainous terrain below. Considering the aircraft's size, it packed a formidable punch. With a wingspan of twenty-seven feet and a length of forty-eight feet, the killer was much smaller than a manned fighter, but could easily carry two Hellfire missiles capable of inflicting tremendous damage to a target protected by thick armor, or hidden in caves of thick rock. If the enemy were close by as reported, they would be found by the drone and completely destroyed.

The craft was the king of the drone world and could remain airborne much longer than its manned counterpart, for up to twenty-four hours. Efficient, it was a drone capable of flying over five hundred nautical miles at an altitude of fifty thousand feet. It had incredible vision, using a color nose camera with daylight variable TV apertures and infrared optical sensors. An all weather killer, the Predator could conduct its reconnaissance day or night, and through clouds or haze. Once the target area was located, the Predator would use a quick reaction laser designator to guide in the Hellfire missiles with deadly conclusions. Today's mission required four Predators and eight Hellfires, the targets – Taliban and Yoorish Shaheed terrorist militants.

Proton and Raza tracked the two Taliban survivors of the mountain firefight for twelve hours, eventually leading the SEAL and his scout up to a hillside enclave of sixty Taliban and Islamic militants. It was just before daybreak when the GPS coordinates of the enemy's location were transmitted to the Predator team. Located at Bagram Air Base in Afghanistan and Nellis Air Force Base in Nevada, the team was made up of fifty professionals, including pilots and ground crew, to roll out and recover the four Predator vehicles. The aircraft would be launched from Bagram and be on target in two hours.

A Navy Lieutenant Commander, a drone pilot, sat in front of a terminal console, watching video images displayed on multiple monitors. She was the strike lead. Three other pilots were sitting at similar consoles adjacent to her, each monitoring the same images. U.S. military intelligence and the CIA had coordinated with Pakistan's Intelligence office, ISI. The position of the Taliban and Yoorish Shaheed operatives was in the southwestern area of the Hindu Kush Mountains, five kilometers east of the Durand line and exactly where Bryan's team had confirmed them to be. They were confirmed to be just on the Pakistani side of the border, therefore the unmanned mission was officially sanctioned. The green light was given to take the terrorists out.

Both the strike lead and her fellow pilots were maneuvering each respective fighter remotely using joysticks and the computer consoles in front of them, flying via Ku-band satellite data link. The target area was now in site on their monitors. The Predators were flying in sections of two drones each, and honed in on coordinates provided by Proton and Raza. The lead UAV banked toward the target area, the Lieutenant Commander then eased the joystick slightly and leveled the unmanned air vehicle's wings. The images were coming in clear from a half a world away.

"General, we have acquisition of the target area. Requesting launch clearance," the pilot said to the Air Force general standing in back of her right shoulder and monitoring the flights of the Mq-1 Predator system.

"How does it look to you?" The general asked the CIA advisor watching along side him.

"Our man on the ground has given the go ahead. Take out the target."

"Cleared to engage Commander," the General advised.

"Roger that sir." She banked the UAV and began a shallow dive toward the target area. The three other UAVs mimicked her flight path, and moments later two of those broke off into a section flight of their own. The two sections of UAVs now established a bracket of the target area.

Fifty plus Taliban and Islamic Yoorish Shaheed militants were outside of a small stone shelter that also served as a storehouse for weapons and ammunition. Two Predators trained lasers on the doorway of the shelter, as the other two UAVs sighted the entrance to a small cave, an enclave that gave temporary protection for the band of militant militia. A dozen or more other Taliban were collecting what little gear they had, preparing to break camp and move out. By effectively bracketing the target area, a flanking strategy using missiles, the attack should be successful in destroying the weapons cache, and severely damaging the capability of this particular element of Taliban and other combatants, if not killing them all.

At an altitude of ten thousand feet, Predators one and two closed to within one and a half miles of the designated target, each launching a Hellfire 114A missile in succession. Using cursors, the pilots, a half a world away, painted the target and guided the beam riders into the stone shelter, both missiles hitting their mark within inches. Packed with warheads of shaped charges, an extremely high velocity jet of metal, so hot it was in a near plasma state, the explosive moved at hypersonic speeds twenty five times faster than sound. The maximum energy of the explosive was focused directly at the shelter, completely obliterating it.

Simultaneously, the third and fourth Predators launched two AGM-114N Hellfires at the largest mass of enemy near the entrance of the enclave, using specially designed warheads of thermobaric overpressure charges and metal, optimized to inflict the maximum damage possible on personnel. The pilots and engineers called it, "a shrapnel concussion bomb." And the black and white images on the monitors spoke for themselves, indicating successful impact and detonation as the screens turned bright white from each of the flashes. Immediately, the Commander and her team fired a second wave of missiles. The devastation was complete, leaving zero chance for survivors. Exultant cheers and handshakes ensued around the control room back at Nellis, and in top secret viewing rooms elsewhere. The drones were flown back to Bagram and landed by the pilots for CIA ground crew pickup.

DJ turned off his monitor back in London. He'd watched part of the evolution while listening to Led Zeppelin's "Gallows Pole."

In Pakistan, Bryan sat down by a rock as the team waited for the Black Hawk and the escort to take them to Bagram. He'd time to use the SATCOM relay and make a quick call on the iPhone Nano.

"Go ahead," the quiet voice acknowledged.

"Mission here's complete. I'm RTB at this time and will be back in Dubai within twenty-four hours. I'll update you once I've made it there."

"Sounds grand. Stay safe and good luck."

"One other thing – the principal here's dead."

"Rehman's dead?" the voice asked.

"That's affirm," Bryan said, preferring not to break protocol by using names.

"Were you there when it happened?"

"Yep," Bryan said, checking his gear before moving out.

"How do ya know it wasn't meant for you?"

Bryan thought for a second before answering. "That's a good question. I don't."

A half a dozen other interested parties were also turning off their own flat panels: at Langley, the head of counter-terrorism; at the White House situation room, the counter-terrorism czar; and in London, MI6 and the Home Secretary's office. In five hours, Bryan would meet with the CIA's area station chief, the principle in charge of covert operations throughout Afghanistan and Pakistan. Between now and then, he'd try to put it all together.

The pilots put down their headsets, preparing for the post flight debrief and review of the video. The Lieutenant Commander thanked her fellow pilots for a job well done, and got right into the mission's pros and cons, "Gentleman, as always good mission. All Taliban and militant elements were destroyed as you can see by the video, as well as the complete destruction of the weapons cache. We'll forward our report to the civilian advisors that were either present during the sortie, or monitored the mission from remote locations."

After finishing the brief and submitting the necessary post-mission assessments, she called together the mission team members once more. "Just want to let ya'll know that my husband and I'll be expecting everybody at our house two weeks from tomorrow. It's his forty-second. They'll be steaks, baked potatoes, burgers, hotdogs, beer and wine. All kids are welcome of course. And bring your bathing suits. The new pool's finally finished. So please don't miss it. That's an order," she said, joking with her flight team.

"Think you'll be able to drink some of that beer with us Commander?" one of the other pilots asked.

"I sure hope so – it'll be reason to celebrate even more. See ya'll tomorrow and be safe," she said.

She walked unescorted out of the building and to her car in the parking lot. A Lexus SUV. It was only a twenty-minute drive back home to the house in the suburbs of Las Vegas. Traffic was light. Arriving home, she pulled into the garage, got out and went inside. Her first stop was the refrigerator. She was hungry. Dill pickles and vanilla ice cream sounded good. She mixed them together in a bowl to enjoy while she relaxed on the sofa in the family room.

"I'm so tired," she said, the empty bowl resting on her pronounced belly. She couldn't see her feet. Looking sideways she caught her profile in a mirror, shook her head and smiled.

"Street – you'll be lucky to get through the next week without going into labor," Lieutenant Commander Crystal Sizemore said to herself as she felt a kick.

* * * * *

JUNE 12, 2008

BAGRAM, AFGHANISTAN

"That confirms what we learned in the mountains," Bryan said, handing the Email to the CIA station chief Grant Ostland.

"After that fire fight up there, you could probably use some sleep," Ostland said as he pulled the Email across the table to read.

"You know what the Spanish say," Bryan retorted.

Ostland stared at Bryan before answering. "Yeah – plenty of time to sleep when you're dead. And you're getting pretty close my friend," he said, observing Bryan's circles. "You look like you're about to hit the wall. You need something?"

"I can manage. Just some coffee, or a Red Bull – maybe something stiffer after we finish," Bryan said.

Ostland shook his head. "I can handle all that, just don't kill yourself on my watch – I don't need the paperwork." Ostland read the message.

```
T O P   S E C R E T

From: Gil Bussmann,
Sent: Sunday, June 9, 2008 23:25 PM
To:    Captain Bryan Craig
Subject: Pakistani Bank Accounts

Bryan,
The two accounts listed below are of high
interest:

    Account 1:
    Islamic Faysal Investment Bank LTD.
    Shaheen Complex,
    M.R. Kayani Road, Saddar
    Acct: 973903120
    FBO: Dupak Ltd.


    Account 2:
    Crescent Bank of Pakistan
    Shaheen Complex,
    Doctor Ziauddin Ahmed Road, Saddar
    Acct: 649783119
    FBO: Tirich Mir Ltd.

Signatories for the accounts in question are the
following:
    Account 1 - Shahid Mahmood
    Account 2 — Afzar Kahn

V/R
Gil Bussmann
```

"Your man confirmed it just before being killed?" the Station Chief asked. Grant Ostland set the paper aside and reached in his pocket for his favorite smoke, a Cohiba Pantella. Lighting the mini cigar, he changed the subject "You been working with Kevin Davis in Dubai?"

"For a few days. My profiler's with him there as we speak."

"Is that a fact," Ostland said, leaning forward to look at the Email again.

"Sir, there's no smoking allowed in the SCIF," the duty officer announced, pointing at sign that read *"No Smoking!"*

Peering over his reading glasses, slightly irritated, "You ever see 'Basic Instinct,' son?" Grant asked the Air Force Staff Sergeant. The CIA man was in his mid fifties, thinning grey hair, a hardcore field operations type, who had seen it all and had the scars to prove it. He had little patience with rules he considered to be "Bullshit."

"Yeah, Davis is working with us," Bryan said.

"Little prick, that guy. Prone to fuck things up, so I'd watch your ass," the station chief said with disdain. Was this an inner agency rivalry between a true "ops type" and a "pencil pusher," or was Grant being sincere, Bryan wondered?

"Well, anyway – enough on that. So the poor bastard sent this out only hours before going over a balcony, huh?" Ostland continued.

"Probably wanted to speak to me in person first, but he put the Email in the system to come in yesterday. Dupak Ltd. was formally Dubai-Pak and set up by Petrov," Bryan said, motioning to the Bagram SCIF duty officer to bring a pen and a piece of paper to the conference table. "Let me draw this out for ya."

Bryan meticulously described the complicated financial network set up by Petrov and Wazir to finance global terrorism operations, including Narco-terrorism: the bogus offshore insurance accounts, the opium trafficking from Afghanistan through the Hindu Kush and into Peshawar to bolster the illegal cash flow used to pay the premiums into the bogus insurance accounts, systematic payoffs to UAE officials to front work visas, and the Dubai labor camps, established to brainwash workers into lethal human bombs. Grant Ostland, the Station Chief responsible for both Afghanistan and Pakistan was impressed by the sophistication, yet yearning to do what was necessary to put an end to it.

"Bryan, I've got my marching orders from the Director – we've got a blank check here to do what's needed based on your directions. You're the QB and callin' the plays, what're we gonna do?" Grant Ostland asked.

Bryan eyeballed him carefully. The veteran CIA man had seen it all, and probably wanted to leave the business with a true feeling of success. "A touchdown," Bryan thought.

Bryan leaned back, his hands holding the back of his head. "So I'm the quarterback, huh? Okay then, how's this for a plan, we're in their territory and it's first down – we've got the ball. First play - we shut down Dupak ASAP. See what intel we can quickly gleam," Bryan proposed. "Look for anything that ties into Amir Kahn or the second account that's in the Email. My guess is that we'll uncover a link between Wazir and Dupak."

"I'm comfortable with that and with you running the show, Bryan. I've known you many years..." the CIA man started to say before being stopped by Bryan.

"You're not gonna start cryin' and tell me how much you love me, are ya?" Bryan said, motioning for a Cohiba from Grant, and drawing a laugh out of him.

Still laughing, Grant said, "Nice touch there, SEAL, but you know I'm not that kind a guy." Poker-faced again, Grant continued, "What I was trying to convey was my surprise that you're so cool about this Wazir Zar Wali character. How's does it make you feel that this guy's Hanif Zar Wali's twin?"

"How's it make me feel? Man, you're soundin' like my FBI profiler," Bryan said. "No proof of that yet, I mean – no DNA confirmation on that," he added.

"Oh, come on – give me a break, Bryan," Grant said, reaching in his briefcase for a bottle of *Grey Goose*. "If I were in your shoes, I'd be hot on the trigger for that guy too. Does he know your connection with his brother, if that's who he is?" Grant asked, pouring them both a shot of the vodka.

"That I don't know. At least it's not been made obvious to me during the one brief meeting with him," Bryan answered blankly. "He's the guy I'm going for now, though."

"It's got to be a little freaky – but I'm here to help you do exactly what you want. I'll arrange for some cash – we've got about two million here now. Let me know where we need to spread it, and we can further tap into our senior warlord network if needed," the station chief said picking the Email up. "Speakin' of money, what about this Bussmann guy?"

"He was good," Bryan said emphatically.

"Yeah, well he got you to this point on the money trail faster than I could have guessed," Ostland commented. "Maybe you'll get a replacement."

"I hope," Bryan said, not imagining who that could be.

Ostland tapped the Email with his index finger. "Who's this Afzar Kahn?" He asked puffing on his cigar.

"Don't know. See what your sources come up with," Bryan said.

"I'll start beatin' the streets with some cash on that one," the CIA man said.

"When will you have some people at the site we took out this morning?"

"I'll have a team fly out early tomorrow - we'll send everything we find to Derrick Johnson – how's that sound?"

"Sounds good, he's the guy," Bryan said.

"You expect to find something valuable there?"

"I'm hoping we find something between there and Dupak, it's a new terrorist arm we're dealing with," Bryan said. "A very dangerous one."

"And they're calling themselves Yoorish Shaheed?" Grant Ostland added rhetorically.

"That's what we've learned."

"That ain't a very diplomatic name – obviously a splinter of militants from Al-Qaeda," Ostland said.

"New leadership – fresh blood. Recruits that show an aptitude for combat are probably brought up to the mountains and receive in-depth training. But I think we're gettin close to putting our finger on the pulse - the blood flow in terms of cash that's financing the operations," Bryan said. "Wazir Zar Wali appears to be one of the principals involved. If I can tie him to Dupak, then he's toast."

"Why not just take him out the old fashioned way?" Grant asked, suggesting they simply cut off the head and be done with it.

"First of all, I need tangible evidence, and I'd like to bring the guy in alive. He's not like his twin – that is, as hard core. This one's an academic," Bryan pointed out.

"In the immortal words of Hank Stram, 'Let's matriculate the ball down the field, boys' - and bulldoze these fuck heads back in the holes from which they came." Ostland said, quoting the legendary football coach and adding his own words.

Bryan hoped for the very same result, and welcomed the enthusiastic support from the CIA operations man, but what he didn't share with the CIA was the fact the second account Gil had listed was wiring funds only to Pakistani Human Rights, the organization run by Shamema. The other element of the compartmentalized message from Gil concerned the Swiss account mentioned by Rodgers Christopher; it was Consul General's own account, and something Bryan wanted to investigate further before divulging that information.

"Now, why put blood hounds on a trail that led straight to him?" Bryan questioned privately of Christopher's account.

CHAPTER 35

JUNE 13, 2008
BAGRAM, AFGHANISTAN

"**S**IR, ARE YOU OKAY?"

Bryan opened his eyes. Standing above him was an Air Force sergeant in a flight suit. He came out of REM - the dream was over. He was groggy. "What's goin' on?" Bryan asked, forgetting the dream, but wondering what the hell he was doing on the linoleum floor.

"There's been an earthquake somewhere, didn't feel that bad though – maybe a five somethin' – you must've slipped off the couch," the sergeant said, not realizing the epicenter was two hundred miles east.

Bryan got up off the floor of the Air Base flight line shack, "shack" being an appropriate moniker. The room was a waiting area for passengers to catch hops and adjacent to a very secure area where flight crew would brief, debrief, check the weather and file flight plans for non tactical flights. There was a SCIF close by too, Bryan's next stop. He needed to call DJ in London.

"DJ, back in the early days of the Soviet invasion of Afghanistan there was a kid that became one of the first heroes of the resistance.

He had blue eyes," Bryan said over the secure phone, thinking about what Shamema had told him.

"Go on boss," DJ said, Zeppelin music playing in the background – "Dazed and Confused."

"There was some U.S. congressman who went to the refugee camps – I think he's from Oklahoma - Republican maybe. He had the press with him. There was a video segment and an Afghan kid featured. He'd shot down a Soviet helicopter. I remember it clear as day. Find that for me ASAP. Check with Dylan Sizemore if need be."

"Whad da want with it?"

"Send it to me when you get it."

"Cheers."

Another tremor began; it had been ten minutes since the last.

Forty-five kilometers below the earth's surface, the frictional stress of the India plate against the Euro-Asia plate finally exceeded the critical value. Now the strain gave way completely, the two hundred fifty kilometer rupture zone releasing an energy equivalent of five hundred thousand Hiroshima bombs; a magnitude eight on the Richter scale. The first of the seismic waves, a primary compression wave, radiated toward the surface at thirty-five thousand kilometers per hour, pushing and pulling, a terra firma jackhammer. Following the P waves were the secondary waves at half the speed, and finally the surface waves with their up and down motion causing the most destruction. Reaching Bagram Air Base after one minute, Bryan started the timer on his watch. The walls of the SCIFF vibrated, causing several pictures to fall. One frame was a quote from Kipling that Bryan had put on the wall almost seven years before.

When you're wounded and left on Afghanistan's plains,
And the women come out to cut up what remains,
Jest roll to your rifle and blow out your brains
An' go to your Gawd like a soldier.

"That's four minutes," Bryan said to the duty officer, the first one to say anything at all during the event. "That wasn't a small one, wherever it came from - it was massive."

The duty officer turned up the volume on CNN. "Maybe they'll have something on it here sir," the duty officer said.

"I'm sure you can count on that," Bryan said, reasonably certain the epicenter was somewhere in the North West Frontier and would quickly be a breaking news story. It was going to be monumental disaster. Bryan's ride to Dubai was already late; the earthquake may delay the flight even more.

"Sir, call for you," the duty officer said, pointing to a secure phone on a conference table.

"Go ahead DJ," Bryan said.

"Es on its way te ye boss. An hours worth o video."

"Thanks – may be delayed getting outa here DJ. Let Shannon know for me, would ya?"

"Any problem?"

"Maybe, just had an earthquake here thirty minutes ago, something's coming up on the news about it now."

"Yeah, see it ere on the news," DJ confirmed.

"I'll call you after I've reviewed this video."

Confirming the delayed departure for the KC-135 as two hours, Bryan settled into a chair at a desktop station to review the archived news story. The Congressman, Jack Smith, was from Tennessee, and known as "Happy Jack" for his first name, love of parties, and propensity to knock back bourbon on the rocks from time to time. A staunch anti-Soviet, he was adamant in immediate support of the Mujahideen at the start of the invasion and was ultimately instrumental in having stingers smuggled to them via the CIA and ISI.

Bryan watched the monitor as a film crew followed the Congressman around the Afghan countryside. Doing their best to avoid getting killed, all Westerners dressed in traditional clothing of the area, hoping to blend in. One segment covered the Congressman as he greeted Pashtun refugees, including a thirteen year old who the year before shot down a Soviet Hind. Bryan froze the image, saved the JPEG and picked up a secure phone.

"DJ, run FaceScan – check Sultan Amir against the boy in the story. I sent you a JPEG," Bryan said looking at the boy, astonished. There was no doubt in his mind that the boy and Amir were one and the same.

"Already ahead of ye boss. Got a real nice JPEG on its way back."

Bryan checked the Email, opening the JPEG. The image had been greatly enhanced, and he could clearly see the blue eyes of the boy. The nodal comparison would only confirm what was obvious.

"Checks across the board boss, thet's im," DJ said.

"How do I figure out if he's related to the old Mehtar in Chitral?"

"Ye got DNA?"

"Sorry, not at the moment, and it might be hard to get Sultan's DNA. What about using FaceScan to match up characteristics?"

"Not very exact, en fact won't 'old up en court."

"I just sent you a copy of an old photo, check it against the guy on the Mehtar's left."

"Give me about twenty minutes boss – call ye back."

Anxious to learn the epicenter and the area hit hardest by the earthquake, Bryan paid attention to the SCIF's television as he waited. Activity in the secure area was picking up as intelligence officers and various military commanders verified the earthquake and made calls to "boots on the ground." Concern would be highest for special ops teams operating near the epicenter. Fortunately, Bryan's team was safe, back at Bagram, but he was worried about Shamema. He'd call her office in Islamabad before he left the base, he decided.

The news finally broke, confirming the epicenter northwest of Peshawar, and if anything like the quakes of three years before, it would be an ongoing tragedy, a humanitarian challenge. Seismologists measured it at an eight, one of the largest ever recorded.

Reviewing the JPEG of the boy again, Bryan saw the Congressman, a short, bald, Gandhi looking man with some children, a girl and younger boys, but Bryan's attention was on a bearded man in his twenties standing near Amir. His hair was light brown, and he looked as though he could be an uncle. Assuming the man was with the Congressman's contingent, Bryan shrugged off any other possibility. "Yeah, that's gotta be it. Probably one of 'Happy Jack's' staffers," Bryan thought.

"Analysis done boss – thes es what aye can tell ye – it's doubtful thet the bloke ye said was the Mehtar's brother could've ad a son with blue eyes," DJ said with certainty.

"Why's that?" Bryan asked.

"Set up the video conference boss, I'll show ya."

Internet video cameras working on both ends, DJ began his detailed explanation, "The copy's creased o'er the Mehtar's son, 'is face is obscured, an aye can't get anything on 'im, but the other three blokes in the foreground came out good. Aye recalled thet ye said the one son 'ad blue eyes."

"Yeah, that's right," Bryan replied, confirming Shamema's story.

"An yer lady friend also has light blue eyes, her grandfather's got baby blues, and this Afzal bloke's wife had blue eyes."

Something was getting very interesting about the direction of the conversation. "Everything you've summarized is what I know to the best of my recollection. Go ahead."

"Well aye thought thet aye'd let FaceScan ave a whirl with their eyes in the photo – an by the way, it's actually a copy of a tintype an the images may be reversed."

"Figured that much out before, but I'm intrigued with your direction on this yet again," Bryan said.

"Well the tintype ye sent me, or rather the photocopy of the tintype, et's pretty good. Thet's te say, the equipment thet's used back then, though not on par with digital imagin, was pretty good. And they ad great lightin as well - another thing - the subjects must ave stayed very still. Thet also elped with the resolution of the old photo."

"Helped how?"

"Black and white photos can be colorized by predictin the known color values from grayscale. FaceScan data has virtually all colors and shades in the color and gray spectrum. Thet's millions upon millions of millions, boss."

"Yeah, NASA does the same thing when turning black and white photos of Mars into color photos," Bryan said.

"Rayght. FaceScan also knows whot those shades look like en grey scale. FaceScan fixes anomalies by usin the program's gamma correction. There are a few things aye need te input of course, such as shadow values, an so forth. The tintype ye ave there was made under a slight overcast."

"True, non of these guys are squinting," Bryan agreeing with DJ's observation. "Look's like a nice day in the mountains."

"Thet of course elped me a great deal, boss."

"So you colorized the photo?"

"Sure did. Check yer Email."

Bryan did just that. And there it was, a color JPEG of the photocopy of the tintype, completely cleaned up, looking as though it had been taken recently.

"This looks great DJ," he said, impressed.

"Look closer boss. An by thet, aye mean zoom in." Bryan complied with DJ's instructions. He was amazed how much detail he could now see. "Truly great stuff DJ, the detail is fantastic."

"Look at their eyes, boss."

Bryan did just that. "Okay, the Mehtar has nice baby blues, and the son's got the crease." Bryan moved the cursor on the JPEG over to the Mehtar's brother, wishing he had a clear picture of Afzal. "And the evil brother has brown eyes. Interesting, Shamema had said it was rumored that Shir's son had very blue eyes." Genetics was not his strong suit, but he thought he knew where DJ was going. "Help me out with this a little DJ."

"First ye need te understand ow eye color is inherited. People ave two genes thet are responsible for the color of our eyes - *bey2* and *gey*. Each of those has two possible forms known as alleles. *Bey2* has a brown allele and a blue allele. *Gey* has a green and a blue. The eye color of the child depends on the alleles inherited from the parents."

DJ's explanation was a little above Bryan's baseline biology, where he'd fallen short during school, but he was following along so far.

Bryan editorialized, "If the beautiful bride came from a family that had blue eyes, and we are assuming that she did - and the new husband had brown eyes, who of course would be Shir..."

"Okay. Yer gettin warmer boss. Realize thet among human phenotypes, blue eyes are very rare. Ye'll find people with blue ave an ancestral tree thet goes back to Northern, or Eastern Europe, an fewer from people along the coastline of the Mediterranean, or Asia."

"That makes sense to me, but what are the odds that their child would have blue eyes, and light blue at that?" Bryan asked.

"Aye's hopin ya'd get around te thet question - the answer is ten point six percent. So it's possible, but not statistically likely."

"Ten point six, huh. That's low," Bryan said. One in ten chance, but not out of them realm of possibilities, he considered.

"Let me put it up on the grease board for you to visualize." DJ wrote it out and then zoomed in the Internet video-cam for Bryan.

bbbb	bbGb	bbGG	Bbbb	BBbb	BbGb	BBGb	BbGG	BBGG
10.6%	10.6%	0.0%	39.4%	0.0%	39.4%	0.0%	0.0%	0.0%

Blue	Green	Brown
10.6%	10.6%	78.8%

"The baby blues are the four lit-al b letters. The Genotype, which is the combination of the *bey2* an *gey*, will give ye the Phenotype - ere ye see the probabilities, an' for the baby blue et's thirteen point six. Now, there are many other various eye colors, like hazel, black, and gray. "

DJ paused to allow Bryan a moment to take in the volumes of information, and continued, "There are also combinations of each, like blue-green, violet, and so forth. An of course green eyes - very common among the Pashtuns in Afghanistan. But blue eyes are very uncommon in thet area of the world. Light blue eyes, even more rare still. So thet's why for this illustration aye stuck with just blue, green, and brown, and the combinations of those basic colors," DJ explained.

"And if the murdered groom with the light blue eyes got there first? What would the odds be that his child would have light blue eyes, too?" The next answer was the key.

"No need to rewrite as a visual boss. Thet one's easy. One undred percent the child would ave blue eyes and bright blue at thet. Lit-al b times four."

"So chances are that a blue eyed Mujahideen from northern Afghanistan, who was running around killing Soviets as a pre teen was a descendant of the rightful heir of the Mehtar of Chitral," Bryan summarized.

"Gives a whole new meaning to "The Man Who Would Be King," doesn't it?"

Bryan cropped the JPEG so that he had only the image of the murdered son Afzal. "You couldn't be more right about that DJ," Bryan said. "But how do we prove it?" Bryan asked.

"Now if ye notice, the Mehtar an his brother don't exactly look much alike."

"That's because they're stepbrothers."

"Do ye ave a photo somewhere o the Prince?"

"I don't – but let's do this - put the images of the Mehtar and his family side by side with Amir Kahn – both the recent and childhood photo of Amir," Bryan asked. Studying the images, he was becoming more convinced that Amir was somehow related to the group of men in the old photo. *How?* Within the JPEG of the Tennessee Congressman and the Afghans surrounding Amir he found a partial answer.

"DJ, I thought the young guy – the one standing next to Amir and Happy Jack – I thought he was a staffer, just in local garb, you know – when in Afghanistan he grew his beard out," Bryan said.

"Well, e looks allot like em, an e also looks like the Mehtar an his sons."

"For good reason – I recognized him because I saw his photo yesterday," Bryan said, feeling adrenalin surge in his tired body. "I'd swear that's Shamema's father."

"Thet's a scoop there boss."

"I also think I know where there's proof – maybe. If I can make it back to the same village I left yesterday, I could find out one way or another," Bryan said. "And I'd also like to make sure that Shamema gets some help for her people after this earthquake."

"It's a disaster boss. It's all o'er the news. Aye'm watchin the telly now."

Thinking about Shamema's father again, Bryan asked, "What's the date of the archived news broadcast with Congressman Smith?"

"September, nineteen eighty three."

"Well there you go DJ – Shamema said her father was killed in nineteen eighty. What's he doing alive in this picture then? I've got to get back up there. I could probably be in and out in twenty-four hours," Bryan said, thinking twenty-four hours might be optimistic.

Communications in and out of Pakistan were bottlenecked, but after several hours Bryan was finally on the phone with Shamema's office, an office that was in a total state of confusion, inundated as more news poured in, no one knew what to believe. Her assistant Jamil was there, but Shamema had never come down from the frontier prior to the earthquake. She could be trapped, injured, or worse.

"All passes will probably be blocked. It could be a weeks before the Pakistani government can get proper medical teams up there, let alone first responders for rescue," Bryan said to Jamil, understanding the dire situation and the reason for urgency.

"I don't know vat to do – if it takes so long, how many more vill perish from injuries or starvation?" Jamil asked, despondent over the frustrating situation. "Dere are many towns dat I'm sure are severely damaged just to de north of Peshawar - and de government vill send de military to dose places first. Many other peoples in de North West Frontier will be ignored." Jamil was thinking of the Kalash village, and other infidel tribes.

"Maybe I can help," Bryan said. "Where would Shamema have gone after she left Chitral town?" Bryan asked the overworked relief worker.

"After the earthquake she vould have gone back to de Kalash village, maybe dere are peoples who survived. It would be important to get the peoples away from de steep slopes. Aftershocks vould cause many landslides. It vould be too dangerous for de peoples to remain in de villages," Jamil said rapidly and at wits end.

"Where would they go?" Bryan asked.

"Dere is a lake dat people have gone to before after earthquakes. It's flat dere, and safe. It would be de best area to give emergency medical help," Jamil said.

Which lake? There are dozens! "I'll need coordinates for the lake, a latitude and longitude. Please get that for me. Also, let me know what it is that you'll need for the first responders – and that's medical equipment – things like that. I'll figure out a way to get you and the equipment up there. Call me as soon as you know that information," Bryan explained. "Do you understand?"

"Yes, I understand."

Bryan's plate was getting full, but the earthquake had set new wheels in motion. He had to do what was right, and he knew going back to the village was part of that; not to mention finding Shamema, which was as important as anything. He needed to make arrangements. "They'll need air support, tents, food, water, all necessary for remote triage – the CIA cash may come in handy," he thought.

Searching secure message traffic for Special Operations, Bryan verified three teams operating out of Bagram, including the team he'd just been with. Assets would be available; he'd need to make it happen. "I'll call in some favors," he decided.

* * * * *

JUNE 14, 2008
BAGRAM, AFGHANISTAN

Kicking up Afghan dust, the combat vehicle bounced along an unpaved perimeter road of the airfield, the Hindu Kush jutting up in the distance. The mountains were particularly spectacular, a phenomenon created by the massive amounts of fine dust stirred up and now airborne from the quake. The afternoon sun illuminated the magnificent peaks and the dusty, light orange veil, surreal against a foreground of tactical airplanes, helicopters, and tanks; nature's art, a vivid painting masking the human tragedy that lay on its slopes and in its valleys.

Normally buzzing like an active beehive, Bagram was standing down for twenty-four hours as its own damage assessments were made following the catastrophic earthquake. The combat vehicle, a jeep, was Bryan's ticket to a Black Hawk helicopter, the crew performing preflight checks on the north end of the field. An old acquaintance was in the back of the jeep, and his escort to a devastated North West Frontier.

"Captain Craig, ets good ta see ya sahr."

"And great to be seen, Sergeant Major MacLean,"

"Hop in sahr, aye understand we're goin' ta the frontier again."

"Yes, we are," he said, happy to be teamed with the SAS man again after so many years.

Not as concerned with secrecy this time into Pakistan, they jumped off the UH-60 Black Hawk Medevac helicopter, the pilot managing to find flat ground a quarter of a mile from the village. The flight then continued on with three CIA investigators to the militant encampment destroyed by the Predators. The flight back to Pakistan had been uneventful, and the destruction caused by the earthquake hardly evident from the air; but once on the ground, Bryan and the Sergeant Major, medical kits in hand, could see the extent of the damage. They were certain the Kalash village that was their destination, would be in shambles, along with dozens of other villages.

The first of the shocked Kalash survivors welcomed the two Westerners with tears in their eyes, their village unrecognizable. Bryan began asking for Shamema, but no one had an answer.

"Da ya know which way to go sahr?" the Sergeant Major asked as Bryan surveyed the rubble that was a village teaming with activity.

"First we'll do our best to find Shamema, if she's here, maybe help out some, then shove off to the lake," Bryan said. If Shamema were unhurt, she'd be there with other first responders.

"Which way's the lake, sahr?" Wolf MacLean asked.

Bryan looked at the GPS. "I've got the lat and long, so we can use the handheld," Bryan said. He looked up and followed a track of people over a low ridgeline, some carrying injured on wooden litters. "But I imagine we can also simply get in line with those people."

As they walked through what appeared to be the center of the Kalash village, Bryan saw the remnants of a sign sitting atop a pile of rocks, partially covered by corrugated tin. "Hold on a sec Wolf, I need to check for something here," Bryan said, as he set the medical bag down. Carefully stepping onto part of the razed structure's roof, he began searching through the piled up debris.

CHAPTER 36

JUNE 14, 2008

HINDU KUSH RANGE, PAKISTAN

USTING OFF THE BOOK, he opened it. Difficult as it was to believe, it escaped damage, all pages intact, none torn. The leather bound cover avoided even the slightest bruising, front and back remarkably unscathed. As if by miracle, the nineteenth century registry seemed to be the one inanimate object untouched by a massive earthquake that destroyed almost everything else man-made.

"I'll be damned," Bryan commented.

"What's that there, sahr?"

"Some history, Sergeant Major – just some history," Bryan said, as he balanced himself on top of the loose pile of rocks and wood.

From his new vantage point he surveyed the slopes of the hills down to a tight valley. They were very close to the epicenter of the earthquake. Confirmed as an eight on the Richter scale, it shook the region to the very core, toppling hillsides, rock avalanches razing villages. Officials predicted at least one hundred thousand dead, and more than two million homeless across the North West Frontier of Pakistan and Kashmir. It was complete turmoil and utter chaos, made worse for a land isolated by lack of proximity.

First responders were just now arriving, not quite two days after the first major tremor, much quicker than previous events. Bryan wanted to stay and help, and he would for a time. However, his primary mission was not earthquake rescue. He had to get back to Dubai, but wanted to do what he could here first. These people needed help, and their dead Mehtar had helped him. It simply was the right thing to do. First, get the old book and its contents if possible; the answers to some questions might be inside.

It came suddenly and with surprise, although the people living in the mountains had warnings of sorts, living with earthquakes, knowing them to be a recurring event. But seismologists couldn't predict exactly when the natural disasters would occur. So instead, the people went about their daily lives as normal, oblivious to the imminent danger. In retrospect, it struck Bryan that the event was a metaphor, the victims' apathy similar to the denial of many where he came from, an ignorant bliss in the face of their own imminent dangers, albeit man-made circumstances. Bryan cast off the notion of worry however, "If you worry about it, then terror and fear win. But be very prepared however, and live everyday to the fullest, without fear," he reasoned. "But most of all - be prepared."

Regardless of the difficulty to predict the earth's shifting faults, the Pakistani government nevertheless failed to adequately prepare for the inevitable, or quite possibly, "Humanity had failed, not just one government, but all governments collectively failed these people before the disaster, and the many other disasters that preceded this one," Bryan privately suggested. So the earth punished them once again, as it had done twice only three years before, and twelve times before that, over an equal number of centuries. It was a certainty to return and kill again, and it did, resulting in a humanitarian catastrophe of epic proportions, an historical cataclysm.

The North West Frontier was still licking wounds from the quakes of 2005. Large seismic events that also left more than one hundred thousand dead, scores of villages destroyed and millions homeless. Structures not reduced to rubble then, had been severely fractured, finally taken down by the new earthquake and its aftershocks. Bryan was seated on a pile of that debris as he perused the valuable book he'd just recovered from the rubble of a stone house.

Trying to preserve the artifact as much as possible, he delicately cut along the edge of the inside back cover with a penknife. The fine opening was just wide enough to carefully remove the contents, meticulously placed there many years ago, a kind of time capsule. There was a square piece of tin, which he hastily looked over, and behind it, a single sheet of paper folded twice into quarters. The metal square was somewhat familiar; almost identical to one he'd seen before, so instead he focused his attention on the old piece of paper, unfolding it. It was a drawing in pen and ink - a falcon.

"Well that's interesting," he said to himself, somewhat disappointed. "This is all that's in here? It seems to pose only more questions," he thought, as he put the contents in his vest pocket. Picking up the knapsack of medical supplies that he'd brought, he stood up just as another intense aftershock began to rumble.

Deep within the earth's interior, its crust floated on a superheated mantle, but not as one large piece, but rather as ten major pieces, tectonic plates broken apart, in direct conflict with one another. The Hindu Kush-Kashmir quake was the result of such a conflict, a collision that had been going on for fifty million years.

Carrying the entirety of the Indian subcontinent, the India tectonic plate was crashing into the more massive Eurasian plate, initially at a speed of sixteen centimeters per year, now reduced to a third of that, yet still in motion. As the two giants met, great forces thrust the earth upward in a "mountain generating" process the Greeks defined as *orogeny*.

The Himalaya *orogen* gave Asia an immense mountain range stretching from the plains of Afghanistan to the northeastern border of China and India. In geologic time it was a young topographic relief, still reaching higher, creating the world's tallest water tower, and supplying fresh water for one fifth of the earth's population.

With the lofty geologic upheaval came growing pains, natural stressor releases in the form of volcanic eruptions and earthquakes. In recent years the movement of the Indian plate was responsible for more than the just the large quakes three years before, but also the huge Indonesian interplate earthquake the year before that as it ever so slowly slips under the Burma plate. And each major earthquake was followed by hundreds of secondary quakes and aftershocks, such as the six point two magnitude that was occurring at that very moment.

"Goddamn it," he said as he helplessly watched the ground give way beneath him. His footing completely disturbed, he lost balance, dropping the book and bag of medical supplies. He watched helplessly as the valuable items disappeared under a pile of rocks and debris.

Luckily unhurt, he looked up to see the side of a steep hill nearest him, only a hundred meters away, begin to break up, and turn into a deadly rockslide. Bulldozing through the remnants of the north side of the village, it pulverized temporary shelters, survivors and rescuers. Screams from the injured, perhaps a dozen or so, some young, most not, could be heard as Bryan picked himself up, aided by the SAS commando.

Grabbing the dropped items, they hurriedly made their way with others to the rescue area, running across broken land as fast as they could to render help. It was an unconscious, involuntary reaction. Most people just did it.

"Hurry, people are buried. We need to get them out, quick – help us," a man screamed in English at them as they ran hard uphill to the pileup of trees, rocks, earth, and people.

They began pulling away boulders, boards, and whatever was in the way. Rescue was priority number one, and as he pried away debris, he could see a hand, a mangled arm, and then a face. It was a woman; she was alive. They pulled her to freedom and to life; now for the next person, and so on. Amazingly, all survived. They were the lucky ones, lucky that others were there to help, or else their fate would have been sealed, like so many others before.

Moving away from the steep hillside slopes of the village, they joined an endless procession of survivors, many badly injured and being carried. Over the next fifteen hours they trudged along en masse, solemn, across a small, narrow valley, over a ridgeline and down to a glacial lake, arriving mid morning. The banks provided the flattest and best area for rescue helicopters conducting relief flights out of the earthquake zone to hospitals in Rawalpindi and Peshawar. The steep cliffs of the surrounding terrain were also far enough away from the mobile hospital so as not to pose an immediate threat to relief workers when an avalanche did occur.

In the center of four tents for triage were Shamema, three English volunteers, and an American from the International Rescue Corps, administering emergency medical assistance to the critically injured. They were surrounded by dozens of hurt and homeless, thousands more were on their way.

Shamema looked up, brushing her light brown hair to the side, smiling at Bryan, her bright blue eyes registering deep feelings of gratitude for his being there, and maybe something more. He handed her the medical kit as he spoke, "Morphine, antiseptics, antibiotics, and a few odds and ends."

"Thank you, thank you so much," she answered, putting her hand on his face. He looked tired, she thought. She wanted to help him too.

"Just a start and probably won't last you an hour," he said, noting the medical emergency camp was already being overwhelmed.

"Yes, but at least a start," she said, her eyes sparkling with hope.

She was a beautiful person, both inside and out, he believed.

Another rumble from an aftershock stopped them in mid conversation. Several people strolling near the lakeshore were knocked to the ground. In the distance, a gigantic ice sheet that was part of a cirque, previously cracked and dislodged from numerous tremors finally gave way and began a slide into the dark lake, the displacement creating a five-foot wall of water. The wave, and smaller ones, moved in all directions towards the banks. The panicked ran haphazardly in all directions, frightened for their lives. But as swiftly as the shockwave arrived, it dissipated, sparing more from being hurt. All breathed a sigh of relief.

Bryan calmly resumed, "Shamema, I spoke with officials in Islamabad, there's a Chinook helicopter on the way here with more emergency equipment. I'm hoping there'll be several flights coming here - unfortunately their resources are stretched thin."

"Clean towels – can you please ask them to send more clean towels - and bandages?" Anything clean was at a premium.

"We'll call on SATCOM for you, and whatever else you need," he said, putting his arm around her small shoulders.

"Thank you again. I'll make a list for what we need, but I must attend to them first," she said pointing to the crowd outside the tent. "What are they bringing now?" Shamema asked, as she motioned for a man holding a child in his arms to come towards her.

Bryan stepped aside, shocked at the condition of the new patient, whose tattered clothes were covered in dried blood.

"Well besides medicines, antibiotics, I believe generators, lights, and water purification equipment. Two teams have dropped in just to the east of here – they've got fiber optic probes and thermal imaging cameras. Maybe they'll find more survivors," he said, hoping for more rescue, and less recovery, but time was running out.

"I pray that we can do more for them," she said.

"We'll do everything we can," he said, as he rubbed dust stirred by the last aftershock from his eyes.

He looked at the man with the child as Shamema helped the two. A young boy; perhaps only three or four years old - badly injured and near death, eyes partially opened, mouth gaping. He was in dire need. Even the boy's father looked as though he too needed immediate medical attention, clothing torn, soiled with dried blood and dirt. Shamema took the boy from his father; the man's face registering complete hopelessness and loss, his wife and daughter dead, the boy was all he had. Shamema laid the unconscious youngster on a cot.

"He's a high fever, and absolutely dehydrated - I can barely feel a pulse," she said checking his vital signs. "What's his name?" She asked the father in a Dardic dialect of the region.

"Latif," the man said brushing away tears. He began speaking very rapidly to Shamema; she held his hand to calm him.

"His home and village are destroyed, most people are dead. He found his son this morning. The boy was underneath his mother, she protected him as a wall collapsed on top of them - all of his family was lost, his brothers, sisters, wife and daughter," she said, translating for Bryan's sake. Another relief worker approached them to render assistance, he could see the boy was critical and wouldn't last long.

"Wa'da we got ere?" He asked with a heavy Brooklyn accent.

"His name's Latif," Bryan said looking at the boy's near lifeless face, his pupils partially covered by his eyelids.

"Okay little buddy, wha 'da we got? Unconscious – dehydrated – pulse, but slight. Let's get ya goin, we need some fluids in this litta fella, stat," the New Yorker said as he looked for a place on the boy's small body to insert an IV. "He's got nowheres on 'is uppa body that's any good. How's a'bout's your leg Latif, ya tough little guy," he said.

Bryan watched as the American went to work. He was obviously experienced in rapid treatment, as he expertly felt the boy's legs for a good spot to place the needle. The man's hands were big and strong, surprising for a doctor, Bryan thought. In fact, the man himself was powerfully built, like a football player, Bryan concluded.

"There we go, right ere. Tell 'is old man ta start prayin ta Allah," the American said as he finally found the right spot. "Come on now kid – show me what ya got – live," he said, squeezing the bag of saline solution to encourage the flow.

Latif's father, a pathetic site, stood close by sobbing, hungry hands clenched near a heavy heart. He feared the worst, and for good reason, for these survivors the worst was generally the result. The unfortunate man believed his son was already lost, soon to be in a grave with the rest of his family. Then to the father's astonishment, unexpectedly the lifeless face began to show color, and his eyes, big, dark eyes, opened wide, suddenly full of life.

Shamema was cleaning dirt off the boy's face when cries of discomfort bellowed from his tiny mouth, cries of being alive again. Tears of overwhelming joy streamed from his father's face. The Muslim Pashtun from North West Frontier embraced the American, thanking him over and over in Pashto and English. *"Sta na shukria – tahnk you, sta na shukria – tahnk you,"* he said gripping the American's hand with both of his.

"Doctor, the name's Bryan Craig," he said, introducing himself to the fellow American.

"Hey, there - how ya doin – Angelo, John Angelo, and sorry pal, but I'm no doc," he said, as he carefully examined the boy for broken bones and other maladies.

"What kind of medical training do you have then?" Bryan asked curiously.

"Firefighter – ladda twenty four, F D N Y," he said proudly. Now it was beginning to make some sense, Bryan thought, including the man's size and apparent physical strength.

"What brought you here, helping these folks – you know, as a volunteer?" Bryan asked, somewhat surprised.

"What brought me ere? Because they need help - yeah, that's why I'm ere – anyway, I was a medic in the Army too – so I jumped on a plane ta help out. Tol' my wife I'd be back when I got back. Arrived just a couple of hours ago," the firefighter said.

"These people will be very thankful, I'm sure of it," Bryan said looking out at the endless advance from the devastated land.

"I go where people need help, simple as that," John added, as he too looked out at the hoards. Bryan felt pride in meeting a man with such unselfish qualities. A true humanitarian and citizen of the world, he exemplified the best of mankind as a whole, Bryan thought.

"We thank God that all of you have come to help us," Shamema said, as she continued to care for Latif. "We would lose many thousands more without you."

"Yeah, at least we can give em somethin they can hold onto, ya know? That man there," the firefighter said nodding toward the Pakistani man standing by his son's cot. "He's gonna remember I saved his son - an American saved his only son. He'll never forget that. That's how to win their hearts and minds," he emphasized. "Ya see, the best approach is to take the high road, if ya know what I mean."

The high road, what a curious a phrase, Bryan thought.

"I wouldn't doubt you're correct on that one," Bryan said, seeing the irony of a New York firefighter, one who had no doubt lost so much to Islamic terrorists; friends, perhaps a brother or father, yet here in Pakistan helping the helpless. Helping Muslims. No, helping people.

"Captain Craig, sahr, just spoke tae Lieutenant Thomas – 'e says tha's on the way ere, ten minutes tae pick ye up," the British SAS man said as he entered the tent.

"Thanks Sergeant Major. Well, I should get ready to shove off then," Bryan said, turning to Shamema. "I'll be taking this." Bryan held up the book. "But, I'll make sure that it gets back to you safe and sound Shamema," he promised.

She silently nodded her head and smiled.

Bryan stepped outside the tent as the first Chinook was landing nearby, throwing up dust as the pilot searched for a level place to set down. The firefighter and Shamema were rushing the boy and IV to the helicopter; he wasn't out of the woods just yet, the next few hours would be critical. The emergency flight would take the boy, and as many injured as the helicopter could safely carry, to the Holy Family Hospital in Rawalpindi, a facility with experience in caring for earthquake victims.

As the helicopter flew south and out of site, Bryan faintly heard a jet engine somewhere nearby. Looking up, he tried to follow the sound to its source, finally spotting the aircraft high up in the sky over the lake. It was an F-16 dispatched by the Pakistani Air Force for a quick reconnaissance of new damage caused by the latest aftershocks.

"Hmmm, a falcon," Bryan said to himself, thinking it coincidental, reminding him of the contents in his jacket pocket. He felt for the items, the piece of paper and the tin square, removing them. Studying the drawing again, he admired the artist's quick sketch, and thought it remarkably accurate. He looked at the tin, a family portrait, and he could clearly see Afzal for the first time. Younger than Amir Kahn at the time of the time of the tintype, maybe in his late teens, Afzal looked remarkably similar. *Like twins!* He felt something rough on the back of the tintype. He turned it over and found writing, etched into the metal. He read it. Bryan then pulled the old book out, opening it to the back, suddenly realizing that there was more there. The book had a false back, hiding more pages. He ripped the cloth away. "There's writing here," he said out loud to no one. There were more pages, old pages of handwriting. *Letters, a journal!*

CHAPTER 37

M Y MOST BELOVED ANNE,

Or who else should read my words. Let this be of proof, true to testimony of to the unfortunate events that may have unfolded here, and befallen my charges at the Fort of Chitral, British India. I shall convey my sentiments and leave for those that shall find my journal, in written, and of sound, deliberate mind, those facts. Our nine, all officers of the British army, we are certainly doomed. Time is but the only delay. Seduced through deceit, by yet by what could only be said as commonplace, we are held as captives, with Afzal, the Mehtar, most assuredly having met his demise. My eyes, although wide open to hope, fear that God, in all his benevolence, may not dissuade the plans of Shir and the zeal of the Mahommedans. To all—officers, non-commissioned officers, and men—I return my best thanks for the ready and willing support which was always accorded me in carrying on the duties of my post. With such support and good-will command becomes easy. It will always afford me the greatest pleasure to learn that mutual good-will, ready and willing obedience to authority, a zealous and fearless discharge by all of the duties of their several stations, continue as heretofore to mark their character.

To therefore, I shall place part of my journal here in this book that I gave to the Mehtar in the last year, for the chance that a fortunate God fearing soul, may one day find. Shuja has said he will look after it. I believe him, for he truly is his father's falcon. I love my wife. I miss my children. May God speed, and God Save the Queen.

Captain John Graham Robinson
Royal Engineer Corps
Twenty Six June Eighteen Hundred Ninety Three

10 July 1892
I have been here now for two weeks, and I dare say, am quite tired of trout. The lake is absolutely overflowing with the fish, only trout, and I have explored every possible way of preparing trawl to find another water dweller, to few results. Therefore, the meals have become routine, using all imagination, that in forethought, myself and my Sergeant Major, a good man, have brought. Planning was to of no avail, for he, as for myself, were remiss. I long for simple chips.

11 July 1892
Mr. Kipling, a charming young man from Lahore, and champion of the Viceroy's imperialism, has joined our troupe of few gentleman of England in this Godless place. A man of many interests, he is familiar with the customs of the indigenous subjects, having been born

along with them, but as yet the English chap that he is, first and foremost.

18 July 1892
As routine, Mr. Kipling has quickly opened the heart of the Mehtar, as no diplomat, or offering of Enfield rifles could ever. Kipling's affability may prove to be a fondness that may help to form a hopeful foundation of trustworthiness with the Mehtar.

20 July 1892
Lessons of the previous Afghan campaigns have been, and are chiefly the subject of conversation. Forever an advocate, much to my disagreement, is Kipling, of the policies of the current and previous Viceroys. Occasionally, have the British army succeeded in absolute defeat, yet never without heavy consequences. The impulse, there upon I perceive, is but to satisfy the minority of Parliament, of who maintain control, and as yet however, fail in understanding, but continue to furiously administer war upon those they do not influence. Should the policy of the Crown be that this place is only but a buffer, then I must adamantly disagree.

I have expressed that opinion to Kipling, who whilst playing with a wooden stick, the game of his choice, must always disagree.

He has informed me that the stick is a "Brassie," and the small ball he hits with the peculiar instrument is a "gutta percha." I pray that I shall never have such an attachment to this peculiar endeavor. The game as I understand, is named Golf. Kipling has deemed it as 'a frustrating folly of the idle,' and to be avoided at all costs for one's own sanity.

22 July1892

Kipling and I have spoken at length of the variety of warrior like tribes here in the north area. Sir Durand, having set a timetable for the completion of the British boundaries, has caused uneasiness amongst the numerous Koms and Kafirs. Mehtar Aman, a benevolent and magnanimous ruler, is beset with the trials of his rule.

25 July 1892
Kipling, a soul of discourse as no other, diplomatically has courted the Mehtar's sons; particular to that fact has been the youngest of the ruler's heirs, Shuja. Fixed in Kipling's grasp, as always, has been the brassie, as Shuja, now in schooling of falconry, and both, conversing endlessly, admire each and their mutual fondness of sport. They have been in constant agreement.

I attempted a pen and ink today, of the Mehtar's prized falcon. Kipling praised my attempt. Perhaps I have other skills beyond that of engineering.

30 July 1892
We, having moved from the enchanting place on the lake, have came to a village of heathen idol worshippers, peaceful people called Kalash Kafirs. Ignorant to civilized man, they are a child like culture, and unusual in appearance for other peoples here. Fair and benevolent, the Kalash have only enemies being Kom Kafirs from the opposite boundary of Sir Durand's line. They are converts to Kabul, and I fear their bombastic approach to the proposed boarder may result in an outbreak of misfortune.

03 Agust 1892
A Russian is in our midst, and has, unfortunately, caused a very dire circumstance by killing a Kalash with his pistol. I believe the act to be an act of murder;

*it has but forced a complexion of aggression, here to
fore problematic. The Russian has, as been reported by
Kipling, engaged in deceit at the hand of Kabul. The
Mahommedans fanatics, as hand-grasped by the rule
in Afghanistan, have painted an attractive
circumstance for those in the Mehtar's cadre. In the
peaceful village today, the Russian instigated the
murder of several Kom Kafir. They, being the related
to Kalash, are not necessarily cruel, being kind to
children and to animals, and protective to the weak
and the old. Family ties and the claim of blood even
triumph over jealousy and covetousness. The men
killed were not deserving to be gunned down without
trial, particularly at the hand of the Russian. Kipling
has informed me that there are sinister cabals at work,
and the Russian is complicit in that deceit. Whisked
away are the young, only the young boys, to Kabul,
where in they are learned to become human sacrifices
in the name of their God. It is an affliction that is
encouraged by a decree of the King in Kabul.*

03 Agust1892
*The signs are obvious, yet the Mehtar, always hopeful,
believes that peace will come for all the people,
including the pagans. I am not so sure. The ruler in
Kabul, Amir Abdur Rahman, is at once set about
enforcing his authority, and the curtain partially lifted,
I fear will fall again as it has done before, with misery
and darkness. As for this day, only rumours shall have
been received by the outside world, rumours of
successful invasions, of the wholesale deportation of
boys to Kabul for instruction in the religion of Islam,
of rebellions, of terrible repressions. Now, finally even
rumours have ceased.*

*A powerful Mahommedan has the means of ensuring a
silence which is final, absolute, and nothing will be
ever known from Kabul except what the Amir desires
to be known. Probably larger numbers of the growing*

boys and young men of the Hindu Kush are fanatical Mahommedans, fanatical with the zeal of the recent converts, while the older people and the majority of the population cherish their ancient customs in hiding, worshiping a degraded religion in fear and trembling—waiting dumbly for a sign. I have heard the name for the zealots to be the invasion force of the martyrs. The Yoorish Shaheed, whose goal it is but to have the second coming of their messiah. A Mahommedan so omnipotent that can stand along side Christ as they believe their scriptures to point to, yet may instead result I fear, in a dark cloud that shall fall over everyone for many years."

Bryan folded the old papers as they had been. He'd be back in Dubai the next day.

CHAPTER 38

JUNE 15, 2008

DUBAI

THE THUNDER CLAPPED OVERHEAD as foreboding lightning lit the grey afternoon and skyline, unusual for Dubai.

"I hope you realize the weight of the circumstances that you've brought upon on me," Rodgers Christopher said as he adjusted himself in his seat of the embassy's Cadillac Escalade.

Shannon stared uncomfortably outside the car; water was streaming along the surface of the window as the rain began to fall from the ominous clouds. She listened for Dylan's response, fastening her seatbelt, compensation for their driver's tight turns.

Shannon had spent the last two days researching, building profiles and personality analysis, developing a background report of her own on Amir Kahn and Wazir. Studies that summarized what they knew so far. It was sadly incomplete, she thought. Unfortunately, the SCIF, where she now spent most of her time following Gil's murder, was two doors down from the Consul General's office. The proximity was an open invitation for Rodgers Christopher to routinely share his dissatisfaction over Pegasus' efforts in Dubai, his opinion being the team was more disruptive than helpful. It was Dylan's turn to field Christopher's frustrations as they rode along the highway.

Sitting directly across from the diplomat, Dylan defended his news report, swatting Christopher's critical volleys like a tennis ace at the net, "I don't see the connection between the embassy and the labor camps. I'm simply reportin' on important stories, Rodgers."

"Excuse my dim view, but was it really necessary to stir the pot on the cusp of one of the biggest international business deals ever?" Christopher lamented the veteran journalist. "Let's hope that your report doesn't frighten the U.S. interests away," he said, lightning highlighting his unpleasantness.

Thunder lightly grumbled. "My timing – and my reporting isn't driven by business deals, nor is the intent to bring the deal down," Dylan said, unperturbed. "The story is about people, and their suffering. Clearing this messy business up, and putting an end to the condition the laborers face is in your best interest, don't ya think?"

"Well of course," Christopher responded, sullen over yet another potential disaster. He stared out at the lightning ballet dancing quieter in the distance.

"If there's money to be made, they'll still do the deal mate," Dylan said. "In fact, I remember some Afghan governor wantin' to turn Tora Bora's caves into a vacation resort, in spite of the Taliban and terrorist militants all around the area," Dylan added with a grin. "You'll get your deal done."

"This is not some backwards shit hole - this is Dubai," Christopher said, not appreciating the Australian's wisecrack.

"Then it's a good bet that if ya improve the workin' conditions for the laborers here in this non shit hole, then ya won't have terrorists bein' created under your noses," Dylan said. "Right now you've got the fanatics givin' ya the middle finger."

"Did the story have to be that damn hard hitting though? I mean, Jesus Christ – it almost seemed as though you insinuated that not only are the bad guys using the camps as terrorist Madrasahs, but that the powers that be in Dubai know it and are turning a blind eye to that fact," the Consul General said, now sulking and staring blankly out the window.

Shannon, doing her best not to agitate Rodgers Christopher any further, kept her thoughts to herself. It had been a long day and she was happy to be going back to the hotel, now always accompanied by an armed escort, a Regional Safety Officer. She checked her watch. It was only 5:30. Bryan should be returning sometime early the following morning, and she had a list of things that needed to be addressed, from "A to Z." Tonight though, she was going to self-indulge a little; what a "seven star" hotel could offer would be welcomed. A good, hard workout on the stair-master came to mind, followed by a deep tissue massage, a nice dinner, and then a few hours to jump on some work. It was a perfect plan, she thought.

The car got quiet as they rode along in the rain, and Shannon liked that silence, enjoying the smooth ride of the SUV's state-of-the-art independent suspension. They turned off the main highway following a marked detour. As the driver slowed to negotiate the chicane, Shannon could see several workers in blue on the side of the road, "part of the highway construction," she assumed. They were motioning for the driver to slow even further.

"Menacing looking," Shannon thought, peering out their car at the construction men. She felt safe though, seemingly in a different world, the tight seal of the heavy doors blocking the outside elements, even the noise. Maybe too quiet, she thought; perhaps some music would be nice. But for the moment the three passengers were content to be in their own thoughts. Without warning, their moment of quietude was broken violently by the thunderous noise of a roadside improvised explosive device.

Placed inside of a car parked on the side of the road, the VBIED, or Vehicle Borne IED was fabricated with scavenged munitions, and detonated remotely, enough explosives to throw the two-door BMW into the path of oncoming traffic. The target was the U.S. Embassy's diplomatic SUV and was executed with precision, tossing the BMW directly on the hood of the Escalade. The Consulate driver, doing his best to protect his passengers, braked without swerving, but the force of the three thousand five hundred pound 330i on the hood of the large SUV flipped the Cadillac onto its roof. Dazed and disoriented, the targets were easy game for armed perpetrators, who quickly descended on the disabled vehicle, shooting the driver and the Consulate's Regional Safety Officer. Five minutes later, when Dubai traffic police arrived, they found the wreckage, two dead men, and the vehicle's passengers gone.

CHAPTER 39

JUNE 16, 2008

U.S. EMBASSY, ABU DHABI

C LINGING TO THE EDGE of the cliff with both hands, Bryan was holding on for dear life. He'd nearly reached the summit, only ten feet away, but the Nuristanis were closing fast. A British officer was just above yelling encouragement, begging him to climb faster, give it a little more effort.

"Keep moving Craig. Don't stop. You've got to keep moving higher," the officer yelled.

The British soldier was wearing a uniform of the Empire, the British Indian Army. Dazzling red, his uniform appeared to be ready for inspection, his pith helmet spotless, brilliantly white. Woven gold shoulder boards attached to a red overcoat. "He's an officer, in fact, a captain," Bryan decided. Precariously dangling in the air, one hand gripping a crag above him, in the other he held his Webley .45 caliber service revolver. Between shouts to Bryan, the officer would randomly fire his sidearm at the hoards of Nuristanis below.

"Where in God's name did he get that?" Bryan asked himself, thinking of the vintage weapon.

The Nuristanis were barefooted, effortlessly climbing the steep cliffs, clamoring over each other in waves. Their red turbans belayed a menacing appearance. Some were carrying shields, curved swords, and sheathed I-handled daggers attached to colorful belts. Most were carrying rifles of some sort, each with ornate designs carved into wooden stocks.

He struggled to move at all, a massive effort to climb higher, all the time being encouraged to do so by the Brit. But each movement he made, whether it be his arms, legs, or hands, were in slow motion and nearly impossible, bordering on paralysis.

"For God's sakes man, move - they're at your heels. Climb as never before. You can make it to the top. It'll be safe up there," the Englishman encouraged, the ends of his large mustache fluttering as the officer barked at Bryan. He pointed to the top of the mountain with his revolver. Bryan could barely see the summit. It was white, covered with snow at the top.

Bryan strained with all his might as he tried to go up the side. He was laboring, very tired and it seemed hopeless. He was making very little progress. The British captain had almost reached the goal when he was suddenly snatched off the cliff's wall by a bird. It was a falcon.

Shocked at the fate befalling the Captain, Bryan nevertheless was mesmerized by the grace of the raptor as it carried the man away in its talons. The falcon flapped its wings a few times and circled while the British Officer was continuing to yell at Bryan, seemingly impervious to his own circumstances, and the fact that the predator had him in its clutches.

And then without warning, the falcon released the Captain. He began an endless fall, hollering encouragement to Bryan, tumbling out of sight into a dark abyss. "Go man. You've got to make it," he yelled, pith helmet still riding on his head. The image was unnerving to Bryan.

Impelled to avoid the plight of the British officer Bryan frantically searched for a way out. The Nuristanis were shooting at him with muskets that seemed never to need reloading. And they were everywhere, like bees swarming from a hive.

"Captain Craig. Captain Craig."

"Who is that?" he wondered, hearing the female voice.

"Please come this way. Hurry. Hurry please, before the falcon comes back."

"It's Shamema," he thought. He could see her beautiful eyes. She was pleading with him, beckoning with her hand. Standing on a ledge just ten feet from him, she called to him again. But his body was immobile, paralyzed.

"This way Captain, follow me," she said, turning the corner of the ledge. She was gone, vanished into the recesses of his mind. Another image replaced Shamema, this one pathetic.

"Save us. Please save us," pleaded a very thin man wearing dirty clothing. He was clutching Bryan's arm. Aghast at the man's appearance, he was obviously malnourished. The eyes were tired, darker folds of skin hanging beneath them. The man's face began to draw very close to Bryan's. Suddenly his eyes grew wide with fear as he pointed skyward over Bryan's shoulder. There was no need for Bryan to turn his head; he could see the reflection in the man's pupils. The falcon was returning. His wings were tucked back in attack mode.

Bryan turned and could now see its eyes as the bird was swooping in, talons raised. Its eyes were large, dark, and malevolent. No, wait. Or were they blue, Bryan wondered?

As the bird bore down on him, Bryan's footing gave way. The rocky ground was crumbling around him, tremors shaking the cliffs.

Earthquake! **Bryan woke up**, his arms flailing. A duty officer was staring at him as he lay on the couch.

"That's right, I'm back," he remembered. The dream was vivid. Bryan looked around. *Must have zonked out!*

A solemn mood hung over the Embassy in Abu Dhabi. Although far from out of the ordinary, especially in places such as Iraq, or Afghanistan, even Pakistan, assassinations, bombings, or kidnapping were rare occurrences in the U.A.E, let alone an American target. Everyone associated with the embassy felt the pain, a direct attack on Americans. Remarkably, the Consul General and the journalist had been released. The significance, Bryan could only venture to guess: unsure as to why only Shannon was held. Maybe a ploy, designed to attract him only, he wondered?

Rodgers Christopher was in the Hospital with a broken neck, a hairline fracture very close to causing complete paralysis, yet miraculously had not. Dylan Sizemore was fine, other than a few bumps and bruises. The driver and an embassy security person were shot at close range during the attack. Shannon was missing, no word as yet from he abductors.

Having just arrived at the compound by Black Hawk, Bryan went straight to the SCIF and organized assets in preparation for a rescue. He was thankful they'd taken precautions earlier having insisted on a nano-tracker. Drumming his fingers on his thigh as he waited, he checked his watch, 9:45 AM. Dylan arrived at the SCIF from the hospital moments later.

"Glad you're back and unhurt," Bryan said, standing up to greet his war reporter buddy.

"I wouldn't worry so much about me, mate – jest doin' my job. What about you anyway? I heard you've had some excitement in the last several days," Dylan said, making a beeline for the freshly brewed coffee pot being held up by the duty officer.

"I'm doin' my job, too. Tell me what happened."

"We'd just come off Zayed Highway, turning ta the Burj al Arab. That's where we were hit," Dylan said, taking a cup of the java. "I'd my seatbelt on, an so did Shannon. When we flipped upside down, I guess we stayed in place. Rodgers went flying, got the worst of it – of course, except for the RSO and the driver."

"Did you see them?" Bryan asked.

"There were four that came to the car, their faces were covered by checkered schumaggs - then they bagged our heads, throwing us in vehicle of some sorts - maybe a van or SUV – not really sure – smooth ride though," Dylan said, thinking about previous rougher blindfolded trips he'd been on.

"There wasn't any traffic video surveillance available – the cameras were out," Bryan said. "And that's when the driver and the RSO were shot?"

"They may've been dead before that – I mean it was fuckin' violent – the explosion, and then the fuckin' BMW landin' on the damn hood," Dylan answered. "I heard the gun shots after we were tossed in the other car."

"What about Rodgers?" Bryan asked.

"We were all taken away together at first. Then they threw him out on the highway after a few minutes, they might've thought he was nearly dead anyway," Dylan said, seeing the Ambassador enter the secure room.

"They're right, he was nearly dead, and still unconscious – we're flying him to Germany once they can stabilize him. He'll undergo surgery there," the Ambassador said. "But you don't seem to be any worse for the wear, Dylan."

"What about Kevin Davis?" Bryan asked, surprised at the absence of the CIA man.

"He'd left the consulate probably about an hour before us," Dylan said.

"I understand he's following up on a few things right now," the Ambassador said. "Had a message from him."

"Back to the captors, did they give you any instructions?" Bryan asked.

"None, never said a word to me until I was let go. Just gave me the CD-ROM," Dylan said, removing it from the pocket of his jacket. They popped it in a computer.

The disc was of Shannon, dressed in a full burqa, all black. Only her eyes were visible as she sat against a blank wall, flanked by two men, their faces also covered by schumaggs. Watching the video without sound, they wouldn't have any idea who it was, but she said her name as she spoke for the camera. Bryan recognized her voice right away, although speaking in Arabic; she still had the Indiana, Midwestern flatness to her accent. She was delivering a standard hostage speech, read from a prepared statement by her captors, announcing the name of the group as Yoorish Shaheed. Which was all Bryan needed to hear to jump into action immediately.

"Mister Ambassador, I think it's time that I get to work – I don't want Shannon there any longer than she needs to be," Bryan said.

"Of course the Dubai police don't have anything yet, but I take it your not waiting for their authorization," the Ambassador said. Bryan only smiled, enough of an answer for the diplomat to understand. "Gentleman, if you'll excuse me. I think this is the part I don't need to hear. I believe my clearance doesn't go that high," Ambassador Evans said as he got up to leave the room. "Glad you're doing fine Dylan – good luck, Bryan."

"Dylan, you feel like going back on the air again?" Bryan asked after Evans left the room.

"Wha' da need mate?"

"Hold on a sec," Bryan said, picking up his cell phone. He called Madrid, and after confirming tight surveillance of the Russian girls, and the location, ordered their immediate capture.

"I need a spot this afternoon – a spot on the Yoorish Shaheed again. That you were captured by them, they let you go and gave you certain information on a disc that you've turned over to proper authorities and so forth," Bryan suggested, thinking he should throw out some more bait. "No details other than 'reliable sources have indicated it's being studied by counter-terrorism experts, and could lead to a major break in the Memorial Day bombings'."

"Is that exactly how ya want me ta say it?" Dylan said with a chuckle.

"Sorry, didn't mean to write your copy, but at the end of the piece I want you to segue to the Russian girls and Gil's death. Let's play that card now."

"I think I can come up with something that'll work for ya," Dylan assured him.

Three hours later, Dylan was on the air live with a classic "Breaking News" report. The trap was set.

* * * * *

JUNE 16, 2008

DUBAI

Robert Rowley was deeply concerned, and for good reason, a potential personal windfall was unraveling before his eyes, rapidly becoming a nightmare. In a rare moment of dark humor, he chuckled at the image of himself in his own episode of the "Twilight Zone." He feared for more than just the end of a bright career though, or even the possibility of prison. He knew it could be much worse. Rowley had jumped to the "dark side" for personal gain and a grab at money. More than he ever could have imagined. But know he was in bed with unforgiving types, who had little regard for life, especially that of an infidel.

Rowley thought of Petrov, and his demise, hoping that he may somehow be spared the same fate. He didn't perceive himself as being evil like the Russian. Maybe there was a chance Wazir would spare him, possibly even help him to escape, to hide from authorities. He reasoned that Wazir would recognize the benefits, possibly appreciate his skill, an expertise that would still be useful. There was a possibility to cover up the damage caused by Gil Bussmann's work, he thought.

"Damn those bastards," Rowley said. He was incensed over the skills of a dead man, one that had so quickly disassembled what took him years to build, and equally incensed with a certain Australian journalist. He replayed the end of the news report that aired just five hours earlier, a DVR recording of Dylan Sizemore.

"In a related story, top counter-terrorism officials from the United States and Great Britain have apprehended two suspects wanted in connection with the death of an American embassy official, killed in Malaga, Spain one week ago. The suspects, Russian citizens, Marfa Popov and Victoria Hubik, pictured in custody here..." the newscast cut to the women being led into a police van by Spanish authorities. "With known residences in Spain and Dubai, are said to be cooperating with investigators. Officials have said the murder may have been connected to an ongoing investigation of the Memorial Day Bombings."

Rowley turned off the conference room television. He couldn't bear seeing the report another time, but was somehow addicted to it, a story foretelling his own fate. The women would directly link him with Petrov, and beyond the Russian being only a client of the bank. Hush money and pay-offs, bribes – Rowley was sure he'd be ruined, that was a certainty. So he waited and sullied about the bank.

The conference room was dark, the only light coming from the display in the center of the table, the Burj al Baaz spiraling upward towards the ceiling, lit up in multiple hues of blue, and fuchsia. As he stared at the hologram of the immense Baaz development, Rowley's heavily pock marked faced looked eerie, more lunar in the strange light. He'd been sitting, almost motionless for ten minutes, still breathing heavily, close to a wheeze, waiting.

His secretary announced over the intercom, "Excuse me sir, but he's on his way up. Should I just have him come straight back, as you wanted?"

"Send 'im back" Rowley said.

"It's 6:00 PM, I'm leaving for the day then," she said.

"Good night,"

The glass door of the conference room was closed. Inside the room Robert Rowley held his head down, forlorn. He never heard the footsteps approaching; never saw the man ease the door open. Rowley looked up, his face again lit from the hologram. Now breathing harder, his heart raced. He smiled grimly and started to speak. Before he could utter a word, the silence was broken by the hissing "phump," of a Walther P5 suppressed by a silencer. Matter from the exit wound splattered on the glass pane in back of his chair as he tumbled onto the marble floor with a thud. The man calmly walked around the conference table and looked down at Rowley's large body sprawled against the glass wall of the room. The banker's mouth was gaped open, his eyes dilating and blank, an entry wound in the center of his forehead. The shooter was amazed to see Rowley's chest still heaving, a wheeze accompanying the vegetative exhale. The muzzle now aimed directly at the heart, the trigger was squeezed twice more. The killer, satisfied with his work, quickly exited the private bank, carefully stepping over the body of the secretary on his way out.

Unusual circumstances sometimes require a unique response, Bryan recalled. Thankfully, Shannon had the embedded tracker under the skin in her arm. He knew where to look; she was in the Burj al Baaz. He'd need to move fast. There was only a slim chance the abductors would find her nano-tracker, but a chance he nevertheless didn't want to take.

Kevin Davis nervously eyeballed his cell phone as it vibrated. Closing a door in back of him for privacy, he finally answered.

"You're no longer MIA, where ya been?" Bryan asked.

"Just following up on some leads I've got. My Dubai sources tell me that she's being held somewhere in the Burj al Baaz," Kevin said. "And I think it may be a valid tip. The building, in fact an entire block, has just gone black. Could be the unusual weather."

"The power grid to the block's out?" Bryan asked, doubting the weather explanation.

"Yep, I'm at the base of the building now – waiting for them to restore power. There's no way to get in right now," Kevin said. "I understand you're at the embassy in Abu Dhabi?"

"Yeah, that's right – arrived earlier today."

"It's gonna be at least a couple of hours before they get power back on, maybe more - I've seen this happen before, usually a construction snafu, and these incompetents are slow as shit around here," Kevin explained.

Curious about Kevin's "Dubai sources," Bryan asked, "Where did you get your information about Shannon?"

"Can't go into that over the phone. Let's just say it's the same source where I got the info on Petrov," Kevin replied calmly.

Bryan thought hard before making the next statement. "I know for certain that Shannon is that building."

"Do you know what floor she's on?" Kevin asked quietly.

Why's he whispering? "I don't," Bryan said, not wanting to give up any more information. "But I'm going to find her."

"Like I said before, the power's out, so you're gonna have to be patient - even the emergency generators are out, it'd be impossible to find her in that place without power anyway, even if ya got in somehow."

"Can't wait," Bryan said.

"Well don't pull any John Wayne shit, I'm workin with the locals here on gettin things going – then if she's there..."

Bryan interrupted. "That's not your lane Kevin, so stay out of it," he demanded of the CIA man.

"Hey, fuck you. I'm not lettin my career go down the drain because some FBI shrink gets whacked on my watch. This ain't gonna be another Dubai Ports for me," Kevin seethed.

Bryan ignored Kevin's last comment, closing the connection. A disturbing departure from Kevin's demeanor, Bryan thought. Confirming the power blackout at the work site, Bryan concluded the outage was intentional sabotage. Based on the telemetry from the tracker, Shannon was near the top of the building, and coming in from the observation deck was one way to get in, the other alternative being two hundred stories of stairs. He'd check the satellite imagery to see what he was dealing with.

"Fortunately for ye boss, we've been keepin' daily updates on Dubai since you an' those billionaires were there – this is from this afternoon when we 'ad the last bird fly over," DJ said as he zoomed in on the skyscraper. "Fortunately, there was a break in the clouds, et's a good image." he added.

Bryan followed along on a large monitor at the SCIF. It didn't look promising at first glance, the building was nearly complete, and all constructions cranes gone, yet he noticed something. "The observation deck is covered and there's an overhang, what's that rectangular thing there off the side?" Bryan asked, seeing a strange anomaly.

"Et looks like a powered platform of sorts, boss," DJ said after zooming in and fine-tuning the focus.

"The kind for washing windows," Bryan suggested. "Should be an easy way in from up there."

"Most likely, yeah – they probably just washed the buildin' for the VIPs. Yeah, thet's it, aye can see a roof anchor 'ere, which means when the bloke's done washin', 'e's got ta get in," DJ said. "Must be through the observation deck."

"Yeah, I concur with that conclusion," Bryan said, beginning to mentally prepare for the coming task. Coming up though the stairwell was out of the question. Three thousand feet straight up would take too long once he was on site, and the stairwells were surely being monitored for anyone ascending. "I guess coming in from above is to my advantage," Bryan said, noting the time – it was 8:05 PM.

"I can lower you from our winch Captain, I've had harder assignments – just don't ask me to try and land on it," the Marine Corps Second Lieutenant said confidently, confirming it could be done. "Anybody going to be shooting at us?"

"Let's hope not," Bryan said, thinking the quiet blades, and darkness would allow him to get in undetected. "Ready to launch?"

"Yes sir, whenever you're ready."

Suited up for night special ops, Bryan was ready. "Let's roll."

The flight to the Burj al Baaz was surreal, a commando mission that Bryan had not anticipated. Fortunately he been prepared for it though, ingrained in his training from years as a Navy SEAL. But this mission would have severe international repercussions if things went array. He thought about Shannon, the victims of the attacks, the young boy – Danny, and of Shamema; her people. It made sense to him; he had to do what was necessary. Lastly, he thought about his father.

"Captain Craig, I've got embassy on the radio for you – it's urgent," the pilot said, pointing to a headset on the cabin wall. Bryan picked up the headset. It was the Ambassador.

"Bryan, passing some news – Robert Rowley and his assistant were found murdered at their bank. They were both shot. It was professional. That's it, just wanted to let you know," the Ambassador told him and hung up. Bryan thought about what the Ambassador had said, now convinced that his decision to get Shannon now, was the correct one. *But who killed Rowley? Was it because of the news story?*

Coming in on the world's tallest building from above gave him a view of the entire city, from one end to the other. It was spectacular at night; the modern world's Metropolis. The building's spire came into view, the skyscraper pitch black, as well as several blocks around the building. Then the rain came, not a thin veil, but a blanket, a downpour.

"This is not good sir," the pilot said as Bryan pulled on his black watch cap and night vision goggles.

"I'm an all weather SEAL, son," Bryan said with grin. "Get me hooked up," he directed the crewman, who did so in disbelief. After Bryan stepped into the harness, the staff sergeant fastened the locking hook from the winch, tugging on it to be sure. Bryan felt for his side arm, before stepping out into the rain, prop wash, and wind. The platform was just below him, seventy-five feet. The ground was more than a half of a mile below that.

"Just try to get me close. I'll grapple it and pull myself in the rest of the way," Bryan said as he checked his watch, it was just after 9:00 PM. He stepped out. The pilot gave a thumb's up, and began his approach, the winch operator lowering Bryan towards the building. His body spinning initially as he came down, he steadied the rotation by grabbing onto the thick wire above his head. It was wet, and he was already soaked. He said a prayer that the night-vision goggles would hold up.

Shannon wrists were beginning to feel the irritation of the ropes that kept them together. Although she could see her captors, they'd long since removed any blindfold, she didn't believe her life was threatened, other than the possibility of being killed during a disastrous rescue attempt. She'd come to the conclusion that Wazir wanted her alive. The men had been talking to her, generally a good sign, and in particular, Wazir, who was intrigued over her aptitude with languages. He'd conversed with her in Arabic, Urdu, Pashto, and also Spanish, however the topics were light.

An irony, she thought, her abduction gave her an opportunity to study her subject matter close at hand. If she got out of the situation alive, she'd have quite a bit more on the job research available for her report, she reasoned. Puzzlingly to her though, she was never interrogated. Her captors were actually kind, asking if she'd sustained any injuries, seemingly concerned for her welfare. Therefore, she was the one asking questions, however, rarely answered when the subject was about their organization's goals.

"What are you trying to accomplish," she asked Wazir, who was holding a large flashlight pointing at the ceiling, illuminating the twelve by fourteen foot room with dim yellow light. Failing to respond, she'd directed a question at one of the four other men in the room, "Are you laborers from Pakistan?"

"Please don't ask them questions, doctor," Wazir said, pointing the flashlight at her face.

"They're wearing blue laborer clothing – I just wanted to know their feelings, you know, how they're being treated at work," she said squinting from the beam.

"You want to know this, and in the situation you're in?" Wazir asked with a laugh. "You should worry for yourself, not for them."

"I believe it must be relevant, or they wouldn't be apart of ..." She stopped herself in mid sentence.

"Of what, doctor? What I've done, or about our cause, perhaps?" Wazir asked.

"That's what I was going to say," Shannon said, listening for emotion of any kind from Wazir.

"It's something you can't understand, no matter how many people you analyze," Wazir said coldly.

Realizing the depth of her captor's intelligence, and the complexity of his personality, Shannon fished for more information, "What prompted you to become this way?"

"Your question is foolish, but I admire your persistence, and your bravery. You're a woman that should be admired. A woman like my sister," Wazir said.

"Your sister, tell me about her? What did she do that's worthy of such admiration?" Shannon asked, seeing an opening into the terrorist's psyche. *Maybe he's not a complete sociopath?*

Wazir pointed the beam back at the ceiling. "Very clever doctor, and I can see what you're attempting to do - so I will tell you this – she risked her life to save and protect what she loved under the worst circumstances imaginable."

"Protect you how?"

"I didn't say protect me, and I think we've spoken enough for now," Wazir said, now bored with the conversation.

Bryan's boots touched down on the non-skid metal of the powered platform that hung directly below the unfinished observation area. Double-paned windows were stacked on the deck above still waiting to be fit on the steel framing. He unhooked his harness, signaling to the Black Hawk that he was safely on the building. He looked down following the flight of the rain droplets falling alongside the darkness of the unlit glass and steel.

He cleared left and right seeing a small dome shaped glass object near the temporary ceiling of the observation deck. "A security camera - must be inop," he figured. "Okay up and over," he said as he clamored onto the covered area. It was dry there. He pulled out a rag and began wiping himself down.

Now less soaked than he'd been moments before, he decided to investigate the surveillance system further. Security was maintained by a skeletal crew until completion of the building, and with the power out, the system would be out too. Nevertheless, Bryan checked the camera's dome as best he could. It was out of his reach, but it appeared to be disabled. So he pressed on looking for the way inside. *"Who could be watching anyway?* As he moved away, the camera's aperture widened, tracking Bryan's movements in the darkness.

Walking the perimeter of the unfinished area, he found the steps to the two hundredth floor, and the door. It was locked, but easy to pick open. Using a tension tool and a narrow straight pick, Bryan maneuvered the tumbler pins.

"Come on," he said, coaxing the pins to open. "Bingo." He turned the doorknob, opening the observation deck door. The nano-tracker put Shannon somewhere between one ninety-five and one ninety, and of course, with a margin of error that might have her higher or lower; he'd check each floor. Fortunately, the massive building spiraled to the spire, and the top ten floors were much smaller spaces, about four thousand square feet each. He'd simply follow the dot to Shannon using the hand held GPS, but first, he had to find the stairwell.

Stepping into the hallway, it was dark, and without emergency lighting, impossible to navigate without a flashlight or night vision goggles. He wiped the water off the lenses and fixed them over his eyes. Walking carefully, measured steps, he turned a corner after clearing the hallway. The space was still unfinished, drywall and cement ground marking time for marble cover. The night vision goggles flickered once, and then failed completely.

"Fuckin piece of shit," Bryan silently said to himself as he fumbled with the technology, realizing water must have gotten inside the old goggles. "Might as well be in a cave," he thought. He pulled out a red, directional penlight, providing little illumination for his periphery, but enough to keep him from running into any wall that might be directly in his path. He stood motionless for a time, his eyes adjusting to the darkness. He heard some voices, followed by a deafening sound and bright light. Bryan flattened under a door jam.

Three loud gunshots and their brilliant, white muzzle flashes had gotten his attention. They came from around the very next corner. The momentary light from the shots revealed a clear lane down the hallway. Bryan pulled out his Heckler & Koch .45 and moved quickly, but silently, toward the source.

CHAPTER 40

JUNE 16, 2008

DUBAI

FINDING THE WAY OUT and who fired the gun was Bryan's first and foremost concern, and without getting shot in the process. He prayed that Shannon wasn't hurt, or at least, still alive.

Turning the corner, he could feel under his first few steps that the floor had changed from cement to marble. Suddenly he slipped, landing hard and dropping the penlight as he slid along the slick floor. Putting a hand down to get up, he slipped again, the cause - a warm, tacky liquid. He was covered in it. His immediate thought was that some cleaning oil hade been spilled, but then he could smell the familiar thick essence hanging in the air. It was blood.

Bryan felt a body just as the red emergency lighting blinked on. Some power was restored, and he had the blinking red lights, along with a loud, irritating alarm. Bryan looked at the body. It was a Paki laborer, and he was dead and laying face down, an exit wound on the back of his head, blood saturating his blue clothing to an indigo hue. The man had been shot multiple times, once in the neck, hitting an artery, which explained the massive amount of blood on the hallway floor. *But who'd done this?*

He heard a door slam; a heavy sound, like an emergency exit door. Picking himself up, Bryan ran to where he believed the source of the noise emanated. "It's close by," he thought. Reaching the door and quietly opening it, he could hear the sound of a struggle from perhaps two or three flights below. He heard another single gunshot.

"Quick, move," a familiar voice commanded, followed by the sound of another door open and close. "It's Kevin," Bryan thought, perplexed. "How the hell did he get up here?"

Making his way quietly down the emergency steps, Bryan found another body, Wazir, shot once in the chest. But he was alive, just barely, and as the wounded man turned his head seeing Bryan, he smiled. Wazir motioned for him to come closer; he wanted to say something.

Bryan held Wazir's head as the dying man whispered, "You should grow your beard again." He coughed and added, "*Baaz.*"

"What?" Bryan remarked, startled, surprised, his mind racing. *Did he say Baaz?*

"Talk to me Wazir."

"You know me Captain Craig," he said in Pashto with a slight smile, his voice weak and drifting off.

"Talk to me, damn it," Bryan demanded. The man's eyes were glassy and his words barely audible. Bryan put his ear directly on the man's lips, hoping to hear something, anything. He felt the warm faintness of Wazir's fading breath. The fanatic's words echoed loudly in Bryan's mind, stirring deep memories, drowning the clamor of the alarm. Bryan's eyes widened as the man spoke one final time, loud enough to be heard.

"*Ma as-salama - Baaz,*" he said, exhaling, and then was dead.

Cracking the door just enough to peak down the hallway, Bryan saw Kevin getting in an elevator with someone. He was armed and with a woman in full black burqa, a hood over her veil and her hands tied. He assumed it was Shannon. They were alone. The doors closed.

"One ten - they've stopped on Amir's floor," Bryan said to himself as he waited for the next elevator. The hundred and tenth floor was still one of the few currently occupied. Arriving at the floor, he found it completely powered, running on its own backup generators. Bryan walked the ornate private hallway to the main entrance of what was Amir's office/residence in Dubai. The passageway was as elaborate as he would've presumed, including a large double door, which was open. There was a security camera above it. "Someone is watching this after all," Bryan realized, as he quietly continued down a beautiful granite hallway, lined with jasmine shrubs. Just then he heard shouting - it was Kevin.

Peering into the massive main room, Bryan saw three people. The woman in the burqa no longer had the hood, but her back was to him. He knew it was Shannon, who standing next to Kevin was facing Amir.

The Sultan smiled. "Captain Craig, nice of you to join us," Amir said, as Kevin and Shannon turned to look.

"Come on in Bry - glad you're finally here - I was just gonna call you," Kevin said glibly, his gun pointed at Amir. Bryan strolled in, his handgun at his side, positioning himself ten feet from Amir, who was calmly standing with his gyrfalcon on a gloved arm, the other behind his back. Taking in his surroundings, Bryan counted no less than eight surveillance cameras.

"I think this is our man, Bry," Kevin added. "He's the one that was in back of it all."

"Is that so?" Amir said coolly.

"You're goin down Amir," Kevin said smiling. "And put your other fuckin hand where I can see it."

"Are you okay, Shannon?" Bryan asked. She nodded her veiled head. "Put the gun down, Kevin," Bryan added, motioning for Shannon to move away from him.

"What are ya talkin about? Here's the face for the wanted poster," Kevin said motioning the gun at Amir. "And put that fuckin bird down before I blow his head off," he added.

"I don't think so Kevin - the face for the wanted poster is upstairs where you left him. But you left him alive, not dead," Bryan said.

"What?" Kevin asked, dismayed. "That's impossible."

"I spoke with him before he died - I know everything Kevin – the bogus bank accounts; Rodgers Christopher – you put the files into the Embassy computer under his name; the contract on Gil, and the fact it was me that you tried to have killed in Pakistan," Bryan moved toward him while he was speaking. "So put the gun down," Bryan added, as he raised his own weapon at Kevin.

"You've got nothin – it's him, Amir Kahn," Kevin said, grabbing Shannon's arm, pulling her close, his gun now at her head, hammer cocked.

"Kev, please..." Shannon started to say before being silenced by Kevin's grip.

"Shut up bitch, I don't really care for your analysis at this point," he said, with one hand on her throat, his small fingers barely maintaining a grip. "Now you put your gun down, Bry. Ya hear me?"

"Kevin, there's no way out for you. We can link you to the bombings, the accounts, even Petrov's phony staffing company," Bryan said, seeing the fear in his eyes.

"I said put your fuckin gun down before I scatter her brains all over the room."

"Easy Kevin. Now watch me carefully, I'm going to put the gun down." Bryan said, both hands rose in the air, his finger off the trigger.

"Yeah, just put the gun down there and kick it away from you," Kevin ordered.

"No problem Kevin, just calm down, we don't want anyone else killed," Bryan said hoping for Kevin to calm down and lower his guard.

Setting the handgun on the white marble floor, Bryan noticed the falcon keeper's equipment by the Patio of Lions fountain, including the lure, only five feet away. As he stood up, he kicked the gun halfway in the direction of Kevin. "How's that? Bryan asked as he stepped toward the lure.

"The bombings weren't my idea. I had nothin to do with them - that was all Wazir and Petrov," Kevin offered nervously. "And I said put the damn bird on the perch," he demanded again of Amir.

"I was told something very different, Kevin - that you're the one that gave up the security camera plan. It was also your idea to frame Christopher, which must be why you targeted cities connected to PDI," Bryan said. "What did Wazir promise you Kevin? Did he say that you'd get equity in the development, maybe a vig from the laborer racket – or was it just plain old cash?"

"Shut up," Kevin yelled.

"The plan Wazir had in mind included you taking the fall, Kevin," Bryan continued, startling Kevin, as if he learned it for the first time. "Wazir set you up, don't you get it? All part of his master plan, and now there's nowhere for you to go. Just give it up," Bryan said, looking at Amir, as he got closer to the lure.

"Why should I do that?" Kevin said, nervously shuffling his feet.

"The Dubai police are downstairs Kevin, and soon the embassy MPs will be here as well. Now that the emergency power back on, they should be up here any minute," Bryan said, bluffing.

"That's good for me then, isn't it?" Kevin said, looking to his left at Amir. Bryan motioned with his eyes at a camera for Shannon; maybe she could see that he had something in mind. Her eyes follow his. She nodded he head.

"Did you already forget, I've got the gun," Kevin said, pressing the barrel with into Shannon temple. She stiffened. "It'll just look like I'm the only one left, but saved the day by killing the kingpin and his henchman," Kevin explained as a matter of fact. "You and the Doc here - were just unfortunate collateral damage."

"Why'd you do it Kevin?" Bryan asked, noting the make of the handgun in Kevin's hand, a Walther P5, the same gun from the Mercedes glove compartment.

"To get what I have coming, that's why."

"From whom, Kevin? Who owes you so much that'd you'd resort to such extreme measures?" Shannon asked, her black veil billowing as she spoke hurriedly.

"Just shut up bitch," Kevin retorted, but after thinking for a moment, offered a limited explanation. "Our urbane Consul General fucked me over, that's about all you need to know."

Shannon shook her head. "You planned this to get back at Rodgers Christopher because he blamed the failure of PDI on you?" Shannon said. "That's all?"

"You never shut up, do you," Kevin said, becoming increasingly fidgety. He moved the gun haphazardly, carelessly. The stress was getting to him. "Alright, we're gonna take a little walk. The four of us." Kevin and Shannon moved towards the entrance, stepping backwards, as Bryan and Amir kept their ground.

"That's why you chose to attack the cities with ties to the deal," Shannon said.

"I said I didn't plan that, so quit sayin I did."

"But you did nothing to stop it - all those people killed. Innocent people, whose lives were taken away, their families' lives ruined; just for revenge?" Shannon asked, pressing him more.

"Don't you get it? My hands were tied, I couldn't do anything – they'd kill me, or my family. So I decided to get my payback. My 'fuck you money' for a career ruined by a bunch of assholes," Kevin said angrily. "PDI was not my fault, but I took the rap for it."

Bryan could see he was nearly overwrought and if he panicked, could begin shooting indiscriminately. Bryan moved closer to the lure, almost on top of it. Noticing Bryan's position, and reading what he had in mind Amir, lowered his hand on the perch, fingers next to the creance. They were ready, and in synch with each other. Needing a distraction, Bryan improvised.

"So are you going to shoot us with your gun?" Bryan asked.

Kevin to turned his hand to see the weapon, moving the gun away from Shannon's head. He looked at the handgun, baffled. "What the fuck?"

Bryan added "And I believe you, when you said that you had nothing to do with the mall security camera plans, I mean, you aren't smart enough, are you?"

"What?" Kevin asked, looking back at Bryan.

"After all, someone with that kind of smarts wouldn't have said what you said – at least not with eight security cameras recording them," Bryan said, smiling and pointing up at the twenty-foot ceilings. "Would they?"

Looking up, Kevin released Shannon's neck. Centering her energy, as she was instructed to do at Quantico, she readied herself.

"What the…" Kevin's sentence was halted by the onset of intense pain resulting from the force of Shannon's heel into his groin, a direct hit. The years of stair-master had paid off. She sidestepped with her left foot, then pivoted and swung her bound hands, clenched together, as hard as she possibly could; a two handed backhand striking Kevin hard in the face. He staggered several steps, injured and dazed. Still in agony from Shannon's assault, he righted himself, as the lure, perfectly tossed by Bryan, landed over his shoulder. Immediately excited at the sight of prey, the falcon launched from ten feet away. Kevin looked up at the incoming hunter; wings fully outstretched four feet, talons aimed directly at the target of prey. He fired the gun haphazardly twice, one bullet passing harmlessly between the falcon's tail feathers, the second hitting a wall.

The sharp talons of the raptor struck Kevin's chest and neck, digging in. Shrieking, he swung his arms wildly as the blood vessels in his paltry skin gave way, small droplets of blood immediately appearing on his golf shirt. The handgun now hanging down at Kevin's side, Bryan moved into him. Recalling rugby days of old, Bryan hit him hard, lifting him in the air, and throwing him into a marble column. Kevin's head cracked against the hard surface, and he collapsed to floor, unconscious. Bryan retrieved Kevin's gun, stuffing it in back of his pants and then looked for his own.

Walking over to Shannon, Bryan remarked, "I don't ever want to play tennis against you - are you okay?"

"I'm fine," she said, "Just untie my hands and let me get this damn burqa off." Bryan pulled out his knife as he looked at Amir. The Sultan was coaxing the gyrfalcon back on the perch with a treat.

"Your predator's learning, isn't she," Bryan said.

"Yes, indeed she is," Amir said, stroking the gyrfalcon's chest.

Hearing a moan, Bryan looked toward Kevin. Three men in blue, faces covered with red-checkered schumaggs, were with Kevin. Two of the men quickly dragged him away. The third, slightly built, raised a SIG 550 assault rifle as Bryan reached for his .45. The man shook his head. Bryan could see the man's eyes, a vivid blue, piercing, staring directly into his own. Someone whistled, the man turned and left.

"He has nowhere to go Captain," Amir announced, grabbing Bryan's arm with his large hand, restraining him from the chase.

Bryan heard what sounded like the hollow sound of a steel pipe making contact with something, followed by a loud grunt. He looked at Amir, who let go of his arm. Reaching the elevator, Bryan saw the doors close, the elevator bound for the two hundredth floor.

"He's gone. They took him to the top," Bryan said returning to the main room. "Who are they Amir, some of Wazir's men, or are they yours?" Amir didn't answer.

"What's going to happen to him?" Shannon asked.

"Only what's necessary, I'm afraid – but the important thing is that you're safe," Amir said. He pointed a remote control at the balcony, opening the large sliding glass doors.

First glancing to the security cameras, Bryan looked at the Sultan, who now had taken a seat on a large sofa, covered in red silk. Amir's cell phone rang. He picked it up, listened for a moment, and spoke one word, "*Ha.*"

"You said 'yes' in Urdu. Who were you speaking with Amir?" Bryan asked.

"My diplomats," he answered.

From the open balcony they heard Kevin's scream as his body passed their floor, a blue streak after being thrown from the observation deck.

"What he would be thinking as he fell those long twenty seconds is anyone's guess?" Bryan asked out loud.

Amir smiled at Bryan. "For the sins they do by two and two must be paid by one," he said, quoting Rudyard Kipling.

Seated next to each other, and safely in an embassy SUV inbound to the consulate, Bryan and Shannon could finally relax. He read a message from the Ambassador on his Blackberry confirming the details of Rowley's death, and then looked at Shannon.

"You did good, Shannon," he said, patting her leg.

"Not something I'd like to go through again, that's for sure," Shannon answered. "How did you discover it was Kevin? Did Wazir give him up?"

"No, he never mentioned Kevin - hardly said anything at all in fact," Bryan said.

"How did you pick up on it then?"

"The events were just too big for him, way over his head – so he made mistakes, but I have to thank Dylan as well. He gave yet another brilliant performance - using reliable sources," Bryan said.

"I'm not sure that I understand."

"He went on the air with a story about your kidnapping and the connection with the memorial bombings – it was just bait."

"The story was a ruse to flush out Kevin?" Shannon asked.

"No, the story was true, and I didn't know what Kevin's involvement was, if any at all. But I had suspicions - I figured the news report would elicit a response of some sorts – at least from Rowley or Wazir," Bryan explained.

"I'm still a little hazy on how you deduced that Kevin was so dirty."

"Kevin gave himself away. He called me - said he was outside the building, yet was upstairs on the two hundredth floor when I got there. From the time I hung up the phone with him to being inside the building was one hour. The elevators were out, and there's no way that Kevin Davis could've climbed three thousand feet in that amount of time. That means that he was already inside the building when the power went out, which I don't think he knew was going to happen."

"But he knew where I was?"

"I think he helped plan your kidnapping – he just didn't know what the rest of the plan had in store for him, which called for Kevin to be the fall guy."

"So that's how you put it together?" Shannon asked.

"For the most part, yes. I figured out the rest on the spot. There were a number of orchestrated events that unfolded, the last being your kidnapping and the fact that Rodgers Christopher was almost killed in the process. That meant the Swiss bank account was a bogus account, and he was set up."

"Accounts set up by Rowley," Shannon added.

"That's what they needed - a banker, working at a bank in Dubai - who, by the way, was shot tonight."

"He's dead?" Shannon asked.

"Yeah, Ambassador Evans told me earlier, his secretary too. I would imagine that ballistics will match this," Bryan said, pointing to the Walther P5 shoved in his belt.

"You're not going to give them the gun, are you," Shannon said.

"No, I'm not."

"Why's not?"

"In the end, and it wouldn't be my decision anyway, but what we've got is closure to tragic events, and it needs to have a pretty little bow wrapped around it."

"I think that I understand, but of course it doesn't sit too well," Shannon remarked. "Who was that called a few minutes ago, by the way?" She asked.

"That was Dylan. He called to tell me that the security cameras at the Bank of Dubai showed nothing."

"But you still believe Kevin went there and killed him."

"After the news report, Kevin went to see Rowley, but not to kill him. It was a professional hit, and Kevin wasn't an assassin. Once

Kevin got there and found Rowley – he got scared and must have gone back to the Burj al Baaz to confront Wazir. After he was inside, the power was cut."

"So they wanted him inside?" Shannon asked.

"It played out exactly the way that Wazir hoped for."

"It's strange though Bryan, I mean I'm still trying to make sense of it all," Shannon said, then took a deep breath. "I was in a room, completely pitch black, when I heard Wazir speaking with someone outside the door."

"Do you know who the other person was?'

"No I don't, but he sounded similar to Wazir and they were speaking a strange dialect of Pashto, which I don't know. Wazir came in the room, put a hood over my head, and led me down a hallway to the stairwell. We went down several flights and waited. The same person I heard outside the door was there – it sounded like him, but it was hard to hear – they were whispering and I had the hood over the burqa. Wazir told me to sit down."

"What happened after that?"

Shannon explained, "Maybe five minutes went by, and I heard what sounded like gunfire, but I didn't know. The stairwell door slammed and someone ran down the steps."

"Wazir?"

"I think so, because he told me to stay where I was, but I also believe someone else was there too, but they just continued down the steps. I can't be sure though, I was pretty rattled at the time, and couldn't see anything."

"That's when Kevin showed up?"

"The door nearby to me opened, and it was Kevin. I heard him greet Wazir – then it sounded as though they started fighting, there was a gunshot – terrified, I screamed, and Kevin grabbed me. From there we went to an elevator and down to Amir's."

"Did he say anything during the elevator ride?"

"It was a very fast ride, but he did say that he 'was going to fix things,'" Shannon said. Bryan contemplated what he'd just been told. Most of the answers were clear.

"So what did Wazir say to you before he died?" Shannon asked.

"You mean before he sacrificed himself," Bryan said, shaking his head.

Puzzled, Shannon asked, "Are you saying he martyred himself? It was intentional?"

"It's obvious now. Probably something he'd planned on doing for a number of years. He owed it to his brother for the sacrifice he'd asked him to make. The laborer on the two hundredth floor was sacrificed as well as Wazir."

"Are you sure?"

"Yes I am, you see, he said something to me that cleared up things from the past. He said - *Baaz*."

"What's the significance?"

"The same word was spoken to me six and a half years ago, and by the same man," Bryan said.

"You spoke with Wazir then?"

"I wasn't sure until you described what'd happened - no, I've never spoken with Wazir – that was Hanif Zar Wali that died tonight at the top of that tower. Wazir died six years ago in a Gitmo infirmary."

"It was Hanif planning everything all along," Shannon said, nodding in agreement. "I knew Wazir didn't fit the profile."

"That's right. Remember when I was told you about the riot at the jail where he was being held before going to Gitmo?"

"Of course."

"I'm sure they did the switch a-roo then, during the confusion. Wazir, who was the detainee that died at Gitmo, was never struck by me, and it's possible may have been injured years before that, which could've caused the aneurism."

"One brother sacrificed himself so the other could carry on their cause," Shannon said.

"That's the way it looks to me. Had we known that Hanif was still out there, rather than dead, none of this may ever have happened."

"So then who killed Rowley if Kevin hadn't?" Shannon asked.

"I imagine Wazir – rather, make that Hanif Zar Wali" Bryan said, still somewhat amazed at the game the twins played so brilliantly.

"That's impossible Bryan, he was never gone from me longer than the time it took for me to go to the bathroom."

"Then maybe one of men that took Kevin," Bryan said, as he checked the clip of the Walther for the first time. It was empty. They didn't leave it to chance, he thought. *They knew I was coming!*

"Well I'm glad you found me," Shannon said, as she leaned over and hugged him hard.

"So am I," he said, holding her.

* * * * *

Bryan accompanied the CIA case officer, a marine guard from the U.S. consulate, and a Regional Security Officer to the parking garage where a valet from the Bank of Dubai building had parked Kevin's black Mercedes sedan. They found it on the fourth level, alone, in a corner. They checked the car carefully, combing the exterior, then underneath the chasse, the RSO using a pole with a mirror, the marine deciding to crawl under the car, just to be sure.

Bryan opened the driver's door and got in, adjusting the seat for the seven-inch difference in height. The RSO and CIA man watched as he checked the interior carefully. Bryan saw another bag from McDonalds on the floorboard. He popped the hood and trunk while the others were busy on both ends of the car. He opened the glove compartment.

"The car looks fine Captain Craig," the RSO said, a retired CIA man himself. Able to see in the open glove compartment, glimpsing a portion of a handgun, he added pointing at the weapon, "So, did Davis think he was some sort of James Bond? What's that he had in there?"

Bryan answered nonchalantly. "A Walther P5." The clip was full.

CHAPTER 41

JULY 15, 2008
WASHINGTON, D.C.

"THEY CALL THEMSELVES YOORISH, meaning 'the invasion' in Urdu," Bryan said to the Director of National Intelligence, Admiral Jack "Rabbit" Barnes, flanked by Homeland Security and the Director of Central Intelligence. It was a closed-door, "compartmented" meeting.

"A sect more than a hundred years old. The new version initiated plans shortly after 9/11, and took root fast. They focused on the recruitment of Pakistanis working as laborers in the United Arab Emirates. The plan was simple – a Madrasah that followed these premises: control the staffing company; control the housing; control the payroll; control religious practices and indoctrination; control information, meaning news, books, television – essentially, control everything. The result was total brainwashing and the second coming of Yoorish Shaheed, the Martyr Invasion. The leadership could direct their minions to all corners of the globe, engaging our deepest fears, anxieties and dreads." Bryan took a sip of water.

He was relieved that he was not at a Senate briefing, and instead briefing only Rabbit. And if it had been a public hearing, and the media were present, he'd have to suffer though each Senator's speech, as they pontificated their opinions. But Pegasus was still Top Secret, and there was not a "need to know," with the exception of the people in the room.

"Based on the most nefarious paradigm, the Yoorish Shaheed could be sent anywhere they were needed - creating havoc - Iraq, the West Bank, Afghanistan, Pakistan, the United States, and Great Britain; all corners of the globe with no limitations, not even Mecca. The supply of ready-made terrorists seemed unlimited. What changed once Petrov was killed was that they became more focused in carrying out their mission against non-Muslims – no longer supplying Shaheed bombers for sectarian causes as Petrov would."

"Bryan, how many do you estimate were indoctrinated from the start of the Yoorish Shaheed?" Rabbit asked him pointedly.

Rabbit's appearance compared to the two sitting on either side of the DNI bemused Bryan. Rabbit was still very fit to that day, carrying one hundred and seventy pounds squarely on his five foot ten inch frame. The other two men were overweight bookends in pinstripes. The Navy men were both wearing their summer "working" whites, a uniform the Navy called "The ice cream suit." Rabbit's was far from that, as was Bryan's. The Admiral's shoulder boards were predominately gold, and each had a silver anchor and four stars. Below his gold aviator wings were ten rows of ribbons, most denoting medals, two more than Bryan's below his gold trident. "This looks like a Navy club," he thought.

Bryan exhaled deeply and finally answered. "How many from the Yoorish Shaheed?" He repeated the question and paused. "Just the Islamic militant Madrasah established in Dubai alone may have turned out sixty thousand."

"A martyr-learning center that graduated sixty thousand - sounds like an awful lot Bryan," Rabbit said, peering over the top of his cheaters as he followed the written version of the brief.

"There are many other sleepers just waiting in the wings sir, but allow me to describe where the resources are coming from - Pakistan is the ideal terrorist factory for Islam. The country has a population of two hundred million, and expected to be three hundred million in fifteen years. To put that in perspective, it took the United States thirty-seven years to do the same thing. It's the fastest growing of the nine most populous countries in the world at three percent per annum.

The male to female ratio is fifty-three to forty-seven, and the literacy rate is thirty-six percent. The country is poor and many cases, the people are isolated by the highest mountain ranges in the world, creating the best formula for the fanatical Islamist organizers."

"For example?" Homeland Security asked.

"The mountainous areas still have more than a million homeless, disenfranchised by their government for many years, and vulnerable to the philosophy of *Yoorish Shaheed,* of course unless someone else is in there helping these isolated people. Poverty, deprivation, isolation are key ingredients for terrorist organizations that simply only need make the effort to show up in those areas. They gain control of pockets when the governments won't, and it spreads from there. Combine all those factors and it becomes easy picking for the terrorist recruiters. Since the earthquakes of 2005, the government in Pakistan was grossly negligent in providing for many who were hungry, injured, homeless, or simply in despair. Taliban and Yoorish Shaheed were right there though – and took advantage of the situation."

"Pick on the illiterate, starving, homeless that are incapable of helping themselves," Rabbit summarized, leaning back in his chair.

"That's what Doctor Parker suggested as well, Mister Director. Obviously if we're more proactive..." Bryan was cut off.

"You're not being asked to establish policy Bryan," Rabbit interjected. "But I hear you loud and clear regarding the hearts and minds. That's up to the American people to decide what to do though, or for the politicians to sell it to them."

"Isn't it our job to sell it to the politicians. We're looking to win the war on terrorism, well that's just one of the battles. Only one, sir, but still it's a start," Bryan said, thinking of Shamema.

"Pakistan."

"Yes sir."

"I'll take that under advisement the next time I see the President, or if you're ever in the Cabinet, you can do it yourself," the DNI said in a straightforward, businesslike manner. "What about Sultan Kahn?"

"That's the other alternative," Bryan said.

"That Kahn becomes the new caliph?"

"He's a hero to the millions of workers throughout the UAE that have now seen, at least for the time being, real wage increases – in some cases four times that of the old wages, and they now have protections enforced by Dubai's Labor Ministry. He's an icon to most Muslims throughout Southwest Asia and the Middle East, a national hero in Pakistan and Afghanistan. He's the largest single shareholder in the most ambitious development ever planned, and his equity is already worth a billion dollars, with an insurance policy. No matter what happens regarding the economies of the West, or to Dubai for that matter, he's golden in the people's eyes. He's brought them up from despair at the expense of the West, yet he moves easily throughout the West. He is in fact already a legend in the Muslim world. A possible caliph?" Bryan shrugged his shoulders. "It was a calculated bet with odds always in his favor – influenced mostly by the greed of Western capitalism. He's similar to a modern day Saladin that can now cut a swath throughout the West with a double edged sword – and he travels with a cleric that's as close to him as a brother."

"Who's the cleric?" the DCIA asked.

"Mullah Afzar Kahn ul Mulk," Bryan said.

"What about this Alexander the Great complex that was in Doctor Parker's report? Is there anything to that?" Rabbit asked.

"Well, you've seen him," Bryan said.

"Photos only, but he does look European," the DNI said.

"His nickname is Sika – short for Sikandar, or Alexander – so as for the Alexander complex, if there is such a thing, I'll agree with her to a certain extent. I'm not sure that he believes he should be conquering the world though."

"What about the Islamic world - or rather what it used to be?" the CIA director asked.

"The Islamic world, you ask – well, he legitimately comes from royalty in the North West Frontier, and it is believed by some that he's descended from the Greeks, hence the Alexander comparison. He's a born leader, and has demonstrated that from an early age that leadership, and unflinching bravery. Certainly he wants to unify the Muslim world into a peaceful coexistence. How far that Muslim world extends remains to be seen."

"Does he have a nuke, or nuclear capability?" the DNI asked, with real concern on his face.

"From reports we're getting now, he's become such an icon in Pakistan that there's a movement under foot to call for a referendum – new elections," Bryan said.

"Take power in Pakistan, you're saying," Rabbit said, finishing Bryan's thought.

"That's exactly right. His popularity has exploded in only one month – Sultan Amir Sika Kahn is on everyone's lips. He's also seeded Humanitarian coffers with his own money – or rather it looks like his own money – and it's being used to aid the earthquake victims. And since it's been disclosed that he was actually of Pakistani heritage – a direct descendent to the last King of the North West Frontier – he's savior of his own people, much the in same way that Gandhi was to the people of India."

"And he's got the backing of fundamentalists," Rabbit added.

"And he's got their backing, that's correct," Bryan agreed.

"So he doesn't need to build a bomb of his own, you're saying," Homeland Security said.

"Precisely, just take over the country, by popular mandate – a free election – a country that already has a bomb," Bryan said.

"I see. But he may not take over tomorrow, let's say, I mean after all there is a political process?" Rabbit asked.

"How many times in Pakistan's history has someone taken over in a single day though," Bryan said.

"I see what you mean," Rabbit said nodding, his mouth in a slight grimace.

"But that gets back to his current capability now, or possible capability," Bryan said, taking a sip of water before continuing. "He's a physicist, understands the technology, and possibly has already obtained weapon's grade plutonium or uranium, and he also knows how to build a stacked centrifuge system to rapidly enrich his own uranium. He has the knowledge, the real estate to build it on, or under – with the material he can make whatever he wants – dirty bomb, a limited nuke around one kiloton, or even something much bigger."

Leaning forward, Rabbit's hands together, resting on the table, "What kind of yield?"

"Fifteen kilotons, say in a device the size of, umm - a love seat," Bryan said, purposely thinking of the most inappropriate analogy.

"Fifteen kilotons, huh - Hiroshima size. That's some tough love, Bryan," Rabbit said, leaning back in his chair.

* * * * *

JULY 16, 2008

CIA HEADQUARTERS

LANGLEY, VIRGINIA

"Now you're certain of that?" the Director of Central Intelligence Agency asked.

"I'm not implying that I'm certain the Sultan Kahn would be a friend of the United States permanently, but he's a moderate and has the confidence of Dubai and Abu Dhabi, and their Sheikhs. Amir Kahn's presence there will give a modicum of safety from attacks by fanatical elements," Bryan said.

"A buffer of sorts, from Islamist extremists such as Iran, or independent radicals like the Zar Walis," the CIA Director clarified.

"They were independent of the Sultan to great degree, but they recognized the Sultan as the one to unite the Muslim world. For them, the ends justified the means, and they were ruthless as well, yet not barbaric. The barbarism they deferred to the Russian, until he was eliminated," Shannon analytically pointed out.

"Anyone waiting in the wings to replace these two sociopaths as the leadership for Yoorish Shaheed?" the FBI Director asked.

"There's always someone wanting to replace those taken down in the battle, but whether they have the skill sets, or rather the aptitude required, remains to be seen. We haven't been able to identify anyone yet," Shannon said.

"Well, all in all, I'd have to say this has been a great success then. We caught the perpetrators and shut down their terrorist factory," the CIA Director said nodding his head while looking at his FBI counterpart. "And we have a face to put with the success," he added, tapping the personnel file on his desk.

"Kevin Davis," Bryan stated flatly, flabbergasted at the comedy, the irony of the matter.

"That's right Captain Craig – Kevin Davis, our agent on location in Dubai, who saved the day, caught the terrorists, and now is a posthumous recipient of the CIA Intelligence Star for Valor," the CIA chief said as he opened the file. Bryan and Shannon looked at the photo of Kevin now visible on the inside cover of the open file. Their hero had almost brought down an entire diplomatic policy, helped terrorists bomb multiple cities, implicated diplomatic officials, participated in the sabotage of a Dubai power grid, linked to the killing of a British banker, and now was probably going to be an award winner. Bryan thought about Gil, who's death had been officially termed "an accident." Gil was the one that deserved the awards and accolades, Bryan thought.

"What about the fact that your man had on a blue worker's outfit. It was even in the papers 'Embassy man killed in fall - found wearing blue laborer clothing' – I believe that's how the story read," the FBI Director pointed out with accurate recall.

"We're saying he was undercover sir," Bryan said.

"Right, of course. That should do it," the FBI director said cynically. "Opened and shut."

"It was the only thing that made sense sir," Bryan said, knowing full well that the story was flimsy if scrutinized in depth, with many holes in it; the rest of the intelligence communities would see right through it. Obviously, Petrov must have been undercover as well, Bryan mused to himself. They had no other angle though, over the proverbial "barrel" – the security cameras in Amir's palace in the sky; complete with an "embassy man's" confession.

"Now what about the PDI issue, the fact that New York was never successfully hit; is there a sleeper in the States that's gonna follow up on that with another *Shaheed* belt soaked in smallpox?" the FBI Director asked.

"You know sir, I honestly can't say for sure, but it appears now that the threat posed by Hanif and Wazir's cells have been neutralized. Yet I wouldn't tell the CDC, or Homeland to lower their guard and put away the vaccine. By the same token, I think we need to be very, very proactive – think tanks focusing on the obvious – the thing that hasn't been used yet," Bryan said. "Because it will be."

"Very good. Well Captain Craig and Doctor Parker, thank you very much. I think we have what we needed, I mean - what wasn't already asked by the DNI," the CIA Director said as the foursome stood up. "I hope you both have a nice flight back to London."

"Speaking of the embassy - how's the Consul General, what's his name again?" the FBI Director asked.

"Rodgers Christopher is expected to make a full recovery. He should be back on the job within a couple of months," Bryan answered.

"He's been appointed Ambassador to Afghanistan in Kabul," the DCIA said.

"Oh, well good for him," the FBI Director said.

"You think so, huh?" Bryan asked rhetorically, looking at Shannon and remembering the fate of a British diplomat murdered in Kabul and ripped to pieces almost one hundred seventy years before.

* * * * *

JULY 26, 2008
LONDON, ENGLAND

"You never noticed this before?" Bryan asked DJ, as Bryan, Shannon and the wizard were enjoying afternoon drinks at the Crescent in Chelsea, a stylish bar known for its great selection of wines.

"Not thet aye didn't notice et boss, but et FaceScan corrected etself every time. Yet aye wasn't satisfied an wanted ta tweak her a bit more. Every node matches perfectly, 'cept for the eyes," DJ said.

"But only the eyes of the faceprint from the W Hotel in New York," Bryan said.

"Exactly boss. The twins match exactly from the Gitmo photos and the JPEG ya sent me from the camel race. The eyes match perfectly, but the one from the 'otel stops short on the eyes."

"Could it be the color? Maybe it's off," Shannon said.

"No, it's the depth. Like e's wearin contacts."

"We know that's not the case DJ. I'm sure it's just some anomaly. Both men are dead anyway, so I wouldn't worry too much about it,"

Bryan said, trying to get DJ to relax. "Look, there ya go DJ, the band's comin out now."

"Rayght boss, the bloke's an amazin guitarist. Plays perfect Jimmy Page." DJ kicked back in his chair as the three-piece band took the small corner stage.

The bar was beginning to fill up, but it was a small place, as most pubs in London. Quaint, loud, and smoky, it was just the perfect spot to meet up with an old friend.

"Gidday ya old bastard, and same ta you folks, especially you Shannon. This es a nice little billabong ere ta knock back a few coldies," Dylan Sizemore said as he shook Bryan's hand.

"Our tech wiz, DJ," Bryan said as Dylan sat down at the outside table with them. "Congratulations are in order, aren't they Dylan."

"Yes, very happy for you and your family," Shannon added.

"That's right mate, rounds on me. Little boy – name's Jimmy," Dylan said, beaming.

"How's mom?" Bryan quizzed with eyebrows raised.

"Aw, jest great, still flyin video games, and Street gives her love to ya," Dylan said, as he lit up a smoke. Looking at DJ, he added as he exhaled "Owe it all to your boss. I met my wife through him. In fact I believe he introduced me on purpose, before he got in trouble."

"That was a few years ago," Bryan said.

"So Captain Craig, we free to speak?" Dylan asked.

"On the QT?" Bryan asked.

"As always mate."

Removing the tintype and the drawing from his jacket, Bryan asked, "What do think about these?"

"Ah, so there they are - little pieces of the puzzle, ay." Dylan picked up the tintype. "That's an old photo there mate – who are these gentleman?" Dylan said, laying down the tintype and picking up the drawing of the falcon.

"It's your big scoop Dylan," Bryan said with a laugh. "The man in the center was the King of Chitral, Mehtar Aman ul Mulk II, and he's surrounded by his sons and brother, plus a few attendants. Here's the book I told you about." Bryan pulled the registry out of a computer bag, opening it to the first page for Dylan to read.

"Some historical figures here mate," Dylan said as he read the entries.

"Look at the inside back cover – that's where I found the tintype, drawing and Captain Robinson's writings."

"Where's the British officer's journal?" Dylan asked.

Bryan removed it from his bag, unfolding the fragile paper carefully. "Here, read this."

Dylan read the British officer's words twice. "Jesus Christ mate – the pommy bastard must have had a crystal ball," he said dismayed. "Either he'd predicted the future, or things never change."

"How about the latter?"

Dylan put the papers down and picked up the tintype again, studying it. "The man standing next to this King looks just like Sultan Kahn, or very close anyway," Dylan commented with some surprise after looking closer.

"Let's just say the man's a direct ancestor of the Sultan," Bryan responded. "Turn the tintype over."

Dylan needed his glasses to read the small letters of the poem etched on the back of the tintype:

It rises from the tower,
Soaring upward and higher,
To the sun it flies.

Sky and blue, the realm;
Vision and speed, its advantage.
Talons and cunning, the weapons.

Tuck, plummet and dive.
Faster than anything ever.
Fearlessly, strikes like lightning.

Dominating all below,
Supremacy and majesty,
Beware the falcon on the tower.

"Is this a Kipling?" Dylan asked, putting the cigarette out.

"That's what I thought, but once we got back to London I had DJ do an analysis on the book, the tintype, and the drawing," Bryan said, holding up his empty glass for the waitress. He motioned for another round for the table,

"This is gettin interestin mate, what ya find out?"

Bryan looked at DJ, so engrossed in Led Zeppelin, he didn't glance their way, but Bryan knew he heard every word. "Custard Pie" was being played.

"The ink from the drawing and the paper date to the late nineteenth century. It's the drawing that Robinson referred to in his journal," Bryan said. "The inside back cover had four types of glue," he added.

"Three types really," DJ interjected.

"Right, three types, just four applications. The cover had been sealed three times since the original," Bryan added. "Once, when the book was first bound and the cover put on; the second time when someone opened it in the last thirty years or so; the third was recent."

"How the hell do ya know that?" Dylan asked, pulling out another cigarette. "Mind if ah have another smoko?" They nodded their heads in approval. Although violating London's smoking ban Dylan's secondary smoke seemed insignificant and nobody seemed to care anyway.

"Aye dated the type o glue. The way glues work are..."

"That enough analysis DJ, get back to Led Zeppelin," Bryan said, stopping DJ from a twenty-minute lecture on glues. "Now look at the engraving again – that's a fresh carving – something else DJ figured out."

"What do ya think the meanin is?" DJ asked.

"I think it was put there for me to find. A message of some kind, and I think that Amir Kahn was the one responsible."

"He put it in there?"

"Someone else put it there on instructions from Amir - he wanted me to read that poem and understand the symbolism," Bryan said as he took his beer from the waitress. "And he wanted me to read the journal, and then come back to Dubai and finish everything he'd put in motion. What no one could have guessed was that such a tremendous earthquake would've happened, nearly destroying the book. But unless I'd been killed, the outcome would've been the same."

"But with the book gone - that still wouldn't have stopped you from finishin the mission though, and completing what you'd started. Catch the falcon, so ta speak," Dylan said.

"Would it have the same conclusions though? I don't know. Amir wanted me to finish what he had in mind. Was I just one of his instruments – one of his falcons? I can't say," Bryan said staring earnestly into space. "Deep down inside, and it's something that I can't prove - I don't even have the slightest bit of evidence, but deep down, I believe Amir designed all this; and the end result was exactly what he wanted."

"The letter and journal?" Dylan asked

"I gave them to Robinson's family – his ancestors, who live here in London," Bryan said.

"Well, in light of that, have you seen the Times today?"

"No I haven't," Bryan said.

"Sultan Kahn has been praised by the current Paki regime for his tremendous personal assistance in helping the Pakistani people – both in the labor situation, and the humanitarian efforts. It even references the Sultan's cousin, Shamema and her father, his cleric."

"There's your story Dylan, the one I said you could have, and the one you wanted so badly."

"That's a fantastic tale mate. Now what?"

"I've got to return the book, that's what I said that I'd do."

"Well I've got a request for ya DJ," Dylan said.

"What can ah do for ye?" DJ asked as he moved his head and shoulders to the beat of the music.

"Please put somethin else on this iPhone besides Led Zeppelin," Dylan said, as he placed the familiar gadget on the table. They all smiled in unison.

FALCON ON THE TOWER

CHAPTER 42

AUGUST 21, 2008
NEW YORK CITY, NEW YORK

A RECORD BREAKING CELEBRATION, the Republican National Convention was underway, the final evening. New York City was playing host once again, Madison Square Garden the venue. The mayor had pulled out all stops to ensure safety, security, and festivities. Security was indeed very tight. More than one hundred twenty million dollars - a record, had been spent on safeguards. The alert levels had been increased to their highest, and the days leading up to the kickoff were tension filled. More than half a million protestors let their voices be heard - a record. Two thousand one hundred twenty people were arrested - a record. New York City's *Hercules Teams*, more than ten thousand five hundred cops in full riot gear and with automatic weapons, patrolled the streets and subways - a record. There were no riots.

Along with bomb-sniffing dogs, brand new technologies were deployed, including *Stoichiometric* diagnostic devices that detect specific chemical compositions such as radioactive particles and other explosives. Able to penetrate metal, concrete, or virtually any dense material, the detectors being use by Homeland Security had an accuracy rate greater than ninety eight percent. There had been no bombings. It was the final hours of the last day, and soon all could breathe a sigh of relief.

"The Garden party" had run very smoothly inside the convention walls, as forty-five speakers had stood on the podium to deliver speeches over the course of four days and nights. Some speeches were dull, the speakers robotic. Other speeches were feisty, attacking. Then there were the dramatic speakers, imbued to biblical quotations, evangelical in their delivery. Finally, there were the visionaries, speakers that rallied the masses, emboldening and challenging the Americans to tackle the future head on, without ducking.

Senator Taylor P. Cox was an exceptional orator, adept at communication, and fell into the category of visionary. He rallied the Republican troops, a speaker whose knack for vocal expression topped all during the four days leading up to the acceptance speech by the presidential nominee. His eloquence was highlighted in a defining moment when he laid out his vision for the continued war on terrorism using forty words:

> *"As Americans we must help all those who ask for our help; vigorously defend our shores, borders, and way of life; show magnanimity and benevolence to those who hate us; and without impunity, crush those who seek to destroy us."*

The final ten words got the approval of the delegates and conventioneers, who if not already standing, leapt to their feet, erupting into ovation, one that lasted five minutes. "Cox for VP" signs filled the Garden. He knew he was at the top of the short list.

The call came to his hotel suite at the Marriott Marquis one hour before the nominee's acceptance speech. Taylor Cox was looking out the window at Times Square. His aide answered the cell phone, handing it to the junior Senator from Virginia. He listened for one minute without an utterance to the man on the other end of the connection, a person he respected, greatly admired, a former Navy man to boot, and one not given to prattle. At the end of the minute, almost to the second, he was asked a question, an easy one for him. "Taylor, I want you on my ticket – how bout it?"

"Thank you sir, and I accept," Taylor Cox answered without hesitation.

"Good man, see ya."

The new Republican ticket stood on the podium amidst the jubilation and confetti, hands joined, arms raised, their families and closest supporters surrounding them, full of patriotism, full of pride. Next came an event that all law enforcement had the most concern for, a fireworks display over the East River rivaled only by the fourth of July. Thirty minutes and sixty thousand stunning explosions, including comet bursts, glittering bursts, and flickering bursts, followed by the grand finale. A million people would be on hand to watch from balconies, rooftops, Battery Park in Manhattan, Liberty Park in Jersey City, from Brooklyn, and on Roosevelt Island. For security reasons, delegates, and conventioneers would watch from giant screens inside Madison Square Garden, the running mates however, would be whisked by motorcade from the Garden to Battery Park, arriving on a stage moments before the grand finale. There the candidates would deliver more rousing speeches to all gathered at the Battery, and those watching on TV. The plan called for coordination between the Secret Service, FBI, the Air National Guard, air traffic control, and local law enforcement, the details worked out well in advance. The fireworks would begin at 10:00 PM.

* * * * *

AUGUST 22, 2008

RAWALPINDI, PAKISTAN

A half a world away, Bryan received the news almost immediately on his Blackberry. It was also being broadcast live on a television in the café near where he was sitting, having a cup of coffee. His friend was the nominee for Vice President. Not affiliated with any particular political party himself, Bryan nonetheless believed it was a good choice. Bryan nodded his head unconsciously with approval as he watched the television, and then returned to the Blackberry, sending a quick congratulatory text message.

Arriving the night before, Bryan had planned to meet Shamema at the Holy Family Hospital at 7:30 in the following morning. The hospital was in an area of Rawalpindi known as Satellite Town, a place busy all hours of the day. Bryan was thirty minutes early, so he passed the time watching CNN on what looked to be a brand new flat panel television. All news concerned live coverage of the convention, and being one of only three people in the hospital's café, very little cajoling was needed keep the TV on the channel. So he sat at the table alone and watched.

Founded as a Medical mission by the Catholic Church in 1948, Holy Family Hospital had grown to become a teaching hospital with over eight hundred beds. The earthquake's trauma victims had stretched it to its capacity. Now only the most severely injured remained. With state-of-the-art MRI and Radiology equipment, as well as CT scanners, many survivors were further treated, or died at this very place. Of the fortunate, the boy Bryan witnessed saved by the New York Fireman. The young boy named Latif had been one of the lucky ones, lucky because a New York Fireman cared to help. Bryan was certain of that fact.

"Captain Craig?" the high-pitched Pakistani voice said.

Bryan broke away from the television to see a middle-aged, short, bald man with glasses, and wearing the white coat of a Physician. Bearing a wide, friendly smile, and thick dark moustache, streaked with gray, the man reminded Bryan of someone. "Maybe it's Gandhi," he thought.

"Yes?" Bryan responded, taking a liking to the little man on sight.

"Good morning, I am Doctor Bokhari. How are you this morning sahr?" the man asked energetically.

"I'm fine. Thank you. Shamema must have sent you."

"Yes she did."

"Well is she here?" Bryan asked impatiently.

"No, not yet, but she called me and asked that I wait with you while she escorts her father to the airport."

"You don't say, so her father's here, huh," Bryan said, wondering how Shamema's reunion was going with the father she thought had been dead for so many years.

"Yes, Mullah Afzar has been here for some time, and has provided great inspiration, both in prayer and."

Bryan finished his sentence. "Money?" He guessed, looking back at the new TV, connecting the dots.

"Well, I was going to say spirituality, but he has brought much money from Sultan Kahn," the doctor said with a smile.

Sultan Kahn! Not a surprise. "Please join me doctor," Bryan said, motioning to a chair at the table.

"Shamema has said many wonderful things about you, Captain. If not for your help with helicopters to the NWF, we would have lost many more people," the doctor said as he sat down.

"Please, don't thank me. I wish that I could've done more," Bryan said, as the Pakistani doctor raised his hand and waved. Bryan, turned his head, and saw Shamema approaching. He stood up to greet her. She was beaming and beautiful as ever, wearing the same white silk shawl, but more elegant and cosmopolitan, Islamic clothing. He wanted to hug her, but instead warmly shook her hand.

She sat down, taking a deep breath. "I have wonderful news. My father has told me that Sultan Kahn will build a brand new facility for our charity in Islamabad. And we will be able to hire ten relief workers, including a fulltime doctor and nurse," she said elated.

"That's wonderful," Bryan said, realizing that he was still holding her hand as he also sat down at the table.

Shamema explained that that her reunion with her father had initially been difficult. At first she couldn't understand why he had kept everyone in the dark for so long that he was actually alive. Not even one communication. Only now was it actually revealed to her, that her grandfather had disowned his only son when Afzar refused to return to Chitral. Instead he chose Quranic training, and would stay in Afghanistan where he believed he was needed. Afzar had become an outcast, barred from contacting his family. He then continued further with his Islamic training, taking the path to become a cleric, and advisor to Sultan Kahn.

Genuinely happy that Shamema was experiencing good things in her life, after such tragic events had occurred, he happily removed the registry from his travel bag and placed it on the table for her. "I believe you've been expecting this," Bryan said, glancing at the TV, noting the fireworks over the East River being broadcast live.

Her eyes lit up. "Why yes, you said that you would bring it back, and here it is. And in better condition than before, almost like new," she said opening it.

"I took it to the company that made it, who amazingly enough, still happen to be around, and they reconditioned it."

"It's simply beautiful," she said, rubbing the cover with her hand. She passed the book to the doctor. "This is the book that I was telling you about, Doctor Bokhari."

"Oh yes, It's very nice indeed," the doctor said.

"Here's something else that you haven't seen yet Shamema," Bryan said, showing her the tintype from the back cover.

"That's quite fantastic too, someone was able to repair the tin you showed me before?"

"No, that tintype had been hidden in back of the registry. The photographer that took the other photo, actually took two," Bryan explained.

"The second one is much better," she passed the tintype to the doctor as well.

"I had my lab enhance the second, it's much, much clearer, and he colorized, being as accurate as a supercomputer can." Bryan produced DJ's new and improved version.

Shamema was flabbergasted at the brilliance of the photo. "I can actually see the colors of their eyes. And for the first time, see Mehtar Afzal. And how blue his eyes were – look at this Doctor Bokhari."

Bryan explained the laws of eye color as he recalled from DJ's short course on the subject, and that the chances were very high that Afzal had a son, as opposed to Shir, King Aman's stepbrother.

"This is simply uncanny, I should say. Most remarkable how much this young man resembles Sultan Kahn when he was young, even the eyes," Doctor Bokhari commented, adjusting his glasses.

"I'd say it's almost a certainty that he's your cousin, Shamema. The Sultan was the boy with the light blue eyes, famous for shooting down the Soviet helicopter. He is probably the direct descendant of Afzal," Bryan said, looking at Doctor Bokhari with curiosity. "Of course, a simple DNA test could prove that," he added.

Something about the doctor, the reason for the familiarity was coming back to Bryan, when it dawned on him that the doctor had said 'Afzal resembled a young Amir Kahn.'

"You knew Amir Kahn when he was young?" Bryan asked, opening up the JPEGs on his Blackberry.

"Of course. I met him when he was just a boy, perhaps only thirteen or fourteen. The refugee camp - I helped there. I was still in medical school. I also tended to Shamema's father after he was injured from a landmine explosion while riding in a car," the doctor said. "He's lucky to be alive, although confined to a wheelchair."

"This is you here doctor, isn't it," Bryan said, holding the screen so Doctor Bokhari could see the JPEG of Congressman Jack Smith surrounded by the group of people from the Pakistani refugee camp.

"Oh my goodness – why yes, that is me. And how young I am there," he said with smile indicative of fond memories. "And look, there are the triplets," the doctor said, holding the screen for Bryan to see clearly. The doctor zoomed in with the thumbwheel until just the boys were in the frame.

Bryan looked hard at the JPEG, silent. Finally he spoke. "The triplets?" Bryan asked, aghast.

"Yes, marvelous little boys. Little Pashtuns, and I believe with Nuristan ancestry. They were favorites of us all - especially Amir. Terrible story though. Their sister, we called her Despoina, brought the boys to the camp after traveling over Afghanistan many hundreds of miles - their village had been destroyed, and everyone had been brutally murdered – I don't even want to describe how, but it was terrible. The four were the only ones to escape," the doctor said.

Bryan sensed what was coming. Anxiously, he looked up at the TV coverage of the convention fireworks. His friend was on stage. The revelry was fever pitched.

The doctor continued, "They were identical triplets, which of course is extremely rare. But there were two ways that I could distinguish between them - one was caused by the war, and the other was caused by nature. The little one on the far left had suffered a bad head injury during the war, causing an aneurism, which he would have for the rest of his natural life. And he was the calmest of the three. His name was Wazir."

The doctor paused, placing his finger on his lip as he studied the JPEG, and continued, "The one in the middle here was a rambunctious one, full of life. His name was Hanif."

The doctor looked at Bryan nodding his head and smiling "But the most brilliant one, strongest character of any of them, and Amir's favorite, was the one here." He pointed back at the screen, adding, "His name was Ahmed Shah. Most fascinating however, were his eyes, the only one of the three boys – the color was a brilliant blue, much like yours, Captain. Everyone called him *Baaz* – the falcon."

EPILOGUE

ARTIN DE LA VEGA disembarked from the pyrotechnics barge two hours before it was towed to the East River. His work for the time being was done. The load heavier than usual, he'd used a crane to carefully lift the last container of fireworks, part of the grand finale. Final checking the container, he had paid particular attention to one sensor attached to a shell; a sensor ultimately controlled by a pyrotechnician using a fireworks master control board. Martin was confident it would perform flawlessly, but only on his command, not the technician's. Ensuring its wires were securely connected, he covered the sensor, protecting it from the elements, and went ashore.

When routine pyrotechnic sensors receive electrical impulses, matches on the fireworks shells are ignited, detonating lift charges and launching the pyrotechnic shells hundreds of feet into the air. This independent sensor however, did something very different. Martin would use a hand-held metal box, when opened, revealed a digital remote control that safely sent an impulse to the sensor. At exactly 10:30 PM Martin would press a button on the remote sending the desired signal. When the sensor received the command impulse it would launch the remaining shells of the grand finale, and a split second later fire a uranium bullet down a six-foot barrel hidden inside the container. The bullet would impact a uranium sphere and generator inside a tamper cover, compressing the subcritical masses together, initiating a fission reaction.

Despoina was in a van expecting her brother any moment. He was on time. Together they drove away taking the New Jersey turnpike south, stopping at a rest area. They waited. At precisely 10:30 PM her brother opened the box.

.

APPENDIX I

Actual Headlines and News Stories:

New York Times, Tuesday, November 14, 2006

Pakistan Link Seen in Rise In Afghan Suicide Attacks
Officials Say Trail of Bombers Crosses the
Border – 2 Nations Dispute Matter

By CARLOTTA GALL

SHAWARN Pakistan, Nov.13
Afghan and NATO security forces have recently rounded up several men like Hafiz Daoud Shah, a 21-year-old unemployed Afghan refugee who says he drove across the border to Afghanistan in September in a taxi with three other would-be suicide bombers.

Every case, Afghan security officials say, is similar to that of Mr. Shah...The trail of organizing, financing and recruiting the bombers who have carried out a rising number of suicide attacks in Afghanistan traces back to Pakistan, they say.

"Every single bomber or I.E.D. in one way or another is linked to Pakistan," a senior Afghan intelligence official said, referring to improvised explosive devices like roadside bombs. "Their reasons are to keep Afghanistan destabilized, to make us fail, and to keep us fragmented."

A senior United States military official based in Afghanistan agreed for the most part... Last week, for the first time, a Pakistani intelligence official acknowledged that suicide bombers were being trained in Bajaur, a small Pashtun tribal area along the border..."They came here to be martyred," he said (Mr. Shah) of his three companions, all Pakistanis, all around the same age, and all also from Karachi.

...After a bombing cell of 12 people was picked up in Kabul recently, two of the men continued to receive cell-phone calls while in custody, urging them to explode their bombs, the intelligence official said. The calls came from an Afghan commander...When Afghan intelligence, at NATO's behest, passed on the cell phone number...their informer, a member of the commander's inner circle, was swiftly killed, his body cut into eight pieces and dumped in the camp.

...In Mr. Shah's case, he and his companions had all studied at the same religious school, madrasa (Madrasah)

REUTERS

Monday, November 12, 2006

UAE: Workers Abused in Construction Boom

(Dubai, November 12, 2006) As the United Arab Emirates experiences one of the world's largest construction booms, its government has failed to stop employers from seriously abusing the rights of the country's half million migrant construction workers, Human Rights Watch said in a report released today. On Tuesday the prime minister of the UAE, Sheikh Mohammed bin Rashid Al-Maktoum, ordered the minister of labor, Dr. Ali bin Abdullah Al-Ka'abi, to enforce the country's labor laws and immediately institute a series of reforms based on Human Rights Watch's recommendations.

"The prime minister's decree to protect worker's rights is a welcome step in the right direction," said Sarah Leah Whitson, Middle East director at Human Rights Watch. "But unless the government starts to hold employers accountable for breaking the law, the UAE's colossal new skyscrapers will be known for monumental labor violations."

Based on extensive interviews with workers, government officials and business representatives, the 71-page report, "Building Towers, Cheating Workers," documents serious abuses of construction workers by employers in the UAE. These abuses include unpaid or extremely low wages, several years of indebtedness to recruitment agencies for fees that UAE law says only employers should pay, the withholding of employees' passports, and hazardous working conditions that result in apparently high rates of death and injury.

After a string of highly publicized strikes and labor demonstrations earlier this year, the UAE government promised to respect workers' rights by legalizing trade unions and vigorously enforcing the country's labor laws, which are relatively good on paper. But the Human Rights Watch report demonstrates that the government has still failed to do so. Human Rights Watch found no public record of an employer in the construction industry forced to pay a substantial fine or suffer any criminal liability even when found guilty of violating labor law.

...The UAE is currently undergoing a dramatic construction boom, and nearly all of the more than 500,000 construction workers in the country are migrants, mostly from South Asian countries such as India, Pakistan and Bangladesh. The country's 2,738,000 migrant workers make up 95% of the country's workforce. "Hundreds of gleaming towers have risen on the backs of migrants working in highly exploitative conditions," said Whitson.

...Employers based in the UAE import foreign construction workers through recruiting agencies located both inside and outside of the UAE. Recruiting agencies unlawfully force workers, rather than their employers, to pay US$2,000-3,000 for travel, visas, government fees and the recruiters' own services. To pay these fees, all of the 60 workers interviewed by Human Rights Watch reported that they had accepted loans from their recruiting agents at steep monthly interest rates as high as 10%. As a result, workers start out burdened with huge debts and use the most of their meager wages to repay these loans during the first two to three years of their employment.

... The wages of construction workers, which range from $106 to $250 per month, contrast starkly with the national average wage of $2,106 per month. Many recent workers' protests have centered on demands for better wages. Although the UAE Labor Law of 1980 requires the government to implement a minimum wage, it has failed to do so for the past 26 years.

"The UAE government needs to implement criminal and financial penalties against employers and recruiting agents who continue to charge workers recruiting and travel fees and withhold their wages and passports," said Whitson.

Hundreds of migrant construction workers die each year in the UAE under unexplained circumstances. The government can account only for a few of these deaths, primarily because it appears not to enforce its own laws requiring employers to report worksite deaths and injuries. In 2004 alone, the embassies of India, Pakistan and Bangladesh returned the bodies of 880 construction workers back to their home countries. Yet the Dubai emirate, the only emirate to keep a count of migrant worker deaths, recorded only 34 construction deaths that year, based on reports from only six companies.

The government does not allow workers to form organizations or trade unions. As a result, there are no institutional mechanisms for advocating on behalf of workers' rights. During the past two years, thousands of migrant construction workers have resorted to public demonstrations. In March, the government promised to legalize trade unions by the end of the year, but instead, in September it passed a new law banning labor strikes and announcing that it would deport striking workers.

"We hope that the government's new promise to enforce its labor laws does not share the same fate as its broken promise to legalize trade unions," said Whitson

Human Rights Watch called on the UAE, as a member of the International Labor Organization, to implement and respect fundamental workers' rights, including the right to freedom of association and collective bargaining and the right to strike. Human Rights Watch urged the government to implement its existing laws to protect and promote workers' rights.

In addition, Human Rights Watch urged the governments of the United States, European Union countries and Australia, which are currently engaged in free trade negotiations with the UAE, to ensure that respect for workers' fundamental rights is a cornerstone of any forthcoming agreements.

- Human Rights Watch

News

Discontent in Dubai

By Tim Mansel
Business Daily, BBC World Service
Wednesday, 12 April 2006

Dubai is a city of towers. Ostentatious towers of glass and steel, 40 or 50 stories high, lined up in rows along the main highways, and each complete with helipads and rooftop swimming pools.

Elsewhere Dubai is a jungle of cranes. Some cluster at the airport, where a third terminal is going up exclusively for the use of the local carrier, Emirates. Or there is Sheikh Zayed Road; home to an enormous construction site dominated by a tower - the Burj Dubai

- which, when complete, will be the tallest building in the world at more than 160 stories. The people behind it are coy about saying exactly how tall for fear of competition, although they do promise the last word in luxury and prestige.

Stress and depression

But Dubai has another face. On the outskirts of the city, where the desert begins, are the concrete barracks where the workers live, thousand upon thousand of them. Dubai is being built virtually from scratch - 20 years ago few of these gleaming towers existed - and the men building it are migrants from India, Pakistan, Bangladesh and Nepal. They work for about $5 a day, sleep four or five to a room, and see their families once every two or three years because it's hard to raise the money to pay for a trip home.

I met a group of workers - from Andhra Pradesh in southern India, from Kabul in Afghanistan, and from Pakistan's North West Frontier Province - one evening after they had returned from work. They were preparing dinner in a small, dingy, communal kitchen with a noisy fan.

Scrawny cats ran across the compound; a cockerel scratched in the dirt. The balconies were festooned with the men's washing.

Many of the workers suffer great stress and depression

KV Shamsudeen, a charitable Indian businessman: "We get 600 dirhams a month ($160)," said one. "They deduct 200 dirhams for our food and it costs another 100 for us to phone home. It's impossible to save anything."

"Many of the workers suffer great stress and depression," says KV Shamsudeen, an Indian businessman, who has set up a charitable trust on their behalf. He says many of the workers have to take out loans in order to pay an agent in their home country to find them a job, even though this type of commission is illegal. "The people who come here aren't able to take loans from the banks, because they don't have any assets," Mr. Shamsudeen says. "So they borrow money from personal lenders. The interest for such loans can be as much as 10%.

Spiral of debt

As a result, many workers find themselves heavily in debt, and KV Shamsudeen says there have been a number of suicides among expatriate Indians: 74 in 2004, 84 in 2005 and 25 so far this year. There's little that workers in the United Arab Emirates can do to improve their lot. Strikes are illegal, although there have been several recently. And because there is no right of association, there are no trade unions. So when, for example, pay is late, there is little the men can do about it.

The lack of redress also means that smaller grievances - like having to wait an hour at the end of the day to clock off - can suddenly boil over into violence. However things look as though they might be about to change.

The UAE government is sensitive to criticism. In 2004, for example, it ordered a magazine to withdraw from circulation an edition in which it had published information on the number of men killed on construction sites. Organizations like the World Bank and the IMF, as well as the United States have all made clear that they want the UAE to improve labour conditions.

The government has now responded by saying that a new labour law being drawn up will allow workers to organize. Current plans, according to the minister of labour, envisage a single union with separate representatives for different industries. The minister has said he expects the proposed law to be in place by the end of the year.

Minister promises to resolve Rapco issue
By Anjana Sankar

8 December 2004

ABU DHABI — The unpaid workers of Rapco Roads and General Contracting Projects at last see light at the end of the tunnel as the minister of labour promises to find a solution to their pressing problems.

The workers yesterday handed over a complaint to the Labour Minister Dr Ali Bin Abdullah Al Kaabi, and he has promised to work out a feasible solution at the earliest. "One of our representatives went to the Labour Ministry yesterday and the minister received our complaint in person," the workers told 'Khaleej Times'.

The workers were seemingly elated and expressed hope that they will receive their pending dues now that they have expressed their grievances to the right authority. "The minister told us that he is very much aware of the present crisis and assured that he will do his best to settle the matter with the company," they added optimistically.

Earlier, the workers had threatened to commit mass suicide if their woes were not addressed within a month. Of the Rapco's promise to pay the workers their pending dues once the company receives payments from outstanding issues, the workers said they will not be convinced until the receive their money.

Following the reports in 'Khaleej Times', exposing the plight of over 1,400 workers who are living in dire straits in Rapco's labour camp in Mafraq without job, money and worse on expired visas, Rapco had come forward and promised to settle the issue at the earliest.

APPENDIX II – Author's Comments:

The plight of unfortunate Pakistanis young and old, whether they are victims of human rights abuses, such as the trade in flesh or child slavery, or whether they are victims of degraded treatment, child abuse, or simple civil rights abuses, has been the focus of the Ansar Burney Trust. The trust, founded in 1980 by Mr. Ansar Burney, is based in Karachi and was Pakistan's first true organized advocacy for Human Rights. Their non-profit network seeks better treatment for disadvantaged human beings caught in a world still struggling to overcome human trafficking, forced labor, and domestic violence or even murder in the name of family honor. In addition, the trust provides relief to save lives following natural disasters such as the devastating earthquakes in 2005.

Human Trafficking comes in many forms, each having destroyed the lives of millions of innocent people around the world. In many cases children and their mothers are forced to become "mules" for drug trafficking under the threat of harm to either the children or other family members. Quite often the human mules are caught smuggling in Middle Eastern countries with severe penalties, such as death. In other cases, young girls are lured into forced prostitution under false pretenses such as a better future for themselves and family.

The fact that children are sold into slavery for the purpose of Camel Racing has been well documented, and although banned in Dubai and the UAE as a whole, unfortunately it is still continuing to this day throughout the Middle East. Oil rich nations have found it very easy to purchase children, ideal for their small size, from poorer countries such as Pakistan, India and Indonesia. Children as young as three years old are used as ballast, and are often maimed or killed when thrown from the humps of camels traveling at thirty miles per hour, then stampeded. The injured receive no medical treatment and the dead find an unmarked grave in the desert. In a disgusting parallel to chimney sweeps of the early nineteenth century, the children if recovered by Human Rights organizations and returned to their family, are usually kidnapped again and resold back into slavery. The camel jockeys are forced to work up to eighteen hours per day, and those that disobey their "owners" are punished with electrical shocks, tied up in chains and beaten, and deprived of their daily meal of two biscuits per day.

Throughout the world, women have suffered at the hands of discrimination, slavery, and violence more than any group. Pakistan in particular has fought an uphill battle to end the horrific violence against women that include such practices as being covered with gasoline and set on fire, or engineered kitchen accidents, causing them to be set ablaze. Many victims are simply doused with acid. All are honor punishments, and the disfiguring injuries are used as a means to force suicide, a punishment for women who wished to be divorced.

Another common practice often used to punish women in Pakistan that have caused dishonor to a family is called "Karo Kari," and involves the simple murder of the woman. Infractions that lead to their death include the refusal to participate in an arranged marriage, divorce, and adultery. Up to fifteen hundred women are murdered in the name of honor each year in Pakistan by brothers, fathers, or husbands.

To find out more information or what you can do to help, please contact the Ansar Burney Trust:

Ansar Burney Trust (Pakistan)
6 Hassan Manzil. Arambagh Road. Karachi. Pakistan
 Phone: + 92 21 262 3382 / 83 FAX: + 92 21 262 3384

Email: contact@ansarburney.org

Ansar Burney Trust (UK)
18 Peterborough Road.
Harrow. Middlesex.
London. HA1 2BQ
United Kingdom
Phone: + 44 20 8422 2277
FAX: + 44 20 8423 4555

APPENDIX III – The world's tallest completed buildings:

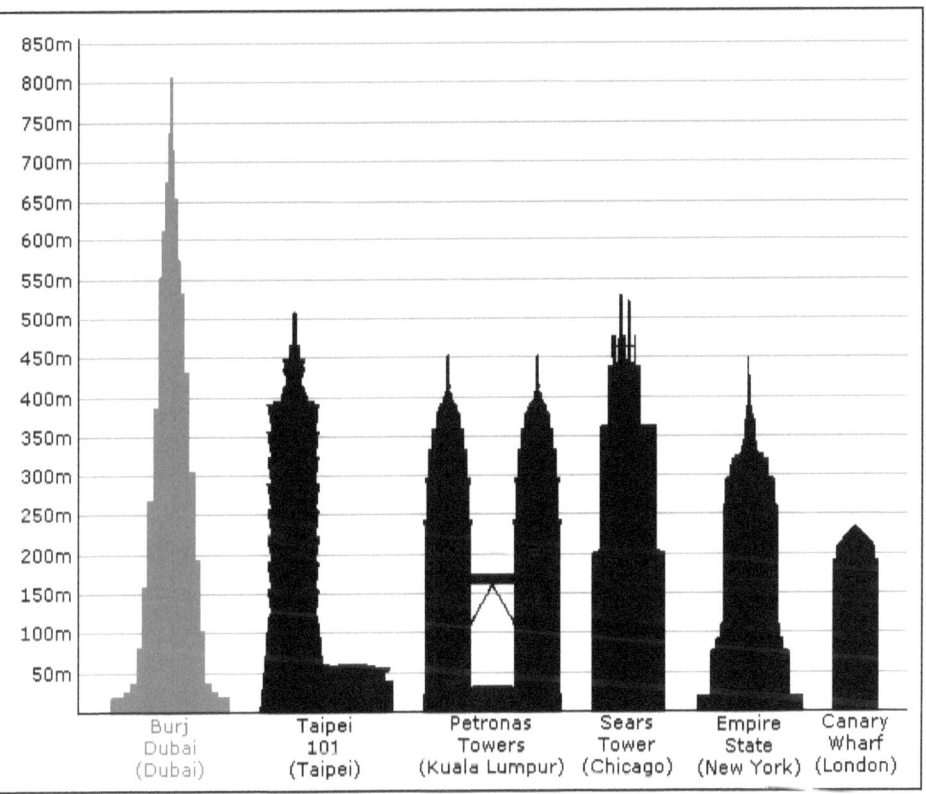

(PD)

The above diagram depicts height as defined by the tip of the highest structural elements. When measured from the ground to the highest attached component, at 818 m (2684 ft) the Burj Dubai is the tallest building in the world, followed by the Sears Tower, and Taipei 101, however the antennas aren't structural. The antennas not being considered part of the building, the Sears Tower building, therefore is shorter than Taipei 101 and the Petronas Towers. Taking into account decorative spires, but not antennas, the tallest towers go in order from Burj Dubai, Taipei 101, Petronas Towers, and then the Sears Tower followed by the Jin Mao Tower. The Burj Dubai also has the most floors at 160.

At their convention in Chicago, the Council on Tall Buildings and Urban Habitat the establishment of "highest" are covered by four categories in which the "world's tallest building" can be measured as defined by CTBUH:

1. *Height to the structural or architectural top (including spires and pinnacles, but not antennas, masts or flagpoles)*
2. *Height to the highest occupied floor*
3. *Height to the top of the roof*
4. *Height to the top of antenna*

"The height is measured from the sidewalk level of the main entrance. In all of these categories, Sears Tower had held the second and third category. Petronas held the first and the original World Trade Towers held the fourth. Within months, however, a new antenna was placed on the Sears Tower, giving it hold of the fourth category. On April 20, 2004, the Taipei 101 in Taipei, Taiwan was completed. Its completion gave it the world record for the first three categories.

Today, Burj Dubai leads in the first category with 818 m (2684 ft), and in each category thereafter. Coming in second is Taipei 101, as well as in the second category with an occupied floor at 439 m (1,441 ft), and in the third category with 449 m (1,474 ft). The first category was formerly held by the Petronas Twin Towers at 452 m (1,483 ft), and before that by the Sears Tower at 442 m (1,451 ft). The second and third categories were held by the Sears Tower, with 412 m and 442 m (1,451 ft) respectively."

Skyscrapers on the drawing board:

• "Murjan Tower" in Manama built on the tiny Island of Bahrain is planned to be 1,022 meters (3,353 ft) in height. Designed by Danish firm Henning Larsens Tegnestue A/S and comprises 200 floors. If built, it will be the world's tallest building, surpassing the proposed Mubarak Tower in nearby Kuwait City.
• The proposed Mubarak al-Kabir Tower in Madinat al-Hareer, Kuwait, is 1,001 m (3,284 ft). No date set to begin construction.
• Near Fuento el Fresno in Spain, the construction of a 750-meter solar tower is being planned.
• Burj Dubai in Dubai, UAE is a 2700 ft skyscraper currently under construction in Dubai. With projected completion in 2010, the Burj Dubai would own the number one spot in all four of CTBUH's categories, as well as make it the tallest manmade structure in history.
• The Center of India Tower in Katangi, India is designed to be a 2,222 ft skyscraper with 224 stories. Ground breaking is scheduled for 2008.
• The 610 meter, or 2000 ft Chicago Spire (formerly Fordham Spire) would surpass the Sears Tower as the tallest tower in Chicago as well as North America. The building is planned to break ground sometime in early 2007 with completion expected in late 2010.
• The Freedom Tower of the new World Trade Center in New York City will stand   1,776 ft (541.3 meters) to its spire, and approximately 1,368 ft (417 m) to its roof.

APPENDIX IV – Author's comments regarding Dubai:

Although severely slowed by worldwide economic downturn that began in 2007, Dubai continues to amaze the development world as newer and more ambitious projects are continuing to be announced. The world's construction crane supply had at one time been strained with the ground breaking of each new mega-project. It had been estimated that up to 25% of the world's cranes were being used in Dubai at any given time during 2006. The surge in construction was caused as the Emirate shifted from an oil-only based economy to one that's diversified. The current oil reserves will more-than-likely begin to run thin in 2010, and the Sheikhdom has made considerable strides to attract tourism and ex-patriots from both the United States and Europe. The first step was to make the land available to outside developers and owners, therefore all property has been deemed "freehold," or on 99-year leases.

Future developments planned besides the Burj Dubai, Falconland, and the Palms, include Dubailand, three billion square feet of development that is twice the size of Disney World have been placed on hold. Contained within its six zones are theme parks with rides and aquariums, horse racing, equestrian and polo club, sporting arenas, planetarium, center for arts, shopping and retail, resorts and hotels. In addition to Dubailand is Dubai Waterfront, the largest waterfront development of any kind in the world, which will extend Dubai's coastline by eight hundred and twenty kilometers, an area seven times the size of Manhattan.

Dubai Business Bay (AP)

Also in development is Business Bay, a collection of two hundred and thirty skyscrapers with names such as Churchill Towers, the Regal Court, Park Lane Tower, and B2B Tower. Business Bay hopes to attract financial institutions from around the world. The first of the buildings were to be occupied in 2007.

A true progressive Arab city-state Dubai has made great strides in providing leadership for the Muslim world by demonstrating religious tolerance and allowing open worship of many religions, including Hinduism, Sikhism, Christianity, and Buddhism. The government in fact, has donated Land for the specific purpose of the construction of four Protestant and one Roman Catholic Churches. All has been in an effort to court the West to Dubai, and for the most part has worked very well. Dubai, however still continues to astound Human Rights watchdogs around the world.

Clearly leading all neighbors for their progressive Muslim views, labor injustices continue, as well as a dramatic increase in prostitution. Although prostitution is illegal, the demand for sex from Dubai's majority foreign population has caused a flood of young women to arrive to meet the demand. Primarily from Eastern Europe, Russia, Ethiopia, and Asia, the closet industry has caused further scrutiny of the Emirate by Human Rights organizations. Purportedly a highly sophisticated trans-oceanic organization is in back of the "flesh" network.

APPENDIX V – The Kalash of Chitral

In researching *Falcon on the Tower*, one of the most pleasant insights came about from my personal discovery of an innocent, peaceful tribal people from a region in the North West Frontier known as the Kalash. Unlike their portrayal in the novel, the Kalash are still devoted to primarily to carving idols rather than rifle stocks. As is depicted in the novel, the Kalash live in an area of the Hindu Kush extremely difficult to access, and as a result have been virtually untouched by modern man.

Believed to have been the direct descendants of Alexander the Great, the Kalash demonstrate physical characteristics unlike any other people on the Indian Subcontinent. Physical characteristics are just the start of it, as the Kalash also pray to deities and participate in rituals unlike any in Pakistan. Closely resembling the practices of the ancient Greeks, the Kalash hold very close old traditions that were passed down over two millennia by just word of mouth. The Kalash don't have written language, but believe their forefathers had at one time. It is thought that their ancestors wrote down all of their collective traditions, as well as the knowledge to write, and then buried the written document in a secret, and sacred place. Tradition holds that one day, God will return the book and all the knowledge that it contains. Other Kalash traditions include: traditions of measurement, traditions for making a house, traditions for the temple, traditions for high pastures, traditions for property, farming, weddings, clothing, eating, sickness, birth, and death.

Ceremony is of primary importance when carrying out any of the Kalash traditions, and the two ceremonies this author thought most intriguing were marriage and death. The marriage ceremony begins with a sacrifice for both the bride and groom, and is usually done using a goat or cow, followed by a feast and the wedding ceremony. The wedding is planned in a manner not unlike Christian ceremonies. A planner will arrange for music, site of the ceremony, and refreshments, including wine. Death is also celebrated as a festive event.

The Kalash use the example of a leaf falling from a tree when considering the death of someone. "Man can not do anything against God's will. As a leaf falls from a tree and is separated from the tree, a man also leaves his friends and family and goes in Gods hands in the paradise. The dead one goes to a better place than where we are." Believing that it's a sin to be unhappy over God's decision, the Kalash pull out all stops when it comes to celebrating the decision of God, shooting guns in the air, drinking, and dancing for up to two days. All relatives will have a viewing of the body before the person is buried. The dead are buried in above ground coffins, or placed on top of each other in a form of mausoleum.

The Kalash religion is focused on offering prayer for virtually everything. First a fire is built, harkening the pagan rituals of ancient Greece and the twelve gods of Mount Olympus. The following are a list of just some of the translated (not by this author) prayers and may result in a smile or two:

1. *When goats are about to be taken to the high pastures.*
2. *When goats arrive at the high pastures.*
3. *A prayer done at an altar before starting the wheat harvest. The wheat ears are burned together with a branch to give thanks for the crop.*
4. *When a corn ear in the field is found to have two heads, an animal is sacrificed and blood is sprinkled on the special corn ear while giving thanks.*
5. *In autumn when the goats are brought back from the high pastures and the unsaturated male goats are allowed to mate, prayer is offered in the ceremony called "bus' bira mishek." Also known as the ceremony of letting the goats mate.*
6. *When the wheat is sowed in the autumn, prayers are offered by making a fire in the wheat field and by pouring wine and wheat grains in the fire while facing west.*
7. *When women are purified by the custom "s'is; or when they are sick or for other reasons.*
8. *A prayer is given when a sacrifice is made for a sick woman. The animal is sacrificed in the woman's house.*
9. *Seven sacrifices are performed on occasion for purification reasons after a husband's wife has died.*
10. *A sacrifice is made for anyone that has not been able to keep a promise or for someone who swears falsely.*
11. *A woman who gives birth to a child is purified after a certain time with a sacrifice.*
12. *When anyone's life has been saved from a disaster or tragedy a sacrifice and prayer are made to give thanks.*
13. *Sacrifices are made for all the offerings and prayers during festivals and feasts, other than those mentioned above.*
14. *A sacrifice is made to purify adulterers.*

The Kalash are a people that truly represent both innocence, and the resulting protection the Hindu Kush can offer with their high granite peaks. Yet, unfortunately what has made these people so attractive and interesting to the rest of the civilized world threaten to their very existence. Tourism has encroached on the Kalash and their way of life. Foreigners desiring to see these usual people firsthand, adorned in their colorful tribal costumes, have attempted to force conversion to other forms of religion, and tried to abolish their many tribal ceremonies and customs. Many anthropologists believe that the days of the Kalash are numbered, particularly should an unfriendly theocracy become their ruler.

Acknowledgements

First and foremost, I wish to thank my good friend and editor Susan Cromer Garcia, whose editorial skills are unmatched. It is imperative that I give special thanks to Harry Sargeant III without whose support the ultimate distribution of Falcon On The Tower Second Edition would not have been possible. I am also grateful to David Zubero and the International Swimming and Cultural Foundation, whose early contribution to Falcon On The Tower ensured its ultimate success. His is a friendship that goes back to our freshman year at the Bolles Prep School, and a person whose advice I have continually sought over the years.

The subject matter of Falcon On The Tower required many endless hours of research and the accuracy would not have been possible without the direction of Admiral James Stavridis, Rear Admiral (Ret.) Tom Zelibor, and Navy Captains (Ret.) Rick Neidlinger and Tom Lindner. I would also like to thank NASA Astronaut and Navy Captain Robert Curbeam, who as my RIO while an F-14 pilot with the Red Rippers, kept me alive and able to include that beautiful airplane in the novel. I wish to also thank all of those men and women of the Armed Forces who are on the tip of the spear each and every day.

I also must thank Paul Anderson, Paul Barros, Pete Davis, and John Stafford, whose critiques and encouragement helped me to complete the manuscript.

I would also like to thank Meghan Mariman, Naval Academy Class of '94. Her encouragement and help were instrumental.

Finally, I must thank my mother Kathy and the memory of my father Ken, who this novel is dedicated to. It was their decision to have a son born in the North West Frontier of Pakistan that was truly responsible for Falcon On The Tower.

Illustration of Peregrine Falcon pg. 388 – Courtesy of Roger Hall – http://inkart.net

Ron Clark Ball was born in the North-West Frontier of Pakistan, and grew up in Germany, Thailand, Laos and the United States. After college at the University of Florida and two years in the open pit coalmines of Wyoming and Gulf of Mexico oilrigs with Shell Oil Company, the United States Navy called. A legacy of military service, his grandfather was a World War I "dough boy," father World War II paratrooper and career CIA officer (recipient of the CIA Intelligence Star for Valor), and brother a decorated Naval Aviator in Vietnam. Following the call to service, he became a Naval pilot as well, flying the famous F-14 Tomcat, and flew reconnaissance missions during Desert Storm. As part of collateral intelligence assignments with the Navy he worked extensively throughout Europe and the Middle East, as well as lived in Spain and Greece. Leaving the Navy after his U.S. Navy Junior Officer tours, he spent ten years on Wall Street before serving as a Director of Business Development for International Oil Trading Company USA. A managing partner of Nøka World Energy, he is an avid sportsman and calls Florida and Virginia home.

888

GROUPE PRIVÉ

Kickback Books

.

www.ingramcontent.com/pod-product-compliance
Lightning Source LLC
Chambersburg PA
CBHW030748030726
47497CB00001B/188